Br...
a Billionaire

Caught by a tycoon!

Three passionate novels!

In January 2008 Mills & Boon bring
back two of their classic collections,
each featuring three favourite
romances by our bestselling authors…

BRIDE FOR A BILLIONAIRE
The Billionaire's Contract Bride
by Carol Marinelli
The Billionaire Takes a Bride
by Liz Fielding
The Billionaire's Passion
by Robyn Donald

JUST THE THREE OF US…
His Miracle Baby by Kate Walker
The Pregnancy Bond by Lucy Gordon
The Pregnancy Proposition
by Meredith Webber

Bride for a Billionaire

THE BILLIONAIRE'S CONTRACT BRIDE
by
Carol Marinelli

THE BILLIONAIRE TAKES A BRIDE
by
Liz Fielding

THE BILLIONAIRE'S PASSION
by
Robyn Donald

◎ ™ MILLS & BOON®
Pure reading pleasure

Harlequin Mills & Boon Limited,
Eton House, 18-24 Paradise Road, Richmond, Surrey TW9 1SR

BRIDE FOR A BILLIONAIRE
© by Harlequin Enterprises II B.V./S.à.r.l 2007

The Billionaire's Contract Bride, The Billionaire Takes a Bride and
The Billionaire's Passion were first published in Great Britain by
Harlequin Mills & Boon Limited in separate, single volumes.

The Billionaire's Contract Bride © Carol Marinelli 2003
The Billionaire Takes a Bride © Liz Fielding 2003
The Billionaire's Passion © Robyn Donald 2004

ISBN: 978 0 263 86117 4

05-0108

Printed and bound in Spain
by Litografia Rosés S.A., Barcelona

THE BILLIONAIRE'S
CONTRACT BRIDE

by

Carol Marinelli

100 Reasons to Celebrate

We invite you to join us in celebrating
Mills & Boon's centenary. Gerald Mills and
Charles Boon founded Mills & Boon Limited
in 1908 and opened offices in London's Covent
Garden. Since then, Mills & Boon has become
a hallmark for romantic fiction, recognised
around the world.

We're proud of our 100 years of publishing
excellence, which wouldn't have been achieved
without the loyalty and enthusiasm of our
authors and readers.

Thank you!

Each month throughout the year there will
be something new and exciting to mark the
centenary, so watch for your favourite authors,
captivating new stories, special limited
edition collections…and more!

Carol Marinelli recently filled in a form where she was asked for her job title and was thrilled, after all these years, to be able to put down her answer as 'writer'. Then it asked what Carol did for relaxation and, after chewing her pen for a moment, Carol put down the truth – writing. The third question asked – what are your hobbies? Well, not wanting to look obsessed or, worse still, boring, she crossed the fingers on her free hand and answered 'swimming and tennis', but, given that the chlorine in the pool does terrible things to her highlights and the closest she's got to a tennis racket in the last couple of years is watching the Australian Open, I'm sure you can guess the real answer!

Don't miss Carol Marinelli's exciting new novel, *Billionaire Doctor, Ordinary Nurse,* out in May 2008 from Mills & Boon® Medical™.

For Mario, with love and gratitude
for all your support, Carol

CHAPTER ONE

'THEY'RE never going to believe us.' Taking Aiden's hand, Tabitha stepped out of the car, her mouth literally dropping open as she watched the guests milling on the steps of the grand old Melbourne church like a parade of shimmering peacocks.

'Why ever not?' Aiden didn't look remotely fazed, waving cheerfully to a couple of familiar faces in the crowd.

'They're never going to believe us,' Tabitha repeated, after taking a deep steadying breath, 'because I don't look like a society wife.'

'Thank God,' Aiden muttered. 'Anyway, you're not a society wife; you're merely pretending to be my girl-friend. So if it's any consolation, you're allowed to have sex appeal. They'll think you're my last wild fling before I finally settle down.'

'They'll see through it straight away,' Tabitha argued, refusing to believe it could all be so simple. 'I'm a dancer, Aiden, not an actress. Why on earth did I agree to this?'

'You had no choice,' Aiden reminded her, before she could bolt back into the car. They started to walk, albeit slowly, towards the gathering throng. 'I played the part of your devoted fiancé at your school reunion in return for you accompanying me to my cousin's wedding. Simple.'

'No,' Tabitha said, pulling Aiden's hand so he had to slow down. 'Simple would be telling your family that

5

you're gay. It's the twenty-first century, for heaven's sake; it's not a crime any more!'

'Try telling that to my father. Honestly, Tabitha, it's better this way, and don't worry for a second about not looking the part—you look fabulous.'

'Courtesy of your credit card,' Tabitha scolded. 'You shouldn't have spent all that money, Aiden.'

'Cheap at half the price; anyway, I wouldn't dream of throwing you into the snake pit that is my family without a designer frock and shoes. Oh, come on, Tabitha, enjoy yourself. You love a good wedding!'

After slipping into the pew and idly scanning the Order of Service, Tabitha let her jade eyes work the congregation, and though it galled her to admit it she had never been more grateful for the small fortune that had been spent on her outfit. What had seemed appropriate for the multitude of weddings she had attended this year definitely wouldn't have done today.

Her dress had been a true find, the flimsy chiffon fabric a near perfect match for her Titian hair, which she wore today pinned back from her face but cascading around her shoulders. Her lips and nails were painted a vibrant coral that matched her impossibly high strappy sandals and beaded bag perfectly, and Tabitha felt a million dollars. It was a colour scheme Tabitha would normally never even have considered, with her long red curls and pale skin, yet for once the gushing sales assistant hadn't been lying: it all went beautifully.

The guests that packed the church seemed to ooze money and style—for the most part, at least. But there were more than a couple of garish fashion mistakes to giggle over that even Tabitha recognised—born, she assumed, from a bottomless wallet and an utter disregard for taste. Aiden took great delight in pointing out each and every one, rather too loudly.

An incredibly tall woman with the widest hat imaginable chose to sit directly in front of Tabitha, which ruined any hope of a decent view of the proceedings. But even with Aiden's and Tabitha's combined critical eyes there wasn't even a hint of a fashion *faux pas* in sight on this ravishing creature. Height obviously didn't bother this woman either, judging by the razor-sharp stilettos strapped to her slender feet. Oh, well, Tabitha shrugged, it must be nice to have so much confidence.

Only when the woman turned to watch the bridal procession did Tabitha start with recognition. Amy Dellier was one of the top models in Australia, and, judging by the extremely favourable write-ups in all the glossies Tabitha devotedly devoured, she was all set for international fame. Suddenly the golden chiffon and coral which she had been so pleased with only a few moments ago seemed a rather paltry offering, standing so close to this stunning woman.

As the organ thundered into the 'Bridal March' they all stood, every eye turning as the bride entered and started her slow walk down the aisle. Every eye, that was, except Tabitha's. She had seen more brides this summer than a wedding photographer. Instead, some morbid fascination found her gaze constantly straying to Amy Dellier. She truly was beautiful—stunningly so. Not a line or blemish marred her perfect complexion, and her make-up highlighted the vivid aquamarine of her eyes.

'Excuse me.' A deep voice dragged her back to the proceedings. 'I need to get past.'

The voice was deep and sensual, and as she turned her head Tabitha almost braced herself for disappointment. It probably belonged to some portly fifty-year-old who did voice-over commercials part-time. But there was nothing disappointing about the face that met hers. If Amy Dellier was the epitome of feminine perfection, then standing before Tabitha was the male version. Jet hair was brushed back from a strong haughty face, and high cheekbones forced her attention to the darkest eyes she had ever seen. At first glance they seemed black, but closer inspection revealed a deep indigo, framed with thick black spiky eyelashes. The heady scent of his cologne and his immaculate grooming indicated he was freshly shaven, but the dusky shadow on his strong jaw conjured images of bandanas and tequila, a world away from the sharp expensive suit he was wearing. He looked sultry and masculine—animal, in fact. As if no amount of grooming, money or trappings could ever take away the earthy, primal essence of man.

'Of course.' Swallowing nervously, she pushed her legs back against the pew in an attempt to let him past—but her bag was blocking the way, with Aiden's foot on the strap. Aiden, totally mesmerised by the wedding, was happily oblivious to the obstruction he was causing.

'Sorry.' His apology was mere politeness, exactly as one would expect when a stranger had to push past—the same as at the movies, when the inevitable hordes returned with their dripping ice-creams and you had to lift your legs up and squash back into the seat to let them past. Except demi-gods like this never appeared at the movies Tabitha attended—at least not off screen—and this moment seemed to be going on for ever.

If he didn't want to fall, he had no choice but to steady himself briefly on Tabitha's bare arm as he stepped over the small bag. The pews were impossibly close, each jammed to capacity with guests. As his hand touched the flesh of her arm Tabitha found she was holding her breath; two spots of colour flamed on her carefully rouged cheeks as he brushed past her, the scent of him filling her nostrils.

Aiden turned then, a smile of recognition on his face as he mouthed hello to this delicious stranger. The bride was passing, and he had no choice but to stand between Tabitha and Aiden as the procession slowly passed.

So slowly.

It was probably only a matter of seconds.

It seemed to last for ever.

Never had she felt such awareness—the whole focus of her attention honing in on this everyday occurrence. Her skin was stinging as she stood next to him, every nerve in her being standing rigid to attention, so painfully aware of his close proximity. But all too soon it was over; the procession had dutifully passed, allowing him to slip into the pew in front and Tabitha to finally breathe again.

He moved directly into the seat reserved next to Amy, and by the way her hand coiled possessively around his she was only too pleased to see him.

Tabitha found herself letting out a disappointed sigh while simultaneously admonishing herself for overreacting. Well, what did you expect? she reasoned. That someone as utterly gorgeous as that would be here alone?

Only she wasn't talking about Amy Dellier.

'Dearly beloved...'

The congregation hushed as the service started, but it held no interest for Tabitha. Instead her attention was entirely focused on the delicious sight of the man who had sat himself in front of her. His thick hair was beautifully cut and absolutely black, without even a single grey hair. It sharply tapered into a thick, strong and tanned neck, and his suit was superbly cut over his wide shoulders. As they stood to sing the first hymn Tabitha stared, mesmerised, her eyes unashamedly flicking downward. Despite her height, Amy Dellier seemed almost petite beside her partner; he was incredibly tall. It was no wonder she could get away wearing heels with him around.

'Don't even think about it,' Aiden whispered into her ear as the congregation sang heartily.

'What are you talking about?' Tabitha flushed, snapping her attention to the hymn book she was holding in front of her.

It didn't work. 'You're supposed to be on page forty-five, Tab.' Aiden grinned. 'That, my dear, is my brother Zavier.'

'I don't know who you're talking about.'

But Aiden had known her far too long to be fobbed off. 'You know exactly who I'm talking about, Tabitha, and take it from me—he'd crush you in the palm of his hand.'

Tabitha winced at the expression. 'Meaning?'

'Just that. Zavier might be a dream to look at, but he's bad news.'

Their heads were huddled over the hymn book, and they spoke out of the sides of their mouths, but it wasn't enough to prevent a few withering looks being cast in their direction. 'Then it's just as well I'm not interested,' Tabitha hissed.

Aiden gave her a knowing look. 'On your head be it, but don't say I didn't warn you.'

She sang tunelessly, her eyes straying all too often to the delectable diversion so achingly close in front of her. Despite her recent aversion to weddings, this one was turning out to be a sheer pleasure; even the endless wait while the happy couple went off to sign the register passed in a blur of delicious fantasy. Never had she felt such a strong physical attraction to someone—someone she knew absolutely nothing about. He was completely unattainable, of course. Way, way out of her league.

Despite her protests, Tabitha had to admit that hob-nobbing with the seriously rich had its perks. There was no question of standing bored and thirsty as the photographer clicked away for hours. Instead, a small marquee had been set up in Melbourne's Botanical Gardens and delicious fruit and champagne were being served as the family mingled, disappearing when the photographer called them to do their duty.

Accepting a glass of champagne, Tabitha smiled as she was introduced to Aiden's parents. Despite Aiden's gloomy descriptions, Tabitha was instantly won over and utterly in awe of Aidan's mother, Marjory, who oozed glamour and wealth.

'A lovely wedding, wasn't it? Though I'm not sure Simone's dress was quite the part. I really don't think thigh-length splits are appropriate attire in a church. What did you think, Jeremy darling?'

Jeremy Chambers had none of his wife's effervescence. His black eyes were as guarded as Zavier's, his haughty face as stern and unyielding as his favourite son's. 'She looked like any of the other brides I've seen this year,' he answered loudly, not remotely bothered who overheard him.

'I know the feeling,' Tabitha groaned, then instantly regretted her comment. 'I've been to rather too many weddings myself this summer,' she offered by way of explanation, taking a good slurp of her champagne. As

Jeremy's stern gaze turned to her she wished that she'd stayed quiet, but Jeremy actually smiled.

'Tell me about it,' he said gloomily. 'How many have you been to?'

'Ten,' Tabitha exaggerated, then did a quick mental calculation. 'Well, six, at the very least,' she added, rolling her eyes. 'All my friends seem to have taken the plunge *en masse*.'

'That's just the start of it,' Jeremy said knowingly. 'The next few years will be taken up with christenings, and before you know where you are all your friends' children are getting married and the whole merry-go-round starts again. Marjory loves weddings, unlike me, and feels duty-bound to attend each and every one—no matter how distant the relative. Speaking of which, I'd best go and say hello to a few. It was a pleasure meeting you, Tabitha.' He went to shake her hand, but halfway there seemed to change his mind and instead kissed her on the cheek, much to Aiden's wide-eyed amazement.

'My goodness, you've actually made a hit—my father doesn't usually like *anyone*.'

'He seems charming,' Tabitha scolded. 'I can't believe all the awful things you've said about him.'

'He is charming, if you happen to be the right son—and talk of the devil...'

'Zavier!' Marjory exclaimed, kissing him warmly on the cheek. 'I thought you weren't ever going to make it to the church. Where on earth did you get to?'

'Where do you think I got to?' Tabitha noticed his haughty demeanour was somewhat softened when he addressed his mother. 'I was working.'

'But it's Saturday,' Marjory protested. 'Not that that ever stopped you, Zavier. But that's quite enough about work—I, for one, intend to enjoy myself today. Have you met Tabitha, Aiden's darling, er...' the pause was interminable, but Marjory eventually recovered. '...er, friend?'

Aiden took a hefty swig of his drink, avoiding Tabitha's eyes. Only Zavier's gaze stayed steadily trained on her.

'Briefly, in the church.' He offered his hand and she shook it gingerly, noticing how hot and strong his grip was.

'Where's Lucy?' Marjory asked.

'*Amy,*' Zavier corrected, 'is touching up her make-up.'

'Lovely girl,' Marjory said warmly. 'She'd make a beautiful bride.'

'Subtle as a brick, as always,' Zavier groaned.

'Well, what choice do I have? I've got two sons in their thirties,' she said, her eyes on Tabitha, 'and not even the tiniest hint at a wedding, let alone grandchildren. Simone's barely twenty; no wonder Carmella's grinning from ear to ear.'

'The reason she's grinning is because Simone's actually managed to nab someone rich enough to get them out of debt—not because of her daughter's eternal happiness.'

'Ahh!' Marjory wagged a playful finger. 'Being out of debt practically ensures eternal happiness.'

'For you, perhaps,' Zavier quipped. 'Anyway, given that you can't even get Amy's name right, I think that says a lot for your motives. Forget it.'

'It would make your father so proud.'

Tabitha was actually enjoying the conversation. She liked the gentle verbal sparring between mother and son, and even Zavier didn't seem so formidable up against the feisty Marjory. But as she mentioned his father suddenly the temperature seemed to drop, and the affectionate, teasing reply that Tabitha eagerly awaited never came. Zavier Chambers, the epitome of confidence, suddenly seemed lost for words.

'It *would*, Zavier,' Marjory said, a note of urgency in her voice. 'It's your father's dearest wish.'

'What's your father's dearest wish?' All eyes turned as Amy appeared. Immaculate, gorgeous, wafting expensive perfume, she sidled up to Zavier and wrapped her arm around him. But Zavier barely acknowledged her presence. 'What did I miss, darling?' Amy persisted in a low, throaty purr.

'Nothing,' Zavier said darkly, shooting his mother a warning look. 'At least nothing that you have to worry about, Amy.' And, extracting himself from her clutches, he nodded to the photographer who was hovering on the sidelines. 'I think we're wanted.'

Even though she had just checked her make-up, Amy whipped out a mirror from her bag and started dabbing at her lips.

'Come on, Tabitha.' Aiden beckoned, but Tabitha shook her head.

'You go. I'm hardly family.'

'What's that got to do with it? Come on.'

But Tabitha was insistent. Immortalising a lie seemed wrong, somehow. 'The photographer said family only. Please, Aiden, don't make me feel any worse about this.'

'You'll be all right on your own for five minutes?'

'For heaven's sake, Aiden, just go. They're all waiting.'

Sipping on her drink, she watched as they all lined up; it was easy to tell which side they all belonged to. The Chamberses reminded Tabitha of a Mafia movie— all their suits seemed darker, all the men taller, all their hair cut just that little bit more neatly. The fatal combination of money and a perfect gene pool—only Aiden didn't quite fit in with the masses. His features were gentler, his gestures more expressive than the tight-lipped brooding looks of his relatives. Zavier stood out also. If the Chambers family were a formidable bunch then Zavier was the pinnacle—taller, darker, and, from the reverent way everyone treated him, the most powerful.

'So you've been relegated to the role of bystander as well?'

Startled, Tabitha turned, only then registering that Amy wasn't up there amongst them.

'It's a bit early in the piece for me to start appearing in family albums,' Tabitha said lightly, somewhat taken aback that someone so famous was actually talking to her.

'And a bit late in the piece for me; I think I've just been dumped.'

'Oh.'

'Bloody Chambers.' The sob in Amy's voice was one of raw anguish, and Tabitha watched, startled, as tears slid down the oh-so famous face. With a strangled cry she attempted to run off, but soft grass combined with six-inch heels didn't make for a dignified exit, and Tabitha cringed as she watched her trip away.

'It's the effect I have on women,' Zavier quipped as he joined Tabitha. 'They can't get away quickly enough.'

'What on earth did you say to her?' Tabitha asked, even though she knew it was none of her business.

'Not much. I just pointed out it was pretty stupid for her to be in the family photo when she wasn't going to be around long enough for the films to be developed.'

'But that's horrible,' Tabitha gasped. 'Couldn't you have finished with her in a nicer way?'

Zavier shrugged. 'Believe me, I tried. Unfortunately she either didn't want to hear it, or it was beyond her comprehension that a man actually might not want her.'

Tabitha stole a closer look, and knew it must be the former. Zavier had a haughty, effortless arrogance that must be a natural by-product when you were so beautiful. And beautiful just about summed him up: an immaculate prototype that left all others as a pale comparison. No wonder Amy hadn't wanted to hear it was over. To have known such perfection, no matter how briefly, would ensure a lifetime addiction.

He didn't seem remotely bothered by her scrutiny, and calmly stood as Tabitha surveyed him. Only when she realised the pause had gone on far too long and that she was obviously staring did Tabitha flush, instantly snapping back to the conversation in hand. She was cross at herself for being caught unguarded, and the scorn in her voice came easily. Gorgeous he might be, but beauty was only skin-deep, and it would serve her well to remember that fact.

'Well, I think you treated her appallingly.'

He raised an eyebrow. 'My, you do get worked up easily, don't you? I assume that hair colour didn't come out of a bottle, then?' Picking up a mass of curls, he pretended to examine them as Tabitha stood burning with indignation. Suddenly he was close, far too close for comfort, the dark pools of his eyes so near she could see the tiny sapphire flecks in them.

'Of course it didn't.' Flicking his hand away, she felt her hair tumble down over her shoulders. The brush of his hand on hers was electric, and she felt a blush stealing across her chest, working its way up her long, slender neck to meet with the scorching heat of her cheeks. 'I don't know why any woman would put up with you.'

'I can answer that for you.'

Tabitha shook her head angrily. 'It wasn't a question; it was a statement. Just because you're rich and good-looking you think you can treat women…' Her voice tailed off as she realised he was laughing—laughing at her.

'So I'm good-looking, am I?'

Tabitha snorted and instantly regretted it; the undignified noise hardly did her gorgeous frock justice. 'You know you are, and you think that gives you a licence to hurt people.'

'Considering we only met…' he glanced at the heavy gold watch on his wrist, his eyes narrowing slightly as he did so '…an hour ago, you seem to have formed a rather hasty opinion, and from the venom in your voice I'm assuming it's not a good one. Can I ask why?'

She stood there, searching for an answer. Why had her reaction to him been so violent? Why was she angry at him for so carelessly discarding Amy when if the truth were known Tabitha knew nothing about the circumstances that had led to the conclusion of their relationship? 'I just don't like seeing people hurt,' she said finally, while knowing her response was woefully inadequate.

'Amy's not hurt,' he answered irritably. 'She got exactly what she wanted from me: her picture in all the social pages and a fast ticket to fame. As for rich and good-looking—I don't think she has any trouble qualifying for that title either.'

'She *was* hurt,' Tabitha insisted, but Zavier just shrugged nonchalantly.

'Maybe,' Zavier conceded, but any surge of triumph

for Tabitha was quickly quashed when he carried on talking, a wry smile tugging at the corner of his full sensual mouth. 'After all, she's just lost the best lover she's ever had.'

'You're disgusting,' Tabitha spluttered, her cheeks flaming as her mind danced with the dangerous images that had suddenly flooded her mind.

'Just truthful. Look, we had a good time while it lasted. Amy wanted more, and I wasn't prepared to give it to her.' He gave a dry laugh. 'The grass is a bit damp here to go down on bended knee.'

'She wanted to get married?'

Zavier nodded.

'But that's even worse.' Tabitha was genuinely appalled. 'She loves you and you ended it like that?'

But Zavier just shook his head. 'Who said anything about love?' He saw the confusion in her eyes and it seemed to amuse him. 'You think Amy loved me?'

'Why else would she want to marry you?'

'Oh, come on, Tabitha—surely you're not that naïve? For the same reason that you're here with my brother: money and position. Why let a little detail like love get in the way of a good deal?'

'But I'm not with Aiden for his money.' She was stunned that he thought this of her.

'Please,' he scoffed.

'I'm not,' she retorted furiously, but Zavier wasn't listening.

'Sorry I took so long, Mr Chambers.' A waitress rushed over, a glass of ice and a bottle of mineral water in her hand.

'Just the bottle will do.' He took a long drink as Tabitha searched frantically for Aiden. Finally catching sight of him, Tabitha groaned inwardly. The bride was chattering to him now, which meant there was no chance of imminent rescue; she'd just have to make the best of it.

'So what do you do?'

'Excuse me?'

'For a living.' Her patience was starting to run out now. 'I mean, I assume that you work?'

His brow furrowed for a moment before he answered. 'I work in the family business; I would have thought you'd have at least known that.'

Tabitha frowned; there was obviously rather a lot of ground that she hadn't covered with Aiden, and his brother's resumé was one of them. Still, she was happy to attempt a recovery. 'That's right! Aiden did mention it, of course. I'm useless with names and details like that.'

'So how did you meet my brother?'

'At a party.'

'Well, it wouldn't have been at work, would it?' He flashed a very dry, guarded smile. 'We both know the effect that four-letter word has on my brother.'

'Aiden does work,' Tabitha bit back. 'He's a very talented artist.'

'Oh, he's an artist all right.' Zavier's black eyes worked the crowd and they both watched as Aiden knocked back one drink, grabbing a couple more from the passing waiter. 'Dedicated too,' Zavier mused. 'So, what do you do for a living?'

Tabitha swallowed. Normally she loved saying what she did for a living, loved the response it evoked in people, but somehow she couldn't quite imagine Zavier's face lighting up with undisguised admiration when she revealed her chosen profession. 'I dance.'

He didn't say a word, not a single word, but his eyes

spoke volumes as they slowly travelled her body, one quizzical eyebrow raised in a curiously mocking gesture as she blushed under his scrutiny.

'Not that type of dancing,' she flared. 'I work on the stage.'

'Classical?' he asked, in the snobbiest most derisive of tones.

'A—a bit,' Tabitha stammered. 'But mainly modern. Every now and then I even get to do a poor man's version of the Can-Can.' The bitter edge to her voice was obvious, even to herself, and she blinked in surprise at her own admission.

A sliver of a smile moved his lips a fraction and his eyes languorously drifted the length of her long legs. 'Is that the sound of a frustrated leading lady I hear?'

'Possibly.' Tabitha shrugged. Hell, why was she feeling like this? Why did one withering stare from him reduce her to a showgirl? 'But, for your information, I'm actually very good at what I do,' Tabitha flared. 'You might mock what your brother and I do for a living, but you don't have to pull on a suit to put in an honest day's work. We happen to give a lot of people a lot of pleasure.'

'Oh, I'm sure you do.' Again those black eyes worked her body, and again Tabitha mentally kicked herself at the opening she had given him.

For something to do Tabitha drained her glass and accepted another from a passing waiter. But still Zavier's black eyes stayed trained on her, making even the most basic task, such as breathing, seem suddenly terribly complicated.

'Don't worry.' He smiled at her for the first time, but just as Tabitha felt herself relax his cutting voice set the hairs on the back of her neck standing to attention. 'I mean, once you get that ring on your finger you'll be able to hang up your dancing shoes for ever.'

Her jade eyes flashed with anger at his inference. 'I'll have you know that I happen to enjoy my job—very much, in fact. If you really think I'm seeing Aiden for the chance to marry into his charming family—' she flashed a wry smile '—you couldn't be more wrong.'

Her fiery response to his provocative statement did nothing to mar his smooth expression, and he stood there irritatingly calm as Tabitha flushed with anger.

'We'll see,' he said darkly. 'But something tells me I'm not going to be pleasantly surprised.'

Aiden appeared then, oblivious of the simmering tension. 'Glad to see you're getting along.' He smiled warmly. 'Isn't she gorgeous, Zavier?' He squeezed Tabitha around the waist as he haphazardly deposited a kiss on her cheek.

'Gorgeous,' Zavier quipped, his smile belying the menacing look in his eyes. 'Now, if you two will excuse me?' He flashed the briefest of nods vaguely in her direction as Tabitha stood there mute. 'It was a pleasure meeting you.'

Not a pleasure, exactly, Tabitha mused as he walked away, but it had certainly been an experience; the only trouble was, she couldn't quite decide whether it was one that she wanted to repeat.

CHAPTER TWO

THE meal seemed to go on for ever, the speeches even longer. Tabitha spent most of the time smarting over Zavier's comments, pushing her food around her plate and drinking rather too much. She hated Zavier Chambers for his cruel suggestion that she was some sort of gold-digger when the actual truth was she was doing his damn family a favour: saving Jeremy Chambers from the news he didn't want to hear.

Aiden was unusually on edge—an inevitable by-product, Tabitha guessed, of being in such close proximity to his family. His promise to stay by her side all night diminished with each drink he consumed, and rather too much of the night was spent sitting like the proverbial wallflower as Aiden worked the room, only returning to reclaim his glass every now and then.

'Go easy, Aiden,' Tabitha said as Aiden knocked back yet another drink.

'I need a few drinks under my belt to face this lot.' He gave her an apologetic grin. 'Sorry, I'm not being very good company, am I? They just set my teeth on edge. How are you finding it?'

Tabitha shrugged. 'Not bad, but then I've only got to deal with it for tonight. I didn't realise your family was so well heeled—I mean, from what you'd told me I'd guessed that they were wealthy, of course, but nothing like this. You should have warned me.' She gestured to the room.

The Windsor Hotel was Melbourne's finest, and the ballroom where the wedding reception was being held was quite simply breathtaking. Everything was divine, from the icy cold champagne and the canapés that had been served as they entered, to the lavish banquet they were now finishing up.

'Why would I do that? I had enough trouble getting you to come in the first place. If you'd known it was going to be like this wild horses wouldn't have dragged you here.'

Aiden was right, of course. Here amongst Australia's élite, with vintage champagne flowing like water, Tabitha felt way out of her depth.

Aiden hiccoughed softly, staring moodily into his drink. 'Tab?' he said gently. 'What's the matter tonight? And before you say "nothing", just remember that we've been friends too long to pretend everything's all right when it clearly isn't. It's not just the wedding that's upsetting you, is it? What's going on?'

She didn't answer, her long fingers toying with her red curls, coiling them around her fingers in an almost child-like manner.

'Is it your grandmother?' As she bit into her lip Aiden knew he'd hit the mark. 'What's she done now?' There was a touch of humour in his voice as he tried to lighten the mood and cajole the problem out of her. 'Sold the family jewels?'

Tabitha's eyes weren't smiling as she looked up. 'My family's not like yours, Aiden; we don't have "family jewels". Sorry,' she added, 'this isn't your fault.'

'What isn't? Come on, Tab, tell me what's going on.'

'She remortgaged her house.' Tabitha let out the long breath she had inadvertently been holding. 'To pay off all her gambling debts.'

'You already told me that—last month, if I remember rightly,' Aiden pointed out. 'You went to the bank with her and helped organize it. Can't she manage the repayments?'

'She withdrew the loan,' Tabitha started in an unusually shaky voice, 'and promptly fed it back into the poker machines at the casino.'

'All of it?'

Aiden's open mouth and wide eyes weren't exactly helping, and Tabitha nodded glumly. 'So now she's got all the old debts that were causing so many problems plus a massive new one, and it's all my fault.'

'How on earth do you work that one out?'

'I shouldn't have left her with access to so much money. She's like a moth to a flame where the casino's concerned; I don't even think it's the gambling she's addicted to, more the company. I should have made her pay off her bills...'

'She's not a child,' Aiden pointed out, taking Tabitha's shaking hand.

'She's all I've got.' Tears were threatening now, and Tabitha put her hand over her glass as the waiter returned, but Aiden had no such reserve. 'Just leave the bottle,' he ordered while waiting for Tabitha to continue. 'Gran brought me up after Mum and Dad died, devoted her life to me, and now she's old and lonely and terrified and there's nothing I can do. I've asked the bank for a loan, but the second you put "dancer" down as your occupation you might just as well rip up the application form.'

'Let me help you.' He ignored her furiously shaking head. 'Come on, darling, it would be a drop in the ocean. I haven't told you my good news yet. I sold a painting yesterday.'

'Aiden!' Despite her own problems, Tabitha's delighted squeal was genuine and, wrapping her arms around Aiden's neck, she planted a kiss on his cheek. 'That's fantastic news.'

'Please let me help you, Tabitha. You can always pay me back. We're on our way, darling.' Aiden grinned. 'I can feel it.'

But Tabitha shook her head. 'You might be, Aiden, but in my case "on my way out" would be a more apt description.' Her gloom descended again, but she did her best to keep the bitter note from her voice. 'I've been asked to audition for the next production.'

'So?' Aiden shrugged. 'You'll walk it.'

'Maybe, but it's always been automatic until now— I've always had a part. It's because I'm getting older.'

'You're twenty-four years old, for heaven's sake.'

'I'm twenty-nine,' Tabitha corrected, grinning despite herself. 'And twenty-nine-year-old dancers have a lot to prove. I can't borrow money from you when I've no idea if I'll be able to pay it back.'

'Please,' Aiden insisted, but Tabitha was adamant.

'No; I mean it, Aiden. I'm going to have to work this one out for myself.'

'You're sure?'

She nodded resolutely, and after a brief shrug Aiden let it go. 'I know it's abhorrent, seeing all this wealth when your grandmother's so broke, but money can be a curse, sometimes. The people here are so busy looking over their shoulders, sure everyone's after their last dollar, they honestly don't know who their real friends are. For all the highbrow people here you could count the true friends on one hand. If the money disappeared tomorrow so would ninety per cent of the guests, and that's probably a conservative estimate.'

'Your brother seems to have the impression that I'd be amongst them.'

Aiden's eyes narrowed. 'Tab, I'm sorry if he's been

giving you a hard time, but, though I'm loath to defend him for treating you appallingly, out of everyone here Zavier's got the most reason to be suspicious of people's motives, especially where women are concerned. He was let down pretty badly recently.'

'She must have been mad,' Tabitha mused.

'Stay clear, Tab. I mean it. A wonderful warm thing like you wouldn't last five minutes in his company. I might adore Zavier, but I wouldn't wish that black heart on my worst enemy. It could only end in tears. Anyway, you're here with me, remember? Don't you dare go blowing my cover by making smouldering eyes at my brother.'

Tabitha laughed. 'I wouldn't worry, Aiden. He's already made it abundantly clear what he thinks of me, and I can assure you it wasn't complimentary.' She grinned as Aiden winced. 'Any hot looks passing between us would probably be better described as fuming rather than smouldering. He's convinced I'm after you for your riches.'

'God.' Aiden added a couple more inches to his glass. 'Zavier couldn't be further from the mark if he tried; he'd have a fit if he knew the truth.'

Tabitha filled her own glass from the bottle, but unlike Aiden accepted a hefty splash of soda from a passing waiter. 'He has no idea, then?'

Aiden shrugged. 'I'm not sure. He tried to talk to me once—a big brother pep-talk would best describe it. You know the type: sort yourself out, grow up, what the hell's your problem?' He drained his glass in one gulp. 'He actually came right out and asked if I was gay.'

'So why didn't you tell him then? Would he have given you a hard time?'

Aiden shook his head. 'Zavier wouldn't care about something like that. Despite the fact he practically wears a suit and tie to bed he's pretty laid-back about that sort of thing.'

'Then why not tell him?'

'I figured it wouldn't be fair on him. There's no way I could tell my father, he'd have a coronary, and it would just be one more thing for Zavier to worry about. He carries the lot of us, you know.'

Tabitha was intrigued and leant closer. 'In what way?'

'Zavier runs the business. Dad's too sick now. I know he doesn't look it, but he's a walking time bomb—he needs heart surgery, but he's too much of a risk for an anaesthetic. No surgeon would touch him, particularly with the name Chambers.'

'But surely he can afford the best treatment?'

Aiden gave a low laugh. 'And the best lawyers. I'm no cardiac surgeon, but I can see where they're coming from. He's just too high-risk to even attempt surgery. And with his heart so weak that's even more of a reason not to tell him about me. It's better Zavier doesn't know—better that no one does.'

'Well, he doesn't,' Tabitha said soothingly. 'So you've got nothing to worry about.'

Still, as she took a sip, her eyes smarting as the liquor warmed its way down, she found her eyes instinctively combing the room, as if constantly drawn to the dark and foreboding man that utterly enthralled her.

He'd only break your heart, she consoled herself. But what a delicious way to go!

The party was getting louder now. People were dancing—kicking up their heels. Aiden swirled Tabitha around the dance floor a couple of times, but his heart clearly wasn't in it and he was only too happy to get back to the table and his never-ending supply of alcohol.

Tabitha was starting to wonder when they could reasonably make an exit to their hotel room upstairs. Her feet were killing her in the impossibly high sandals, and she thought her face might crack soon with the effort of smiling. There were also a couple of videos on the movie channel she wouldn't mind watching while Aiden slept off his excesses. She had more than returned Aiden's favour, and tomorrow she would tell him this had been the first and last time she would play the part of his girlfriend. Zavier's snide comments had seriously hit a nerve; the whole thing was starting to get out of hand. She would join the family for breakfast, make all the right noises, and then that would be it. Aiden would have to find someone else to fool his family.

Her hopes for a discreet exit were foiled, though, when Marjory descended with a grim-faced Zavier.

'There you are, darlings. How come you're not dancing?'

Tabitha forced a bright smile. 'Aiden's feeling a bit tired.'

'Well, that's no reason for *you* not to be dancing.' For an awful moment Tabitha thought Marjory was suggesting they grab their handbags and dance around them together! The reality was far worse. 'Zavier, why don't you take Tabitha for a dance?'

She braced herself for rejection. Zavier Chambers didn't look like the kind of man who did anything he didn't want to, and after the way he had addressed her earlier she was dismally confident of one thing: dancing with a money-grabbing gold-digger wouldn't be high on his list of priorities. Not that she wanted to dance; ten minutes alone with this man had truly terrified her.

'I'd love to.'

She looked up with a start, and as he offered his hand had no choice but to accept. Standing, she turned somewhat anxiously over to Aiden for some support, but he really was the worse for wear now.

Zavier's hand was hot and dry, closing over hers tightly. As he led her to the dance floor Tabitha had the strangest urge to make a bolt for it, to wrench her hand away and run to the safety of her hotel room. As if sensing her trepidation, he closed his hand more tightly on hers, only letting go when they were in the middle of the tightly packed dance floor.

Slipping his hand around her slender waist, he rested it there. She could feel the heat through her flimsy dress. A couple dancing past bumped her, forcing her closer to him. Zavier gripped her more tightly, steadying her as she toppled slightly.

'You're having a terrible night, aren't you?' He had to stoop to meet her ear, and as he did he held her closer. His hot breath tickled her earlobes, and despite the heat of the room Tabitha broke out in goosebumps as she felt his hands tighten around the small of her back.

'Of course I'm not. Everyone's been charming,' she lied, in what she hoped was a convincing voice.

But Zavier begged to differ. 'You've been sitting on your own most of the night, trying to pretend you don't mind. I've been watching you.'

That he'd noticed Tabitha found strangely touching; that he'd been watching her she found pleasantly disturbing. But she didn't answer at first. His hands on her back were having the strangest effect. All she wanted to do was rest her head on his chest, to let the heavy beat of the music fill her, to lose herself in the moment.

'So this is a sympathy dance?'

'No, I don't do anything out of sympathy.'

She wanted so badly to believe him, wanted to believe it was her stunning good looks that had brought him over—hell, she'd even settle for her witty personality—but the facts spoke for themselves: Marjory had commandeered the whole thing. 'I'm sorry.' Her voice was high and slightly breathless.

'For what?'

Dragging her eyes up, she was stunned to see the change in him; the icy stare had melted, replaced by the moist sheen of lust, but his dilated pupils in no way softened the intensity of his gaze. Running a tongue over her lips, she forced a reply, confused at the sudden shift in his demeanour. 'For you being forced to dance with me.'

He didn't say anything at first; then he bent his head and she felt the brush of his face against her hair. All her senses seemed to be standing rigid to attention.

'Don't be sorry,' he said huskily. 'After all, it's only a dance.'

This was the man who thought she was a conniving gold-digger—the man who had blatantly told her he was suspicious of her motives. But he was also the man holding her now, making her feel more of a woman than she had ever felt in her life. Everything about him forced her senses into overdrive: the exotic heady scent of him, the expensive cut of his suit beneath her fingers, the quiet strength of the arms holding her, the scratch of his cheek against hers. She gave up fighting it then. Nestling against his chest, she swayed slowly against him, relaxed under his skilful touch. Closing her eyes she inhaled deeply, every sense in her body attuned to the perfection of the moment.

It wasn't only a dance.

To describe it as such was a travesty.

CHAPTER THREE

'LET'S get you upstairs.' Aiden was slumped over the table but still managing to cling on to his half-empty glass. Shaking him on the shoulder, Tabitha whispered loudly in his ear. 'Come on, Aiden. People are starting to look—you really ought to be in bed.'

'Having trouble?' She could hear the derisive tone in Zavier's voice as he took in the situation.

'We're fine,' Tabitha said through gritted teeth, unable to meet his eyes after the dance they had shared, confused at the response he had so easily evoked in her and determined not to let him see.

'You don't look it,' he said knowingly.

'Well, we are. Aiden and I are just about to head off upstairs to bed.'

'Have you already called for a forklift or did you want me to ring for you?' His biting sarcasm only inflamed her taut nerves.

'He's just tired.' Tabitha said defensively, but she knew she wasn't fooling anyone—least of all Zavier.

'Ah, that's right; he's had a busy week at the studio. And there I was assuming that, as per usual, Aiden's the worse for wear. God, I'm such a cynic sometimes.'

People were really staring now; she could see Jeremy Chambers starting to make his way across the room, a questioning look on his face. A drunken showdown with his father was the last thing Aiden needed—her too, come to that.

Swallowing her pride, Tabitha bit back a smart reply.

31

Jeremy was nearly upon them now, and she had no choice but to accept Zavier's help if she wanted to avoid a scene.

'I could use a hand,' she admitted reluctantly.

'A "please" would be nice.'

She wasn't that desperate! 'Look, are you going to help or not?'

He smiled then—a real smile, that for a fleeting moment lit up his face. 'Okay, come on, let's get him upstairs.'

Which was easier said than done. They managed to get him out of the function room in a reasonably dignified fashion, but once they got to the lift Aiden slumped on his brother and proceeded to snore loudly.

Tabitha willed the lift to move faster; Zavier's close proximity in this confined space was not having the most calming effect on her. Still, it was just as well Zavier was there, Tabitha conceded, or she'd never have managed otherwise.

Aiden steadfastly refused to wake up, let alone walk, and in the end Zavier had to resort to giving him a fireman's lift—something he managed amazingly well, considering Aiden stood well over six feet. Tabitha retrieved the swipe card from Aiden's top pocket, holding the door open as Zavier made his way in and deposited his younger brother unceremoniously on the bed.

'Be sure to tell him how badly he behaved in the morning.'

'Oh, I'll tell him all right,' Tabitha said, her annoyance with Aiden apparent in her voice. 'And thanks for all your help getting him upstairs,' she added grudgingly.

'Don't mention it. I'm just glad he had the foresight to book a room here or we'd be stuck in the back of a taxi now. As you probably gathered, it's not the first time

I've had to come to my hapless brother's rescue. I'm sure it won't be the last.' He stared at her then, openly stared, until Tabitha was blushing to the tips of her painted toenails. 'I would have thought he'd have toned things down a bit by now, though—the love of a good woman and all that.'

'But I'm not good…' The words slipped seductively from her mouth before she could stop them, and she saw the start in his eyes at her provocative statement. Stunned, confused at her own behaviour, Tabitha attempted to retrieve herself. 'I mean from what you said to me at the reception…'

'Oh, I'm sure you have your good points.'

Despite the fact they were occupying one of the Windsor's most opulent suites, suddenly the room seemed incredibly small. There was something big going on here—more than just a gentle flirting. Everything about Zavier screamed danger. Every nerve in her tense body seemed to be on high alert, the fight or flight response triggered by his proximity overwhelming her, but there was nowhere to run and, even more disturbing, Tabitha wasn't sure that she wanted to.

She wanted badly to dazzle him with some witty response, to show she was completely in control, not remotely fazed by his imposing presence, but she wasn't in control here—far from it. Zavier Chambers seemed to trigger a major physiological reaction in her just being in the same room.

Void of any reply, Tabitha busied herself removing Aiden's shoes. Pulling a thick blanket from the wardrobe, she covered his limp body.

She was confident Zavier would go now, which would enable her to at least catch her breath again. After all, he had delivered Aiden safely—had done his brotherly duty. There was no reason for him to stay now—no logical one anyway.

'I ought to put him on his side, in case he's sick,' Tabitha said, more to herself than in an attempt at small talk. Pushing her arms under Aiden, she knelt on the bed, pulling his back towards her.

'Careful—you might hurt yourself.' In an instant Zavier leant over to help her, his hand catching her arm as he attempted to render assistance. But the contact was too much for Tabitha's already shot nerves and she pulled her arm back swiftly.

His coolness only exacerbated her nervousness. She felt his eyes flicker over her exposed cleavage, and as if in response her nipples stiffened, protruding against the flimsy fabric. Even as she swallowed nervously she felt as if he was registering the tiny movement in her throat.

'Tabitha…' Aiden, slurring his words, struggled to sit up. 'Sorry.'

'Don't worry about it now,' Tabitha said gently. 'Just try and sleep.'

Aiden's squinting eyes locked on her. 'I mean it, Tab, I'm really sorry. I've been thinking,' he slurred, resting back on the pillow, 'I should just marry you. You know that? It would solve everything.'

She felt more than saw Zavier stiffen, heard the tiniest hiss come from his lips, and knew that Zavier thought this was a proposal she had somehow engineered. Her own shock at Aiden's suggestion for a moment put on hold, she attempted to quiet her friend. But it was too late. The words had escaped, seeping through the air like a vile vapour, compounding every last one of Zavier's suspicions.

'Don't be silly.' Tabitha attempted a light scold, a

nervous giggle escaping her lips. 'Why would you say such a thing?'

All Aiden could manage was a small shrug before closing his eyes again, but Zavier wanted answers. Reaching over, he shook his brother, rattling him none too gently.

'Come on, Aiden,' he quipped, his light voice belying the muscle pounding in his cheek. 'That's no way to propose to a lady.' She saw the tiny snarl as his lips formed around the words. 'Finish what you've started.'

'It would solve everything,' Aiden mumbled. 'Dad would see a marriage before he dies—' he squinted at Tabitha, who stood mortified '—and your gambling debts would be taken care of, darling. I know how worried you...' He never finished his sentence, instead choosing that moment to go into a deep and rather noisy sleep.

'I can explain...' Tabitha started. 'It's not how it seems.'

Zavier flashed her a thin smile. 'I'm sure it's far worse.'

'It isn't. The gambling debts—'

He halted her with one flick of his manicured hand, his gold watch glinting in the bedside light. 'I don't give a damn what trouble you're in. You, Miss Reece, don't concern me—not one iota. But understand this.' His voice was menacing. 'Stay away from my brother. Marry him and I'll expose you for what you are—a cheap, conniving gold-digger. Do I make myself clear?'

'You don't understand.'

'Oh, yes, I do,' he hissed. Coming around the bed, he stood over her, stepping uninvited into her personal space, so close she could feel the scorn of his words on her cheek—so close, so vividly near, even the batting of his eyelids seemed to be happening in slow motion. 'You think you've got it all worked out, don't you? You think the Chambers family are going to be the answer to whatever mess you've got yourself into.'

'I don't.' She was trying to defend herself, trying to form an argument, but his presence, his closeness, wasn't just intimidating her now; it was overwhelming her, fogging her mind with dangerous images. The scent she had inhaled on the dance floor was stifling her now, conjuring recollections of their one dance, and her subconscious responded as it had when he held her. 'I don't,' she said again, dragging her eyes up to meet his, trying to sound as if she meant it, trying to ignore the surge of adrenaline cascading through her body—the high alert of imminent impact.

His Adam's apple moved as he swallowed. Already he was wearing the dusky growth of a five o'clock shadow, and she imagined the scratch of his cheek on hers, the roughness behind his kiss. Though she hated the venom of his attack, Tabitha was curiously excited, high on adrenaline and champagne and the heady cocktail of hormones his presence haplessly triggered.

His hand moved up slowly and she stood frozen. Only the none too gentle sound of Aiden's snoring broke the silence—only that and the pounding in her temples as he traced a finger along her white collarbone, exploring the hollows of her neck, his fingers brushing under her curls.

And she waited.

Waited for him to jerk her towards him, to expel the tension with the roughest of kisses. She licked her lips, her pink tongue bobbing out involuntarily, moistening her flesh in anticipation.

'I might have known.' In one harsh movement, one

harsh sentence, reality invaded and his fingers flipped out the designer label on her dress. 'Is that the going price for a date these days?'

His words confused her. Struggling to understand his meaning, she stepped back, the distance giving her a chance to collect her thoughts as the contempt in his eyes flared.

'I sign off Aiden's credit cards,' he explained nastily. 'I should have worked it out earlier. Your outfit is the only tasteful thing about you.'

'Get out.'

'Oh, I'm going, and in the morning, Tabitha, so are you. As far from my family as humanely possible if you know what's good for you.'

Only when the door was safely closed, when only the heavy masculine scent of him remained, did Tabitha breathe again.

Not trusting her legs to stand, she sat on the edge of the sofa, practically trembling just at the thought of him. He was vile, loathsome, full of his own self-importance—and yet… Never had a man made such an impact on her. Those few moments on the dance floor with him had tapped rivers of passion she hadn't even realised existed. His eyes had seemed to tear through her, his mouth, his smell…

And there wasn't a single thing she could do about it! Even if she could stretch the boundaries of truth and imagine someone as completely stunning as Zavier Chambers ever in a million years being attracted to her, she was supposed to be his brother's gold-digging girl-friend—with a gambling problem to boot! Completely out of bounds by anyone's standards.

Stretching out on the long sofa, she lay staring at the ceiling, almost weeping with frustration at the unfairness of it all. Even the movie channel held no attraction now. What was the point? The real thing had been in this very room only moments before!

It was only a few seconds later when she realised she'd left her bag down at the party.

Rolling on to her side, she battled with the urge to go and retrieve it—battled with the urge to return to the party and a chance of glimpsing Zavier again. It would look stupid, she reasoned. He would surely realise the motive behind it. But her reasoning, however logical, however sensible, was no match for her desire—her need to somehow finish whatever dangerous game had been started, to put him right, to draw a conclusion or open Pandora's box.

She simply couldn't just leave it there.

Opening the door, Tabitha made her way along the thickly carpeted corridor, her heart beating loudly, her pulse rapid and out of time with the music pounding below.

The dark, shadowy figure making its way towards her was so broad, so tall, it could only belong to one person.

A couple more steps and his face came into focus, his eyes glittering and dark, a curious look of triumph on his face.

'Looking for this?' He held up her bag, the splash of feminine colour an enticing contrast against such a masculine backdrop. 'I was back down at the party and I saw it lying under the table.'

'Thank you.' She accepted the bag but didn't turn back, unable to tear her eyes away from his penetrating gaze.

'Fancy a nightcap?'

Even as Tabitha nodded her acceptance she knew he didn't intend to take her back down to the bar, and for that moment at least she wouldn't have had it any other way.

His room was amazingly tidy. A few heavy bottles and brushes adorned the dresser, and a half-drunk glass of whisky was on the coffee table. Tabitha noticed the ice-cubes undissolved; he hadn't gone straight back down to the wedding after he'd left her.

His eyes followed hers to the glass; his steady voice answered the unasked question.

'I was trying to figure out a legitimate excuse to see you again tonight. Contrary to the lecture I'll be delivering to Aiden in the morning, sometimes the answer does come in a bottle.' He looked at her bemused expression. 'I was sitting here thinking about you, wondering if I could risk ringing you, then it dawned on me you didn't have your bag…'

'Why did you need an excuse? I mean, why did you want to see me again? Haven't you quite finished lecturing me?'

'Lectures over.'

Could this be happening to her? Had Zavier Chambers sat nursing his whisky filled with the same trembling desire that had overcome her as she lay on the sofa? Surely it wasn't possible? 'So why did you come looking for me?'

'Isn't that obvious?'

She had stared at the glass long enough. Dragging her eyes up to his, she was shocked and strangely excited to see the same blatant desire emanating from them that had turned her to liquid on the dance floor. 'I thought you hated me.'

He shook his head slowly, deliberately. 'It's a rather more basic feeling you evoke in me at the moment.'

How could this be happening to her? How could

someone as charismatic and overtly sexual as Zavier possibly be interested in her, possibly want her? He could have any woman he wanted. He held her gaze, pinning her with his eyes. Everything about tonight seemed surreal, as if she were caught up in some strange erotic dream.

'Come here.' His voice was low, his request direct.

Tabitha knew that she should have left right there and then—picked up her bag, thanked him for his help and got the hell out of there.

But she didn't.

Tentatively she stepped towards him, drawn by an overwhelming longing that transcended all else.

She was completely out of her depth, overcome with desire. Never in her wildest dreams could she have imagined acting so boldly, yet Zavier imbued in her a feeling of wantonness—desires so basic, feelings so overwhelming that for now she couldn't even begin to deal with the consequences, couldn't contemplate anything other than what was happening right here and now. One look into his dark brooding eyes and a whole lifetime of scruples needed rewriting.

'Dance.'

Mesmerised, she nodded, her hand reaching out for him, desperate to feel him again, to revisit the magic they had created on the dance floor. But Zavier had other ideas. Almost imperceptibly he shook his head.

'No. Dance *for* me.'

His eyes left hers for the briefest impatient moment, his fingers working a remote control and the room filling with the low sensual throb of bass, the straining tears of a violin. And though it moved her, though the music fuelled her, it didn't even come close to the rush of desire that flooded her as his gaze returned.

'I can't.' Her tongue flicked over dry lips. 'I can't,' she said again when he didn't answer. 'You'll laugh at me.'

Again he shook his head. 'I'm not laughing, Tabitha; I want to see you dance. Dance for me like you do when you're alone.'

He knew! Like a child caught singing into a hairbrush, she felt the sting of embarrassment. It was as if he had an open ticket to her mind, her dreams—as if he had seen her pushing back the coffee table at home, pulling the curtains and dancing as she would have if only her ambitions had been fulfilled.

It was the most ridiculous of requests, one that under absolutely any other circumstance would have been laughable. But there was no mirth in his voice, not even a note of challenge, just the thick throb of lust and a million fantasies that needed to be fulfilled, imbuing her with the confidence of a woman who could fulfil them, the empowering realisation that though it was Zavier calling the shots it was she, Tabitha, fulfilling them.

The straps on her sandals were fiddly, her hair falling forward as her shaking hands worked the tiny buckles. She was incredulous that she was even contemplating obliging him, but as the music filled the room it overtook her awkwardness, the throbbing sensual rhythm fuelling her. Slowly she slid her toes up the long length of her calf, the wraparound dress falling apart to reveal taut flexed muscles. Instinctively tightening her stomach, she felt the imaginary string that pulled dancers taller snap taut. She let the music take over, washing over her body as, like liquid silk, she moved to the beat, swaying, turning, dancing the most private of dances for the most captive of audiences. And when the music slowed, when, breathless, her body glimmering, she dared to look at

him, the blaze of desire emanating from his expressive
eyes took the last of her breath away.

'Come here.'

It was the second time he had beckoned her, the second time he had summoned her, and Tabitha knew the
interlude was over—knew this time when she went to
him exactly how the scene would end.

Tabitha had never been promiscuous; to date her relationships had always been taken seriously. She wasn't
a woman who could be bought with meals and flowers,
her heart wasn't something to be given away lightly, but
as she crossed the room, as she took that tentative step
off the cliff-edge and into areas unknown, her mind was
whirring, her love-life passing before her eyes in those
fateful final moments before passion completely took
over.

With blinding realisation she knew why she was doing
this—or, more importantly, why she wanted to do this.
Meals, flowers—they all made her feel wanted, feminine, sexy. Zavier Chambers had done in a few hours
what most men took months to achieve. He had made
her feel completely a woman.

He stood absolutely still as she crossed the room,
drawing her towards him with an animal magnetism, but
as she drew nearer his arms shot up, pulling her close,
dragging her from her cliff-edge as if one split second
was too long to be apart.

The weight of his lips on hers was explosive, hungry.
She almost cried out at the impact of him against her,
her lips parting as he probed her with his tongue. She
could taste the lingering traces of whisky, the sharp scent
of his maleness filling her senses.

His hair was thick and silken under her fingers, his
thighs hard and solid as he pulled her nearer, and she

could feel his arousal, urgent and solid. Pulling at her hairclips, he threw them almost angrily to the floor, his fingers spilling her Titian curls, coaxing them around her face. Pushing her head back, he let his lips explore her neck, scratching the soft skin with his chin as his sensual mouth located the flickering pulse there.

He pulled away. 'Are you sure?'

His voice was thick, rasping, and the question was thoughtful. But she was beyond any rationale. The whys and wherefores would have to wait; for now only the moment mattered. She stood quivering, only his arms holding her up. The only thing she was sure about was that if he stopped kissing her now, stopped ravishing her, adoring her with his body, she would die with frustration. Her voice came out gasping, unsteady. 'Please,' she urged, 'don't stop.'

For the first time since their lips had met she opened her eyes. He was staring down at her, his pupils dilated, desire burning in every facet of his being.

'Don't stop,' she urged again.

It was all the affirmation he needed to continue and, swooping her into his embrace, Zavier carried her towards the bedroom. Ripping back the smooth counterpane, he laid her on the huge bed.

What Tabitha had expected she had no idea—for him to tear at her clothes, for her to rip at his shirt? But the animal passion that had gripped them in the lounge suite dimmed a notch, replaced instead by a sensual hum, an almost reverent admiration as he slowly pulled down her zipper, savouring each first glimpse of her exposed flesh.

Planting slow, deep kisses on her shoulders, he pulled down her straps, exploring her clavicle with his tongue. She heard his sharp intake of breath as the chiffon slipped over her breasts. Her pink nipples begged for the coolness of his tongue, flicking each taut nipple until it was swollen and aching, dancing to his probing attendance. Down ever down, he moved, across the white hollow of her stomach to the glistening silken Titian curls hiding her amber treasure box, which he opened with wonder, his tongue working its magic again, making her gasp as he brought her ever nearer to the brink of oblivion. Then, abating slightly, leaving her hovering on the brink, on the edge of the universe, he worked slowly on the delicately freckled expanse of flesh that spilled out over her sheer stockings.

With cat-like grace he stood up, his eyes never leaving hers as he undid his shirt, and though the music had stopped long ago his hips gyrated slowly to a beat of their own. Only his eyes were still, watching her reaction at the first glimpse of the ebony mat of hair on his chest, inking down over his flat stomach. She heard his zipper slide down, followed the plane of ebony as his trousers slid down his solid thighs, revealing the first heady glimpse of his manhood, trapped and writhing in his underwear. She reached towards him, her trembling hand aching, desperate to touch him, but Zavier shook his head, taunting her a while longer as he slowly took off the last remnants of clothing.

It was the most sensual thing she had ever witnessed, a teasing ritual that whetted her appetite. What she had expected from his lovemaking she hadn't dared even imagine. A cool aloofness, perhaps, a distance despite their closeness? Not this teasing disrobing for her benefit, this naked display of sensuality, this sheer, delicious decadence. He pushed her gently back onto the bed, the rough hair on his thighs scratching through the silk of her stockings as he parted her legs, diving into her with such precision and force that she cried out in abandonment, her legs coiling around his waist, whilst her coral-painted nails dug into his taut buttocks.

And finally the only dance left was the dance of lovers entwined, their bodies making music of their own, dancing to a private rhythm, a jazz of harmonic idioms in tune with each other, improvising as they went. The rhythm filled them, fuelled them, spurring them on, finding out what worked, what mixed—and it all did. Every last cell in their bodies seemed to be sated with desire until she could hold back no longer. Every pulse in her body had aligned, focusing towards her very epicentre as he exploded within her. Gasping, her body throbbing, she opened her eyes. She needed to see him at this moment—see the man who had brought her to this magical place. For he was the perfection she craved, he was the ultimate fantasy, and she was living it, loving it.

To close her eyes now would only taint the dream.

'What about Aiden?'

His question filtered through the haze, unwelcome and unexpected, the harshness in his voice such a stark contrast to the husky endearments of only moments before.

'Tabitha?'

She heard the impatient note, the summons for an explanation. Pulling up the heavy white sheet, she tucked it around her, her eyes darting to his, reeling with shock at the contempt so visible, stunned at the change in his demeanour.

Sitting up, she pulled the sheet closer, covering her breasts while knowing it was way too late for false modesty, bemused at the sudden change in him. 'I can explain...' she started, running a hand through the riot of curls, searching her mind for an answer. But she didn't have one. Telling the truth to Zavier might redeem her somewhat, but at what price? Betraying her dearest friend simply wasn't an option; Aiden's secret wasn't hers to share.

He turned his head then, just a fraction, enough for his eyes to burn into her shoulder, to see her stiffen as he carried on. 'If you love him then tell me, Tabitha, just what are you doing in bed with me? I mean, surely even you can see that this is stretching the boundaries of decency. I guess anyone can make a mistake in the heat of passion, but surely you would have put up a bit of a fight if you truly loved Aiden? I thought I'd at least have to try a bit harder to get you into my room.'

It took a moment to gather her thoughts, to take in all he was saying, but suddenly with vile realisation she saw what he had done. He might have been attracted to her, he might have wanted her, but going through with it— inviting her to his room, seducing her—had all been a test. A test to see if she truly loved his brother, if she could fight the attraction of another man.

And she had failed, dismally failed.

'You set me up?' Her lips were white, her voice shaking.

Zavier laughed. 'Possibly, though I didn't sense much resistance.'

'You set me up,' she repeated, angry now, shocked and hurt at what he had done. 'You were testing me, trying to see how far I'd go.' With a whimper of horror she recalled Aiden's words. *'He'd crush you in the palm of his hand.'*

Zavier Chambers had done just that. He was as inscrutable as he was dangerous, and she had only herself to blame for playing right into his hands.

Grabbing the sheet around her, Tabitha leapt out of bed. Retrieving her flimsy dress and underwear from the floor, she ran into the bathroom. Slamming the door, she grappled with the lock—but he was too quick for her. Forcing the bathroom door open, he strode in. His nudity embarrassed her now, hurt her, a shocking reminder of what she had done. Averting her eyes, she pulled tighter at the sheet. Her eyes sparkled with tears and she squeezed them shut.

Mercifully, he reacted to her embarrassment and tucked a towel around himself before firmly taking hold of her arm and turning her to face him.

'Stay away from Aiden,' he hissed, his face menacingly close.

'Get your hands off me.' Her voice was amazingly calm—authoritative, even; her shock had been replaced now with a burning anger. 'You don't know all the facts. The truth of the matter is that I'm actually doing your damn family a favour by being here.'

'By making sure we don't find out Aiden's gay?' His sneering reply simultaneously shocked and confused her.

'You already know?'

'Of course I know, and if I hadn't been sure tonight only confirmed it!'

'Why?' Her mind was reeling, shocked by the revelation, wondering what Aiden's reaction would be.

He let her go then, but Tabitha didn't move. Her eyes searched his face, demanding an answer, and when it came it was barely audible, his voice a throaty low whisper that she had to strain to catch. 'Any other man would have been proud to have you on his arm.'

Tabitha let out a nervous giggle that was completely out of place given the animosity between them. 'I'm hardly Amy Dellier.'

'You're ten of Amy Dellier,' Zavier spat. 'And if Aiden had an ounce of testosterone in him just what the hell was he doing holding his whisky glass instead of you?'

'If you know he's gay then I don't see why you're so angry. Surely you know I can't be after him for his money…'

'Oh, spare me the speeches,' Zavier spat. 'Do you really think yours would be the first marriage of convenience? And I'm not talking about the general population either. The whole Chambers family tree is littered with rotten apples—sweet little things on the outside, rotten greedy gold-diggers on the inside.'

'I don't know what you're talking about!' Her voice was rising now, her shame at having slept with him wrestling with her anger at the way she was being treated and, worst of all, her cringing embarrassment at how easily she had let him in, at the side of her she had so readily exposed.

'Take this wedding, my cousin Simone…' He threw his hands up in the air in a wildly exaggerated gesture. 'Love's young dream, my foot.' He looked at her bemused face. 'You want an example closer to home? My parents, then.'

'But—but they seem so happy,' Tabitha stammered.

'Happy, yes. Married, yes. But happily married is another thing entirely. And if you think I'm going to let you get your claws into Aiden you can think again.'

'He was joking,' Tabitha pleaded, but it fell on deaf ears.

'No, he wasn't, Tabitha,' Zavier said darkly. 'For all his arty ways, for all the alternative lifestyle you and Aiden insist on living, you're both as shallow as it comes. You can buck the system all you want but you still like your bills paid, you still like your little luxuries—and what a luxurious life it would be,' he sneered.

'How respectable Mrs Tabitha Chambers would be once her gambling debts were paid off. I can see you now at bridge parties, or at the Melbourne Cup. Far less sordid than the places you probably frequent now. The only problem with that little scenario is you're a hot little thing.' He moved closer now, his breath warm on her already scorching cheeks. 'The gambling tables aren't the only place you get your kicks, are they?'

'You don't know what you're saying.' Her voice was strangled, a strained whisper, yet she couldn't move, standing frozen like a rabbit trapped in headlights.

'Oh, yes, I do. You'd have to take a lover—discreetly, of course. Was that what this was about? Some sort of audition to see if I have the staying power to sustain you through a lonely loveless marriage?'

'Of course not.'

He dismissed her response with a toss of his head. 'I assume I passed.'

'You *assume* one hell of a lot,' Tabitha flared. 'You know what? I actually feel sorry for you. You're so sure everyone's out for your money, so sure we're all as hard as you. Is it so hard to believe in happily-ever-after?'

'After what?'

For a second she thought he was being facetious.

'After what?' he demanded again.

Still she thought he was joking, but on closer inspection he looked genuinely perplexed. 'Happily ever after,' she repeated, but still there was no reaction to indicate he understood. 'Like in the fairytales. Didn't your mother read you bedtime stories?'

Zavier laughed, but there was no humour behind it. 'You've met my mother. Can you really imagine her tucking us in with some namby-pamby fairytale?'

It had never entered her head that she might feel sorry

for Zavier Chambers. After all, he had everything she didn't—money, power, parents. And yet… Looking over at his haughty face, his brooding eyes, Tabitha was assailed with a sudden tidal wave of sympathy. Sure, she had only had her parents for seven years, but she wouldn't trade her memories for a lifetime of Marjory and Jeremy—tucked up in bed with her mother reading aloud as she took her on journeys to castles and princes and happy endings. A world where the good guy always won.

'You've got it all wrong,' Tabitha said, but more gently this time.

'Oh, I don't think so.'

Picking up her dress, he flashed one more look at the designer label before throwing it towards her.

'Stay away from my family, Tabitha Reece. You make me sick.'

CHAPTER FOUR

DANCING had always been her escape. So much more than a job, so much more than a means to an end. The throbbing music, the darkened audience, the sensual smell of bodies dancing, writhing. Losing herself to the rhythm, living only for the moment, the world on hold till the heavy dusty curtain descended.

But tonight there was no escape.

There hadn't been for five days.

Five long days and five even longer nights. Days spent chasing banks, building societies, waiting for the call that would save her grandmother, the gnawing panic of debt snapping at her heels. But they paled in comparison to the agony of the nights. Lonely nights waiting for a call of a different kind, tossing and turning, watching the moon drift past her window, the Southern Cross twinkling in the inky sky a constant reminder of her insignificance.

There was no refuge.

Now, as she danced, every response in her body, every surge of emotion seemed paltry, a pale imitation of what she had felt under Zavier's masterful touch.

A one-night stand. It sounded cheap, sordid—sexual gratification for the sake of it. A primitive meeting of desires, then walking away without a backward glance.

But it hadn't been like that for Tabitha. She hadn't walked away without a glance. Her mind was constantly there, remembering the bliss of him. He had hurt her, embarrassed her, humiliated her, yet…

In his arms, wrapped around his body, when the velvet endearments had poured like silk from his lips, she had found the solace she hadn't realised she'd craved, felt the mastery of his touch, glimpsed the impossible fantasy of being loved by Zavier.

Loved.

The word echoed through her mind like a mocking taunt.

There was nothing transitory about it.

So tonight Tabitha danced, danced because she had to, because it was her job, her livelihood, and she danced well—but nothing like the way she had for Zavier. And this time when the curtain came down she didn't rush off stage with the other dancers, because tonight there was no rush to get home, no haste to get into her large lonely bed and dream her impossible dreams.

The high-spirited chatter, the buzz of euphoria that came with the end of each show seemed to be in another language as she listlessly pulled off her costume, her dusty tights discarded on the even dustier main dressing room floor as Tabitha rummaged in her bag for her wrap.

'There's a Mr Chambers here to see you.' Marcus the stagehand sounded as put out as ever, and Tabitha gave him an apologetic smile as she turned to greet her friend. Aiden was becoming a regular feature backstage, his excuses to Marcus legendary as he wrestled with a reason not to drink alone.

'So what was the crisis tonight? Has your pet goldfish finally succumbed…?'

Her teasing sentence died on her lips as she stared into the face of Zavier, as familiar as her own, the face that had filled her dreams, fuelled her imagination since the moment she met him.

'Nothing quite so dramatic.' He made his way over,

the sea of dancers parting, staring shamelessly from him to Tabitha, undisguised admiration on their faces. 'I have to go to America in the morning and I thought we ought to go over some details.'

'Details?' Her perplexed voice was barely audible as she stared at him dumbfounded.

Only as his eyes flicked down to her pink, glistening body did she become acutely aware of the fact that all she was wearing was a flesh-coloured G-string. It had never been an issue—the changing room was permanently littered with naked bodies—but under Zavier's gaze there was nothing casual in her nakedness, no innocence in the way her body responded to his mere presence. She had dreamed of this moment, determined that when—if—she ever saw him again, she would look cool and aloof; she had even gone so far as to practise in the mirror—a gentle furrowing of her brow, a slight snap of her fingers as she tried to recall his name.

A wasted effort.

There was nothing sophisticated in the way he had found her, nothing aloof about the burning blush creeping over her near-naked body.

'The wedding—it's only four weeks away. We really ought to be finalising a few things.' The usual post-performance gaggle was deathly quiet, every ear straining to hear, every eye on them. 'Marcus?'

She vaguely registered Zavier turn to the stagehand, noticing how strange it was that he knew his name, how even Marcus seemed only too happy to please the might that was Zavier Chambers.

'Is there somewhere we could go? Somewhere a bit more private?' He flashed a malevolent smile at a mute Tabitha. 'My fiancée looks as if she might need to sit down.'

It only took a moment to dress, to drape her wrap around her, to pull on her short Lycra skirt and slip on some sandals, but it felt like a lifetime. The eyes of her colleagues, her friends, her boss, were on her, but they didn't compare to the heavy stare of Zavier, the impatience in his stance as she fiddled to tie her wrap.

Of course when you are Zavier Chambers your affairs aren't expected to be discussed in a dusty backstage dressing room. Doors open, or rather *private* dressing room doors open. Five-star ones, with mirrors and mini bars. And, though it was a world she inhabited daily, such sumptuous surroundings were painfully unfamiliar. Zavier immediately made himself at home, tossing aside his jacket and pulling a bottle out of the fridge with all the arrogance of a man who was used to having the best of everything.

'What's all this about?' Her voice, which had failed her for the past few minutes, didn't sound as assured as Tabitha would have liked, but it would have to do. 'How dare you just barge in here? How dare you stroll in and drop a bombshell like that, only to leave me to pick up the pieces? I have to work with these people.'

'Chambers wives don't work,' came the swift riposte. Annoyingly unmoved by her anger, he popped a champagne cork with ease and filled two glasses. He handed her one, topping up the pale liquid until the bubbles flooded her trembling hands.

'I mean it, Zavier. I want you to tell me what all this is about!'

'It's really very simple.' He flashed that dangerous smile. 'It's about us.'

Us?

It was hard to remain focused on the words coming

from him as she lost herself in the simple word. Us. You and I. Him and I. Me and you. You and me.

The simplest of words with the biggest of connotations.

'What us?'

'Us getting married.'

He said it so lightly, so easily, that for a moment Tabitha didn't even register his words, her mind too much filled with remembering when his lips had been closer, the taste of his cool tongue exploring hers. It was only after a few seconds that she parted the fog where her brain had once been and his statement filtered through.

'Married?'

'That's right.' Zavier nodded.

'Marry you?'

'Right again.' The dressing room, not big, seemed to have taken on minuscule proportions. It wasn't just his size that was daunting; everything about him oozed confidence and over-abundance. She felt like Alice in Wonderland in reverse, as the walls seemed to close in around her. Actually—Tabitha shook her head ruefully—maybe she wasn't so far off with her fairytale analogy. A proposal from someone like Zavier Chambers was the stuff of pure fantasy. It must be every girl's dream that a man as infinitely desirable might say those three little words while looking into your eyes. Except there wasn't a hint of romance in the air, and from the way he was distractedly examining his fingernails, tapping his well-shod foot on the floorboards as he waited for Tabitha to speak, it was clear Zavier wasn't about to whisk her off to live happily ever after.

'Why on earth would you ask me to marry you?' The

anger had gone from her voice now, replaced instead by sheer bewilderment.

'Because for once one of Aiden's hare-brained schemes actually has some merit.'

'But all I agreed to was a date. The marriage proposal was as much a surprise to me as it was to you. Why won't you believe me when I say I'm not after your brother? I never have been. It was a simple matter of helping him out—not some contrived plan to rob him blind. And for your information I spoke about it with Aiden the following morning, when he repeated his offer, and again I said no.'

'I'm aware of that,' Zavier replied easily, examining his manicured nails closely, not even bothering to look up as he spoke. 'And I must admit somewhat surprised too. Were you holding out for more?'

Dumbly she shook her head.

'I can't say I blame you,' Zavier carried on, ignoring her denial. 'After all, Aiden's hardly a safe bet.' He shot her a dry smile. 'We all know how you like a gamble, but why stack the odds against you with a penniless artist who could be disinherited? Why expose yourself to the risk of his family finding out the truth behind your little sham and run the risk of ending up penniless?'

'You've got it all wrong.'

'I don't think so,' Zavier said with a thin smile that definitely didn't meet his eyes. 'Anyway, for once in your life, Tabitha, you win. This time, darling, you've hit the jackpot.'

'What jackpot?' Her lips were curled in the beginning of a sneer, her nerves at seeing him momentarily overridden by the preposterousness of his words.

'I'm raising the stakes.' His eyes narrowed and he left his nails, examining her closely now, watching her colour mount under his scrutiny. 'That's the bit you like, isn't it?' he hissed.

But Tabitha refused to be bullied. Yes, he was intimidating, and, yes, he was undoubtedly the most powerful man she had ever come up against. Yet she had seen another side to him, been held by him, ravished by him, adored by him albeit fleetingly.

Fear didn't come into it.

'If I was confused before, you've completely lost me now,' Tabitha admitted with a slightly exaggerated sigh, then gratefully took a sip of champagne, because it was the only thing she could do other than look into his eyes.

'For once in his gormless life Aiden actually had an idea that might have some merit.'

He watched as she sat down at the dressing table, watched as she took some tissues and wiped the livid red lipstick from her lips, pulled out the jangle of pins that held her Titian locks.

He remembered with total recall the feel of those silken curls beneath his fingers, releasing the tight pins, running his hand to free them, the cool tumble of her hair as it cascaded down her pale shoulders, and realised he was clenching his fists, having to physically restrain himself from crossing the room and helping her.

'Maybe this will make things clearer.' His voice came out too harsh, too sharp, the quilted muscles in his face refusing nonchalance as he reached into his suit and laid a cheque in front of her.

'This is a joke, right?'

'I've never been more serious in my life.'

Her hands were working faster now, pulling out the pins with impatience, and apart from a brief cursory glance downwards, to see what he was doing, her eyes never left the mirror. She had no desire to examine it

more closely—no desire to see the undoubtedly ludicrous figure he was offering for her services.

'I suggest you take a closer look,' he said, his voice
deep, his eyes boring into her shoulder. 'It's not every
day one gets offered this amount of money.'

'It's not every day one gets to be made to feel a tart.'

Her words were like a slap to his cheek and Zavier
involuntarily winced. 'That isn't my intention.' His response sounded genuine, almost apologetic, but, clearing
his throat, he carried on in a more impassive voice. 'It's
merely a solution to a problem.'

'What *problem*?'

'You have major financial problems; I have a father
who longs to see one of his children married. Time isn't
on my side, and from what Aiden's told me you're up
against the clock to come up with some money. You're
up to your neck in debt.'

'No.' The violence behind her denial literally brought
Tabitha to her feet. 'I'm not.'

He didn't move a muscle, didn't even deign to look
at her. 'Why do you need money, then?'

It did enter her mind to tell him—she even opened
her lips to speak. But it dawned on her then that telling
Zavier the truth would end things here and now. If
Zavier knew the debt was her grandmother's rather than
hers then their conversation would effectively be over.
And, though his suggestion of marriage was as preposterous as it was ludicrous, Tabitha was intrigued and,
perhaps more pointedly, ten minutes more of Zavier's
time were ten minutes she craved.

'I don't want to talk about it.'

'I bet you don't,' he snapped, before taking a deep,
steadying breath. 'I'm offering you a way out, a solution
to our respective problems.' He pushed the cheque to-

wards her again, and this time Tabitha did look, her eyes
flicking down to the extravagant scrawl, widening as
they saw they impossibly huge figure. 'This is part-
payment.'

'Part-payment?'

'On acceptance,' he said, his tone businesslike.
'You'll get the same amount again after the wedding,
and double that in six months—providing, of course,
you've been a good wife.'

'A good wife?' The bewilderment in her voice was
audible even to Tabitha, and she mentally kicked herself
for repeating his words. She sounded like a parrot.

'No scandal, no talking to the press, and no objections
to a quick divorce.'

'D-divorce?' A parrot with a stammer, Tabitha
thought ruefully, focusing on anything other than the
ridiculous conversation that was taking place.

He gave a wry smile. 'I'm not expecting you to sign
your life away—just six months.' He gave a small shrug,
but Tabitha knew the nonchalant gesture hid a lot of
pain. 'My father's been given three months to live at
best. Six months will give a respectable time-frame before the family hits the headlines again. Otherwise, it
might look a touch callous for you to leave me so soon
after his death. I'm not out to trash your reputation.'

'Just to trash my self-respect.'

'I think you've already taken care of that,' he said
nastily, and Tabitha felt her colour rise as she remembered just how quickly she had jumped into bed with
him. But as he continued she realised he wasn't alluding
to their one night together—her vice, as he saw it, wasn't
for impossibly handsome dark-haired men with enough
sex appeal to set the world on fire. 'There'll also be no
more gambling. Naturally, given your weakness and the

nature of our marriage, you'll understand that I shan't be making you a joint signatory on anything, but of course you'll have a substantial allowance. Aiden informs me that your debts were incurred in a casino, so I just ask that you stay away from gaming tables unless I'm present—at least while we're married. What you do after that is your business. You can put the whole lot on black, for all I care, when the divorce comes through, but it might be wise to use this time to get some help. I'm happy to pay for a counsellor.'

'That really won't be necessary.'

'Fine.' Zavier sighed. 'Addicts are always the last to see they have a problem. But if you change your mind the offer's there. Anyway, it's all outlined in the contract.'

Tabitha was about to repeat his last word, but managed to bite her lip as he produced two documents from his briefcase.

'I suggest you sit down to read it. It will take some time. I want you to be absolutely sure you know what you're getting into before you sign.'

He was talking as if she had agreed, as if the result was a foregone conclusion, and Tabitha's bemusement turned to anger. 'You really think I'm going to say yes to this ludicrous proposition?'

'Of course you are,' Zavier replied assuredly. 'This amount of money will change your life.'

'I'm quite happy with my life, thank you very much.'

'How long do you think you can carry on like this, Tabitha?'

She braced herself for a short, sharp lecture on the pitfalls of gambling, smugly confident that Zavier didn't have a clue what he was talking about, but when he spoke, the words that came from his lips literally floored her, chilled her. Every raw, shredded nerve, every silent fear, every sleepless night, were all summed up in one callous sentence.

'How much longer will you be able to earn a living from dancing?'

'I'm only in my twenties,' she said indignantly. 'You make it sound as if I'm shuffling around the stage on my Zimmer frame.'

'You're nearly thirty,' Zavier pointed out mercilessly, ignoring her reddening cheeks. 'And furthermore you've been asked to audition for a part that up until this point would have been yours as a matter of course.'

'It's just a formality,' Tabitha spluttered. 'And Aiden had no right even discussing it with you.'

'We're brothers.' Zavier shrugged. 'And it was hardly an in-depth discussion. I just happened to read in the paper about the glut of talent in Melbourne, about the plight of dancers looking for work…'

'I don't recall any such article,' Tabitha retorted, her eyes narrowing. 'And for your information I do read the papers now and then; I'm not a complete airhead.'

'Ah, but my brother is. You're right—there was no such article. But the suggestion of one was all it took for Aiden to sing like a bird, to tell me how hard it was for his dear, ageing Tabitha, how cruel the world of theatre was for a delicate creature like yourself.'

'But why would my career—' she gave a sharp laugh '—or lack of it, interest you?'

'It doesn't.' He tapped the side of his temple. 'You know what they say—knowledge is power. Before that, for all I knew agents could have been clawing at the door to get your signature on a contract.' He held a mocking hand up to his ear. 'Quiet as a mouse. So now

I know how precarious your situation is: you need money, and to boot your work's not exactly secure.'

'I could get a job in an office,' she flared.

'Wearing that?' His eyes ran the length of her body, taking in the ridiculously short skirt, the long expanse of pale, freckled thigh. 'The dress Aiden bought you might see you through Monday, but on your current form I doubt a night at the casino is going to stretch to a full wardrobe.'

'But why me?' Tabitha asked, more to herself than Zavier, her green eyes only finding him once the words hung in the air. 'Why me? Why would you risk your reputation…?'

'My reputation can take it,' Zavier said darkly. 'It would take more than a showgirl with a gambling problem to ruin it. Anyway, marry me and the casino's out of bounds; it's all been taken care of in the contract.'

'Why didn't you ask Amy? It was what she wanted, after all.'

'Because Amy wanted to pretend that love came into it,' Zavier answered irritably. 'Amy wanted the works. You might think this is a big figure, but my *real* wife— the mother of my children—would stand to gain a lot more. With you, Tabitha, it would be entirely a business agreement. You'll walk away independently wealthy and my father will die knowing one of his sons is married and with a tangible hope that grandchildren are on the horizon.'

'Am I supposed to produce a baby?' Her voice was dripping with sarcasm, loaded with scorn. Not for a moment did she expect him to take her question seriously. But again she had misjudged him. Not only did he have an answer; he had it typed up and leatherbound.

'Absolutely not. There will be no children. You might

be happy to gamble your life away, but we're not gambling with the life of a child. I expect you to take adequate precautions, and before you accuse me of being chauvinist, we both know there's an undeniable attraction between us—our previous lovemaking showed no restraint, and certainly birth control wasn't on either of our agendas. I need to know if there have been any consequences from that night before we go any further.'

'Consequences?'

'Are you already pregnant? If you are then that puts an entirely different light on the subject.'

'The deal would be off?' she sneered.

'Let's say it would make things more complicated. Although I wouldn't deliberately put a child into this position, if it's already happened then naturally I'm prepared to stand by my responsibilities and address the issues. So are you?'

Tabitha flushed. Discussing her monthly cycle with Zavier was the last thing she had expected to do—or almost the last, she conceded. Discussing marriage in such businesslike tones hadn't even figured as a distant possibility. But hearing those words—however crudely said, however impossible the dream—hearing Zavier discuss marriage and babies in the same sentence had her senses reeling, her mind wandering, dancing in the delicious faraway realms of impossible fantasies.

Zavier's seed planted inside her. Dark-haired children the image of their father coming from inside her. Zavier's body lying beside her at night, awakening her with its arousal in the morning, the bliss of yielding again and again to his touch.

'Tabitha.' He snapped her back to reality; the surreal reality he had forced upon her. 'Are you pregnant?'

'No.'

'You're sure?'

'Do you want me to pop out to the chemist and buy a kit?'

'That might be the most sensible thing to do, but I'm going to take your word for it.'

Again he deflected her sarcasm; again he floored her.

'I'm sure you will agree that as we will be sharing a bed for the next six months there are bound to be repeats.'

'You're sure, are you?' Her comment was sneering, as if the answer was negotiable, but when Zavier answered she knew her attempts were futile. The fact they would make love again was as inevitable as breathing.

'Positive.' His eyes met hers. He looked so removed from the man who had held her, loved her, but the essence of him still moved her, still made her feel more sexually alive, aware, more feminine than she had ever felt in her life. He wasn't being arrogant, just truthful. Sharing a bed with Zavier and not touching him, holding him, sleeping beside him and not moving her body against him would be equivalent to being told not to breathe for the next six months. Even if she were superhuman, could somehow restrain herself while awake, what would happen as she slept? When the self-imposed barriers slipped and only her subconscious remained, her body would respond to him like a petal reaching to the sun. Her resolve would be dashed the second she closed her eyes.

'I'm asking for six months, Tabitha. Here.'

Snapping her mind back, she realised he was handing her a pen.

'You expect me to sign, just like that?'

'Of course not,' he answered irritably. 'I want to go through the whole document with you. No doubt you're going to demand a few changes, but I warn you I'm no push-over.'

The warning was absolutely unnecessary, but with a jolt Tabitha realised the conversation had shifted. From her initial abhorrent reaction, her absolute rejection of this most preposterous idea, slowly, unwittingly the tempo had changed. It was more a matter of when than if.

How, rather than not.

Her mind reeling, she sat down, trying to ignore the trembling undercurrents as he shifted his chair around the desk so they were sitting side by side, for all the world trying to concentrate on the contract that would change her life.

'We'd be married in four weeks. My family owns a holiday home in Lorne. It's right on the beach, very pretty, and my father has a lot of fond memories and ties to the place. We'll hold the service there, unless of course you're strongly opposed. I don't know if you're religious and would rather get married in a church?'

She looked up at him from under her eyelashes. 'Even if I am, given the circumstances it would hardly be fitting.'

'Good—at least we agree on something.'

With a small wail she flicked through the contract. 'It's twenty pages long. Are we supposed to discuss everything?'

'It's for your protection as well as mine,' Zavier answered, unmoved by her protests.

'Can we at least go out to eat and do it? I'm starving.'

'One thing you'd better realise before you agree to this, Tabitha: you're no longer anonymous.'

She stared at him, nonplussed, and he didn't make any

comment when her teeth distractedly nibbled on the end of his expensive pen.

'The second we become engaged you'll be a Chambers in everything bar name, and this time next month even that detail will be taken care of.'

'Which means?'

'Mess up or play up and, much as you might want to forget about it, there'll be some journalist only too happy to remind you of your misdemeanours. And sitting in a restaurant going through a prenuptial agreement would be over the newspapers in a matter of hours. It's the way it is for us. It's the rule we live by daily.'

'Aiden doesn't,' Tabitha argued.

Zavier shook his head. 'God, are you just a good actress or are you really so naïve? Aiden's scared to cough in case Dad finds out. Why do you think he dragged you along to the wedding? The press have already made a couple of comments about his lack of partner at social occasions—did you really think he wanted you there for your sparkling repertoire?'

'Actually, yes.'

'Please.'

'I know you might find this impossible to fathom, but Aiden actually likes me for me. So don't try and belittle our friendship; that's one argument you're never going to win. I have no doubt if his family were less judgemental and less critical there would have been no need for me to be there.'

A tiny smile was tugging at the edge of his lips, embroiling her in further anger. 'I notice you didn't add "present company excepted" to your little outburst.'

She held his gaze, her tiny face taut and defiant, her eyes wary but with a fire that burned brightly.

'I assure you the omission was intended.'

Even conjugal rights were addressed, right there on page eighteen, with an endless ream of sub-clauses.

Mutual consent…adequate protection…no indicator of the marriage's longevity; the words blurred before her eyes. How could something so beautiful, so intimate, be relegated to a sub-clause in a contract?

Even Zavier managed a small cough of embarrassment as he read out the details. 'I'm sorry, but this had to be put in. As I said, we're kidding ourselves if we pretend it's not going to happen.'

She nodded, a small, sharp nod, not trusting herself to speak.

'It would only complicate things if the legalities weren't addressed now.'

'Of course.'

'Then I think that just about covers everything. Do you have any questions?'

How austere and formal he sounded, as if he had just concluded an interview rather than arranged their marriage.

'Just the one,' Tabitha said with false brightness to hide her nervousness. 'What star sign are you?'

'Pardon.' He looked back at the contract and Tabitha actually laughed.

'You won't find the answer there. We need to know each other's star signs.'

'Why?' he asked simply.

'Because we're supposed to wake up and turn to the horoscope page in the newspaper to find out what the other one's thinking, to find out what sort of day we're going to have, to see if the other's in the mood for romance. You've no idea what I'm talking about, have you?'

For once Zavier was only too happy to agree he was none the wiser.

'One of the first things Marjory will ask is what star sign I am.'

'Of course she won't. It's all a load of rubbish,' he answered irritably. 'I know my mother.'

'I'm sure you do. But she's not only a mother, Zavier, she's a woman, and women do these things. When she asks—which I can practically guarantee she will—if you don't know the answer then an Oscar-winning performance isn't going to save us.'

'Libra.'

'Oh.' The surprise in her voice was evident. Librans were supposed to be warm, loving, tender. 'Were you premature?'

'I was actually on time—to the very day,' Zavier added. 'So what sign are you?'

'Virgo.'

He gave a low devilish laugh. 'Which proves my point: it's a load of rubbish.'

And suddenly there were no pages left. No 'i's to dot or 't's to cross, just a big space for them to sign and date. And as complicated as it was, as intricate as the details were, even Tabitha, with the legal brain of a gnat, understood the gist of the black writing on the wall. She would love him and adore him, in public at least, never embarrass him or jeopardise his status, never waver from the dictated path of the contract. She could have it all— riches, respect, his body, his bed. But there was just one thing the contract left out. One small detail that hadn't been addressed by the nameless lawyers who had created this document.

Love.

The one thing that couldn't be defined, legalised, or rationalised was the only thing missing.

'It's a business deal, Tabitha.' Zavier seemed to sense her hesitancy; his words were surely meant to make her feel better, so why then did her eyes unexpectedly fill with tears?

'I loan out my heart; you pick up my bills?'

'Something like that.' His voice was unusually gentle. Reaching forward, he caught her face in his hand, a heavy thumb smudging away a stray tear that had splashed on her cheek. The surprisingly intimate gesture confused her almost as much as the contract itself. 'But it *is* a good deal, Tabitha. Nobody loses.'

Nobody loses. He watched as a frown flickered across her face. How could he say that? How could he look into her eyes and tell her there would be no losers when six months from now she had to walk away?

'Don't we need a witness?' Tabitha asked, stalling at the final hurdle.

'No,' Zavier said slowly. 'We need time.'

The businessman was back. Clicking into action, he stood up, shuffling the contracts together before tossing them into his briefcase. The strangest thud of disappointment resounded in her chest as she realised he didn't expect her decision just yet, and the thud was coupled with a start of astonishment at her own willingness to sign.

'Sleep on it,' he offered. 'I don't want you feeling forced into anything.'

Picking up the cheque, Tabitha handed it to him, noticing the tremor in her hand as she did so. 'You'd better take this.' She gave a slightly shrill laugh. 'After all, I might just run off with your money.'

But Zavier merely shook his head, refusing the cheque

in her outstretched hand. 'Oh, I don't think there's any need for that.' His eyes narrowed thoughtfully, and though his voice was still soft Tabitha heard the warning note behind it. 'You wouldn't be that stupid, now, would you?' But just as suddenly as the hairs rose on her neck, just as she felt the confines of the contract closing in, heard the warning bells start to ring again, his features softened, an easy smile instantly relaxing his face. 'Come on, you, I'm starving; get dressed and we can go and eat.'

'But I am dressed.' Tabitha shrugged, glancing down at her long bare legs, her pink cleavage spilling out of her wrap-over. 'What's wrong? Don't I make a very good fiancée?'

Zavier laughed, really laughed, and for once it was with real mirth.

'On the contrary, you make a wonderful fiancée. I'm just wondering how I'm going to survive a three-course meal with you looking so appetising.'

CHAPTER FIVE

'WHAT would we tell Aiden?' They were sitting in a sumptuous restaurant, with waiters fluttering like butter-flies, filling her glass, placing vast white napkins in her lap.

'You'll tell him nothing.'

Which helped not one iota. Tabitha made a mental note to ring Aiden first thing; the news could only be better coming from her.

'Or tell him an offer you simply couldn't refuse came up.'

'Can I at *least* tell him the truth—that it's a business deal?'

Zavier's eyes narrowed.

'He'll know,' Tabitha insisted. 'After all, it was his idea in the first place.'

'Okay,' Zavier relented. 'But only Aiden. I mean it, Tabitha, no one else can know. Not your best friend, not your hairdresser, not even your parents.'

Tabitha's hands tightened around her glass. 'My parents are both dead.'

If she had expected sympathy she didn't get it. 'Well, at least you won't have to lie to them.'

Shocked at his callousness, she opened her mouth to protest. But Zavier was in full swing. 'No wonder you and Aiden are friends. You're exactly like him.'

'We're nothing alike,' Tabitha protested.

'Oh, yes, you are. Neither of you have ever had to

worry about meeting a mortgage payment—no doubt you inherited your house?'

'What on earth has that got to do with anything?'

'Well, it goes some way to explaining why you have such a reckless attitude to money, why you've spent your life to date indulging your fantasies. It must be pretty easy to call yourself a dancer when you don't have to worry about mortgage payments—worry about keeping a roof over your head.'

'You're so bitter,' Tabitha snapped, but Zavier merely shrugged.

'I'm a realist.'

'A bitter realist.'

'Perhaps.' Leaning forward, he lowered his voice. 'We met at the wedding, we fell head over heels in love, we're as stunned as we are delighted.' Tapping his fingers, he reeled off the platitudes then leant back in his chair. 'That's the story we'll tell everyone. No wavering, no deviation—not without discussing it with each other first.'

'Won't your parents find it strange?' Tabitha chewed her lower lip, simply refusing to believe it was all that simple.

Zavier shrugged. 'Why would they? Aiden only ever passed you off as a close friend; it was all innuendo. Just remember: we met at the wedding…'

'…fell head over heels in love…' Tabitha continued as Zavier raised his glass to hers.

'…and are as stunned as we're delighted,' he finished as their glasses chinked. 'Good girl—you're getting the idea.'

Strange that any praise from Zavier made her blush.

'Look, Tabitha, as long as we keep pretending they'll believe us.'

'I'm just nervous, that's all. I can't quite believe it myself; I guess that makes it harder to believe that everyone will fall for it.'

'Why wouldn't they?'

'Does anyone fall in love so quickly?'

For once Zavier was off the mineral water, and he took a long sip of his Scotch before answering. 'Who said anything about love? The fact I'm getting married will be enough for my parents.'

'Speaking of your parents, how are we going to tell them?' Tabitha ventured, but her words trailed off as a beaming, smiling man appeared

'Is everything to your satisfaction Monsieur Chambers?' The owner, obviously thrilled at his clientele, appeared at the table.

'Actually, now you mention it, Pierre, no! Everything is not to my satisfaction.' His haughty upper-class tones filled the restaurant and Tabitha slid down in her chair as every face turned to the impromptu cabaret.

Pierre clicked his fingers and a multitude of anxious waiters appeared. 'What is the problem, *monsieur*? Tell me now and I fix it this instant.'

Zavier's face broke into a smile, and Tabitha's blush only deepened as he reached across the table. Taking her hand, he kissed it deeply, and the coolness of his tongue instantly replaced her embarrassment. In a flash her audience was forgotten as the liquid silk of his eyes met hers, the velvet of his lips slowly working its way over her palm.

'My problem is…' Zavier drawled between kisses, his eyes never once leaving hers.

'*Oui?*' Pierre answered, desperate to please.

'That there's no champagne. Tell me, Pierre, what's

a wedding proposal without your best French champagne?'

It was all clicking fingers, corks popping, bubbles fizzing and congratulations being offered as Zavier dug in his suit, producing a tiny black velvet box.

'I haven't said yes yet,' she whispered furiously across the table, but her indignation at his brazen presumption was brushed aside as he took her hand and closed her fingers around the box, his voice a low drawl and for her ears only.

'You can dump me tomorrow.'

The surprise on Tabitha's face when she fiddled with the tiny gold clasp and the box finally opened was genuine. As the ring caught the candlelight and glittered mockingly in her face she found herself staring at the darkest, largest ruby—beautiful in its simplicity, perfect, even. Everything this relationship wasn't.

'You look surprised.'

She swallowed, then grasped his hand back, aware of their audience. 'Isn't that what you're paying me to look?'

'There's a necklace that goes with it.' He gave a dry laugh. 'I'm supposed to give it to you on our fortieth wedding anniversary.'

As he leant over to whisper in her ear they looked for all the world every bit a young couple in love, on the threshold of the universe with all their lives before them waiting to be lived and loved together. Even Pierre's eyes filled with tears as Zavier pulled her closer.

'This ring is on loan. I'll replace it with one of equal monetary value when the deal's completed. Just don't go getting too attached to it; this stays in the family.'

There was no malice in his voice, no offence meant, just a coolly delivered statement of fact.

The only thing Tabitha had to comfort her was the fact that the tears that inexplicably formed in her eyes had Zavier almost gasping in admiration. 'You're wasted as a dancer, Tabitha; you should try your hand at acting.'

It was only when their main meal had been served and Zavier had waved away the attendant waiters, insisting he was perfectly capable of pouring his own wine, that they started to talk again.

'You still haven't answered my question. How will we tell everyone?'

'That's already been taken care of.'

'You mean you've told them before I've even agreed? Are you so sure that I will?'

Zavier shrugged. 'No to the first; yes to the second.'

She stared at him, nonplussed.

'You'll soon see.'

And despite the initially strained atmosphere, despite the awful lies that bound them, sitting there across the table from him, gleaning tiny details about him, watching his features soften in the candlelight, hearing his voice, his occasional laughter, she saw another side to him. Learnt about the man instead of the icon. Discovered that he could be nice and funny—sensitive, even.

Maybe it was the champagne, the crêpes dripping in dark chocolate and raw sugar. Maybe it was the company. Whatever the explanation, as she sat running her spoon in the rivers of chocolate sauce on her plate, when the bill discreetly arrived in its velvet folder, Tabitha felt like a child watching the Christmas tree being taken down. Automatically she reached down for her bag, ready to pay her share, but as soon as she had done so she immediately righted herself.

Of course Zavier noticed. 'Good girl. You're learning fast.'

Pierre was back, positively beaming. 'I am so delighted you chose my restaurant for this most special night. May I say, Monsieur Chambers, what a beautiful fiancée you have, sir. You make a very handsome couple. Tell me, how did you meet?'

Zavier took her hand before he answered. 'At a family wedding, Pierre. It was only a few days ago, yet I feel I've known Tabitha for ever. She swept me off my feet.'

Pierre clapped his hands together in delight. 'A whirlwind romance. How romantic.'

'Isn't it?' Standing, he offered Tabitha his hand, which she accepted.

As the night air hit them Tabitha let out the breath she had inadvertently been holding. 'Do you think he believed us?'

'Why not? I think we did bloody well, actually. Anyway, Pierre can only benefit, so it's in his interest to believe us.'

'Why?'

He turned, the light from the restaurant enhancing his strong profile, his eyes unreadable. 'You've got so much to learn, little one.'

'But what's Pierre got to do with it? He seemed genuinely delighted at the news.'

Zavier gave a cynical snort. 'Genuinely delighted at the publicity, you mean.'

She opened her mouth to question him further, but before the words even formed in her mind a great weight came upon her, the force of his body literally pinning her against the wall. Her breath literally knocked out of her, all she could do was stare in surprise as his hungry mouth searched for hers, his body pushing, pressing against hers in unbridled passion. Amazingly, she wasn't scared—not for a single second. Even though there was nothing gentle about the way he was holding her, nothing restrained about his searching mouth and hands, the scratch of his chin against her cheek like a million tiny volts coursing through her face.

He tasted of champagne and decadence and danger, his kiss a symbol of the very real danger of the man, the inexplicable thrill of the reckless desire that blinded her. How she would love to resist him, to coolly push him away, but it was an impossible feat. Her hand instantly jumped up, grabbing at his hair, pulling his face closer as she kissed him back deeply. His manhood pressing into her left her in no doubt that he was as aroused as her. For a crazy second she thought he might take her there and then—and what was crazier was that she would have let him. In one swoop he had rewritten her values, the very standards she lived by. Her morals, her inner rules were discarded as she kissed him back. But just as suddenly it was over. He pulled away, barely breathless, triumph blazing in his eyes.

'It's all been taken care of,' he said slowly.

They walked along the river in silence, her face raw and tingling from the weight of his kiss, her body a twitching confused mass of desire. Every few steps Tabitha slowed, lifting her hand to her face, the sheer beauty of the jewel a necessary reminder that she wasn't dreaming.

'Look at that.' The wonder in her voice stopped him momentarily and he joined her as she gazed at the chalking on the pavement. His eyes briefly flicked to the self-portrait, a mirror image of the young artist who sat beside his work, torture in his eyes, the pathetically thin body a mocking reminder of the unjust world in which they lived. An abundance of raw talent reduced to begging on the street. She half expected Zavier to deliver some derisive comment, to pull at her arm, discourage her from lingering; instead, to her infinite surprise, he nodded at the artist.

'This is quite beautiful.' There was no patronising undertone, no superiority, just genuine admiration. 'Can you draw my fiancée?' No price was discussed, no figures traded. Zavier's word was his bond and the young man sensed it, gesturing Tabitha to sit down.

Embarrassed, she wanted to refuse, to walk away now, but it was too late for that. Already bony fingers were sharpening charcoal, those tortured eyes were studying her face, and Tabitha knew that leaving now would probably deny him a meal.

More than a meal, actually.

When Zavier took the rolled-up sheet she watched as he shook hands, then, peeling a large amount of notes, handed them to the artist without a word.

'Can I at least see?' she asked as Zavier motioned her to go.

Briefly he unrolled the work, deigning to give her the briefest of glances.

'It's beautiful.' Tabitha flushed. 'I don't mean *I'm* beautiful, just the drawing.'

'That's talent for you.'

'Aiden sold a painting.' His step quickened at the mention of his brother's name and Tabitha had to half run to keep up with him. 'He's talented as well.'

'Rubbish. Some no-name who probably knows nothing about art happened to buy a picture.'

'Why are you so scathing of him?'

'Because I hate waste,' Zavier spat. 'I hate to see him

throwing his life away, chasing dreams, not facing up to his responsibilities.'

'Why?'

'Why?' He spun around then, his hand gripping her arm. 'Don't you think I have dreams, Tabitha? Do you really think that sitting in an office staring at stock markets is where I want to be every day?'

'But you love your work,' she interrupted.

'Says who? Aiden? My mother?' His eyes flashed and his hands moved in unusual animation. 'They're wrong.'

'Then why do it?'

A small hollow laugh escaped his taut mouth. 'My father put his life into that business, but even when he retired, lucrative as it was, it wasn't going to keep my family in jewels and furs and mansions for the rest of their lives. It wasn't going to keep Aiden in Scotch and designer suits. I've turned it into a bloody empire, ensured my family have carried on living the lives they're used to. If I'd walked away, bummed out like Aiden did, sure we wouldn't have starved—but there wouldn't have been the trappings there are now.'

'So?' Her words seemed to incense him, but Tabitha carried on talking quickly, determined to have her say. 'Money's not everything. I know you think I'm a gold-digger, but I know this much—if you didn't want to do it you wouldn't be there.'

'You mean I should walk away and watch my father's dream evaporate, along with my parents' marriage?'

'Surely there's more to them than just money?'

'Maybe, but my mother has never looked at a price tag in her married life, never thought twice about refurbishing the house, putting in a pool or a tennis court, and somehow I can't quite picture her sticking around if the going gets tough. If Aiden had just met me somewhere in the middle, put in a couple of days a week, maybe we both could have had a life outside the business.'

There *were* two sides to every story, Tabitha realised. Aiden's bohemian lifestyle didn't sound quite so romantic now. Chasing his dream had cost his brother dear, and she could almost see the selfishness in her friend's actions.

Almost.

'He's got talent, Zavier,' Tabitha said urgently. 'It isn't just a dream.'

'Said the dancer to the stockbroker.' His voice was dripping with sarcasm, but Tabitha refused to be deflected.

'I'm a good dancer,' she started slowly. 'But not a brilliant one.' Her hand reached up to his face and turned his taut cheek to face her. 'I can't believe I've just admitted that. I've always kidded myself that one day there'd be that nameless face in the audience, the one that was going to whisk me away, ask me why I was wasting my talent in the chorus line. It isn't going to happen for me. It never was, and that really hurts to say.'

His eyes moved slowly to hers, the pain and honesty in her voice forcing his attention,

'But Aiden... He's got more talent in his little finger than I have in my whole body. His paintings are so beautiful they make me cry. And not just me. You should see them—go to the gallery and look at his display, watch people's reactions when they see his work. You should take your father as well,' she added. 'Maybe Aiden was selfish, chasing his dream, but with raw talent like that I don't think he had a choice.'

Zavier didn't answer. Her heartfelt speech was left hanging in the air, without comment or acknowledgment, and Tabitha could only wonder if it had even registered as he took her arm and they carried on walking. Zavier was so broodingly silent that she knew the end of the night was imminent, that her allocated time slot was over.

With terrifying clarity Tabitha knew that she didn't want it to end.

Idly she stared at the casino as they passed it, watching the huge gas chimneys blasting flames into the air in their half-hourly performance, lighting up the night sky in a huge phallic show of power. But of course Zavier misconstrued her vague interest.

'Is this where your money goes?'

'What? Do you think that I'm going to dash back there once you've taken me home?'

Only Zavier wasn't joking, she realised as he glanced over, a look of contempt curiously interlaced with pity on his face.

'I wouldn't put it past you.' Under the brightly lit forecourt it was as light as midday, but his expression was unreadable. 'Come on, let's go in.'

'I thought it was out of bounds,' Tabitha remonstrated, realising her lie by omission might very easily be exposed once Zavier saw her attempts at gambling. Still, the relief that flooded her at the prospect of prolonging their time together made her protest audibly weak.

'We haven't signed the contract yet. Anyway, if you'd been paying attention you'd know that you're allowed to come to the casino so long as you're with me.'

'But why on earth would you want to bring me here? And why tonight? Is this another one of your bizarre tests?'

'I'm afraid so!' A smile tugged at the edge of his mouth. 'A lot of my clients like to be entertained here when they visit Australia; sometimes you'll be expected to accompany me.'

'Oh, and I suppose you want to be sure I can contain myself, that I'm not going to pull out a pack of cards at the dinner table or descend into a catatonic state at the poker machines in front of your important clients?' She snapped her mouth closed as his grin deepened.

'I think they're a bit too high-rolling for the poker machines. Is that where you spend your time when you're here?'

Tabitha gave a half-nod, consoling herself that at least she was telling the truth—or sort of. Her friend Jessica's hen night had ended up at the casino, and Tabitha had fed a whole twenty dollars into the machines—she was hardly the addict Zavier so clearly thought she was, unless they were talking about shoes!

They were walking through the casino's arcade now, row after row of designer shops, their wares glittering invitingly in the window, their doormen insuring only the truly well heeled even made it past the threshold.

'You know they're expensive when there's no price tag,' she said, pressing her nose up against one of the windows and letting out a low moan. 'Did you ever see anything more heavenly?'

Zavier took in her glittering eyes, the rosy cheeks flushed from champagne and the tendril of red hair cascading from her ponytail and working its way down her long slender neck. He was about to agree when he forced himself to concentrate on the focus of Tabitha's attention.

'It's a pair of black slippers,' he drawled in a bored voice.

'They're not slippers,' Tabitha corrected knowingly. 'They're mules…' She eyed the petite shoes with the cheekiest little kitten heels, the heavily jewelled uppers winking back at her. 'And they're divine.'

'The dress is nice,' Zavier mused, looking at the simple full-length velvet with its shoestring straps. 'It would suit you.'

'But not my bank balance. And, no, I'm not fishing. This is just window shopping, at which I'm an expert.'

'I'm sure you are. Right, where do you want to go?'

Tabitha had no idea, but she took his offered hand and they wandered around for a while. People looking, she mused, would think that we were just an ordinary couple. Stealing a look at her escort, she corrected herself—no, they wouldn't. There was nothing ordinary about Zavier. Such was his aura, his effortless grace, even the most groomed and sophisticated heads turned when he walked past.

She was enjoying herself, Tabitha realised, really enjoying herself. Back at the river she had thought the night had almost ended, the fairytale was over; but here amongst the bustling crowds, clutching her picture, walking beside him, his hot dry hand around hers, in the false day the casino created Tabitha felt that the night might last for ever.

'What are you grinning at?'

'I was just thinking what a good time I'm having.'

'Of course you are. This is what turns you on, isn't it?'

She dropped his hand and stopped walking then. At first he didn't appear to notice, but after a couple of steps turned back.

'What now?' he asked irritably. 'Has a Tiffany ring just caught your eye?'

'I was actually thinking how much better it was when you were being nice to me.'

'Oh.' Zavier managed to look uncomfortable, which gave Tabitha the confidence to continue.

'And if this is going to work, Zavier, surely we should at least try being nice to each other—and not just in other people's company. It's going to be a long six months if we're constantly sniping at each other.'

'Okay,' he mumbled, but Tabitha was on a roll.

'We've already established that where sarcastic one-liners are concerned you're a master, but I for one don't need my faults and shortcomings being constantly rammed down my throat. Yes, this is a business deal, and, yes, if I do accept then I'll come out of this with a huge financial advantage. But you were the one who approached me, not the other way around.'

'Okay, okay,' he snapped.

'That's not being nice,' she retorted.

The champagne had worked its way down to her toe-nails now, and combined with the undeniable euphoria of finally having an answer to her grandmother's problem it was proving an intoxicating combination. A smart reply, easily as witty as one of Zavier's, was forming, but just as it reached the tip of her tongue a wedge of flesh pushed her against a boutique and he kissed her far too thoroughly, his cool tongue parting her lips like a hot knife through butter.

'Is that nice enough for you?' he growled as she licked her stinging lips, and without waiting for her response he dragged her back into the sea of people.

Tabitha could see how her grandmother's problem had started. The lights, the noise, the hum of the place—the whole extravagant package, actually—gave her a thrill of excitement in the pit of her stomach. Of course the fact she was also on the arm of one of Australia's most eligible bachelors amplified the effect, but Tabitha could certainly see the attraction it must hold for a lonely old woman whose days and nights stretched on endlessly.

Zavier had disappeared to a bar and, after feeding her last note into a change machine, Tabitha took her bucket of dollar coins and settled at a poker machine, trying to assume an air of knowledge as she attempted to locate where to put her money.

Love hearts whizzed around before her eyes, cupid's darts took aim as the machine started singing, arrows flew as dollar signs appeared, and an earsplitting electrical fanfare belted out of the machine.

'Aren't you going to take your free spin?'

He was back, and Tabitha instantly stiffened on her stool, sorely tempted to put her arm up and shield the machine from his sight. But she knew that wouldn't stop Zavier. She could imagine him as a sulky schoolboy, finishing his spelling test first and then peering over with mocking scorn at her futile attempts. And she was positive he was laughing at her—positive at that moment he knew the fraud that she was. Taking her drink, Tabitha pretended to concentrate, pushing the flashing button before her. She could feel the boredom emanating from him and fiddled with the buttons a few more times, watching her credit limit dissolve to zero in two minutes flat.

'So what now?' Turning, she gave him a smile.

'You mean you're already finished?' His eyebrows shot up in surprise. 'I thought we'd be stuck here for hours.' Picking up her bag, he handed it to her. 'Is this your attempt to show me how controlled you can be?'

Tabitha shrugged. 'Something like that,' she muttered, while privately wondering how people could sit for hours staring at the blessed things. Mind you, not everyone had a diversion quite as delicious as Zavier to lure them away. 'Are we going home now?'

He stared at her for a moment, watching as her colour deepened under his scrutiny. 'I thought I'd have to drag you out of here kicking and screaming.'

Mentally chastising herself, Tabitha realised she wasn't exactly behaving like a woman with a gambling problem. 'Sorry to disappoint you,' she said lightly, jumping down from her stool and making to go. But Zavier didn't move. He just carried on staring, his eyes narrowing as he looked at her thoughtfully.

'Come on.' Taking her hand, he led her easily through the crowd and without a further word led her up mazes of escalators until the thronging masses eased off. Suddenly the fairground-like, carnival mood of the casino had evaporated; suddenly they were back in Zavier's world. The world of the well dressed, with dimmed lights and discreet music, a world where doormen greeted you by name and *never* asked for ID, where even the bar staff never thought to charge.

A world away from Tabitha's.

A vast wooden door was opened as if by magic, and Tabitha blinked a couple of times as the heavy cigar smoke that filled the air reached her eyes.

'Why have you bought me here?' she asked slowly, terrified he might ask her to play one of the tables.

'To teach you a lesson.' His hand was still wrapped around hers, and he pulled her nearer but didn't bother to drop his voice. 'The minimum bet here's a thousand dollars. I'm going to show you just how easy it is to lose money.'

'Oh, come on, Zavier.' She turned to go but his hand gripped hers ever tighter. 'There's no need for this.' She let out a nervous giggle. 'I gamble away the odd twenty dollars or so; this is the big league.'

'It's all relative.' His eyes narrowed. 'Anyway, I'm not the one in debt here.'

'Well, you might be soon.' Tabitha gestured to the tables. 'Look, Zavier, this has gone too far…' She had to tell him, had to stop him—everything was getting way out of hand. 'I don't have a problem with gambling. I don't know how you got the idea—'

'So you're suddenly cured?'

'I never had a problem in the first place—'

'Save it,' he snapped.

'But I don't—'

'You see that guy over there?' This time his voice did drop. 'Hands clenched, sweating buckets?'

Tabitha followed his gaze, nodding as she saw the unfortunate gentleman who was now fishing a large silk handkerchief out of his undoubtedly expensive suit. 'I bet if you asked he'd tell you that he hasn't got a problem either. Yet he probably just lost his house, or his car, maybe his business, and no doubt he lost his wife a while back. And see that woman there? The one in the green dress?' He didn't wait for her response. 'See how she's chewing on her lip, taking a drink every few seconds? Well, if she had any sense then she'd get the hell out. Like I said, it's all relative, whether it's twenty dollars or twenty thousand. If you can't afford it you shouldn't be here.'

Despite her awkwardness Tabitha listened, enthralled, his insight was amazing, his descriptions spot-on. 'And I suppose you'll just stand there calmly?'

'That's right.' He led her over to a soft low sofa and they sat down, drinks seemingly miraculously appearing before them before the waiters discreetly melted away. 'I'll set my budget and stick to it.'

'Oh, very controlled,' Tabitha said sarcastically. 'It must be hard, being so perfect all of the time.'

'Hey, I thought we were being nice to each other.'

'We are,' Tabitha grumbled. 'Except when you start lecturing me.'

'I'm not lecturing you. Well, maybe a bit,' he admitted. 'But it's for your own good. The difference between us, Tabitha, is I know when to stop.'

'Fine,' she snapped, nervous at the thought of him gambling money to prove an extremely unnecessary point. 'You do what you want. Just don't expect me to join you.'

'So the poker machines are more your thing, then?' His upper-class accent was mocking now. 'You don't fool me, Tabitha. The only reason you don't want to join in is because you don't know how to play the tables.'

'Look,' Tabitha said very definitely, her hand pulling at his suit sleeve as he turned to go, 'I don't have a gambling problem.' She allowed him one long bored sigh before tentatively continuing. 'I really don't. The debt you heard Aiden and I discussing is my grandmother's... I hardly ever come here!'

He didn't look at her. Pointedly removing his sleeve from her grip, he took a long sip of his drink before finally turning to face her. 'Then why the sudden euphoria, Tabitha? Why the flushed face and the sparkle in your eyes? The second we walked in here I could feel your excitement—feel it,' he reiterated. 'So if it isn't the casino that's doing it for you, why the sudden change?'

'Zavier!' She almost shouted his name, but he didn't even blink. 'Why do you think I'm so excited? It's not every day a girl gets a marriage proposal. It's not every

day…' Her voice trailed off, and from the shuttered look
in his eyes she knew she was wasting her time; a word
like love simply didn't factor in here.

'You've got a problem,' he snapped. 'You can deny
it all you like, but the only person you're fooling is
yourself, Tabitha.'

Sinking back into the sofa, Tabitha nursed her drink.
'Oh, I've got a problem all right,' Tabitha muttered as
he stalked off towards the table. 'Six foot four's worth.'

She didn't have to worry about her cover being blown.
She could take a full-page ad out in the papers telling
him about her grandmother and he'd still just put it down
to denial. But why had she let him think she had a problem in the first place? Surely a gambling addict was
hardly a flattering light to put oneself under? Looking
over, she watched him. Not a muscle flickered in his
face, not a single bead of sweat marred his brow. His
brief nod at the croupier was friendly and relaxed.
Turning momentarily, he caught her eye.

'All right?' he mouthed, and Tabitha nodded, a
strange feeling suddenly welling in her. Despite his protests, despite his attempts to prove otherwise, Zavier
Chambers was a nice man.

His back was to her now, but she could just make out
his strong steady hands moving a pile of chips across
the table. The woman in green was taking another nervous sip of her drink as Zavier stood unmoved next to
her. She watched the woman walking away, tears in her
eyes, shaking her head in disbelief at her loss. Perhaps
the magnitude of what she had gambled was only now
starting to dawn.

She could end it all here—walk away now and have
lost nothing. It was Tabitha taking a nervous sip of her

drink now, her hand tightening around the glass as she mentally rolled the dice.

Standing, she made her way over, one hand gently touching Zavier's shoulder as she quietly observed the game in progress.

'I thought this wasn't your scene?' Zavier turned briefly as an inordinately large pile of chips was pushed towards him.

'It seems you were right after all,' Tabitha murmured, breathing in the heady scent of him as she edged just a fraction closer, feeling the solid warmth of his legs against her barely clad thighs. 'Maybe I don't know when to stop.'

CHAPTER SIX

'THANKS for the lesson, by the way.' Tabitha let out a gurgle of laughter as his car pulled up outside her house. 'You've definitely cured me.'

'I'm never going to live this down, am I?' Even Zavier was laughing as he pulled on the handbrake. 'I couldn't have lost my car keys tonight if I'd tried; I made a bloody fortune. So much for trying to show you the error of your ways.'

'Lesson well and truly learnt,' Tabitha answered in a solemn voice, then broke into hysterics again.

'You're a bad girl,' Zavier said gruffly, and something in his voice stopped her laughter. Something in the way he turned his head, his dark eyes glittering in the moonlight, made Tabitha's heart-rate accelerate alarmingly.

'Maybe I am, but I make great coffee.' Running her tongue nervously over her bottom lip, she watched his hands tighten on the steering wheel. 'Do you want to come in?'

'Better not.' His words were clipped, and Tabitha felt the good mood of earlier evaporate, steaming up the car window as she sat there suddenly void of anything to say. The tension in the air was palpable. 'It's been a good night, though.' His voice was strained, forced. 'I really enjoyed myself.'

'Don't.' The single word was out before she could stop it, and it hung in the air as she forced herself to continue. 'I mean, you don't have to pretend now; I know you're just being nice.'

For an age he stared at her. 'I thought nice was what you wanted, Tabitha.'

'It is....'

'Well, then, don't complain.' He nodded to the house. 'You'd better get inside. The neighbours' curtains are starting to twitch.'

'How did you know where I lived?' It suddenly dawned on Tabitha that he had taken her home without direction, and her mind reeled from impossible scenario to scenario. 'Did you have me followed? Have you been watching me?'

'Nothing so exciting, I'm afraid. I looked you up in the phone book.'

'Oh!' She let out a nervous giggle and Zavier smiled, but the drumming of his fingers on the steering wheel indicated her allocated time slot was over.

'When will I see you again?' It came out wrong, needy and unsure, and his idle drumming on the steering wheel stopped momentarily. 'I mean, what do we do now?'

'That's up to you.'

'So I passed the test back at the casino?'

A smile skated on the edge of his lips and Tabitha ached, ached to put up her fingers, to catch the glimmer of light in his tired, jaded face.

'You passed,' he said simply. Leaning over to the passenger side, he pulled the contracts from his briefcase, then flicked on the car light. She watched, her breath hot in her lungs, as he scrawled an extravagant signature on each of the documents before handing them to her. 'Drop them off at my solicitor's if you decide to go through with it.'

'That's it? That's all I have to do?' The simplicity of the action truly terrified her.

'That's it.' Zavier shrugged. 'Look, I really am going to the States tomorrow, to close off some deals. Anyway, it will be easier that way—playing the part of the devoted fiancé for the next month or so might prove a bit too hard. I'll ring you with all the details once I've worked things out, and my driver will pick you up, take you shopping for the wedding and take you to Lorne. In the meantime keep your nose clean. I'll be in touch.'

'But surely I have to do something. What about invitations, my wedding dress…?'

'It will all be taken care of.'

And with that she had to make do. Stepping out of the car, she half expected him to call her back, to pull her into his arms, to end the perfect evening in the perfect way. But he didn't—just sat there watching as she let herself in.

She watched from the darkened lounge window as his car slid off into the darkness, the ring on her finger heavy and unfamiliar.

Unable to fathom what had just happened, the enormity of Zavier's proposal only now truly registering, she expected to be awake for hours, to lie in the darkness staring at the ceiling, wrestling with her conscience. But for the first time since the wedding Tabitha fell into a deep and dreamless sleep, as if seeing him had somehow stilled the restlessness in her soul.

Only when the sun arose, when the trucks in the distance shifted their gears noisily and schoolchildren chattered excitedly outside her bedroom window as they passed by on the way to school, did her sleepy eyes open as the door below was pounded.

Her mind was whirring, the ring still heavy on her finger, her mouth dry from the champagne, her heart hammering as the previous night's events repeated themselves.

Surely it was a dream—a strange, vivid dream? Surely it could never have happened?

Wrapping a robe around her, she pulled the bolt on the door, half expecting to see Zavier telling her it was a joke—a mistake, perhaps.

'Delivery for Miss T. Reece.' A huge white box was thrust into her arms, and as she wrestled to hold it and somehow sign the delivery note her heart-rate quickened as Aiden made his way purposefully up the garden path, his grim face a million miles from the gentle man she loved and knew.

'What the hell have you done?' Ignoring the delivery boy he burst past, slamming the door as she stood there in the hallway. 'Page four,' Aiden practically spat, flinging the morning paper at her. 'The headline reads "Marriage made in Financial Heaven".'

Shaking, she put down the box and struggled with the newspaper, a small gasp escaping her lips as she turned the pages. There she was—at least, there her hands were—lost in Zavier's hair, the glint of the ruby on her finger, the searing memory of his kiss immortalised in a photo now.

Aiden grabbed back the paper, reading it aloud in a taunting voice. '"Met at a wedding! Swept off his feet! A whirlwind romance!" My God, Tabitha, what have you agreed to?'

Pierre must have rung the press the second the first champagne cork had popped. So that was what Zavier had meant when he'd said it had all been taken care of.

'I haven't agreed to anything,' Tabitha answered quickly, playing for time.

'That's not what it says here,' Aiden snarled. 'Do you want me to carry on reading?'

'I was going to tell you,' she begged. 'I was going to ring you this morning.'

'To tell me what, exactly? You mean this is all true? You really are marrying him?'

'I don't know…'

'It was Zavier you were with the night of the wedding?'

'How did you know I was with anyone?' She was stalling, dreading the questions her answers would lead to.

'I got up to get a glass of water—you know, mouth like a carpet and all that. I never said anything at the time because I figured it was none of my business. But if it was Zavier you were with then I'm damn well making it my business.' He was struggling for control now, and Tabitha stood speechless as he hurled the newspaper at the wall. 'It was him you were with, wasn't it?'

She nodded, staring dumbly at the carpet, unable to meet her friend's eyes.

'I told you not to get involved. I warned you about him. Honestly, Tabitha, he's no good for you. He may be my brother but he's still a bastard.'

'He's not. Honestly, Aiden, we went out last night and he was really nice…' Her voice trailed off as she recalled Zavier's shuttered eyes in the car.

'Can't you see that he was just being nice because you were doing what he wanted?'

'Of course I can.' Tabitha swallowed hard, hating the fact but knowing it to be true.

'You're going to get hurt, Tab.' He was nearly crying now, and Tabitha wasn't far off herself. 'You're going to get so hurt.'

'How can you be sure?'

'Because I know him. Why, Tabitha? How did you get into this? And please don't quote the newspaper—I need to know what's happened?'

'He offered me money.'

'*I* offered you money.'

'He offered me more.'

Aiden refused to buy it. 'I know you, Tabitha, as well as, if not better than, I know Zavier. I offered you enough to get your grandmother out of debt and a bit more, and yet you refused.'

'It's a lot more than you offered,' she admitted, shame filling her. 'A lot more.'

But still Aiden steadfastly refused to believe her. 'He could have offered you the Crown Jewels and you'd have turned him down.' Sitting on her sofa, he stared moodily out of the window. 'You love him, don't you?'

'This has nothing to do with love.'

'Bull.' He practically spat the expletive and Tabitha winced. Seeing Aiden so angry was something she hadn't reckoned on. 'You love him, and you're hoping in time he'll love you too.'

'Of course I don't love him, Aiden. I hardly know him.' But the uncertainty in her voice was audible even to herself.

'That didn't stop you sleeping with him,' Aiden pointed out nastily. 'Just what the hell's going on between you two, Tabitha? And don't feed me this line about money; I just won't believe it.'

'There is an attraction,' Tabitha admitted slowly, unsure how to explain what she couldn't even articulate to herself. 'But I'm not stupid enough to believe a marriage can survive on sex alone. It's a lot of money, Aiden. It will change my life. I can open up my own dance school.

Yes, you offered me money and, yes, you offered me marriage. But, Aiden, how long would it have lasted? How long before we'd be exposed? At least this way…'

His eyes locked on her hand, his face growing more incredulous by the moment as he lifted it up and examined the ring. 'He gave you the ruby?'

'It's a loan,' Tabitha said breathlessly. 'He made it very clear he wanted it back.'

'He said he'd never let it out of his sight again.' Aiden's voice was one of utter amazement. 'Swore on his own life the next time a woman wore that ring it would be the real thing.'

'The next time?'

Aiden looked up at the question in her voice. 'He was engaged a couple of years ago, to this sweet young thing—or so we all thought. Two weeks before the wedding Louise went and got herself some hot-shot solicitor to draw up the most complicated prenuptial agreement, figuring that Zavier wouldn't back out of the wedding at that late stage.'

'And did he?'

'Yep.' Aiden gave a wry grin. 'The one thing she didn't bank on when she worked out her plan was Zavier's exacting standards. The day he realised it was more about money than love he dropped her—and there was nothing dignified about Louise's exit, let me tell you. Even as we speak there's a court action against him for breach of contract and emotional trauma. But this isn't about money,' Aiden insisted again through gritted teeth. 'You can deny it all you like, Tab, but this *isn't* about money. You know it and so do I.'

She did know it, yet was too terrified to admit it— even to herself. 'He thinks the gambling debt is mine.' Watching his uncomprehending face, Tabitha took a breath before venturing further. 'I tried to tell him the truth but he just refused to hear it. Please, Aiden, don't tell him otherwise.'

'He'll find out anyway,' Aiden was shouting again. Tabitha put her hands over her ears but he carried on relentlessly. 'Hell, he probably already knows. He's using you, Tabitha. You can't win this one.' He quietened then, his voice softening when he saw her pain, saw the tears coursing down her cheeks. 'It's not too late to say no. Your surname's not in the paper. Zavier can shoot the rumours down in five minutes flat—he's done it for me before... He'll demand a retraction and it will all be forgotten. You won't need to go through this ridiculous charade.'

Which was what terrified her the most.

Tabitha closed her eyes. 'Please don't hate me, Aiden. I couldn't bear it.'

'I don't hate you, Tabitha, I'm just scared for you—for me too, come to that.'

'What have you got to be afraid of?'

'You're my best friend, Tabitha, and he's my brother. I don't want to lose either of you, and when it all goes bad—as it surely will—I don't want to have to choose.'

There was so much finality in his voice, such a jaundiced air of inevitability, that the gnawing sense of foreboding she had awoken with multiplied with alarming speed and a surge of panic swelled within her.

'It won't come to that.' Her voice wavered and there was nothing assured about her response.

'I hope not.'

'Will you give me away?'

'You're going to go through with it, then?'

'*If* I do go through with it,' Tabitha corrected, 'will you give me away?'

Aiden let out a low whistle. 'You're pushing it, you know?'

'Please, Aiden. I'll be nervous enough; at least I won't have to lie to you, pretending to be the blushing bride and all that. You know it's just a business deal.'

'But is it?'

She nodded, slowly at first and then more certainly. 'You know it is. Please, Aiden, I really need you to be there for me.'

He stared at her for a moment. 'Okay, then, but I'm not buying you both a present. I'll save my money for the mountain of tissues and chocolate I'll undoubtedly have to dole out when it's all over.'

'I'll be fine,' Tabitha said resolutely. 'I know what I'm doing.'

'I hope so,' Aiden said simply, and, giving her the briefest kiss on the cheek, he let himself out.

Only when she was alone did Tabitha remember her parcel. Her hands still shaking from the confrontation— from everything, really—it took for ever to open, but as the box slid open she let out a gasp of delight. The dress and shoes she had admired so lovingly last night lay on a mountain of tissue paper, only they weren't black. Instead the softest, palest lilac beckoned her hands, which she ran over the soft velvet of the dress. In a second Tabitha's robe was discarded and the dress skimmed over her head. Slipping the shoes onto her feet, she searched through the tissue paper until she found what she was looking for.

It wasn't quite the declaration Tabitha had secretly been hoping for, but just the sight of his purple signature somehow soothed her.

Funny that a hastily written note with a noticeably absent kiss gave her more pleasure than several thousand dollars' worth of clothes, Tabitha thought as she sat there dressed in all her finery staring at the piece of paper.

'Six months,' she whispered to herself.

Six months of sleeping beside him, waking next to him in the morning. Six months to show Zavier how good and sweet love could be if only you let yourself taste it.

Six months to make him love her.

In a corner? Maybe.

Making a mistake? Probably

Taking the biggest gamble of her life? Definitely.

Of course there was never a pen when she needed one, but a rummage down the side of the sofa finally delivered the goods, and with a shaking hand Tabitha held the contract and added her signature beneath Zavier's— not quite with flourish but with definite determination.

There were a million reasons she should have said no to Zavier, and only one truth. The simple fact that she loved him was the real reason Tabitha said yes.

CHAPTER SEVEN

'WE'VE put you in here.' Marjory Chambers flung open the shutters. 'I know you and Zavier will probably think it old hat, but until you're married at least I've put you in separate rooms. Jeremy wouldn't hear of anything else.' Marjory gave her an engaging smile, misinterpreting the look of relief that flooded Tabitha's face as she pointed to a door. 'Of course the rooms are adjoining, so what you get up to is your business.'

Everything about today felt surreal. She expected grandeur after the wedding, but the Chambers holiday home was practically a mansion. There was nothing dark and stately about it, though. Wall-to-wall floorboards, huge white walls littered with black and white photos, sumptuous white leather couches and artefacts each meriting more than a cursory glance. If this was their holiday home heaven only knew what their main residence must be like. Her bedroom jutted out onto the ocean, its vastness glittering before her, the bay view to end all bay views.

'Jeremy's having a lie-down, but we'll be having drinks on the patio at seven before dinner. He can't wait to say hello. But please, Tabitha, feel free to come down before then—make yourself at home. I know this last month can't have been easy on you, with Zavier being away, but it's over now, he'll be here within the hour and finally we can get on with this wedding. Now, do you want me to look after your dress? Zavier simply mustn't get even a glimpse; you're going to look stunning.'

Marjory was so nice, so disarmingly friendly, that as Tabitha unzipped her suitcase—new, of course—and passed her the wads of tissue paper that contained the lilac dress and shoes Zavier had sent her, she was suddenly assailed by the biggest wave of guilt.

'I brought you these chocolates.' She hadn't known what to bring. What did you give to someone who'd got everything? No doubt there was a cellar bursting with the finest wines, which had ruled out anything Tabitha could pick up at the local supermarket, and anticipating gardens trimmed and manicured to perfection had made flowers seem rather paltry. So she had settled for chocolates—wasn't that what everyone did? And not the usual half-kilo slab that she occasionally treated herself to. Tabitha had splurged on the best she could find in the department store. They had cost a small fortune; hopefully she'd get a taste!

Thrusting the package at Marjory, Tabitha felt a blush spread over her cheeks.

'I didn't know what to get.'

She was taken back by the sparkle of tears in Marjory's well-made-up eyes.

'Oh, Tabitha, you're such a dear thoughtful girl.'

Tabitha shuffled her feet. 'I know it's not much.'

She was enveloped in a hug within Marjory's heavy scented bosom. 'They're perfect, and so are you…' Her voice trailed off as the sound of tyres crunching on the gravel broke the moment.

'Aiden is here!' Marjory exclaimed, but the excitement she reserved for Zavier was noticeably absent. 'I must go and welcome him. Won't you come down?'

Tabitha politely declined; another lecture from Aiden

was the last thing she needed right now. 'I'll stay and unpack, if you don't mind.'

'But the staff will take care of that.' Marjory's voice softened then. 'Silly me. You'll want to spend some time getting ready for Zavier.'

As Marjory rushed from the room Tabitha set about unpacking, and finally, when every last thing had been put away, when she had fiddled with her hair long enough and rouged her cheeks, sprayed scent over every inch of her body, there was nothing else to do. Nothing but wait with mounting trepidation for the crunch of gravel that would bring her future husband to her side. Since the day she had met him, since the day he had burst into her life, knocking her sideways with his sheer presence, he had dominated every facet of her life. As surely as any major trauma he had inflicted more drama, more emotion than she had ever experienced to date. Though her days had been filled with work, with time spent sorting out her grandmother, explaining her sudden wedding to her stunned friends, the practicalities had been a breeze compared to the torturous mental abacus that had overwhelmed her: counting the weeks, the days, the nights, the hours until she saw him again.

She felt him approaching before the low snarl of his engine was even audible. A cynic would say it was guesswork—after all, his plane landed at four, the timing was inevitable, perhaps her subconscious heard him without realising—but she knew as sure as her heart was beating that there was something deeper going on here, some mental telepathy that had invaded her. This very moment had sustained her through the uncertainty of the last few weeks, but now that the moment had actually arrived she was completely overcome with nerves, and the all too familiar sense of foreboding, Zavier randomly triggered, assailed her again. She was playing with fire here, and someone was bound to get burnt. Tabitha held her breath, standing just far back enough from the open window so she couldn't be seen.

Perhaps she moved, maybe a shadow fell, but whatever the reason he lifted his head, his eyes searing into the room in which she stood. Ducking backwards, Tabitha caught her breath; she knew he hadn't seen her, knew it was impossible, but there was no safety in logic.

Trembling, she sat on the bed, berating herself for the impossible situation she had thrust upon herself. She wasn't just messing with her own life here; she was playing Russian roulette with every person in this house. How was she going to face him? How was she going to look at him after all these weeks and not betray what was seared in her heart?

Love wasn't in this equation.

Yet.

'Tabitha!' The happy shriek from Marjory made her jump. 'He's here!'

Painting on a smile, she made her way out of the bedroom, reaching the top of the stairs as Marjory pulled the front door open.

Tabitha had hoped that the passage of time would somehow diminish his beauty, that the man who stepped gracefully into the entrance hall would hold only a distant charm. That she could play along with the charade and still keep a semblance of control.

She was wrong on all counts.

His beauty literally knocked the breath from her, and she stood there stunned as his eyes slowly lifted to hers, her breath coming out in short bursts, her nerves snapping to attention, deprived for so long and only now awakening as the master returned.

'Don't I get a welcome home kiss?' he drawled.

Slowly she made her way down the stairs, but as she reached the last couple the violence of her desire, the magnetism that surrounded him, made her literally run into his arms. It was him she needed, his strength was all that could get her through, and she fell into his arms and he pulled her close and kissed away the salty tears that had unexpectedly sprung from her eyes.

'Hey, I'll have to go away more often if that's the welcome I get.'

Embarrassed at her emotive display, she kept her head trained on the floor.

'Don't you dare,' Marjory scolded. 'You have to learn to delegate, Zavier. You're going to have a lovely wife to come home to now; you can't be jetting off at a moment's notice.'

'Someone has to work,' Zavier quipped.

Tabitha wasn't a big drinker, but never had she been more grateful for the gin and tonic Marjory thrust into her hand. Taking a large sip, she sought some refuge as the sharp taste hit her tongue.

'You look stunning, Tab.' Aiden finally acknowledged her, squeezing her hand and taking a hefty sip of his own drink as he did so.

She knew it must have been hard for him and she smiled gratefully, happy they were friends again.

'Every bit the bride-to-be.'

She almost felt it.

This whole week had been spent in a frenzy of preparation. Her legs being waxed, eyebrows tweezed, eyelashes dyed, shopping for bathers and cocktail dresses. Zavier's driver had indeed picked her up and taken her shopping. Had handed her a credit card with a discreet nod and a list of instructions that would have caused most women to think they'd died and gone to heaven. The driver had waited outside the most exclusive shops as Tabitha searched amongst the beige and navy suits and fitted dresses for the lilacs and pinks and moss-greens she adored, the velvets and silks that were so much her own style, so much more readily available at the craft markets she frequented. Filling smart bright bags with designer labels, exclusive one-offs, she had felt sick at what she had so effortlessly spent.

Good money after bad.

The weight of her deception was almost unbearable.

'Where's Dad?'

'Asleep.'

'How is he?'

Marjory flashed a perfectly lip-lined smile that every-one in the room knew was false. 'He's doing very nicely; he's just tired, that's all. He'll join us for dinner; now let's go and have a huge drink.'

'Let's not,' Zavier drawled. 'I think I'll take Dad's lead and have a lie-down.' His eyes flickered to Tabitha, who stood there suddenly deflated. What she had ex-pected from this the strangest of reunions she had no idea, but it came as a huge anticlimax that now she had finally seen him he was disappearing so fast.

Just what did you expect? she scolded herself. That he'd be pleased to see you? But her spirits lifted as he pulled her close, running a lazy hand around her waist. 'Perhaps you could bring me up a drink.' He kissed her then, again, and this time it was absolutely unnecessary, for no one had doubted the joy in their reunion.

This blatant display of sexuality Tabitha knew had been entirely for her benefit, and the thought simulta-neously thrilled and terrified her, making even the sim-plest task of pouring a Scotch a feat in itself. Knocking gently, she quietly opened Zavier's door. The drapes were drawn and she stood there for a moment, allowing her eyes to become accustomed to the darkness. Making her way over, she passed the heavy crystal glass to him; the touch of his fingers made her jump and most of the contents of the glass trickled between their fingers.

'Steady. You're really nervous, aren't you?' Zavier observed.

'Terrified,' she admitted.

'Why? They all believe us. Even Aiden seems to be coming round to the idea.'

'Good.' Her voice was strained; she was scared she might reveal it wasn't his family that was unnerving her at the moment, wasn't the charade they were playing, but the impact of him close up that terrified her. 'How was America?'

'Great—didn't you get my postcard?'

Which ended that conversation. Zavier would no more write a postcard than fly to the moon. He had propped himself up on one elbow, and, placing his drink on the bedside table, he pulled his tie looser.

'You must be exhausted?'

'I've spent sixteen hours sleeping on the plane.'

'Oh, that's right.' Tabitha gave a wry laugh. 'There was me feeling sorry for you, imaging you slumming it in economy, but no doubt you flew first class—or does your family have its own private jet?'

'No, but for heaven's sake don't suggest it or it will be on top of Mother's list of "must haves".' It was a tiny joke but it made her smile, though it wobbled slightly as his finger came up to her lips.

'That's better. I forgot how beautiful you look when you smile.'

He was being nice to her, gentle and funny, and she

didn't know how to respond, didn't know what was real
any more.

'Lie beside me.'

'Why?'

'Practice. We're going to have to get used to sharing
a bed, and anyway I don't like sleeping on my own.'

And no doubt he never had to, Tabitha thought, but
she was weakening. 'I shouldn't.'

'Why?'

Tabitha swallowed. 'Your mum put us in different
rooms; it wouldn't be right.' She was fighting for excuses. Marjory had practically opened the adjoining door
for them, handed her consent on a plate, but it wasn't
some delayed moral code that was preventing her lying
down beside him. It was the very real fear that she might
weaken and tell him how she was really feeling. Tears
were threatening, and the emotions of the past few
weeks, the desperate need to see him, the fact he was
actually here, the shock of his tenderness were all doing
unimaginable things to her self-control.

'Come here.' They were the same two words he had
used on their first night together, the same two words
that had catapulted her into his arms, and this time the
effect was gentler but just as devastating. Slowly she
unstrapped her sandals, before stretching out on the bed
beside him.

'We mustn't...'

'I know.' He pulled her into the crook of his arm and
she lay there rigid, her breath hot and bursting against
her lungs. 'How has it been, the last few weeks?' She
didn't answer, just lay there, revelling in his embrace.
'How did your family take it?'

'There's only my grandmother.'

'So how did she react to the news?' His voice was so

deep, so soft, it was almost lulling her to sleep as she lay in the darkness next to him.

'She was surprised, pleased, stunned—the same as my friends, really.'

'Why were they surprised?'

Wriggling slightly, she turned in the darkness towards him. 'Well, the speed of it. They all initially tried to convince me that I'd gone crazy. I guess there's not many people left who believe in love at first sight. How about you?'

'What about me?' He was half-listening, half-asleep.

'Do you believe in love at first sight?'

'There's no such thing as love.'

She stared into the darkness, waiting for him to finish his sentence, waiting for him to elaborate. When he didn't, when the only sound that reached her ear was his gentle rhythmic breathing and the ticking of his watch, she realised he had finished talking. 'You don't believe in love at all?'

'I believe in lust, compatibility, friendship—but love like in the movies? There's no such thing, Tabitha.'

'But of course there is.' Propping herself up on her elbow, she jabbed him playfully in the ribs, but Zavier was deadly serious. Taking her hand, he pulled her back into his arms.

'There's no such thing,' he repeated. 'I thought I'd been proved wrong once, actually thought I'd hit the jackpot.' His voice was detached but Tabitha could feel the tension in him as he spoke, and she listened intently, desperate for insight, for understanding. 'For a while there it was great, but it was just a fantasy, like one of your fairytales. Louise never loved me. Sure, she was attracted to me—liked me, even—but that's not the type of love you're going on about.'

'Just because it didn't happen with Louise it doesn't mean there isn't someone out there for you.'

He gave a low laugh. 'The other half that will make me whole? You've been watching too many films, Tabitha. I'm telling you there's no such thing.'

His words tore through her—to hear him so cynical, so scornful, defied explanation.

'I know Louise hurt you, Zavier, but to write off the rest of the human race because of one bad relationship— surely that's a bit of an overreaction?'

'It isn't an overreaction. I can't think of one marriage in my entire family that hasn't been about money.' He lay there, thoughtful for a moment. 'No, not one—ours included.' He gave a loud yawn, stretching his body languorously beside her, his arms reaching above his head then wrapping back around her. 'Funny, I actually missed you while I was away.'

Stunned, scared to move in case she had somehow misheard him, Tabitha swallowed hard.

'You missed me?' Her voice was a whisper and she finally turned to him, but Zavier didn't answer. His eyes were closed, his mouth slightly open, the sulky look on his face even in sleep. She went to get up, to go to her own room and somehow glean some breathing space, somehow try to add up all the pieces that were Zavier. But, grumbling, he pulled her back, his arm clamping down around her, his face burrowing in her hair with a low moan, and she lay there scared to move, in case the spell was broken.

If this was the hell she was destined to for her sins then Tabitha could take it. Pompous, arrogant, scathing he might be, but the occasional glimpse of what she believed was the real Zavier made up for it all tenfold.

Surely something that felt so right, so natural, couldn't be *all* wrong?

CHAPTER EIGHT

SHE dressed at lightning speed for dinner, terrified that the intimate mood might somehow evaporate while he showered. But out of his arms, as she pulled on a pale lemon shift dress and strapped on her sandals, the demons that constantly sniped at her returned.

Of course he was being nice; he wanted this to work as much as she did, and keeping her on side was one way of ensuring that their audience remained convinced.

Walking down the stairs, he took her hand, and as they entered the lounge his grip tightened. They joined the group and it took only one look for Tabitha to realise that the sudden strength of his grip wasn't about lending her moral support.

Jeremy Chambers sat in a wheelchair. He seemed light years away from the powerful man of just a few weeks ago, his face haggard and thin, his eyes sunken, but his suit was impeccable and there was an air of dignity and strength about him that illness couldn't ravish, no matter what else it took.

'Tabitha.' He took her hand, kissing it gently. 'You look stunning.' He winced slightly as he let her hand go.

She knew he was in pain, but instinct told her that Jeremy didn't want his pain to be acknowledged.

'We're thrilled to welcome you to our family.' He turned to his son, hesitating slightly as he caught his breath, even the minimal exertion of greeting his future daughter-in-law a huge feat in his poor health. 'How are you, son? How was America?'

No flip reply for Jeremy, Tabitha noted. Instead Zavier plunged straight into an in-depth report, reeling off figures as if he was giving a presentation. It was almost inhuman, the knowledge his brain held. Not once did he ask his father how he was feeling, and the wheelchair was dismissed as if it had always been there. Tabitha knew that was exactly how Jeremy wanted it, his face rapt as he listened to his son intently.

'Bores the hell out of me.' Marjory rolled her eyes. 'But just look at Jeremy—it's exactly what he needs: a bit of intelligent conversation. I admit I'm as guilty as anyone. The second he sits in that damned wheelchair I find myself speaking to him louder and even answering for him.'

Tabitha smiled sympathetically at her honesty. 'I'm sure you'll all get used to it.'

'Let's hope we have time to.'

'How are you feeling, Dad?' Aiden's awkward attempt at conversation brought nothing more than a frown and a sharp retort from his father, and Tabitha reflected how austere and formal Jeremy sounded when he addressed his younger son, how sad that it had come to this.

'So, how are the wedding preparations going?' Aiden forced a smile and walked over to the more receptive audience of his old friend.

'I've no idea,' Tabitha admitted honestly.

'Don't tell me—' Aiden grinned '—everything's being taken care of.'

Tabitha laughed at his perception. 'Apparently all I have to do is turn up.'

'Nervous?'

She nodded, relieved at finally being able to be honest with someone.

'What does your grandmother say about it all?'

'She's as stunned as everyone else.'

'Is everything sorted there?'

She went to take a sip of her drink but realised that her glass was empty; instead Tabitha picked up the lemon slice, sucking on it, she gave a small nod. 'For the time being.'

Aiden lowered his voice. 'She needs help—you know that. You mightn't have done her a favour, getting her out of trouble again.'

Tabitha was down to the pith now, but that was more preferable than talking about her grandmother's problem.

'Gambling's an illness,' Aiden continued relentlessly. 'It doesn't just go away. The debt might be cleared but it will just mean the bar's raised higher next time.'

'There won't be a next time,' Tabitha replied indignantly.

'But that's exactly what you said before,' Aiden reminded her. 'And the time before that, if I remember rightly. How can you be so sure that this time things will be different?'

'Because next time the bailiffs come knocking there mightn't be a multimillionaire prepared to bail me out.'

'It's those little things you say that make me love you more.' Zavier slipped an arm around her waist, but there was nothing tender about the kiss he placed on her cheek.

She had meant her words for Aiden only, in defence of her grandmother, her brutality a cover-up for the genuine fear she felt for her only real family, and knowing Zavier had heard made her stomach sink. Sure, they both knew it was a financial arrangement, but the gentle acceptance, the truce she had demanded, was undoubtedly over.

'And for your information, *sweetheart*—' his lip curled around the word '—it happens to be a billionaire bailing you out. But then what's a few more zeroes to a dizzy thing like you? What's a few million here or there when you're prepared to blow your last cent on the poker machines?'

'What are you lot looking so serious about?' Marjory was all smiles, wagging a finger as she joined them.

'We were just discussing my fiancée's little *problem*.' He arched one perfect eyebrow as Tabitha stood there mortified. He wasn't going to mention it? He couldn't— not here!

'What problem, Zavier? Do tell.' Marjory giggled, moving closer. 'Anything that needs a woman's viewpoint? I'd be only too happy to help.'

'You wouldn't know where to start,' Zavier said ominously to his mother, and Tabitha held her breath. 'Unless that is, you've taken a crash course in domesticity all of a sudden. Tabitha's glass has been empty for the past five minutes and no one's bothered to fill it. You really need to have a word with the staff.'

The ringing of the bell summoning them for dinner was the only thing that made Tabitha remember to breathe again.

Dinner was awful.

Oh, the food was perfect, the wine delicious, the conversation scintillating, but dinner really was awful.

Zavier studiously avoided her eyes, and the hand that briefly brushed hers was icy cold. Any headway that had tentatively been made was now seemingly dashed by one inappropriate comment.

The conversation inevitably turned to the wedding,

and Tabitha struggled to concentrate, to laugh at the right moments, to inject some enthusiasm into her voice when she listened to what Marjory had in store for them.

'I've put all the gifts that have arrived so far into the drawing room; we'll have to decide where we're going to display them. It's a shame you didn't want a bridal registry—you've doubled up on a couple of things.'

'How many toasters?' Tabitha's feeble joke fell flat on its face as Zavier leant back in his chair.

'None—well, I can only vouch for my side of the family anyway. Mother, just how many toasters have we received from Tabitha's side?'

'Just ignore him, darling.' Marjory giggled, not remotely fazed by the simmering tension. 'I do believe he's getting nervous. How about you, Tabitha?'

'A bit.' That was the understatement of the century, but unlike Zavier at least she was trying to sound as if she cared. 'Still, at least it's just a small wedding. I couldn't cope with much more than that.'

'The only problem with that…' Zavier's sardonic drawl at least momentarily forced the attention from Tabitha '…is that I've a feeling my mother's version of "small" might differ somewhat from yours. Isn't that right, Mum?'

Marjory clapped her hands gleefully together. 'Well, I can't promise small, but I can guarantee it will be tasteful.'

Zavier rolled his eyes, but smiled affectionately at his mother, and Tabitha noticed how much nicer he looked when he addressed someone he truly loved. Gone was the haughty menacing expression she was becoming so used to, instead his face seemed softer, younger, perhaps, and infinitely more desirable. 'Why don't I believe you? No doubt you've already put in an order for heaven only knows how many helium balloons and a couple of ice sculptures.'

'No,' Marjory said defensively. 'Balloons are old hat now. I'm sticking with fresh flowers.'

'Good choice—and how many ice sculptures?'

Tabitha had thought he was joking, but her face dropped a mile when Marjory shuffled uncomfortably. 'Just the one.'

The groan that escaped Tabitha's lips was muffled by the guffaws of laughter around the table, though Zavier caught her eye as she sank lower in her seat. For the tiniest second he smiled sympathetically, and she knew then she was forgiven. For that brief instant she was privy to a glance from him that wasn't suspicious or malicious, and for all the world it felt like a caress. What was it about him? It was as if he had a hotline to her soul—one small look could wrap around her like a warm blanket on a cold night. She felt the colour in her cheeks mount under his watchful eyes, even managing a small smile back.

Maybe Marjory's ice sculpture wasn't such a bad idea after all, she thought. At least it might cool her down, though the heat that was radiating from her now would melt it in a flash. Clearing her throat, Tabitha dragged her eyes away, smiling around the table.

'Marjory, it's such a lovely night—I wondered if I might take my port out on the balcony?' The vast dining room seemed stifling now, and the need to escape the oppression of her lies overrode Tabitha's usual shyness around the Chamberses.

'Of course, my dear, make yourself at home. It can get rather warm in here.'

Gratefully Tabitha picked up her glass and made her way through the French windows onto the balcony.

It was a beautiful night; placing her glass on the stone wall, she rested her arms and gazed at the magnificent view. The bay shimmered before her, dark indigo as deep as Zavier's eyes but with flashes of silver as the moonlight hit the waves. The endless water glimmered in parts, and she imagined the couples entwined on the dance floors, sharing romantic meals in the bayside restaurants.

She envied them.

Envied them for the uncomplicated lives they must surely lead compared to hers. Envied these unknown people for the gift of requited love.

'You seem miles away.'

She had half expected him to join her; in some ways she had engineered it.

'I was over there, actually,'

Her slender arm lifted and she pointed to a cluster of lights sparkling on the foreshore.

There was no need for further explanation. He seemed instinctively to understand how her mind had wandered.

His eyes followed to where she was pointing. 'And were you enjoying yourself?'

Tabitha laughed. 'Actually, no, the food was terrible.'

'I'm sorry for earlier.'

She swung around, visibly stunned; never in a million years had she expected any sort of an apology from him. If anyone should be apologising it was her.

'Sorry for what?'

'For making you so uncomfortable before dinner—pretending I was about to reveal your gambling problem. It was a cheap shot, not my usual style at all.'

'I'm sorry too,' she admitted. 'What I said to Aiden—I didn't mean…'

'Yes, Tabitha,' he said slowly. 'You did.'

She didn't say anything; instead she reached for her drink, taking a hesitant sip, confused at the change in his demeanour.

'But it didn't give me the right to put you on the spot. We both know it's business; I guess sometimes it's all too easy to forget. We must be good actors. Unfortunately you seem to bring out the worst in me. Or the best in me. I guess it depends what night we're talking about.'

His eyes almost imperceptibly travelled the length of her body and she knew he was remembering not just what had happened but every last searing detail. Knew that as his eyes flicked to her breasts Zavier was tasting her all over again, that when he glanced at her feet, confined in the strappy summer sandals, he was remembering her undressing, the feel of her thighs wrapped around his solid torso…

Swallowing the port she was holding in her mouth, Tabitha resisted the urge to rush over to him, to bury her face in his chest and feel his arms tightly around her.

That night, that one stolen, decadent night. She had brought out the best in him. Oh, Tabitha wasn't the world's greatest lover—lack of experience put paid to that—but they had both brought out the best in each other. Their lovemaking had been wondrous—divine, even—and the memory of his touch, the gentleness she had glimpsed, gave her the confidence to broach a question.

'Doesn't it make you nervous?'

'What?'

Her hands gestured as wildly as her eyes; she couldn't believe he didn't know what she was talking about. 'This. This lie.'

He shook his head. 'Why should it?'

'What if they find out?'

'They won't—at least so long as you show a touch more discretion than you did with Aiden earlier.'

'But what if they do?' Tabitha insisted.

'Then I'll deal with it. Anyway, the Chamberses aren't going to collapse because of another loveless marriage in the family. My father just wants me married; he never said anything about love.' He was so confident, so arrogantly assured it annoyed her. Suddenly she wanted to see him squirm, wanted Zavier Chambers to admit to even a tenth of the fear that gripped her.

'What if I don't turn up? What if I just disappear with your money?'

His eyes narrowed. 'I'd soon track you down. It was a generous amount but hardly enough to disappear on. Anyway, no doubt it's already spent.'

'But isn't this eating you up inside?' The anguish in her voice was evident, and Zavier looked at her thoughtfully before answering.

'Look, Tabitha, you remember those people at the casino—sweating buckets, chewing their nails, clutching their chips, willing themselves on? I'm not like that.'

'You'd set your budget,' Tabitha reminded him, not sure where the conversation was heading. 'You could afford to lose.'

'Okay, then, take work. Every day I make billion-dollar deals, shuffle money. Whether it's a gamble or an educated bet, I roll the dice every day, but the difference is that I can walk away. I'm not like the rest of the guys I work with—compulsively watching the stocks, swallowing ulcer tablets, imagining the worst. They'll be burnt out by the time they're forty, strapped to a cardiac monitor on the coronary care ward and wondering what the hell went wrong. Me, I'll still be playing this game when I'm seventy.'

'So where's the analogy?'

His face broke into a grin. 'What on earth are you talking about?'

'Well, I'm assuming there is one. I'm sure this short sharp lecture on the exigencies of stocks and options is leading somewhere. I do read the business pages now and then,' she added as he muffled a cough. 'I don't automatically turn to the horoscope page.'

'Ah, but *I* will now.' He laughed. 'I can hardly wait to find out what's in store for me tomorrow. You were right, actually. My mother did ask what star sign you were.' His voice hardened then. 'Don't threaten me with mind games, Tabitha; nothing fazes me. If you're there then we'll get married—great. If you're not I'll survive.' His face was menacingly close, his voice a silkily disguised threat, but despite his foreboding stance, despite her trepidation, the adrenaline that coursed through her system had nothing to do with fear.

She could feel the warmth of his body, his breath on her cheek, his eyes pinning her to the wall behind. There was nowhere to go, nowhere to run and absolutely no desire to do either. The air was crackling with sexual tension as his hand brushed her arm. The tiny hairs stood up and her nipples jutted through the fabric of her dress, painfully greeting their master.

'We get married in two days.' Her tongue moistened her lips nervously, and she knew the innocent gesture had aroused him. 'Maybe we should wait.'

'Is that what you want?'

It wasn't. Right now all she wanted was to be in his arms, for him to take her upstairs and for the skill of his lovemaking to obliterate the endless conundrums in her

head, for him to take her to a place far away from the
problems of the surreal world they had created. Picking
up her hand, he ran it across his face, burying his mouth
in it. She could feel his tongue running along her palm,
working slowly along her life line, then up her wrist.
Her knees were trembling; she was sure at any moment
she might faint with longing. Suddenly he pulled her
hand down to his groin. With a start she felt the weight
of his arousal through his dark suit, angry and fiery under her fingers. He pushed her hand still harder against
him.

'Someone might see,' she gasped, trying to pull away,
but his vice-like grip only tightened.

'It's too dark outside for them to see.' He was pushing
her hand against him and he let out a low groan as her
fingers moved independently, tightening around the velvet steel of his manhood. She was stunned at her own
boldness, berating the clothing that separated their searing skin.

'That analogy you wanted,' he whispered. 'I've made
my bet; I've narrowed the odds.' His hand pushed hers
deeper into his groin. 'That,' he growled, but there was
a breathless edge to his voice, 'is the reason you'll be
there.'

His wicked eyes grinned mockingly into hers as she
angrily pulled her hand away. 'Who knows, Tabitha?
You might be the world's first bride to get there early.'

CHAPTER NINE

HER body ached with fatigue. Most of the night she had lain on tenterhooks, painfully aware of Zavier just a few feet away, aching for him and yet simultaneously dreading him coming into her room; wanting him to, yet terrified he might. Finally she had drifted into an uneasy sleep, only to be awoken what seemed like moments later by the sun. For a while she lay there, taking a moment to orientate herself. The lapping of the ocean was so close she felt as if she might reach her hand out of the bed and touch the cool water. How peaceful it all seemed, how serene compared with reality, with the Pandora's box of lies they all were living. One wrong step, one misguided comment and the whole festering mess would burst forth.

Not that Zavier seemed bothered. Did nothing upset him? Did nothing worry him?

Slipping on some shorts and a T-shirt, Tabitha pulled some runners onto her bare feet. Creeping slowly through the darkened house, sliding the bolt, she slipped quietly out onto the driveway.

She had no direction, no purpose behind her steps, but instinctively she made her way to the beach. Slipping off her runners, she walked a while, trying to fathom the hows and whys, the impossible puzzle that was Zavier, until finally, with a moan, she sank to the soft sandy floor, the damp sand cool against her bare thighs, the lapping waves tickling her toes, rushing in up to her knees, skimming the top of her cotton shorts before being pulled back to the ocean, back to where they belonged.

He saw her first. Sitting there alone on the deserted beach, the rising sun catching her Titian locks, setting them on fire, her long limbs blending in with the water. She looked like some exotic surreal fantasy, an auburn mermaid washed ashore, cast out from the ocean and into the chaos of life on land.

Last night his façade had slipped. Despite what he had said he hadn't slept on the plane, and that had been a bad idea. Whisky and jet lag were a dangerous mix, a lethal cocktail that had, for a moment, blinded him to what she was about, had made her seem appealing, tempting. She wasn't a mermaid, she was a vixen—stealing her way in, menacing and dangerous—and it would serve him well to remember the fact. His face hardening, Zavier picked up his pace, running directly towards her.

He watched her face turn, the set of her slender shoulders stiffen as she realised it was him, wariness filling those stunning jade eyes.

Bewitched, yet not in the way he had expected. The passion from before was gone; the calculated moves of yesterday had all evaporated. More bewitching, more achingly appealing, was the undisguised depth of despair in those calcite pools, and, gazing into them, Zavier found himself breathless, as if he had run the length of the beach and back.

'Couldn't sleep, huh?'

She shook her head, drinking in his presence. Dressed only in a pair of faded denim shorts, his hair for once tousled, he was unshaven, unkempt, but infinitely desirable.

'Pre-wedding nerves?'

She forced a small brittle smile. 'Something like that.'

As he lowered himself beside her the beach seemed to implode around them, and Tabitha moved sideways a fraction, as if making room for him to join her.

A silence followed, but it wasn't painful. They both drank in the stunning view, the endless curve of the bay, watching the liquid gold reflections to their right as the rising sun hit the ocean, the pier filled with fishermen, the waves dotted with surfers, taking advantage of the early-morning swell, riding the waves with skill and precision mixed with overwhelming abandonment, in tune with nature. Tabitha fought to focus, to stem the tide of lust his mere presence summoned. And when the silence had stretched on too long, when something finally had to be said, it was Tabitha who broke it, saying the second thing that came to mind.

The first would have been her undoing.

'I wonder if it's like working in a chocolate factory?'

'Sorry?'

'Apparently, if you work in a chocolate factory they let you eat as much as you want. After the first few weeks of gorging yourself, sooner or later you get sick of it.'

'I'm still not with you.'

'This—' She gestured to the ocean. 'I wonder if you lived here whether one morning you'd open the curtains and not notice the view; if you'd become blasé about it?'

He nodded his understanding. 'God's own country, isn't it?'

The sun was up now, the red and gold hues that had filled the air over till the next time. The sky was blue, dotted with tiny wisps of white cloud that would surely burn away within the hour. The beach was no longer deserted. Joggers were starting to appear, and the occasional dog, diving into the sea, retrieving sticks, swimming with pink tongues lolling, seemingly grinning at the splendour of it all.

'Morning, Zavier. Good to see you back.'

An elderly couple walked over to them, their wrinkled hands entwined, an air of peace and contentment about them. Zavier greeted them warmly, introducing her as his fiancée. The pride in his voice fooled even Tabitha for a moment.

The gentleman smiled at her curiously. 'We actually read about it in the paper. We're so pleased for you both. And may I say, Zavier, what marvellous taste you have. The newspaper certainly didn't do your bride justice.'

'The wedding's pretty much family, really, but it would be great if you could come and join us for a drink afterwards.'

'We'd love to.' A dog bounded up to them, dropping a stick, his breath panting from joyous exertion. 'I think we're being summoned. We'll look forward to Saturday, then.' Picking up the stick, the man tossed it into the air before taking his wife's hand and ambling on along the beach.

'There's your answer.' Zavier's voice echoed her own thoughts. 'They're here every morning—at least every morning that I've been here, for the past thirty years or so.' His eyes were squinting as the sun hit them, sparkling now, his teeth white as he smiled, more to himself than to her. 'Every time they tell you what a great morning it is. Rain, wind or shine, they're walking hand in hand, loving every moment.'

'Loving each other,' Tabitha said slowly.

It dawned on her then: she had always known she wanted him, adored him—loved him, even—but the full magnitude of her love hit her then, as her eyes flicked down to her hand, down to the gleaming ruby on her ring finger. It wasn't just the ruby ring she wanted; it was the necklace and the forty years that came in between. To walk along the beach hand in hand with him every morning, their children running ahead.

And later, when the lines around his eyes had deepened, when the jet of his hair was sprinkled with silver, when it was grandchildren playing at Zavier's feet, vying for his attention, she wanted so much to be there, wanted her past to be bound to his, their legacy to last.

Wanted to be the one.

'Why the pensive face?'

She swallowed hard. How could she tell him that she loved him? Always had. That from the second he had walked into the church, into her life, his name had been indelibly scored into her heart. How could a man whose life was run by fact, deadlines and contracts understand something as simple, yet as inexplicable as love?

But how could she not?

The crashing of the waves swirled in time to the pounding in her temples as Tabitha fought for eloquence, struggled to articulate what was written in her soul. 'There's something I need to tell you.'

'Sounds serious.'

His flip remark only unnerved her further; the magnitude of her feelings truly terrified her. 'It is.'

Despite the heat of the morning Tabitha suddenly felt chilled to the bone. Telling him now would surely change everything. Zavier wanted a woman he could discard with ease when the allocated time slot was over. Love wasn't on his agenda, and telling him now might end everything. It was a business deal, for Zavier at least, and a declaration of love could only spell the end, but her back was to the wall now and something needed to be said. 'I don't have a gambling problem.' Okay, so it wasn't the big one—fireworks didn't suddenly start whizzing through the air and cupid's dart might have missed its mark for a moment—but if Tabitha couldn't tell him what was truly in her heart right now, she wanted at least a semblance of honesty between them.

If her revelation was somewhat an anticlimax Zavier didn't notice. He let out a low hiss. Rolling onto his back, he stared up at the sky, his eyes squinting in the glare before he snapped them closed. 'I don't want to go into it again, Tabitha. We've already covered that.'

'But I don't—'

'So you keep saying. I can't make you admit it—it has to come from you.' He let out a low laugh. 'I've been reading up on it.'

His eyes remained closed, effectively shutting her out, but Tabitha carried on talking, her voice breathless. 'I've tried to tell you. It's my grandmother that has the problem.'

'Well, thank God I covered babies in the contract; your affliction must be hereditary.' His eyes were still closed, his voice a sarcastic bored drawl. 'You'll be telling me it's not your fault soon.'

'You don't understand.' He wasn't making this easy. Zavier's absolute refusal to accept the truth had Tabitha wondering if it was even worth it, yet suddenly it was imperative she tell him this. If he couldn't know that she loved him, she at the very least needed to walk up the aisle with as few lies between them as possible. 'I've never had a problem, and if you won't believe me—keep refusing to listen to me—then I can't go through with tomorrow.'

His eyes flicked open. Rolling onto his side, he eyed her slowly as she stared fixedly ahead. 'Does Aiden know?'

She gave a small, hesitant nod.

'So why the hell didn't he tell me?'

'I asked him not to.' Her voice was a strained whisper, her eyes screwing tightly closed as she struggled with his questions. 'Anyway it probably didn't seem relevant at the time whom the gambling debt belonged to.'

'Didn't seem relevant?' For the first time ever she heard Zavier raise his voice. She had seen him angry, livid, even, but always, always in control.

Until now.

Black eyes were blazing at her, a muscle leaping in his cheek, his neck and shoulders absolutley rigid with tension.

'Didn't seem relevant,' he repeated. 'I'll tell you why it didn't seem relevant—this is just another one of your lies, another one of your…'

'It's the truth, Zavier.'

Her small voice did nothing to stop the tirade, and still he steadfastly refused to believe her. 'At the casino…' his hand was on her chin now, jerking her head around, forcing her to face him. 'You were suddenly so alive, so vibrant.'

So in love.

Still her eyes were screwed shut. How could she look at him and lie about the one thing that mattered? But if she wanted to keep him, wanted her shot at paradise, lying was her only option. 'It had nothing to do with the casino, Zavier, nothing at all. If I was suddenly happy it was down to the fact I had the best part of a bottle of champagne inside me and more than a few years' wages in my bag with a promise of more to come. Is it any wonder I felt so good?'

It was the hardest thing she had ever done, the most vile lie of all, and if she hadn't been so wrapped up in her own angst maybe she would have registered the pain in his eyes, the drop of his hand from her chin as he sat there in silence.

'I'm sorry,' she stammered when Zavier didn't say anything. 'I thought you'd be pleased.' Unshed tears sparkled in her eyes, the aftertaste of her words still bitter in her mouth. 'Pleased that I wasn't a gambler.'

'What? Were you expecting a round of applause? Some noble little speech about what a wonderful woman you are, saving your grandmother from the loan sharks with no thought for herself?'

Tabitha looked up sharply. 'No. I just thought it would help us if you knew the truth.'

'The truth is that this is a business deal.' His words were harsh, angry. 'I don't care about your grandmother—or you either, come to that—so save the little speeches, Tabitha. Save the guilt trip and the dramas. The only person getting worked up about this wedding is you. And as for the gambling debt, you were right— who it belongs to isn't relevant.'

She shot a look at him from under her eyelashes. 'Isn't it?'

'You cashed the cheque the day after you got it,' Zavier pointed out. 'What you spent it on is your business, so long as it was within the confines—'

'Of the contract.' She finished the sentence for him. 'It was.'

'Fine,' he snapped. 'So unless you come up with the money by tomorrow you owe me, Miss Reece, big time. The contract still stands.' The anger left him then, and, propping himself on his elbow, Zavier looked at her thoughtfully. 'Any other little gems you want to toss at me? Any other truths you'd like to share while we're being so open?'

His voice was laced with sarcasm. Tabitha managed a brief shake of her head, biting on her lips to stop the tears.

'So nothing's changed, then?'

'I guess.' Her long fingers were dragging through the sand, drawing endless swirling circles in the virgin smoothness.

He watched her, his eyes slowly dragging the length of her body. Her toes were still painted the same shade of coral they had been at the wedding. Her legs were slender and long, pale freckles skimming the translucent skin, her thighs toned yet soft on the underside. The same legs that had been wrapped around him; the same legs that had pulled him closer, driving him on, pulling him deeper. Suddenly Zavier was hit in the groin with a burning longing, and the searing memory of the soft warm flesh against his skin was so vivid his hand un-thinkingly crept closer, his fingers absently stroking the soft marshmallow of her thigh, the need to feel her, to touch her, surpassing all logic.

Tabitha turned abruptly. She had been lost in her own world, oblivious of his mental lovemaking, but as his fingers made contact she jumped, her body tremulous, shocked eyes widening despite the glare of the sun, her pupils constricting against the bright light till the pools of calcite seemed bigger than the ocean.

'What are you doing?' It was a pointless question, one that didn't merit an answer, and he rolled towards her, pinning her to the soft beach, a quilt of flesh and muscle bearing down, burying her with hot needy kisses that almost drowned out reason.

Almost.

With a sob of frustration, of anger, she wriggled away, the tears that had threatened dangerously close now.

'You've just told me you don't care about me, just sweetly reiterated that this is business, and now you have the gall to kiss me, to touch me. This isn't just business, Zavier, and you know it as well as I do…'

He gave a low laugh. 'This is the pleasure. I never said we couldn't mix the two. In fact you signed yourself up for it, remember…'

In one lithe movement she pulled herself up, but he was too quick for her, grabbing at her ankle. He held his hand there in a vice-like grip as she stood, and when he was sure she wasn't about to make a bolt, when the rigid muscles relaxed slightly, he loosened his grip, working his hand slowly up the length of her freckled leg, toying with the top of her shorts. She felt her groin contract, a bubble of moisture welling between her legs.

'This was very much a part of the deal…'

She stared back at him for the longest time. The fact she wanted him was a given, and to deny it would be a lie, but right here, right now, she also hated him. She had told him about her grandmother, her darkest secret, her deepest pain, and he hadn't even graced her with a decent response. She had been right not to tell him of her love, Tabitha acknowledged with relief, and until that ring was safely on her finger she had to be sure he didn't realise her truth.

'You think this is pleasurable?' Her voice was steady, her lips white, and she stared down at his hand with a sneer. 'You think I'm enjoying this?'

For the first time she saw a flicker of doubt in his eyes, felt his grip loosen on her ankle. Freeing her leg, she shook her head ruefully. 'You think you're such a bigshot? Well, I've got news for you. It's business for me too. The only pleasure I get from you is cashing your cheques.'

'You want me as much as I want you.' The words were assured, his voice laced with his usual haughty tones, but she knew she had thrown him; that tiny flicker of doubt still darted in his eyes.

'You once accused me of being a good actress, Zavier. Perhaps for once you actually read me right.' And, turning on her heel, she ran the length of the beach, not once looking back, determined he would never see the tears that coursed down her cheeks or hear the sobs that rasped from her lungs.

She knew, had she stayed one moment longer, he would have seen the truth in her eyes.

CHAPTER TEN

'HERE they are,' Marjory gushed as they stepped out onto the patio. 'We were just about to send out a search party. How long does it take to get changed for lunch?'

'Sorry.' Reaching over, Tabitha planted a long kiss on Zavier's rather taut cheek, determined to keep up the act despite the most unwilling partner. 'I take full responsibility—don't I, darling?'

Marjory's giggles in no way made up for the black look Zavier threw at her, or the visible wince as her lip brushed his cheek, as if her touch was more than he could stomach.

'Where's Jeremy?'

'Oh, Jeremy's gone for a siesta—probably conserving his energy for tonight's dinner. He's not a fan of the sun—not now, anyway.'

A glass of something long, cold and delicious appeared in front of her and Tabitha took a grateful sip. Only the smarting of her eyes and the warm feeling as it reached her stomach told Tabitha that the drink wasn't as harmless as it looked.

Lunch was hell. The man who sat beside her on the patio was positively brimming with anger, not a trace of indigo in the black coal chips of his eyes. Of course the fruity little number Aiden and Marjory were knocking back meant that his sarcastic comments, his biting repartee and dark looks for the most part went unnoticed.

If ever Zavier had been foreboding, brooding, unnerving, to date it had only been a dress rehearsal. The row that had ensued back at the house had been of such humongous proportions it would probably rate a mention on the six o'clock news, somewhere between nuclear missile heads and urban warfare.

And in a perverse sort of way Tabitha had enjoyed it.

Enjoyed the confirmation that Zavier Chambers wasn't completely unflappable, that underneath that ruthless, pitiless shield beat a mortal heart, and questioning his sexual prowess made it bleed. Of course the fact that he was more of a lover than Tabitha had ever imagined, that the very thought of him made her toes curl in anticipation, didn't even rate a mention; why ruin a good thing? Zavier's fury she could almost deal with; it was the truth that could hurt her the most.

By the time lunch was over Aiden had long-ago given up on the fruity number and had worked his way down the neck of a bottle of Scotch—which left more for Marjory. Only Zavier carried on with his mineral water, his eyes never leaving Tabitha, making her acutely aware of her every movement, making every delicately prepared mouthful like sandpaper in her throat.

'This time tomorrow you'll be husband and wife.' Marjory beamed, pushing her untouched dessert aside and signalling for a refill. 'I bet you're so excited, Tabitha.'

'I wouldn't bet on it,' Zavier drawled. 'Apparently looks can be deceiving—can't they, darling?'

Fortunately his below-the-belt black humour was far too subtle for his family, who carried on smiling as Tabitha slid further into her seat.

'Well, I don't know about you lot—' Marjory's voice seemed to be coming at her through a thick fog '—but

I'm going to work off my excesses in the pool. Won't you join me, Tabitha?'

'I'd love to, Marjory,' Tabitha answered in a falsely bright voice as she replaced her napkin on the table with a slightly shaking hand. 'But I'll just watch from the poolside for now. I've eaten so much I'd no doubt sink like a stone if I ventured in the water.'

Thankfully, Marjory's plans to work off her lunch weren't quite so energetic as they had initially sounded. Flopping onto a huge sunbed, she snapped her fingers impatiently at one of the staff and they brought over yet another tray of drinks. Tabitha shook her head as the tray passed her. 'Not for me, thanks. I'd love a mineral water, though, please.'

'You sound like Zavier—him and his water. Come on, Tabitha, have a proper drink.'

'I'd rather not.' A loose tongue was the last thing she needed at the moment. 'I'm not a big drinker, especially during the day. And anyway, I want to look my best for the wedding.'

That seemed good enough for Marjory, and she smiled affectionately as Tabitha slipped out of her dress down to her skimpy yellow bikini—four triangles and shoelaces really—painfully aware of Zavier removing his shorts and T-shirt, every hair on his body, every glistening toned muscle seeming to taunt her with its beauty.

'Do you fancy a swim?'

Mute, she shook her head, remembering the last time he had undressed in front of her. She felt his eyes skim over her and dared to dream he was remembering the same.

The two women watched in amicable silence as Zavier dived into the vast pool in one lithe motion, streaming through the water, his muscular body hardly making a ripple as he parted it. There was no way on earth she'd get in now, Tabitha decided. Her doggy paddle was nowhere near his élite level, and there was far more chance of looking graceful on land than thrashing about in the water.

'Don't let Zavier's mood upset you.' Tabitha looked across startled, surprised Marjory had even noticed. Marjory was carefully examining her face in a large hand mirror while simultaneously smearing vast quantities of sunscreen around her eyes and over her décolletage. 'He's just worried about his father.'

Tabitha didn't answer. No doubt Zavier *was* worried about Jeremy's increasingly fragile health, but she knew his black mood was due to a rather more basic problem.

'We're so glad he found you,' Marjory continued, her eyes never once leaving the mirror. 'I know how difficult he can be, and to be honest we were worried for him.'

'In what way?' She was treading on dangerous water here; insights into Zavier weren't part of the deal, but they were way too tempting to pass up.

'Well, he's so exacting. It's all black and white to him. You know about Louise, I presume?'

Tabitha nodded. 'The girl he was engaged to?'

'Lovely thing—though not as gorgeous as you, of course. She even managed to loosen him up a bit—you know, get him out of a tie on weekends and things. They'd have been so happy, but she messed it up, the silly girl—got too greedy. The day Louise came home with that prenuptial agreement it was all over bar the shouting. He'd never admit it in a million years but she really hurt him.'

'No wonder,' Tabitha responded thoughtfully. 'It's hard enough finding someone to spend the rest of your life with without being filthy rich and wondering if they're just with you for your money.'

'Oh, *please*, Tabitha, money matters. As much as I adore Jeremy, I wouldn't have given him a second glance if he weren't wealthy. Life's hard enough without worrying about money.'

Tabitha blinked a couple of times; even though Zavier had told her, she was utterly stunned at the blatancy of Marjory's revelation.

'But you seem so in love.'

'We are,' Marjory tinkled. 'I'm merely saying our relationship would have been a complete non-starter if Jeremy hadn't a bean to his name. Come on, Tabitha, are you honestly telling me that Zavier's money doesn't influence you in the slightest?'

It was a strange question—and, given the fact it was coming from Zavier's own mother, even more confusing. No wonder he was so mistrusting. She had thought Zavier was being his delightful cynical self when he had said that Marjory was with Jeremy for the money, but here she was, openly admitting that money came first and love a poor second.

'I...' Tabitha didn't know how she could answer. After all, money *was* the only thing binding her and Zavier; it was money that had brought them to the eve of their wedding.

And it was money that would end it.

Tabitha pondered before answering. Dreaming for a moment the impossible dream, dreaming that Zavier loved her. She knew one thing for sure: if he lost everything it wouldn't matter a scrap so long as they had each other. Broiled on the passion of her imagination, Tabitha was at least able to answer the question with conviction.

'Money shouldn't come into it. Marriage should be

about love, taking the good times with the bad, leaning on each other, growing together...'

The slow handclap resounding behind her made Tabitha stop in full flood.

'Bravo.' Dripping, he sat on the sunbed next to her. 'Did you hear that, Mum? Doesn't that little speech restore your faith in the human race?'

'Gorgeous, isn't she?' Marjory agreed sleepily as she lay back and closed her eyes, totally missing the venom behind his words, oblivious of the scorn in her son's eyes. 'Darling, put some oil on Tabitha. That fair skin of hers is going quite pink already. We can't have her looking burnt for tomorrow.'

'I can manage myself.' Hastily Tabitha reached for the bottle, but Zavier was too quick for her.

'Don't be silly. You're as red as a beetroot. Lie down.'

Without making a scene Tabitha was left with no choice but to do as she was told. Her eyes met his; swallowing nervously, she stared at him like a rabbit caught in headlights. He seemed to sense her fear, and the malicious glint in his eye evaporated, the dewy hues of lust softening the black weight of his stare.

'Lie down,' he repeated, but this time his voice came out in a husky caress.

Nervously her eyes darted to Marjory; she was sure she must surely sense the crackling sexual tension. But Marjory was dozing, soft snores coming from her slack lips, and with the tiniest nod of acceptance Tabitha rolled onto her stomach, holding her breath as he fiddled with the gold clasp of her bikini.

The oil was already warm from the hot Australian sun, and as he squeezed it onto her skin the chill she had anticipated didn't eventuate; instead she lay there as the slippery moisture seeped onto her back, jumping only when his cool wet hands came into contact with her rosy skin, or the occasional drop of pool water dripped from his hair onto her taut back.

'What's wrong?'

'I'm a bit sore,' she lied. She damn well wasn't going to tell him just his mere touch had such a strong effect on her.

'Silly girl.' His voice was a velvet whisper. 'With skin like yours you shouldn't be out unprotected in the sun.'

The sun was the least of her worries at the moment! As his skilful hands massaged in the oil Tabitha had to remind herself to breathe. Her stomach knotted as they moved slowly across her shoulders. She could feel her nipples hardening, jutting into the sunbed like soldiers standing to attention; a pulse was flickering between her thighs, her blood running like mercury towards her groin. With one hand still on her back, he squeezed the bottle onto her left thigh and the oil, melting in the heat, ran like a river between her legs.

Almost faint with longing, she felt his hand touch her sun-kissed legs, his fingers working in small circular motions, moving higher, ever higher. Only a gentle snore from Marjory broke the oppressive silence, and Tabitha lay there, grinding her teeth together to hold back the groan in her throat.

Zavier might just as well have been massaging accelerant into her skin; one tiny spark and surely her body would explode in flames. It took a superhuman effort to lie there and for all the world appear detached, to pretend that it wasn't the man she loved massaging her so skilfully.

'That should keep the rays off.'

She felt the sunbed lift as he stood up, and she waited,

waited for the sensations overpowering her to abate, for the burning, aching longing he had initiated to subside. But it didn't.

She lay there another ten minutes or so, her eyes tightly shut, feigning sleep. But she knew Zavier wasn't fooled, that he was more than aware of the passion he had awoken.

'It's too warm for me,' Tabitha said finally, when she could take it no more. Standing, she grabbed at a towel, pulling it around her so he wouldn't see her swollen nipples, the arousal he had instigated. 'I'm going inside.'

'Why?' His voice was low but she could hear the mirth in it. 'Things are only just starting to hot up.'

Oh, the bliss of the icy cool water as she splashed her face then rested her face against the tiles. Tabitha fought the image of his hands on her body, the sheen of lust in his expressive eyes. How could one man have such a hold on her? How could one man turn her world around like this? Why did Zavier Chambers have this effect on her?

Because she loved him.

The answer was as simple as it was complicated. Lust, passion, power—they all played their part. But this was good old-fashioned love. She had loved him from the moment she had laid eyes on him in the church. She loved everything about him.

But Zavier Chambers despised her; he thought she was the worst kind of woman. The pain of that thought was enough to calm her twitching body, enough to temper the wild thoughts that were cascading through her mind.

Peeling off her bikini top, she fiddled with the shower control before catching her reflection in the mirror.

Tabitha gazed back at her own glittering eyes, searching for an answer to the impossible conundrum.

'You've only yourself to blame,' she said darkly to her image. 'You've only got yourself to blame for all this.'

'My thoughts exactly.'

Jumping with shock, she saw the dark brooding reflection of Zavier standing in the bathroom doorway.

'How long have you been there?' Her eyes were glittering now, with anger and embarrassment. 'How long have you been watching me?'

Zavier laughed, but there was no warmth in it. 'Don't worry—I don't need to get my kicks peering through a keyhole. Why would I?' He crossed the bathroom slowly and she shrank back against the sink. 'When we both know I can have you any time I want.'

'How dare you?'

'It's a bit late for false modesty.' He put a hand up to her burning cheek, running his finger along its length and down her neck, halting teasingly as he came to the soft naked mounds of her breasts. 'My, you have caught the sun, haven't you? Perhaps you should have let me oil your front.'

Angrily brushing past him, she fled for the safety of her room. But there was no haven to be found there: the bed seemed to mock her, forcing an instant recall of another place, another time, their tumbling bodies replaying in her mind like some erotic foreign movie stumbled upon by accident, their limbs locked in tremulous unison more erotic than any fantasy.

'Only business, huh?' He strode over to her, one finger flicking her nipple, giving a knowing, mocking smile as it swelled at the merest touch. His other hand was expertly untangling the tie of her bikini bottom. 'All just an act, huh?'

She should have run—slapped him, kicked him—but she stood there rigid, every muscle, every taut nerve shivering with shameful desire.

'I can have you any time I want,' he repeated.

He was poisonous, arrogant and loathsome; but he was right, damn him. He was so right, and there was nothing she could say otherwise.

'You want me, Tabitha.' He spat her name.

'I don't.' Her voice was a mere croak. He had freed one strap and now ran a teasing finger through the damp Titian mound of down as he plied the other strap, his breath hot and hard on her warm oiled body. The towel slinked around his hips slithered down without a sound, and she started in excitement at the angry swelling that baited her, that summoned her body just by its presence. 'I don't.'

She was naked now, exposed. He threw the saffron garment aside, parting her legs with his hand. He slid his fingers into her warmth as her throat constricted against a gasp of protest.

'I don't remember oiling you here.'

Her breathing matched his now, gasping, uneven, and she felt herself contract around his fingers, felt her body arching towards his.

'Tell me to stop and I will.' His thumb was massaging her swollen nub as his fingers snaked inside her slippery warmth. 'Tell me to stop,' he ordered, pushing her back onto the bed, parting her legs further with his muscular thigh.

His erection teased her at the entrance to her Nirvana, a tiny thrust that took her to the edge. She was pushing against him now, urging him to come deeper, but still he held back, the swell of him awaiting the formal invitation that she was loath yet desperate to give.

'Tell me to stop.'

She shook her head, Titian curls splaying over the pillows. 'No!'

'No, you don't want me, or no, don't stop?'

His restraint was agony, his manhood swelling at her entrance as her legs wrapped like a vice around him.

'No, don't stop,' she gasped.

Still he made her wait, inching his way just a fraction deeper as she writhed beneath him.

'Say you want me,' he ordered, and though it repulsed her to beg she was beyond reason, her need for him so urgent nothing else mattered.

'I want you!' She was nearly screaming, her legs coiling around him as he plunged into her, swelling the instant he entered her, their bodies exploding in unison, contracting, tightening as the world rushed around them. With a moan he collapsed on her, groaning, the last shuddering spasms of their union pulsing together as they lay in the moistened sheen of their skins. And as she lay there, listening to his breathing even out, one arm wrapped around her, the lazy hand softly cupping her bottom, his maleness filling the air she breathed, tears sprang from her eyes.

Surely she could tell him now? Surely, deep down, he must already know?

It took a second to register that the telephone was ringing, but her anger at the intrusion paled as she heard the thin, thready voice of her grandmother.

He watched her as she took the call, watched the rosy glow of her cheeks fade as she held the telephone, her knuckles white around the receiver, her lips taut as she mumbled into the phone.

'Was that your bookie?'

His attempt at a joke didn't even raise a smile, and with a start he watched the tears form in Tabitha's eyes, her lashes crushing the moisture as she screwed her eyes shut and fought for control.

'What's happened?' His voice was clipped, formal, even as he snapped into the businessman that he was: ready to deal at a second's notice with whatever was thrown at him.

'My grandmother,' Tabitha started, 'she's sold the house.'

'To pay off her debt?'

Tabitha shrugged; pulling the sheet around her, she covered her breasts. 'I'd already taken care of that.' She looked up. 'Or rather you had.' Her fingers were pleating the sheet; she was chewing her bottom lip as she dealt with the bombshell that had just exploded. 'She's sold up and is moving into a retirement village with a man she's apparently fallen head over heels in love with. She's going to pay me back—that was why she rang. She wanted to tell me before the wedding.'

'So you wouldn't have to go through with it?' His voice was strained, hoarse, his austere façade disintegrating with every word. 'Did you tell her our marriage was all a sham?'

'No.' Tears were streaming now, his apt description the salt in the wound. 'She thought it would make things easier for us—you know, a young couple starting out and all that…'

'We're hardly teenagers.'

'I told her that,' Tabitha agreed, wiping her cheeks with the edge of the sheet. 'And I told her she didn't have to rush—after all, we wouldn't exactly have starved.'

'What do you mean?'

'Well, it's not as if you need the money…'

'I meant why the sudden past tense, Tabitha? What's with the ''we wouldn't have''? Shouldn't you be saying ''we won't''?'

'I can pay you back the money I owe you,' she sobbed, looking at his perplexed face. 'She's sold her house, I tell you. His name's Bruce…'

'I don't give a damn what his name is.' Realisation was dawning for both of them, with aching clarity, and he ran a hand through his tousled hair, the muscle jumping in his cheek the only sign he was anything other than completely calm. 'I could still make you go through with it,' he hissed. 'The contract covered everything.'

Not quite. Tabitha fiddled with the stone on her finger. Not once did it mention love. She could feel the moisture of their lovemaking between her legs, slipping away from her as surely as Zavier was. 'You can't force me, Zavier, you've no hold over me now. I can back out if I want to.'

He stood up, walking over to the window and staring broodingly outside, his nakedness mocking her now, a teasing taste of what she could have had—for six months at least.

'But I won't.' His back was to her. She saw the set of his shoulders, the quilted muscles beneath the olive skin, and she ached to reach out for him. 'I still want to marry you.'

She watched him stiffen more, if that was possible.

'Why?'

Still his back was to her; still he couldn't bring himself to look at her. Tabitha was grateful for the reprieve. This was hard enough without being humiliated further, seeing the scorn, the triumph in his eyes when she told him she loved him.

'Because...' The words were there but her mouth simply wouldn't obey her. 'Isn't it obvious? Do I have to spell it out?'

He turned then. The scorn she had predicted was there in his eyes, but there wasn't even a trace of triumph, just a sneering look of distaste.

'Money?' His lips twisted around the word. 'God, you're even more desperate for it than I thought.'

She could have put him right then, pleaded her case and told him the truth, but what purpose would it have served? He was as damaged as Aiden; sure, he didn't drown himself in alcohol, but his problems ran just as deep, his soul was just as damaged. Not once had it even entered his head that her reason for sleeping with him, for agreeing to this charade, for marrying him, might be love.

'Do you know why I despise you so much, Tabitha?'

She didn't want to know, didn't want to hear his scathing comments, but some sadistic streak made her answer. Running a tongue over her dry lips, she heard her voice come out in a coarse whisper. 'Why?'

'Because beneath that smile, beneath that trusting little face and that easygoing laugh, you're as hard as nails.' He glanced at his watch. 'This time tomorrow you'll be Mrs Tabitha Chambers—if a bolt of lightning doesn't strike you down first.' Slamming out of the adjoining door into his own room, he left her there, on the bed, shocked and reeling at his outburst.

She ached to go after him, to somehow explain that money had nothing to do with this—but what was the point?

She felt sorry for him.

Sorry that his life had left him so scarred, so untrusting that he simply didn't believe in love.

Six months.

Six months of holding him at night, waking to him each morning. The mental abacus was starting again. One hundred and eighty days to shower love on him, to show him that life could be so much sweeter, so much easier with love on your side.

This time tomorrow she would be wearing his ring, would be blessed with the saving grace of time.

This time tomorrow she would tell him she loved him.

CHAPTER ELEVEN

'YOU look beautiful.'

Tabitha smiled at Aiden's reflection in the mirror as he slipped into the room.

'She'd look even better if she stayed still for five minutes,' Carla the hairdresser grumbled as she pierced Tabitha's scalp with yet another pin. Checking the tiara was firmly secured, she almost asphyxiated her client with yet another waft of hairspray before standing back to admire her handiwork. 'He's right; you do look beautiful.'

Even Tabitha agreed. The sophisticated woman staring demurely back at her from the mirror was nothing like the dizzy redhead she knew so well. The wild Titian curls were sleek and straight, caught at the back of her neck in an elegant chignon, her fringe was smooth and silken, falling seductively over one eye, and though she felt as if she were wearing a ton of make-up her complexion looked clear and smooth, with a dusting of rose on her cheeks and her eyeshadow a smudgy brown, accentuating the jade eyes. Only her lips were heavy, the dusky red tones making her mouth look wide and sensual.

'Thought this might help,' Aiden said once Carla had gone. Holding two glasses up, he pulled a bottle of champagne from under his jacket. 'I swiped it from one of the tables.' Expertly popping the cork, he handed her a glass before proposing a toast.

'To my dear friend Tabitha, who after today will also

be my sister-in-law. The sisterly advice will still be freely available, I hope?' he asked in a jokey voice after draining his glass in one.

'Of course.'

'And this is still all about business?' The jokey edge had gone, his voice cautious, his eyes concerned.

Tabitha hesitated, but only for a second. Confiding in Aiden was practically second nature, after all, but this was one thing Zavier definitely deserved to hear first. 'Absolutely.'

'You know, despite my earlier reservations, this wedding isn't turning out to be such a bad thing after all. My father's so delighted with the whole caboodle he seems to have forgotten to be angry with me. I took him for a walk this morning. We couldn't go on the beach, obviously, what with his chair, but I pushed him along the pier and we spoke.'

'How was it?'

Aiden shrugged. 'Better than it has been. He even made a few noises about going to look at my paintings. Apparently Zavier's been to see them and persuaded Dad to take a look.'

'Zavier went to see them?'

'Yep. He's a dark horse, isn't he? After the way he's criticised my painting, never in a million years did I think he'd actually be the one sticking up for me, and to Dad of all people. You just can't imagine how much that meant to me. Dad still managed a few barbs, though, about how I needed to face up to life, grow up and all that, but on the whole it was great.'

After putting on her dress, Tabitha lifted the sheer, simple veil as Aiden pulled up her zip. 'Maybe he's worried about your drinking,' she ventured nervously, slipping on her mules so she wouldn't have to look at him.

'Not you as well,' Aiden groaned. 'Darling, you're even starting to sound like an old married woman.'

'I care about you, Aiden, and…' Her voice trailed off. She was scared of pushing, yet scared to say nothing when it was so obviously needed.

'Go on,' Aiden offered, with a slight edge to his voice. 'Don't stop now.'

'You *do* drink too much.'

'Said the gambler to the alcoholic.'

Tabitha smiled. 'And *you're* starting to sound like your brother; he used the same line on me a while back.' Her hand touched his arm. It wasn't the time, it wasn't the place, but Aiden was her friend and some things just had to be said.

Perhaps it was a day for the truth.

'You're drinking every day, Aiden, and for the best part of it too. I'm allowed to be worried.'

'Not today you're not. Today you just have to worry about looking beautiful.' He stood back and stared at her slowly as she looked at her reflection in the full-length mirror.

'Which you do; if I didn't know otherwise I'd say you look every bit the blushing bride. You know, Tab, if I wasn't gay you'd be the woman of my dreams.'

She gave a small laugh. The simple lilac velvet dress hugged her curves, slipping over the hollows of her stomach. The gentle gathering at the bust accentuated her full soft breasts, the thin straps not detracting from her delicate collarbone where her one and only heirloom glittered—a diamond necklace her father had once given to her mother. She fingered the stone, overcome with sadness for what she had lost so young, for the family

cruelly torn apart and for what her parents had lost: the
dream of seeing their daughter walking down the aisle.

Aiden was right, she looked every bit the blushing
bride, but despite the lies, despite the circumstances, the
guilt was gone.

All of it.

When the music played, when she walked on Aiden's
arm to join her future husband, she would be doing it
with a clear conscience and with her parents' blessing;
she just knew that deep down. As she spoke her vows
her voice would be steady, for she would be speaking
the truth.

Because she loved him.

'I got you this.' Digging in his pocket, Aiden pulled
out a diamond bracelet. He had to hold her shaking hand
steady as he clipped it on.

'It's beautiful. But, Aiden, I thought you said you
weren't getting any presents.'

He shook his head. 'This isn't a wedding present; it's
a friendship bracelet. Even when you're an old divorcee
and moaning about Zavier we're still going to be best
friends. Hey,' he said, alarmed as tears welled in her
eyes. 'You'll ruin your make-up.'

'I'm sorry.' His crack about divorce hadn't exactly
helped, but given the emotion of the moment Aiden let
it pass without too much inspection and gently wiped a
stray tear away. 'Thanks for doing this today, Aiden. I'm
glad you're here with me.'

'I wouldn't be anywhere else.' Glancing at his watch,
he offered his arm. 'Come on, you, let's get this over
with. I'm dying for a Scotch.' A tiny wink creased his
left eye as Tabitha's lips pursed. 'I know I need help,
Tab, and I really am going to do something about it. I

just need to get used to the idea for a while. A lifetime of abstinence doesn't really sound my forte.'

He stood there smiling and she took his arm, her dearest friend holding her as they walked through the house and across the lawn.

An arch of roses was the only barrier between Tabitha and her vows, and she listened as the orchestra paused and the congregation stilled.

'You're sure about this?' Aiden offered for the very last time.

Her heels were sinking in the grass, butterflies jumping in her stomach as she listened to the delicious sound of Wagner trickling through the hazy afternoon air. Stepping on to the carpet, she fiddled with her dress before taking Aiden's arm.

'I'm sure,' she said softly.

'Then let's go.'

Every eye turned as she stepped through the arch. She heard the gasps for a fleeting moment, saw the congregation—her friends, her grandmother with her partner, Marjory, grinning widely, Jeremy pale and proud beside her—and then her eyes were on Zavier.

He swallowed as she entered, his eyes meeting hers, his hands clenched by his sides as his chin jutted upwards. She knew he was nervous, and so was she, but her confidence in this unison, her utter love for him, was enough for them both.

They walked slowly, Aiden steadying her, beaming faces welcoming her as she walked to the man she loved.

And though in the days that followed Tabitha would rewind and replay the scene like a perpetual video in her mind, she would never be quite sure how it actually happened. Whether Marjory's piercing scream or the loud crash came first.

Her first ridiculous thought was that the bolt of lightning Zavier had darkly predicted had somehow come to fruition, but just as she discarded that notion, as she watched the gaze of the crowd frantically turn to the front, she registered that Jeremy was lying on the floor, his grey face darkening, blue around the lips, his body limp, spread-eagled where he had collapsed to the floor.

It was Tabitha who moved first. Everyone else stood frozen to the spot, the video stuck on freeze-frame. With her heart in her mouth Tabitha raced over. Already breathless from the emotion of seeing Zavier, she had to force herself to slow down, to calmly and methodically assess the situation and do what little she could.

'Jeremy!' She called his name loudly, once maybe twice, as her trembling hand reached for Jeremy's neck, her long fingers searching for a pulse. Her eyes moved to his chest, looking for a movement, the tiniest indication that he was breathing. She could feel every eye on her. An eerie silence had descended and there was no need to call for quiet as she placed an ear to the lifeless chest, listening for a heartbeat, listening for the breath of life, frantically trying to remember what she should do, to recall the information she had learnt on a long-ago first aid course.

'He's not breathing; I don't think his heart's beating.' Looking up, she surveyed the stunned and horrified crowd. She had wrongly expected some sort of reaction to her statement, for someone to snap to attention, for some assistance. But no one was moving.

No one except Zavier. Kneeling astride his father, after a momentary pause he took control in an instant. 'Someone call an ambulance—is anyone a doctor?'

Bending forward, he pinched his father's nose and gave him the kiss of life, nodding briefly as Tabitha leant on the lifeless, still chest and pushed as she had seen on the television, berating herself over and over for her lack of knowledge, for the awkward giggles expended in that first aid course when she really should have listened.

'Can I help?'

The oldest man Tabitha had ever seen was being pushed forward by a tearful Marjory, his old bones leaning heavily on a walking stick, small eyes magnified by the thickest glasses imaginable.

'Gilbert's the family doctor,' Marjory sobbed.

A smile that was absolutely out of place tugged at the corner of her lips as she registered Zavier's horror, and, most amazingly of all, when his eyes briefly met hers he returned her smile.

'We're doing fine,' Zavier clipped between breaths. 'Perhaps Gilbert could ring Melbourne, line up Dad's cardiac doctor.'

Her hair was plastered to her head with sweat, her arms aching with the sheer exertion of keeping Jeremy's heart pumping, and she knew she couldn't go on for much longer.

'Aiden, help me here.' She looked at the stricken face of her dearest friend and her heart went out to him, but she needed his help. 'Aiden?' she pleaded.

But all Aiden could do was stand and weep. 'Please, Dad, breathe,' he begged, tears streaming down his face as she worked on the inert body of his father.

'Do you want to swap?' Zavier offered, but Tabitha shook her head, knowing Zavier was working just as hard as her and that seconds lost in moving would be seconds Jeremy needed.

On she worked, the hot sun on the back of her neck,

her eyes blurry from sweat and make-up and mascara that clearly wasn't as waterproof as it said on the tube, almost weeping with relief when finally the sound of sirens in the distance permeated the sultry afternoon air.

Exhausted, she leant back on her heels as the paramedics took over, clipping endless monitors to the still lifeless body, pushing oxygen into his mouth through a bag. Tabitha tried to move back on cramped legs that wouldn't obey her.

'We're going to shock him,' the paramedic said sombrely, and Tabitha knew that it was now or never. 'Everybody back.'

Strong arms lifted her out of the way, and without looking she knew instinctively it was Zavier.

The defibrillator paddles were placed on Jeremy's chest and they all stood back as the paramedic delivered an electric shock in an attempt to restore the chaotic rhythm of Jeremy's heartbeat.

'Again. Everybody back.'

Her legs were trembling so violently she thought she might sink back to the floor. But Zavier's strong arms were still around her, holding her tightly as they stared transfixed at the monitor. Her mind was on Jeremy, willing him to live, and yet with Zavier's arms around her she couldn't help but draw from his strength, couldn't help but lean on him slightly. Never had she felt closer to him.

Surely now there must be a chance for them?

A loud blip emanated from the monitor, and they watched as the flat green line flickered once, then twice, and then again, the blips becoming more frequent. An audible sigh of relief filled the room as Jeremy's heart reverted to a stable rhythm.

'Thank God,' Tabitha muttered, more to herself than

anyone else, but for some reason her words seemed to incense Zavier. As if suddenly conscious that he was touching her, holding her, he dropped her out of his arms as if he was holding hot coal.

'Why the relief?' he snapped, his eyes full of hatred, contempt. 'Were you worried you mightn't get the second instalment?'

With horror, Tabitha swung to face him, her optimism of a moment before, the slim belief that now there might be a chance for them, evaporating in the heat that radiated from his eyes. But there was no time to argue the point. Jeremy Chambers had to take precedence here.

This was no time to tell him she loved him.

'Is there anything else I can do?' Ashen, trembling, she offered her assistance to the paramedics as Zavier organised the guests to clear chairs and prepare a makeshift landing pad.

'The best thing you can do is to have a large brandy, love. Not the nicest thing to happen at your wedding, is it? We're waiting for the helicopter to arrive. We're going to take him direct to Melbourne.'

Aiden, shouting into a mobile phone, came over then. 'The doctors are on standby.'

'I'm coming with him.' Marjory's affected tearful tones carried across the garden.

'Sorry, love.' The paramedic shook his head. 'He's really too sick.'

'I'm coming,' Marjory said resolutely, her voice void of hysteria now. There was an air of authority and a strange dignity as she knelt beside the stretcher and took Jeremy's lifeless hand. Turning briefly, she looked the paramedic square in the eye. 'I won't get in the way; you have my word. If my husband is about to die I want to be with him.'

'I'll look after her.' Aiden was grey himself, trembling violently, his teeth chattering noisily. 'She ought to be with him.'

The whirring chopper blades heralded the arrival of the transfer team. Everyone was moved back as it landed, its whirring blades buffeting the marquee, ladies' hats and dresses flapping as the noise drowned out any conversation.

As they loaded Jeremy into the back Aiden turned to Tabitha, squeezing her hands tightly. 'I'll see you at the hospital.'

But Zavier had other ideas. 'You'll do no such thing. I'm taking her back to her house and then *I'll* meet you at the hospital.'

'But she ought to be there,' Aiden argued.

'What for?' he snapped. 'We both know she's not the caring daughter-in-law to be. Mum and Dad are the only concern here. Look after them and I'll meet you there just as soon as I can.'

The paramedics were ready to go now, and there was no time to debate the issue.

'Keep your chin up, Aiden.' Tabitha kissed him fondly on his tear-streaked cheek. 'Everything will work out.'

If only she could believe her own words.

He stood over her as she packed, not saying a word, his dark eyes watching her every move as Tabitha piled her possessions into her suitcase.

'Could you leave me alone for just five minutes?'

She desperately needed to go to the bathroom, to peel off her dress, undo her hair, to somehow remove every trace of the awful charade she had engineered. Dressed in her best, she seemed to embody the hard-faced bitch

Zavier assumed she was, and suddenly it seemed imperative he saw her as she was, not as the sleek, sophisticated woman of earlier.

'I'm not going anywhere. Just hurry up, will you?'

'Are you scared that I might run off with a few choice items?'

'It did enter my head.'

His patience snapped then. It was almost as if he couldn't bear to watch her a moment longer; couldn't stand being in the same room any longer than absolutely necessary. Pulling out the top drawer of the dresser, he tipped the contents into her case. She watched with mounting trepidation as he strode over to the wardrobe, grabbing her dresses and piling them into the case without even bothering to take them off their hangers.

Her underwear drawer was the next recipient of his simmering anger. Grabbing handfuls of lingerie, his face livid with unvented rage, he tossed them on top of her dresses before snapping the case firmly closed.

'Anything that's been left behind I'll have sent on to you. Now come on.'

'Please, Zavier, can I just come to the hospital? Surely your mother will expect me to be there?'

'My God, you just don't give up, do you? It's over, Tabitha. The wedding is off—we don't have to pretend any more.'

'I didn't mean for that. I just want to see how Jeremy is—how you all are…' The thought of going home without knowing if Jeremy had lived or died was unbearable, but more to the point she wanted to be there for Zavier, to help him through what would undoubtedly be the worst night of his life.

Because that was what lovers did: they were there for each other.

But Zavier had other ideas. 'Save the crocodile tears; I'm taking you home, Tabitha.'

He didn't even wait for her to put on her seat belt, accelerating out of the drive as if the devil himself were chasing them. She sat there shivering and stunned, staring out of the side window, watching the dark inky ocean whizzing past as his car hugged the bay road.

The drive to Lorne had taken hours, probably because she had wanted to get there. But now she didn't want to leave suddenly time seemed to be moving faster, the shimmering night skyline of Melbourne drawing ever nearer. She dreaded arriving. However strained the silence, however huge the loathing emanating from him, any contact, however painful, was better than none. The bleak empty wilderness of her life stretched before her: a life without Zavier.

This had never been part of the game, had never been the intended prize; love had come when everyone had said it would: when she was least expecting it.

And losing it for ever hurt like hell.

He pulled over into a lookout, a move that surprised Tabitha, who sat staring ahead as he opened the door and without a word left the car. Idly staring into the night sky, his profile strong in the moonlight, he stood motionless.

Unsure, she sat a moment in the car, memorising every last detail of him. As if sensing her longing, he turned his head, raising his hand to beckon her to join him.

'It's all right.' His lips hardly moved as he spoke. 'I'm not about to throw you in.'

She managed a shallow laugh as she teetered towards him, her high heels no match for the sandy inlet. 'Thank goodness. I'd sink like a stone with all the cutlery I shoved down my bra.'

The tiny spark of humour between them shifted the mood away from the volatile anger of before; he looked sad now—jaded, perhaps, but infinitely more approachable.

'Shouldn't you be getting to the hospital?' she ventured.

'I don't want to go,' he replied simply.

Honestly.

She didn't know how to respond; hearing the break in his voice tore at her heart.

'I just need a moment; it's going to be pretty messy when I get there.' He swallowed hard and she realised then the pain he was in. How hard it must be for Zavier at times like this. How hard it must be to always be the strong one, to have everyone leaning on you, turning to you for every last thing. The lynchpin of the family, the breadwinner, the organiser, and sometimes the adjudicator.

'He might make it.' She tried to inject some hope into her voice, tried to give him something to cling to, something to sustain him, but miracles seemed in short supply today.

Zavier shrugged helplessly. 'It doesn't look great, though, does it? I know that really there's no chance, that this surely must be it. Tabitha, what I said to you about the contract—I really didn't mean it. I'm truly sorry for my words. You were amazing back there, and if my father does live he owes his life to you.'

Tabitha knew then that this was her only chance. If she didn't say it now, couldn't be there for him, to support him through what was undoubtedly about to come, then there wasn't much point.

Maybe Zavier was right, maybe her grandmother's affliction was hereditary, for she was about to take the biggest gamble of her life.

'I didn't do it for money.' The words were out now, and she swallowed, watching closely for his reaction.

'I know, and I had no right to imply that you did. I just saw red all of a sudden. I thought he was dead...'

'I'm not talking about your father's heart attack.' Her teeth were chattering as badly as Aiden's had been, but she forced herself to take a deep breath and calm down. 'I love you, Zavier. I always have. I wasn't marrying you for money.'

She heard the hiss of his breath as he exhaled loudly, stepped back as she watched his face darken, jumped as she heard the venom of his attack. 'My God, I wondered how long it would take you to play your last card.'

She'd never expected him to take her in his arms, to accept her words without question, but the pungent delivery of his statement was a million miles away from any scenario she had tentatively imagined.

'What do you mean?' Her arms shot out to him, as if somehow by touching him she might reach him, might make him hear the truth in her words. 'I love you, Zavier. I honestly love you.'

'Please.' He flicked her hand away, cruelly, dismissively. 'Have you any idea how many women have said that to me? "Oh, Zavier, this has nothing to do with money."' His voice simpered in a derisive generalisation of the female population, then returned to its harsh reality. 'This has everything to do with money, Tabitha. That was all it was ever about. And do you know what the saddest part is—the saddest bloody part of this whole charade?' He was shouting now, and she shook her head dumbly, shocked and stunned at the anger her declaration had unleashed. 'Believe it or not, I actually loved you.'

He stopped then, as stunned as she was by the admission.

It was Tabitha who broke the silence. 'You love me?' she gasped, her voice choked with wonder. But he broke in quickly, shattering her one second of salvation.

'Loved you,' he corrected. 'Past tense, Tabitha. That's all you'll ever be to me. I've spent my whole life wondering how my father could have been so weak, how he could have stayed with my mother knowing that she didn't love him, knowing she was only there for the life he could give her.' Finally his eyes found hers. 'And then you came along, Tabitha...'

She stood there transfixed, listening with tears streaming down her face to his revelations.

'And suddenly I didn't think my father was so weak any more. I actually understood him. That first night we met, my intention was to get you to my room—a kiss, perhaps, just enough to prove what I already knew—that you didn't love Aiden—to shame you into staying away from him. It was never my intention to...' He closed his eyes fleetingly. 'I don't think I need to remind you what happened, but in case you missed it I fell in love that night—fell so hard it hurt. I spent the next five days trying to work out how I could see you again, how to be with you, how to stop you taking up Aiden's offer of marriage.'

'I was never going to accept it,' she pleaded, but it fell on deaf ears.

'I could have married you knowing it was a business deal. I even figured that once you'd had a taste of the high life you might hang around—we could even have made it to forty years, like my parents. Yesterday, when you told me it wasn't your debt, I felt sick, physically sick at the prospect of losing you. I felt like the biggest heel in the world for still making you stick to the contract, but it was nothing compared to the terror I felt when you realised you could pay me back. I didn't want to lose you, Tabitha.'

'You don't have to,' she argued, tears coursing down her cheeks, begging for him to listen, to finally understand. But her tears didn't move him, didn't sway him an inch from the lonely moral high ground he was taking.

'I could almost have lived with it. Knowing you were with me for the lifestyle didn't seem to matter so long as I had you in my arms at night. But I knew the one thing I wouldn't be able to bear was you pretending that you loved me; the one thing I wouldn't be able to stand was hearing you lie to me.'

'I'm not lying now, Zavier. You have to believe me…'

'You're a con-artist, Tabitha.' The venom returned to his voice then, his words ripping at her very core. 'You've beguiled each and every one of us at every turn. First you're Aiden's girlfriend, then a gambler, then you change your story when it suits you so your grandmother's the one with the problem—and then, when it all falls through, when there's no chance I'll marry you, you throw in the fact you supposedly love me in an attempt to win me round.'

'But I do love you,' she pleaded. 'I have since that first night…'

'I might be weak where you're concerned but I'm not a fool. How can I ever believe a word that you say?'

The full magnitude of her loss hit her then—a loss of insurmountable proportions. This sophisticated, strong, beautiful man had loved her. This aching, gaping void, which would surely be her life now, was the price of her deception.

What had started as a silly game had cost her dearly.

There was no point arguing over the small details, no point pleading her case; she was guilty as charged, and though the sentence was harsh there was nothing to gain from an appeal.

Just the hell of agony prolonged.

The tears that had started at the outlook flowed unchecked as they drove on, the ocean too quickly replaced by the freeway, the city drawing closer and closer and closer, until finally it was upon them. The car slowed down as it drove through the empty late-night streets. Every light was green, of course, as if the whole world was conspiring to ensure the imminent ending was a swift one.

Popping the boot, he stayed in the front, clenching the steering wheel as she hauled her suitcase onto the street and up the path, her heels clipping noisily as she dragged the case along. But he didn't drive off; she had known he wouldn't. Ever the gentleman, despite his wrath, he would see her safely inside.

It only took a second of rummaging through her bag for her to realise that her keys weren't where they should be.

So much for a dignified exit!

Of all the times to misplace the blessed things, this wasn't the one Tabitha would have chosen. Looking up, she saw the irritated set of his chin, his fingers drumming impatiently on the steering wheel. She could almost hear the pained sigh as he threw open the car door and stepped out.

'What now?'

'It doesn't matter.' She tossed her head defiantly. 'You go on to the hospital.'

'I would if you'd just get inside.'

'I've lost my keys.'

The roll of his eyes was too much for her already strained nerves. 'Well, if you hadn't rushed me...' she argued.

'Sorry about that.' His face was white in the street-light, his lips set in a thin line as he strode over. 'I just wasn't banking on my father suffering a cardiac arrest and then having to police my fiancée from rushing off with the family silver. Next time I'll be more patient.'

His biting sarcasm actually helped! Enough anyway to dry up her tears and return the fire to her eyes.

'There's a small window round the back. If I break it I can get my hand in and undo the laundry door lock.'

Without a word he turned on his heel, walking smartly along the side of the house, not even bothering to part the rather overgrown fauna that she'd never quite got around to trimming.

'I can manage,' she said proudly.

'Sure, and were you planning to smash the glass with your bare hand?'

She hadn't thought of that! 'I'm sure there's a towel or something in my case...'

He didn't even deign to give a response. Pulling off his jacket, he wrapped it around his arm and punched the glass out in one quick motion. Slipping his hand through, he promptly undid the lock.

'Not the safest property, is it?' he said dryly as she tiptoed her way through the glass. 'You should see about getting someone in to put some security screens up.'

'Save it, Zavier. My safety's not your concern; you've made that abundantly clear.'

As she stepped into the laundry she lost her footing for a second in the darkness. His hand shot out to save her in a reflex action, steadying her from falling, perhaps, but sending her body into absolute overdrive.

The world stopped for a moment; his skin seemed to sear her flesh. Tabitha half expected to look down and see blisters forming around the strong grip of his fingers. Dragging her eyes up, she held his gaze. His contumelious words, the inscrutable features, couldn't mask the pain in his eyes or the passion that burnt there: a lexicon of the love she would now never know.

'I have to go.'

'I know.' With a sob she pulled the ruby off her finger. 'Here, you'd better take this.'

'Keep it.'

'I don't want it. You said it had to stay in the family…' She stood stricken as he took the ring, her words tailing off as he tossed it out of the broken window.

'What the hell do you think I'd need it for now?'

Stunned and reeling, she stood in the darkness of her laundry, listening to his footsteps echoing down the path, the slam of the car door, the deep purr of the engine as he pulled off into the darkness. And finally when there was nothing left of him to hear, when the draught from the open door had taken away every last trace of his powerful cologne, when the skin on her arm had stopped tingling from his touch, Tabitha flicked on the light. The shattered glass littering the floor, the jagged remains of what had once been her window, were so achingly akin to the remnants of her own life she might just as well be looking into a mirror.

CHAPTER TWELVE

Six months. That was all she had wanted.

Six months to show him how good and wonderful love could be, if only you'd let it.

Wandering home from work in her smart little boxy suit, she thought no one could have guessed the agony in each step, the burden of lugging around a broken heart.

Milk.

The most basic of daily chores took a huge mental effort these days.

Even the local milk bar was agony. Everything seemed to remind her of Zavier, from the mineral water to the daily papers headlining the amazing progress of Jeremy Chambers. How he had been wheeled into Emergency barely conscious, with an unrecordable blood pressure and a grim diagnosis. His appalling chances of survival were the only reason the surgeons had agreed to operate.

After all, you can't kill a dead man.

Amy Dellier even managed to flash a smile from the pages of the glossies, strategically placed at the check-out. It was as if in the short time she had known him Zavier had permeated every facet of her life, taken over every last one of her senses.

Arriving home, she was reminded of him sitting in the driveway as she scrabbled for her keys, and such was her longing she half expected to look up and see him sitting there in the car. As she opened her front door for a moment she was almost sure she could smell him.

Flicking listlessly through her mail, she felt her heart skip a beat as his flashy writing jumped out at her. Her hands shaking, she ripped open the envelope. She ignored the cheque that fell out as she hastily opened the letter inside. It didn't take long to read it—after all, it was only three little words.

As agreed
Zavier.

Just not the three little words she needed to hear.

Sure, Tabitha thought about putting on make-up, combing her hair and dressing up for the occasion. But she knew there wasn't any point. Why dress up for your own funeral?

Lining up at the bank, she watched the teller's eyebrows shoot up a fraction as she gave her withdrawal slip and without a word handed over her driver's licence to verify her signature.

'We normally require some notice when it's such a large withdrawal. We don't always have enough cash on the premises.'

Tabitha wasn't in the mood for games, or lectures. 'Can I have my money now? Yes or no?'

'It might take a few moments. Will you be happy to wait?'

She let out a low laugh. 'I'll wait, but I can't guarantee to be happy.'

A storm was breaking as she reached the high-rise office of Chambers Financiers. There must have been something in her stance, or perhaps it was the determination in her eyes, but even Zavier's receptionist let her past without much argument.

So what if she didn't have an appointment?

Zavier didn't stand as she entered, he didn't even look particularly surprised to see her—just gestured to the chair at his desk, watching as she sat down in a skirt that was too short and a jacket that was too big.

His office was huge. Her entire home could have been dropped in the middle and still left room for a courtyard. But then this was Chambers territory she was stepping into—why would she expect less?

'What can I do for you?' She felt like one of his clients for all the tenderness in his greeting. Even Zavier seemed to flinch at his own formality. 'I'm sorry, how have you been?'

'Fine,' she lied. 'Work's been busy.'

A hint of a frown marred his smooth face. 'Just finished a matinée?'

Tabitha shook her head. 'I've got a job in the box office. It looks a bit more respectable on an application form.'

Still the frown remained.

'What?' she ventured, blushing under his scrutiny.

'You just look…different, that's all.'

'Shackled' was the first word that sprang to his mind, but of course he didn't say it. Her red hair was pulled back, that gorgeous body draped in sombre navy, even the jade of her eyes seemed to have dimmed—but what Tabitha wore, what Tabitha did, for that matter, was her business and hers alone. Still, it was only polite to ask how she was doing…

'How come you're not dancing? If you're having any trouble getting a part because of taking a break, I could have a word—make a few noises.'

'You mean you'll take care of it?'

Zavier shifted uncomfortably in his seat. 'Something like that. Look, I don't want what happened between us to ruin your career.'

Tabitha let out a low laugh. 'It was hardly a career, as you so delicately pointed out on more than a few occasions. Anyway, it doesn't matter now. I'm hoping to start my own dance school some time next year; the office work will help.'

'How?' He gave a derisive laugh. 'It's a box office, Tabitha, hardly rocket science.'

'And you're still a pompous know-it-all.' That stopped him in his tracks long enough for Tabitha to open her bag and catch her breath. 'This came in the post.' She pushed the cheque towards him, remembering with a strange surge of power him doing the same.

Like her, he didn't even deign to give it a glance. 'That's right. It's what's due to you. There should have been a covering letter enclosed. You didn't break the contract, I did, so you're still entitled to the money.'

'I don't want it.'

He waved a dismissive hand and turned back to his computer. 'Up to you.'

Trembling, she stood up and, opening her bag, took out a wad of money and placed it in front of him.

'What's this?'

'What does it look like? You're the financial whizz; I thought at least you'd recognise money when you see it.'

'But what's it for?'

'The first payment you gave to me—it's all there.' She turned to go but he called her back.

'You don't have to do this, Tabitha. How can you afford it?'

'My grandmother paid me back, remember?'

'But what about your dance school?'

'It will happen,' she said assuredly. 'Perhaps not as quickly as I'd like, but it will definitely happen.' Her hand was on the door and she wrenched it open.

'Why didn't you just write a cheque?'

For a second she stiffened, then slowly she turned. Her wary eyes had a strange dignity about them. 'So you could humiliate me further by not cashing it?'

She stared at him for the longest time, trying to somehow entrench his features on her memory, to capture the indigo of his eyes, the beauty of his face, scanning them, filing them, storing them. Saving them up for the dreams she was destined to live on.

'Why the acrimony, Tabitha? We both knew what we were getting into.'

'Maybe you did, Zavier,' she said softly. 'It seems I was naive enough for both of us.'

And then it was over. All she had to do was close the door and he was out of her life for good. The worst part of it was that he didn't even call her back.

She hadn't really expected him to.

'Tabitha?' Aiden met her as he came out of the lift. He was dripping wet, his hair for once out of place. 'What are you doing here?'

'Tying up a few loose ends.' She forced a smile, forced a normal voice. 'I read that your dad's off the ventilator; that's good news.'

'Better than that—they moved him out of ICU today. The cardiac surgeons are still shaking their heads in disbelief that Dad actually survived the surgery.' Taking her elbow, he steered her nearer the wall, away from the traffic of people in the corridor. 'Dad knew all along about me, Tabitha; about me being gay, I mean.'

'He knew?' Even in her emotionally drained state, Tabitha still felt a surge of interest and shock.

'Yep. When the nurses were prepping him for Theatre he called me in; I guess he thought it was going to be a deathbed talk. All that stuff about wanting me to grow up—well, he actually meant to stop living a lie, to face the truth.'

'And did your mum know?'

'Yep.' He gave a low laugh. 'Apparently she knew all along; she just didn't want to upset my father in case he couldn't cope with it. She's fine with it. At least now it's all out in the open, and apparently it's even quite fashionable these days to have a gay son. It gives her something new to talk about at the tennis club. I'm officially out of the closet now. We should have a party to celebrate.'

When she didn't respond he looked at her sadly.

'Poor Tab. I feel so guilty.'

'Why…?'

'Because for everyone else things have worked out. My father's got a few years left in him, my secret's happily out of the closet and no one seems to mind, but as for you, darling Tabitha—well, you're the one who got hurt. You do love Zavier, don't you?'

The tears came then, fast and furious, big sobs that racked at her body. And Aiden stood there, his arm around her shoulder, offering her a handkerchief as she fought for control.

'I'm sorry.'

'It's me that should be sorry—sorry for all that I've put you through. It was me that started the whole thing.' He gave her a long hug. 'Oh, Tab, I did try to warn you. I told you he'd only…'

'Crush me in the palm of his hand.' She finished the

sentence for him. 'It's a pretty accurate description of how I'm feeling.'

'You'll get over him,' Aiden assured her. 'You always do…'

'Not this time.' She blew her nose noisily.

'I did try to talk to him, to tell him what a wonderful woman you are, but he just wasn't interested. Maybe I could have another go…'

'No.' She shook her head firmly. 'He's not interested in excuses. He still insists it was all about money.'

'Which is so bloody like him,' Aiden replied. 'You were doomed, darling, the day you cashed the cheque. My dear brother believes the rest of us should be as infallible and as honest as he is.'

'I can see where he's coming from,' Tabitha said defensively. 'You can hardly blame him for being suspicious of love, given the examples he's been set. I don't exactly come out of this as a paragon of virtue.' She blew her nose again. 'Anyway, it doesn't matter. It's over now.'

'We're still friends? I've been terrified to come over in case you throw a saucepan at me or something.'

She gave a strangled laugh, but it changed midway and she cried instead. 'Of course we're still friends; it's just different, that's all. I can't see you for a while, Aiden. I can't look at you and not think about him. Do you understand?'

He nodded sadly. 'I'll miss you.'

'I know. Look, I've really got to go. I'll call you in a few weeks, a few months—whatever it takes.'

'Please, Tab, wait. I'll have a driver take you home. It's started to storm outside—at least let me do that for you.'

She shook her head. 'I'd really rather walk.'

'But it's pouring.'

'Good, then no one will see me crying.'

He saw her into the lift, stood watching as the numbers carried her down before heading into Zavier's office.

I told you so.

For Aiden there was no pleasure in being proved right. None.

For a little while there he'd actually thought they might make it. His face darkening, he went into the office. Seeing Zavier sitting there, working at his desk for all the world acting as if nothing had happened, only angered him further.

Maybe he wasn't acting, Aiden figured.

Maybe Zavier really didn't care.

'I just saw Tabitha leaving in tears.' Aiden flicked on the television on the far side of Zavier's office, changing the channel from the stock market show Zavier preferred to one of the commercial channels.

Zavier didn't bother to look up, frowning at the noise from the television. 'She just paid me back; it must have hurt.' He expected a laugh, but when it didn't come he finally looked up, watching as Aiden shook the rain off his jacket before carefully hanging it up on the hook. 'Mind you, I'll never work her out. What did she agree to do it for if she was intending to pay me back?'

'You're such a bloody fool sometimes.'

Zavier's eyes narrowed. Aiden, who never got angry, who was always laughing, always joking, suddenly looked as if he might actually hit him. 'What the hell's your problem?'

'I'm gay!' Aiden shouted.

'So what's that got to do with it?'

'I'm gay,' Aiden repeated. 'Yet even I managed to work it out.'

Zavier stared at his brother, utterly perplexed as Aiden waved his hands dramatically in the air.

'What do you think Tabitha did it for? She loves you, you idiot. Though God knows why.'

'It was business,' Zavier said darkly. 'She did it for the money.'

'If that's the case what's this doing here?' Aiden gestured to the notes on the desk. 'And why was she crying in the hall, with unkempt hair and not a scrap of make-up.'

'Her hair's always unkempt.'

'No, it isn't—at least not in that way—and Tabitha *always* wears make-up. Always. I notice these things.'

'Because you're gay?' Zavier asked, his voice bewildered.

Aiden rolled his eyes. 'Because I'm not blind.'

'So what you're telling me,' Zavier said slowly, standing up and walking the long length of his office before finishing his sentence, shaking his head as he did so, 'is that she loves me? Tabitha really loves me?'

'Finally.' Aiden rolled his eyes and lowered himself into one of the sumptuous leather lounges, his calm demeanour exacerbating Zavier's nervous pacing.

'So what should I do?'

'That I can't help you with. But I think it would be much better if you go to her now.'

'Because she's upset?' He was stalling, confused and unsure, wanting so much to believe what he was hearing, yet scared all the same.

'Maybe.' Aiden shrugged, pouring himself a large Scotch. 'But, more to the point, my favourite soap starts in five and I want to concentrate.'

*   *   *

Listlessly she walked up the garden path. Her clothes were drenched, clinging to her body, and her hair dripped in coiled tendrils down her back, but she didn't care. Sure, she wasn't so pessimistic as not to realise this torturous melancholy would abate somewhat, given time, but Tabitha also knew that for as long as there was a breath still in her body she would love him.

The love she felt might rest for a while, might even fade to bearable proportions, but it would never relent.

The sun peeking out from behind a cloud did nothing to cheer her. What was the point of a silver lining when Zavier was gone? A bright glint in the grass caught her eye and with a start she realised it was the ring. Bending, she retrieved it, her eyes filling as she rubbed the soil from it. Painful memories were all she had now.

'Tabitha.'

She froze, the sound of his voice so utterly unexpected, she literally froze—which, Tabitha realised quickly, wasn't the best look when one was half bent over.

'Zavier.' She straightened up, taking the opportunity to force a calming breath into her burning lungs. 'I'm just off to the pawn shop. What do you reckon I'll get?'

'Tabitha, don't.'

She sniffed, wiping her nose with the back of her hand. Not the most elegant of moves, but she was past caring. 'Of course it probably needs a good clean, but I'm sure I'll get a few thousand. I've been digging for days trying to find it.'

'Tabitha, can you stop talking for a moment and look at me?'

'Why?' she asked rudely.

'Just look at me, please.'

She couldn't—couldn't do that without breaking down. So instead she focused somewhere over his shoulder.

'I know that you love me.'

She didn't respond.

'I know that I love you.'

Still she didn't move.

'Aren't you going to say anything?'

'What is there to say? I told you I loved you when your father had his heart attack. You told me that you loved me too then—oh, sorry, *had* loved me. But it didn't stop you walking away.'

'I was scared.'

Slowly, achingly slowly, she lifted her eyes to him.

'But why? How could you be scared of me when you're so powerful…?'

He put a finger to her lips, first to hush her but then the feel of her flesh under the nub of his index finger couldn't pass without recognition. Tracing the outline of her mouth, he gazed at her, his eyes shining with wonder and love.

'Tabitha, work doesn't scare me—that's why I'm good at it. I can look at a pile of figures and reports, scan a spreadsheet in ten seconds flat, and know instinctively what's right. And do you know why I find it easy?'

She shook her head, her curls moving as she did so, tinctured every shade of red as the emerging rays of the afternoon sun lit up her features.

'It's easy because it doesn't matter—not to me, anyway. That's why I'm so good at it. I can totally detach myself. I make a million or I lose a million; at the end of the day it's only money. But love…' He gave a low laugh, but there was a break in it. 'You can read all the signs, think you've got it right, that this is the one—but what if you're wrong? What then? I don't give a damn about money, Tab, but getting it wrong, losing my heart, being hurt, being used—I couldn't bear it. My head and my heart were telling me two different things.'

She knew there was more, knew that he hadn't finished talking. Suddenly they were back on the beach, gazing at the rising sun, taking a moment to regroup, lost in their own pregnant pause.

'I had my life worked out, had everything sorted. I knew exactly what I wanted and a marriage like my parents' wasn't on the agenda. And then you came along, Tabitha, a fiery redhead with an attitude to match, rewriting my rule book as you went along. I almost convinced myself I was trying to protect Aïden and my family when the truth is the only person I was trying to protect was me.'

'Protect from what?' She needed to hear it, to be absolutely sure that she wasn't imagining things, wasn't getting ahead of herself and reading far too much into his words. She closed her eyes as she awaited his response.

'From falling in love with you.' He kissed her then—his lips finding hers easily, their mouths moving in heated unison, the need to seal his words transcending all else. And when, breathless, she pulled away, when the need to finally explain, to justify her actions overcame her ardour, he held her as she spoke, soothing her as he might a child reliving a nightmare.

'I didn't do it for the money—or maybe I did. I sort of convinced myself that was why I was doing it.' Her words were as jumbled as her thoughts. 'I think I knew I loved you right from the start. Aiden certainly did. But

I knew it was impossible, that love wasn't part of the deal. I tried to tell you about the gambling…'

'I knew.' His words stopped the tirade of her confession. 'I knew way before you told me that you didn't have a problem; I just didn't want to hear it.' It was Zavier who was trembling now, Zavier laying it all on the line with everything to lose, Zavier searching her eyes for a reaction. 'For a gambling addict you've got an amazingly good credit rating.'

'You checked up on me?' Her lips were white now, her mind whirring as she relived the past weeks under this entirely different slant.

He nodded slowly; it was way too late for lies now.

'So you knew all along?' His admission had truly shocked Tabitha. Just when she'd thought he couldn't surprise her, that there was nothing left to reveal, again he had floored her. 'That night in the casino…' Her eyes darted down, then back to his, needing, demanding answers.

'My suspicions were confirmed then. You didn't even know how to take your free spin, Tabitha,' he pointed out. 'It was almost funny.…'

Almost.

'But you were so angry on the beach when I told you—furious…'

'Because I didn't want you to say it,' he explained, his only defence the love that blazed from his eyes. 'I didn't want it to be over before we'd even started, and I knew that once you'd told me the truth the only decent thing I could do was offer you a chance to get out.'

'But you didn't?'

'I couldn't.'

The raw honesty of his answer moved her, and the bemusement faded from her eyes.

'Can't you see, Tabitha, I couldn't risk losing you? I was just trying to buy some time.'

'Time's what we've wasted,' Tabitha said gently, her anger evaporating as she gazed at the man she adored, finally allowing the enormity of his love to softly wrap around her, to soothe and comfort her broken, aching heart. 'What are you doing?' She giggled through her tears as he knelt down in the mud swamp that was her garden. 'The neighbours will see.'

'Good.' He laughed, enjoying the sound of her laughter, her girlish embarrassment. The sparkle was back in her eyes now. 'You're not the only one who enjoys an audience, you know. This time we're going to do things the right way.' His voice was suddenly serious, love blazing from his eyes as he knelt before her and with shaking hands offered her the ring—*her* ruby ring. 'Tabitha Reece, will you marry me?'

Tabitha took the ring and slipped it on her finger, back to where it belonged, to where it always would be.

'Say something,' he urged.

'Why? I've already said yes to you,' Tabitha pointed out. 'Six weeks, two days and fifteen hours ago.'

'But that was only temporary,' Zavier said, doubt, angst creeping into his voice.

'No, Zavier,' Tabitha said softly. 'When I said yes I meant it. It was always for ever.'

EPILOGUE

'IT's embarrassing,' Aiden insisted, bouncing baby Darcy on his knee. 'Isn't it, sweetheart? Seeing your nanny and grandad carrying on like a couple of teenagers at your christening?' He peered more closely at his nephew's face. 'Tab, why's he going all red? Purple now—and what's that terrible smell?'

Grinning, Tabitha relieved him of her son. 'Well, I think it's lovely. It might have taken forty years and a heart attack, but seeing Marjory and Jeremy so devoted to each other is a real tonic. There's nothing embarrassing about it. Anyway, if you don't want to be late for your date you'd better push off. I'm going to change Darcy. Thanks for his wonderful present, Aiden, you shouldn't have.'

'Of course I should have, and tell him to hang on to it. That painting will be worth a fortune in a few years. Actually, Zavier—' Aiden lowered his voice '—I was hoping for a word before I go.'

Zavier rolled his eyes. 'How much this time?'

'It's all right for you,' Aiden said defensively. 'Dad's going to live for ever, at this rate, and maybe my paintings are taking off, but compared to you it's peanuts. Anyway, Luigi's got expensive tastes—I can hardly take him to the local burger bar. Have you seen the price of champagne these days?'

'You're supposed to be on the wagon,' Zavier said sharply.

'I am, but that doesn't mean Luigi has to be.'

'If he cares about you,' Zavier started, in a voice that could only denote a lecture, 'he won't mind where you take him. And stop rolling your eyes, you two. I'm right on this.'

'I hardly think a man who had to buy his bride should be lecturing me,' Aiden teased, and Zavier actually blushed. 'You've still never told me how much you had to offer to sway this divine creature.'

Laughing, Tabitha left them to it. After changing Darcy's nappy she pulled on his blue Babygro, admiring his little fat legs as he kicked happily in the air. He really was the most delightful baby, and of course that had nothing to do with his having two of the most biased parents. Gently placing him in his crib, Tabitha stood watching as he rolled onto his stomach, his fat bottom sticking up in the air as he searched for his thumb.

'Is he asleep?' Zavier asked as he crept in behind her.

'He's gone straight onto his stomach. Maybe I should turn him.'

'He'll only roll straight back.' Seeing her tense, Zavier grinned. 'Here.' She watched as his strong hand gently rolled the sleeping baby onto his back, never failing to marvel at how gentle and patient he was with his son. 'He's exhausted. It's been a great day.'

'Fantastic,' Tabitha agreed, nestling against his chest as they admired their sleeping baby. 'Your dad was so proud, and did you see the smile on my grandmother's face?'

'She's looking really happy. Bruce must be good for her—at least she's not gambling now. Mind you, they play a mean game of snap; I've never seen such concentration! I doubt Mum will pull the cards out next time they come for dinner. Anyway, enough about everyone else—there's something for you downstairs.'

'But we opened all the presents,' Tabitha said as she walked behind him. 'What's this?'

'It's for you. Open it.' His voice had gone strangely thick, and he couldn't quite meet her eyes as she snapped open the large velvet box he handed her.

'Oh, Zavier, it's stunning.' It was, too—a delicate neck chain, littered with rubies all different sizes. 'There must be hundreds here.'

'Forty,' Zavier said gruffly. 'One for each year of marriage. It's the one my grandfather had made for my grandmother for their fortieth anniversary.'

'Shouldn't you be doing this in thirty-nine years?' She watched the tiniest frown on his face. 'I'll still be around, Zavier. I'm not going anywhere; this is for keeps.'

'I know.' The frown vanished and his eyes lifted to hers. 'I guess I just want to keep hearing it—anyway, it seems a shame to have something so beautiful locked away when you could be wearing it.'

He fastened it tenderly around her neck and followed her to the large mirror over the fireplace.

'I can't believe I nearly let you go.'

'Don't.' Leaning against him, she closed her eyes, chasing away the nightmare of what could have been.

A world without Zavier.

'Can I ask you something?''

'Ask away,' he mumbled, only half listening as he pulled back the wild red curls, exposing the hollow of her shoulder on which he rained tiny kisses.

'Why don't you sell the business? Your parents are fine, I've got my dance school and Aiden's got his little gallery; what about taking the time to chase your dreams now?'

'What dreams?' He was working his way along her

collarbone, peeling back the thin strap of her dress with his teeth as his fingers worked their magic on her yielding breasts.

'Your dreams.' Tabitha forced her mind onto the one-sided conversation, determined to see it through. 'The ones you spoke about the night we got engaged.'

'I don't remember much talking. In fact all I can remember is this.' His hand was creeping down now, her dress slithering over her softly rounded bottom.

'The night we *first* got engaged, you said you had dreams…'

'Oh, that night.' In one easy motion he scooped her up, carrying her across the hall to the bedroom door, which he kicked impatiently open. 'You talk too much.'

'I'm serious, Zavier. I need to know if your dreams…'

'Chased, caught and fulfilled. Does that answer your question?'

'Honestly?'

Laying her on the bed, he slid down the last tiny remnant of her clothing before adding softly, 'Beyond my wildest expectations…'

THE BILLIONAIRE
TAKES A BRIDE

by

Liz Fielding

Liz Fielding was born with itchy feet. She made it to Zambia before her twenty-first birthday and, gathering her own special hero and a couple of children on the way, lived in Botswana, Kenya and Bahrain - with pauses for sightseeing pretty much everywhere in between. She finally came to a full stop in a tiny Welsh village cradled by misty hills and these days, mostly, leaves her pen to do the travelling. When she's not sorting out the lives and loves of her characters, she potters in the garden, reads her favourite authors and spends a lot of time wondering…'What if…' For news of upcoming books – and to sign up for her occasional newsletter – visit Liz's website at www.lizfielding.com

Don't miss Liz Fielding's exciting new novel, *The Sheikh's Unsuitable Bride,* out in January 2008 from Mills & Boon® Romance.

For the ladies of the eHarlequin Writers'
Auxiliary and Hamster Circle.
Thanks for the laughs.

CHAPTER ONE

THIS was a mistake. A big mistake. Every cell in Ginny's body was slamming on the brakes, digging in its heels, trying to claw its way back behind the safety of the rain-soaked hedge that divided her roof top terrace from the raked perfection of Richard Mallory's Japanese garden, with its mossy rocks, carp pool and paper-walled pavilion.

Previous perfection.

Her boots had left deep impressions in the damp gravel. So much for stealth.

She was not cut out for burglary. Even her clothes were wrong. She should have been in svelte black and wearing lightweight tennis shoes that made no noise, her hair bolted down under a tight ski cap…

Oh, for heaven's sake. It was the middle of the morning and the last thing she wanted to look like was a burglar.

In the unlikely event that she was discovered it was important that she looked exactly what she was. A distressed neighbour looking for her lost pet…

Somebody totally innocent. And an innocent person didn't change shoes, or happen to be wearing the appropriate clothing to battle through a hedge. Her lace-ups, baggy jeans and a loose shirt in an eye-gouging purple—fifty pence from her favourite charity shop—screamed innocent. Of everything except bad taste.

5

She groaned.

Distressed was right.

She had promised herself that she would never volunteer to do anything like this ever again. Not even for Sophie. Famous last words.

Her mouth hadn't been paying attention.

She took a deep steadying breath and firmly beat back the urgent desire to bolt. It would be fine. She had every angle covered and this was for a friend. A friend in trouble.

A friend who was always in trouble.

A friend who'd always been there for her, she reminded herself.

She took another deep breath, then stepped through the open French windows into the empty room.

'Er, hello?'

Her voice emerged as a painful croak. A bit like a frog with laryngitis. She had her story all ready in the unlikely event that someone answered, but that didn't stop her heart from pounding like the entire timpani section of the London Philharmonic…

'Anyone home?'

The only response was the faint whirr of a washing machine hitting the spin cycle.

Apart from that no sound of any kind.

No turning back.

She had fifteen minutes. Maybe twenty if she was lucky. A brief window of opportunity while the cleaner, having opened up the French windows to let in the fresh air, as she did every morning—why had she mentioned that to Sophie?—and put on the washing, was downstairs flirting with the hall porter over a cup of coffee.

Okay. She wiped the sweat from her upper lip. She could do this. Fifteen minutes was more than enough time to find one little computer disk and save stupid Sophie's stupid job.

Excuse me? Who exactly is the stupid one here?

The prod from her subconscious was unnecessary. She was the one burgling her neighbour's apartment while 'stupid' Sophie was safely at work, surrounded by an office full of alibi-providing colleagues. Should the need for one arise.

While quiet, sensible Ginny—who should at this moment be safely tucked up in the British Library researching Homeric myths—was the one who'd be arrested.

All the more reason not to waste any more time wool-gathering. Even so, she took a moment to look around, get her bearings. This was not the moment to knock something over…

Mallory's penthouse apartment, like his garden, tended towards the minimalist. There was very little furniture—but all of it so perfectly simple that you just knew it had cost a mint—a few exquisite pieces of modern ceramics and absolutely acres of pale polished wood floor.

Stay well away from the ceramics, she told herself. Don't go near the ceramics…

There was only one 'off' note.

Spotlit by a beam of sunlight that had found its way through the scudding clouds, a black silk stocking tied in a neat bow around the neck of a champagne bottle

next to two champagne flutes looked shockingly decadent in such an austere setting.

A linen napkin—on which something had been
scrawled in what looked like lipstick—was tucked into
the bow.

A thank you note?

She swallowed hard and firmly quashing her curiosity—she was in enough trouble already—resisted
the temptation to take a look.

Whatever it said, the scene confirmed everything
she'd heard about the man's reputation. Not his reputation as a genius, or money machine. Those went
without saying. The financial papers regularly genu-
flected to his brilliance while salivating over Mallory
plc's profits.

It was his reputation as a babe magnet that seemed
to be confirmed by this still-life-with-champagne tab-
leau.

Despite being his next door neighbour, albeit on a
temporary basis, their paths hadn't yet crossed so
she'd had no opportunity to check this out for herself.
Not that she was the kind of 'babe' he'd look at
twice—she wasn't any kind of 'babe', as she'd be the
first to acknowledge.

Whether or not he magnetised her.

Not that he would. Magnetise her.

No matter how superficially attractive, she didn't
find anything appealing about a man who had a reputation for casual affairs, even if the gossip columns
loved him for it. But then she didn't think much of
gossip columns, either.

She pushed her spectacles up her nose and, putting

her hand over her heart in an effort to cut down on the jack-hammer noise it was making, made a big effort to concentrate on what Sophie had told her.

He'd taken the disk home with him earlier in the week and it would be lying about on his desk somewhere. Probably.

Totally confident of her ability to find the thing—'I mean, how difficult could it be?'—Sophie had been weak on actual details.

About as weak as her reason for not doing this herself. If this was such a breeze, why couldn't she squeeze through the rain-soaked hedge—the very *prickly* rain-soaked hedge—and get it herself? After all, she only lived a few floors down, in the same apartment block.

'But darling, you're living next door to the man. It's just so perfect. Almost as if it was fate. If he even suspects I was anywhere near his study I'll not only lose my job, I'll never get another one. The man's a complete bastard. He has absolutely no tolerance for anything less than perfection…'

Right. Of course. She remembered now. Sophie couldn't risk getting caught. The whole point was to save her job. The only mystery was why she was working for a computer software company in the first place. She usually preferred a little light PR work, or swanning about looking decorative in an art gallery…

Sophie had made it all sound so simple. A quick trip through the hedge that divided her roof garden from his and Bob, apparently, would be her uncle. Which was why Ginny had been nominated to ransack this 'complete bastard's' apartment, 'borrow' the disk, copy and return it—thus saving Sophie's job—without his ever knowing she'd been there.

Piece of cake.

A low groan escaped her lips. She wasn't built for burglary. Or was it breaking and entering? When she hadn't actually broken in?

A fine legal point that she was sure the magistrate would explain as he passed sentence if she didn't find the disk and get out of there before Mrs Figgis returned from her daily dalliance over a double *latte* with the porter.

Unfortunately, although she was sending urgent 'move' messages from her brain to her feet, her synapses appeared to be on a go-slow. Or maybe they were just frozen with terror like the rest of her.

Never again, she vowed, as the message finally got through and her feet came unstuck from the spot to which she had been glued for what seemed like hours. This was positively, absolutely, totally the last time she would allow Sophie Harrington to talk her into trouble.

No. That was unfair. She'd managed to talk herself into trouble. But who could resist Sophie Harrington when she turned on the charm?

Twenty-four years old going on fifteen.

This was just like Ginny's raid on the school secretary's office all over again. That time it had been Sophie's life-or-death need to reclaim her diary before the headmistress read it. Only an idiot would carry such an inflammatory document around with her. Only a complete idiot would be stupid enough to write it in class…

Except that on this occasion if she got caught pulling her best friend's irons from the fire she risked a lot more than a shocked 'I expected better from you' lecture and a suspension of visits to the village for the rest of the term.

She dragged her mind back to reality. Cloakroom, kitchen... She came to a stunned halt as she took in the brushed steel and slate wonder of Mallory's state-of-the-art kitchen. What couldn't she do in a kitchen like that?

Richard Mallory wouldn't need to use magnets on her, she decided, just offer her the run of his kitchen...

For heaven's sake! She had less than fifteen minutes and she was wasting them drooling over his top of the range knives!

She moved quickly across the room and opened a door on the far side of the two-storey-high living space. Desk, laptop... Bingo!

Good grief, it looked as if a madman had been working without cease for a week. In contrast to everywhere else that had looked almost unlived in. Apart, that was, from the champagne bottle and flutes. One of them barely touched.

So, which of them had been in too much of a hurry...?

She really didn't want to think about that and, dragging her mind back to the study, decided that untidy was good. It meant he probably wouldn't be obsessive about locking stuff away.

It also meant there was a lot to look through. Empty water bottles, chocolate bar wrappers—he had seriously good taste in chocolate—and a ton of paper covered with figures littering the desk and floor.

Unfortunately, once she'd looked under all the papers, she could see that was all there was. Not a disk in sight.

She dragged her wandering mind back into line and tried the desk drawers. They didn't budge. So much for the casual-about-security theory. And the key would be with him, on his long weekend in the country. Along with the owner of the black silk stocking.

Although, if that was the case, why the note? She jerked her curiosity back into line.

Why on earth would she care?

She checked her watch. Six precious minutes gone…

Okay. Keys came in sets of two so there had to be a spare somewhere. She ran her fingers beneath the desk, under the drawers, in case it was taped there. Well, no. First place a burglar would look, obviously. Even a first time burglar like her.

If you didn't count the school secretary's office…

Where would she keep the spare key to her desk drawer?

Safely in the drawer so she wouldn't lose it, but then she didn't have anything worth locking up. Okay, there were files and disks containing months of painstaking research. Nothing anyone would want to steal, though. But supposing she did…

In her bedside drawer seemed a likely place. Who would ever find it amongst all the clutter?

But would a man think that way? What did men put in their bedside drawers, anyway?

She had no way of knowing but, short of any other ideas, she abandoned the study and ran up the spiral staircase to the upper floor, emerging in a wide gallery where comfort had been allowed to encroach on the severity of the minimalist theme.

The floor was covered with a lovely old Turkish rug, there was a huge, much used leather armchair and the walls were lined, floor to ceiling, with shelves crammed with books that looked as if they'd been read, rather than arranged by an expensive decorator just for effect. She moved towards them on automatic, stumbling over a low table she hadn't noticed and sending a heap of magazines slithering to the floor.

The noise was horrendous. But it brought her back to her senses. This was no time for browsing...

There was only one door leading from the gallery. Rubbing her shin, she opened it, stepping into a wide inner hallway lit from above by a series of skylights and groaned as she was confronted by half a dozen doors, opening the doors to an airing cupboard and two guest suites before she finally found Mallory's room. It had to be his room. It was in darkness, the heavy curtains still shut tight against the feeble morning sunlight.

She left the door open to give her some light and looked around. There was very little furniture, which rather confused her.

The whole apartment was so different from the McBrides' which, like the apartment block that Sir William had designed, had an art deco feel to it. Even the garden.

But it seemed that Mallory's taste for minimalism

extended even to his sleeping arrangements. A very low—and very large—unmade bed dominated the room. Mounded up with a mountainous quilt and pillows and flanked by a pair of equally low tables, each with a tall lamp.

She crossed quickly to the nearest one. At first, she couldn't work out how to open the narrow, flush-fitting drawer. The lamp would have helped, but her hands were shaking so much with nerves that she was sure to knock it flying if she attempted to switch it on.

Instead, she got down on her knees and felt underneath, relieved to discover that the trick to it was nothing more complicated than a finger ledge.

She pulled and discovered the answer to her question. The drawer contained a quantity of products that suggested Richard Mallory was a man whose guiding principle in life was 'be prepared'.

Frequently.

She closed it quickly. Okay. Enough was enough. She was running out of time here. And Sophie was running out of luck. She'd check the other table so that she could say she had done everything possible. After that, she was out of there.

Then, as she began to get to her feet, something caught her eye. A glint of something small and shiny under the table, right up against the wall, that might be a key. For a moment she was torn. What was the likelihood that this was the key she was looking for?

But then it had to fit something…

She had to lie down and stretch out flat before she could reach it. It felt right—long and narrow—and she emerged, flushed from the effort as she backed out,

holding up the object to get a better look. Light, she
needed more light. As she reached for the lamp it came
on by itself. Startled, she stared at it for a moment,
then grinned. That was so brilliant! She'd heard of
lamps that did that…

But this was not the time to investigate. She turned
her attention back to the small metallic object she'd
picked up. 'Oh, drat…'

'Not one of yours, I take it?'

The voice, low and gravelly, had emerged from the
heaped-up quilt, along with a mop of dark, tousled hair
and a pair of heavy-lidded eyes. It was followed by a
hand which tossed aside a remote and lifted the sliver
of platinum from her open palm and, warm fingers
brushing against her neck, held it up against her ear.

Not a key, but an earring. Long, slender…

And that was just his fingers.

'No,' he said, after looking at it and then at her for
what seemed like an age, during which her heart took
a unilateral decision not to beat—probably something
to do with all the magnetism flowing from those electric blue eyes—before dropping it back into her hand.
'Not your style.'

A sound—something incoherent that might have
been agreement—emerged from Ginny's throat. Re-
cycled charity shop was cheap. That was its attraction.
Whether it could be described as a style…

'If you tell me what you're looking for I might be
able to help?' he prompted.

More of Richard Mallory emerged from beneath the
quilt as he propped himself up on one arm. Naked

shoulders, a naked chest with a spattering of dark hair that arrowed down to a hard, flat stomach…

'Um…' she murmured, mesmerised.

'I'm sorry?' One brow kinked upward. 'I didn't quite catch that.'

The sleepy lids were deceptive. His eyes, she realised, were wide awake. How long had he been watching her? Had he witnessed her attack on his bedside drawer?

She swallowed hard. There was nothing to do but bluff it out and hope for the best. If she could handle a room full of eighteen-year-old undergraduates who thought they knew it all—and who almost certainly knew a lot more than her about pretty much anything other than Greek myth—she could surely handle one man…

As his eyes continued to burn into her, she decided she'd take the lecture hall any day. Unfortunately, it wasn't an option. Bluff would have to do it.

'I said, "um",' she replied, pushing her glasses up her nose as she found her 'teacher' voice. After all he couldn't sack *her*…

He could, of course, call the police.

'Um?' He repeated the word back at her as if it was from some foreign language. One he'd never before encountered.

Bluff, bluff.

It was easy. She did it all the time. It was how she had got through the lectures she had given to help support herself through her doctorate. All she had to do, she reminded herself, was use the classic technique of imagining that he was naked. From what she'd seen so far she wasn't finding it difficult. He probably *was* naked...

Oh, bad idea.

Think of something else. Her mother...

'Not the acme of clear thought translated into speech—' she said, her thoughts—and vocal cords—snapping right back into line '—but then you did startle me, Mr Mallory.'

This, for some reason, appeared to entertain him. 'Do you expect me to apologise?'

'That really isn't necessary.' She finally wrenched her gaze from the wide expanse of his shoulders and, scrambling to her feet, put a little distance between them. 'It's entirely my fault, after all. I didn't realise you were here, or I wouldn't have just...' Her desperate attempt to appear cool in a difficult situation buckled under his undisguised amusement. He was, she realised belatedly, teasing her...

'Just?' he prompted.

'Um...' That foreign word again...

'Just um?'

'I wouldn't have just walked in,' she snapped. Then, because that seemed to lack something, she said, 'I'd have knocked first.'

'Really?' His eyebrows suggested he was seriously surprised. 'That would be a first.'

She frowned, confused, unable to drag her gaze from his shoulders. Or the way the muscle, emphasized by deep shadows, bunched up as he shrugged.

Then she realised what he was implying and felt herself blush. Of all the arrogant, self-opinionated...

She wasn't some Richard Mallory 'groupie', intent on flinging herself on his irresistible body!

'If it's a regular problem maybe you should keep your bedroom door locked,' she advised, perhaps more sharply than was wise under the circumstances.

'Maybe I should,' he agreed. Then, bringing her back to the point, 'So? What *were* you looking for?'

Her heart—which was having a seriously bad morning—skipped a beat. She should have legged it while she had the chance, instead of sticking around to chat. He might have dismissed the whole incident as a bad dream. She'd had worse nightmares.

'Looking for?' she repeated.

'Under my bed.'

'Oh.'

Help…

Her excuse had sounded perfectly reasonable as she'd rehearsed it in the safety of her own apartment. But then she'd never expected to have to use it. She'd be in and out in a flash, Sophie had promised.

When would she ever learn?

What had sounded reasonable as a back-up story, in the event that the cleaner returned early from her morning flirtation with the porter, lacked any real credibility when confronted with the man himself.

Or maybe it was just guilt turning the words to ashes in her mouth.

That was silly.

It wasn't as if she was a *real* burglar, for heaven's sake. She was only going to borrow the disk—it would be back on his desk before he'd missed it. Hardly a matter for the Crown Court.

Unless, of course, she killed Sophie.

'In your own time,' he encouraged.

Faced with a pair of sharp blue eyes that suggested Richard Mallory would not be so easy to flannel as a 'daily' with dalliance on her mind, that seemed a very attractive idea. Right now, however, she had a more pressing problem and she trawled her brain in a desperate attempt to come up with a story that was just a little less…ridiculous.

Her brain had, apparently, taken the day off.

But then why else would she be here?

Please, please, she prayed, let the floor open up and swallow me now. The floor refused to oblige.

She was out of time and stuck with the excuse she'd prepared earlier.

'I was looking for my hamster,' she said.

'Excuse me?' He laughed. 'Did you say your *hamster*?'

Faced with his amusement she felt a certain irritation. A need to defend her story. It wasn't *that* ridiculous.

Okay, so maybe it was. A kitten would have been cuter, but the cleaner would have known she didn't have a kitten. Nothing uncaged was allowed within the portals of Chandler's Reach.

'He escaped,' she said. 'He made a break for it through the hedge and headed straight for your French windows.' And when this didn't elicit polite concern… 'It took me longer to get through it. He's smaller,' she elaborated when Mallory remained silent. 'He was able to scoot underneath.' Then, in desperation, 'It's really scratchy…'

She could not believe she was saying this. Richard Mallory's expression suggested he was having problems with it too, but was making a manful effort not to laugh out loud.

In an attempt to distract him, she took a step closer and extended her hand.

'We haven't met, Mr Mallory, but we're temporarily neighbours. I'm Iphegenia Lautour.' Only the most truthful person in the entire world would own up to a name like that voluntarily, right? 'I'm looking after Sir William and Lady McBride's apartment. For the summer. Next door,' she added, in case he didn't know his neighbours. 'While they're away. Flat-sitting. You know—dusting the whatnot, watering the houseplants. Feeding the goldfish,' she added. Then, as if there was nothing at all out of the ordinary in the situation, she said, 'How d'you do?'

'I think—' he said, looking slightly nonplussed as he took her hand, gripping it firmly for a moment, holding it for longer than was quite necessary '—that I need notice of that question.'

He sat up, leaned forward and raked his hands through his hair, as if somehow he could straighten out his thoughts along with his unruly curls.

It did nothing for the curls, but the sight of his naked shoulders, a chest spattered with exactly the right amount of dark hair, left her with an urgent need to swallow.

He dragged his hands down over his face. 'Along with coffee, orange juice and a shower. In no particular order of preference. I've had a hard night.'

Ginny didn't doubt it. She'd seen the evidence for herself…

She gave a little squeak as he flung back the covers and swung his feet to the floor. Backed hurriedly away. Knocked the lamp, grabbed to stop it from falling and only made things worse, flinched as it hit the carpet.

Mallory stood up, reached down and set it back on the table, giving her plenty of time to see that he wasn't, after all, totally naked but wearing a pair of soft grey shorts.

Naked enough. They clung to his hips by the skin of their teeth, exposing a firm flat belly and leaving little else to the imagination.

It was definitely time to get out of there.

'I'm disturbing you,' she said, groping behind her for the door handle but succeeding only in pushing the door shut. With her on the wrong side.

'You could say that,' he agreed, picking up the remote and using it to draw back the curtains so that daylight flooded into the room.

'Neat trick,' she said. 'Is that how you turned on the light?' It was a mistake to draw attention to herself because he turned those searching blue eyes on her.

One of them was definitely disturbed.

'I'm really sorry—'

'Don't be,' he said, cutting off her apology. 'I'd have slept all day if you hadn't woken me. Iphegenia?' he prompted, with a frown. 'What kind of name is that?'

'The kind that no one can spell?' she offered. Then, 'My mother's a classical scholar,' she added—at least she was, when she could spare the time—as if that explained everything. He looked blank. 'Iphegenia was the daughter of King Agamemnon. He sacrificed her to the gods in return for a fair wind to Troy. So that he could grab back his runaway sister-in-law. Helen.'

'Helen?' he repeated. If not dumb, definitely founded...

'Of Troy.'

'Oh, right, "...the face that launched a thousand ships and burnt the topless towers of Ilium"?'

'That's the one,' she said. Then, 'He got murdered by his wife for his trouble. But you probably knew that.' There was more, a lot more, but years of explaining her unusual name had taught her that was about as much as anyone wanted to know. 'Homer was writing about the dysfunctional family nearly three thousand years ago,' she offered.

'Yes.' He looked, for a moment, as if he might pursue her mother's choice of name... Then, thinking better of it, said, 'Tell me about your wandering hamster. What's *his* name? Odysseus?'

Irony. He'd just woken up and he could quote Christopher Marlowe, recall the names of mythical heroes and do irony. Impressive.

But then he *was* a genius.

'Good try, but a bit of a mouthful for a hamster, don't you think?' she asked, keeping her mouth busy while her mind did some fast footwork.

'I'd say Iphegenia is a bit of a mouthful for a girl,' he said, as if he knew she was simply playing for time. 'The kind of name that suggests your mother was not feeling particularly warm towards your father when she gave it to you. If I gave it any serious thought.'

He wasn't even close.

'So what is this runaway rodent called?' he asked when she made no comment, pushing her for an answer.

'Hector,' she said.

'Hector? Not Harry—as in Houdini?'

No, Hector. As in heroic Trojan warrior prince slain by Achilles. Classical scholarship ran in the family but she thought she'd probably said more than enough on that subject.

'Harry who?' she asked innocently.

His eyes narrowed and for a moment she was afraid she'd gone too far. 'Never mind,' he said, letting it go. 'He must be quite a mover if you chased him up here. Didn't the stairs slow him down?'

She hadn't thought of that. Hadn't thought, full stop. Certainly hadn't even considered the possibility that Richard Mallory would be at home in bed recovering from a hot date instead of where he was supposed to be, in deepest Gloucestershire.

Thank you, Sophie…

She supposed she should be grateful that the woman with the black silk stockings wasn't under the duvet with him. Although she would at least have offered a distraction.

Ginny attempted to recall exactly how large hamsters were. Four or five inches, perhaps, at full stretch? And she realised she was so deep in trouble that the only possibility of escape was to keep on digging in the hope of eventually tunnelling out.

'Hector—' she said, with a conviction she was far from feeling '—has thighs like a footballer. It's all that running on his exercise wheel.' Then, 'Look, I'd better go—' before his brain was fully engaged and he began to ask questions to which she had no answer '—and, um, let you have your shower.'

'Oh, please, don't rush off.'

He was across the room before she could escape, his hand flat against the door, towering over her as she backed up hard against it in an attempt to put some space between them so that he wouldn't feel the wild, nervous hammering of her heart.

In an attempt to avoid the magnetic pull of his body.

'I so rarely encounter this level of entertainment before breakfast.'

CHAPTER TWO

RICHARD MALLORY'S chest, those heroic shoulders, the warm male scent of his flesh, was making it very hard to breathe normally. A fact she was sure he knew only too well.

'I—um—'

'Why don't you stay and join me?'

Join him?

With one hand keeping the door firmly shut, he used the other to deal with a wayward strand of hair that had been dragged from its scrunchy as she'd fought her way through the hedge and was now slowly descending across her face.

It wasn't just his eyes that generated electricity. Her skin fizzed, tightened at his touch and not just on her cheek, her temple. Her entire body reacted as if it had been jump-started like some long dead battery.

No. Not long dead. Never charged.

'Join you?' she repeated, stupidly.

Did he mean in the shower?

Why didn't that sound like a totally impossible idea? And what on earth was he doing to her hair?

She flattened herself against the door, moved her mouth in an attempt to form a coherent sentence. Something along the lines of What the hell do you think you're doing? should do it. No, it would have to be something simpler. Stop…

He plucked a twig from her hair, holding it up for her inspection. 'I hope you didn't do Her Ladyship's perfectly clipped hedge mortal damage.' Then, without waiting for her to elaborate on the extent of the mayhem she'd caused in Lady McBride's exquisite formal roof terrace, 'I won't be more than five minutes. Stay and tell me all about your athletic pet over some scrambled eggs—'

Five minutes? Eggs? Then reality sunk in.

'Eggs?' she repeated. 'You meant join you for breakfast?'

His mouth widened in a lazy smile that deepened the lines bracketing his mouth.

'What else?'

Her own mouth worked soundlessly for a moment before she finally managed to engage teeth and tongue and exclaim, 'Are you serious?' And feigning blank astonishment—which wasn't difficult, blank perfectly described the state of her mind—she covered her blushes by snatching the twig from him and stuffing it into her pocket. 'I had breakfast hours ago. It's nearly lunchtime. I shouldn't be here at all. I should be working...'

'Plants to water, whatnots to dust...?'

'A woman's work...' she agreed, leaving him to complete the saying. It wasn't politically correct—her mother would have been shocked that she could even think such thoughts. But her mother wasn't here to criticise and right at that moment she'd have said anything to escape...

All she had to do was move. All she had to do was remember how.

'How did the McBrides find you?' he asked while she was still thinking about it.

'Find me?' She hadn't been lost… 'Oh, I see. It was a personal introduction. I know their daughter-in-law. Philly. Slightly,' she added. She wasn't claiming any deep personal friendship. 'She knew I needed somewhere to stay in London for the summer and they needed someone…'

'To feed the goldfish?'

'Look, I'd better go.'

But he wasn't quite finished with her.

'Aren't you forgetting something?'

'Am I?'

'Hector?' he prompted. 'Surely you're not going to abandon him?'

Drat with knobs on.

'He could be anywhere,' she offered just a little desperately, discovering too late that a make-believe pet could be as much trouble as a real one. 'He'll have found himself a quiet corner and gone to sleep by now.' He was beginning to assume a presence and character all his own. 'They're nocturnal, you know.' She swallowed. 'H-hamsters.'

'Is that a fact? Then I'll be sure not to make too much noise. He must be tired after all that effort.' And he finally straightened, releasing her from his personal force field which had held her fixed to the spot far more effectively than any door. When she still didn't move he said, 'Well, if you're sure I can't tempt you…'

'No!' Did that sound too vehement? She was beyond caring. 'I really do have to go.'

'If you insist.' He made a gesture that suggested she was free to leave any time. 'It's been a pleasure meeting you, Iphegenia Lautour.'

He was laughing at her now and not making any real attempt to hide the fact. But that was okay. She'd been laughed at before and this was the warm, teasing kind that didn't hurt. In fact, she was beginning to wonder if Sophie had misjudged him. He might be a shocking flirt, but he did seem to have the redeeming feature of a well-developed sense of humour...

'Ginny,' she said, her voice no longer crisp but unusually thick and soft.

It seemed to go with the tingling in her breasts, a curious weakness in her thighs. He had the most kissable mouth of any man she'd ever met, she decided. Not that she'd met many men she would cross the road to kiss.

Firm, wide, the lower lip a sensual invitation to help herself...

She caught her own lower lip between her teeth before she did something truly stupid, cooling it with her tongue.

'People call me Ginny,' she explained. 'Usually. It's shorter.'

'And easier to spell.' The muscles at the side of his jaw clenched briefly. Then, since she was clearly rooted to the spot, he opened the door and held it wide for her. 'I'll keep a look out for Hector, Ginny, and if I find him I'll be sure to send him home.'

She was being dismissed. A minute ago she was desperate to escape. Now he was reduced to encouraging her to leave.

'If Mrs Figgis, your cleaner—' she added in case
he wasn't personally acquainted with the lady who
kept his apartment free of dust '—doesn't suck him
up in her vacuum cleaner thinking he's a lump of
fluff,' she said, before she could stop herself. Her urgent desire to flee evaporating the moment a swift exit
offered itself.

'Perhaps you'd better warn her,' he suggested.

'I will. And I'm, um, really sorry for disturbing
you.'

'I wouldn't have—' he paused, smiled '—um…
missed it for the world. But now I really must take
that shower, so unless you want to come and keep an
eye on me, make sure I don't drown the heroic
Hector…' He stood back, offering her a clear route to
his bathroom.

This time there was no hiding the crimson tide that
swept from her neck to her hairline as she finally
caught on to what he already knew. That she'd become
just one more case of iron filings clinging to his personal magnet.

'No…' She backed through the door, raising her
hand, palm up, in a self-protective little gesture. 'Really, Mr Mallory, I trust you.'

'Rich,' he said. 'People call me Rich.'

'Yes,' she mumbled. 'I know. I've seen it in the
papers…'

Then she turned and fled.

Ginny couldn't believe she'd just blundered into a
strange man's bedroom then lied shamelessly while he
flirted with her. Worse, that she'd responded as if he'd

reached out and flipped a switch—turning her on had been that easy. And, with the game so swiftly won, he'd lived up to his reputation and just as quickly become bored.

She groaned as she ran down the spiral staircase, wishing that it were possible to stop the clock, rewind time…

'Miss Lautour?' Mrs Figgis, standing at the foot blocking her way, a puzzled expression creasing her face, brought her to an abrupt halt. 'What are you doing here? How did you get in?'

The voice of Rich Mallory's cleaner had much the same instantly bracing effect as the proverbial cold shower. Allegedly. She'd never found the need for such self-abuse.

'Through the French windows, Mrs Figgis,' Ginny said, clinging to the truth. Her voice shocked back to crispness. Besides, having bearded the lion in his den and escaped in one piece, she wasn't about to be scared by someone wielding nothing more dangerous than a duster.

Nevertheless, she held her position two steps up. Just to even up the cleaner's height advantage.

A mistake. It just drew attention to her boots. Puzzlement instantly shifted to disapproval.

'Can I ask you to be careful when you're going round with a vacuum cleaner?' she asked. Getting it in before she was on the receiving end of a lecture about leaving footwear at the door—particularly anything as unsuitable as boots—in keeping with the Japanese theme of the décor. 'I'm afraid I've lost my hamster—'

'Hamster?'

What was it about hamsters that was so unbelievable?

All across the country people kept hamsters as pets. As an undergraduate, she'd briefly shared rooms with a girl who'd kept one. It had escaped all the time. It had even got under the floorboards once. Life with a hamster was a constant drama.

That was where she'd got the idea in the first place...

'Small, buff coloured rodent. About so big.' She sketched the rough dimensions with her hands. 'He's called Hector,' she said, her head distancing itself from her mouth as she elaborated unnecessarily. Or maybe not.

She probably thought a woman who kept a hamster as a pet would be a sad-sack obsessive—not true, her room-mate had been the life and soul of any party— but Richard Mallory would undoubtedly mention the incident, be suspicious if Mrs Figgis knew nothing about it. With good reason.

'Easy to mistake for fluff in a dark corner,' she added.

'There is no fluff in any corner of this apartment,' the woman declared indignantly.

'No, of course not. I didn't mean...' Then, 'I'm sure Mr Mallory will explain.'

'Mr Mallory?' Mrs Figgis blanched. 'He's still here?' So she wasn't the only one who'd been caught out. 'He should have left hours ago.'

'Really?' she said. Oh, listen to her to pretending not to know! She was shocked at just how convincing she sounded. 'Well, it's still early.' If you were a multi-millionaire businessman who'd just had a hard night with a girl who wore black silk stockings. 'Actually, I think he might appreciate coffee. And he did mention something about scrambled eggs...'

She didn't hang around to see whether Mrs Figgis considered it any part of her duties to make coffee rather than drink it. Instead, she headed swiftly in the direction of the French windows, legging it across the formerly immaculate raked gravel of Richard Mallory's roof garden before scrambling through Her Ladyship's now less than pristine hedge.

She didn't stop until she was safely inside, with her own French windows shut firmly against the outside world.

Only then did she lean back against them and let out a huge groan.

Rich Mallory straightened under the shower, letting the hot water ease the knots in his shoulders, the ache from the back of his neck. These all-night sessions took it out of him. They were a young man's game.

Then he grinned.

Okay, he was well past the downhill marker of thirty, but he could still teach the whizkids who worked for him a thing or two, even if he did need a massage to straighten out the kinks next morning.

Maybe he should have lived up—or was that down?—to his reputation and taken up the offer in Ginny Lautour's disturbing eyes. They were curiously at odds with her clothes, her mousy, not quite blonde hair caught back in a kid's scrunchy adorned with a velvet duck-billed platypus; he knew it was a duck-billed platypus because he'd been handbagged by his five-year-old niece into buying her one just like it.

But there was nothing childlike about her eyes. A curious mixture of grey and green and slightly slanted beneath finely marked brows, they were intense, witch's eyes...

His grin faded as he shook his head, flipped the jet to cold and stood beneath it while he counted slowly to twenty. Only then did he reach for his robe, towelling his hair as he padded back to his bedroom, trailing wet footprints across the pale carpet.

Orange juice. Coffee. Eggs. In that order. He'd been wise to pass on the side order of sex. Not that he hadn't been tempted. Beneath the shapeless clothes, Ginny Lautour's body had hinted at the kind of curves that invited a man's hand to linger. And her eyes had invited a lot more than that. But he wasn't ready to be bewitched just yet.

He'd beaten off several attempts to break through his security cordon, steal the latest software his company had developed which was now going through the rigorous testing phase. He'd hoped that they, whoever they were, had given up. Apparently not.

But he was smiling again as he picked up a phone, hitting the fast dial to his Chief Software Engineer as he headed downstairs in the direction of the kitchen. Despite the fact that she had been lying through her pretty teeth—not even the most athletic hamster could have got into that drawer—he'd enjoyed watching Ginny getting into deeper and deeper water as she had tried to extricate herself from an impossible situation.

For a girl in the industrial espionage business she had a quite remarkable propensity to blush. It gave her a look of total innocence that was so completely at odds with the hot look in her eyes that a man might just be fooled into believing it.

Maybe he'd be a little less relaxed about it if there'd been anything of any value in his apartment for her to steal. As it was, he was rather looking forward to her next move.

'Marcus.' He jerked his mind back to more immediate concerns as his call was picked up. 'I've finally cracked the problem we've been having.'

Then, as the spiral turned inward so that he was facing into the vast expanse of his living room, he saw the open bottle of champagne standing on the sofa table and belatedly remembered the luscious redhead he'd taken to the retirement party he'd thrown for one of his senior staff.

'I'll be with you in half an hour to bring the team up to speed,' he said, not waiting for an answer before he disconnected.

Well, that explained the earring. It was Lilianne's. She must have taken him at his word when he had told her that he'd just be five minutes, invited her to make herself comfortable.

How long had she lain in his bed, waiting for him to join her? How long before she'd stormed out in a huff? Even he could see that it would have to be a huff. At the very least.

Long enough to write him a note and tie it to the neck of the champagne bottle with one of her stockings, anyway. Presumably to emphasize what he'd missed.

He sighed. She'd been playing kiss-chase with him for weeks and he'd be lying if he denied that he'd enjoyed the game. Hard to get was so rare these days. He wasn't fooled, of course. He understood the game too well for that. She believed the longer she held out, the greater would be her victory.

Not that he was objecting.

He'd been looking forward to the promised pay off. Which would have been last night if he hadn't suddenly caught a glimpse of the answer to a problem that had been giving his entire development team a headache for the last couple of weeks. He checked his wristwatch. The best part of ten hours ago.

He tugged at the stocking, caught a hint of the musky scent she'd been wearing. He really needed to concentrate on one thing at a time, he decided, as the napkin fell into the melted ice.

Work—nine-till-five. Personal life—

Forget it. Work was his life.

He shrugged, picked up the napkin. Her note was short and to the point.

LOSER.

Succinct. To the point. No wasted words. He admired brevity in a woman.

However, there was still the earring found by his uninvited caller. An earring not meant to be found by a casual glance. It suggested that she'd given herself a chance to call him—after sufficient time had elapsed for him to understand that she was seriously annoyed—and offer him the opportunity to tease her into forgiving him. Resume the chase.

And he grinned.

Then, as the scent of coffee brewing reached him, his eyes narrowed. It seemed as if Ginny Lautour hadn't been in as much of a hurry as she'd made out...

He left the note where it was and, tossing the stocking over the arm of the sofa, headed for the kitchen.

'So, you decided to stay for breakfast after all—'

He came to an abrupt halt as he realised it was his cleaner—rather than his interesting new neighbour—who was making coffee. It left him with oddly mixed feelings.

Relief that she hadn't, after all, taken up his casual invitation to stick around, taking advantage of an unexpected opportunity to get close to him. That she hadn't been that obvious.

Disappointment...for much the same reason.

Not that he doubted she'd be back. Like the earring, Hector gave her all the excuse she needed to drop by any time she felt like it. Which was fine. He didn't believe for one minute that she was a criminal mastermind. He simply wanted to know who was pulling her strings.

'Good morning, Mr Mallory. I've made fresh coffee. Would you like me to cook breakfast for you?'

'No. Thank you, Mrs Figgis.' He'd lost his appetite. 'I'll have something at the office.' Then, 'You'll keep a look-out for Miss Lautour's hamster?'

'Of course. I'm sorry she disturbed you,' she said. 'If I'd realised you were home...'

'Late night. No problem.'

Far from it. If he'd left for the office at the usual time, or even taken this Friday off as he had originally planned and driven off into deepest Gloucestershire, Ginny Lautour could have searched his flat from top to bottom at her leisure and he doubted it would have crossed his cleaner's mind to even mention it.

The hamster, he realised, was a clever excuse. It was possible he'd underestimated the girl. No, that wasn't right, either. She might blush like a girl, but she had the eyes, the body of a woman…

'She's staying in the McBrides' apartment this summer?' he asked. It wouldn't hurt to double check.

'That's right. Keeping an eye on the place. She's a very quiet young lady,' she said. 'For a student.'

Maybe. Being quiet didn't preclude dishonesty. The prize of newly developed Mallory software was enough to tempt the most innocent of souls. Or maybe she was doing it for some man.

She might blush like a nineteenth-century village maiden, but those eyes didn't belong to a nice quiet girl.

'She's a student?'

'According to Lady McBride's daily.'

'And she's living there on her own?'

'Yes. She wants some peace and quiet to work, apparently.'

'I see. Well, let me know if you find the creature.'

'Yes, Mr Mallory.'

He poured himself coffee, calling his secretary as he retreated to his bedroom.

'Wendy,' he said, as she picked up the phone. 'I need you to organise some flowers.'

'For the lovely Lilianne?' she asked, hopefully.

'No.' She'd forfeited the flowers and the apology when she'd indulged herself with that cryptic note.

For that he'd make her sweat a bit before he called her again.

'What happened?' Wendy demanded, interrupting his train of thought.

'What? Oh, nothing happened.'

'Nothing? You left the party with the most beautiful woman in the room in one hand and a bottle of champagne in the other. What went wrong?'

'Not a thing. I just had an idea, that's all. I didn't think it would take more than five minutes to check it out—'

'And before you noticed, it was morning. You are the absolute limit, Richard.'

'I'm a total loss as a human being,' he agreed. 'But my computer loves me.'

'A computer won't keep you warm in your old age.'

'No, but it'll pay the electricity company to do the job.'

'You'll end up a lonely old bachelor,' she warned.

'Read the gossip columns, Wendy,' he said, rapidly growing bored with this conversation. 'There are no lonely old millionaires. Bachelor or otherwise.' Then, 'The flowers are for my sister. It's her wedding anniversary.'

'I've already ordered some.'

'Have you? When?'

'The moment the invitation arrived. I offered to have a little bet with the girls in the office on the likelihood of you wriggling out of a long weekend of come-and-join-us marital bliss. Your sister, bless her, isn't subtle. She wants you married and producing cousins for her own offspring while there's a chance they'll be in the same generation. But they all know you too well. I had no takers. Not even the new girl in the software lab.'

She was kidding. She had to be kidding…

'Save the smug gloating for the ladies room, Wendy, and sort out a working lunch for the research and development team in the boardroom for one o'clock. I'll be there in thirty minutes—'

'I really think you should send Lilianne flowers too,' she said, not in the least bothered by his Chairman of the Board act. 'At the very least.'

Wendy had been with him since he'd started the company and had seen him through the bad times as well as the good. She thought it gave her the right to treat him like a rather bossy nanny. Occasionally, he allowed her to get away with it. But not today.

'I really don't have the time for this—'

'Is the situation salvageable, do you think? What kind of statement do you want to make?'

Who did he think he was kidding? She always got away with it.

'No statement of any kind.' But, since he recognised a brick wall when he saw one, and he'd meant it when he had said he hadn't got time for petty details, he went on, 'Okay, I'll concede on the flowers.' And honesty compelled him to admit that Lilianne had had a point. She did deserve an apology. 'But they are not to be red roses. Not roses of any hue.'

'Terribly vulgar, red roses,' she agreed. 'And, besides, you're right. It would be unkind to raise any serious expectations in the lady's breast. She is, after all, just another passing fancy.'

'And what the devil is that supposed to mean?'

'Only that she's out of the same mould as every girl you've ever dated. Only the names—and hair colour—change.' About to protest, he realised it would be quicker to just let her get on with it. 'But you're like all men; you see the pretty wrapping and you're hooked. Temporarily. Of course, the clever women realise very quickly that they're always going to be playing second fiddle to your computer and throw you back—'

Okay, that was it. 'Is this conversation going somewhere?'

She sighed. 'Obviously not. Leave it with me. I'll sort out something that will put her in a forgiving mood. Anything else?'

'No. Yes. Have you ever kept a hamster?'

'A hamster is not a substitute for a proper relationship,' she replied sternly. 'But I suppose it's a marginal improvement on a computer. Why?'

'I'm informed there's one on the loose in my apartment.'

'Then guard your cables. My kids had one and, I promise you, they can chew through anything.'

'Oh, great. Better make that an hour while I make sure that at least my study is a hamster free zone.'

He might not be totally convinced about the hamster, but he wasn't prepared to take any chances.

Miss Iphegenia Lautour might have a ridiculous propensity to blush for a grown woman. He wasn't, however, about to overlook the possibility that she could have let loose a small furry friend in order to provide herself with a legitimate excuse for searching his apartment.

Why pretend when you could do it for real?

An answer immediately offered itself. Why would she complicate things with livestock?

A real hamster would, sooner or later, be found. Maybe too soon. An imaginary one, on the other hand, would provide her with endless opportunities to return.

Just how clever was she? The image might be pure innocence, but the eyes had glowed with something that had warned him not to take any chances.

He'd be well-advised, he decided, not to take anything for granted, but to assume the worst.

Ginny, too agitated to be able to concentrate, didn't make it to the Underground station before she abandoned all thoughts of work. Instead, she bought a sandwich and a carton of coffee and retired to a small park where she tossed crumbs to the sparrows, putting off the evil moment when she'd have to call Sophie and let her know that she'd failed.

But eventually she ran out of sandwiches and time.

She dug out her cellphone, keyed in the number. Her call was answered with an alacrity that suggested Sophie had been sitting with the phone in her hand.

'What happened?' she demanded without preamble.

There was no soft answer. 'I'm sorry, Sophie, but his desk was locked. I tried to find a key but when I went upstairs…' She hesitated. Did she want to entertain Sophie with her encounter with Richard Mallory? Definitely not. 'I was interrupted.'

'Interrupted? Who by?' she demanded.

'It's fine, Sophie. No problem.'

'Oh.' For a moment Ginny had the feeling that she was disappointed. 'Well, that's good, isn't it? You can have another try tomorrow.'

No! 'Look, why don't you just own up? Surely Richard Mallory will understand? You can't be the first person ever to delete a file.'

'You don't understand! I should have backed it up! I should have made copies! I should—'

'Sophie! Pull yourself together!' Heavens, she'd never been in this kind of state about a job before. She must be really desperate to keep it. 'It has to be in the system somewhere. Can't you flutter your eyelashes at one of those clever young men who work for him?'

'No! This is a serious job and I want to keep it. I can't admit to messing up. Besides, it's not that easy. Go poking around in the memory of the mainframe and alarms get triggered off. The man is paranoid about security.'

'Well, thank you for telling me that,' Ginny said drily.

'What? Oh...' Then she laughed. 'Oh, I see what you mean. You're safe enough in his apartment. He wouldn't expect anyone to break in there, would he? And it's not as if it's his precious secret development stuff you're after.'

'But would he believe that?'

'He's never going to know. I've told you, it's his

sister's wedding anniversary and he's playing happy families in Gloucestershire.'

Maybe that's where he should have been, but he'd clearly been distracted by a pair of silk clad legs…

'Listen to me, Ginny. It is absolutely vital that you get that disk. I have to prove to my father that I can keep a job.'

'Why?'

There was a pause, then a sigh, then Sophie said, 'He's had enough of subsidising me, that's why.'

Something she'd never have to worry about, Ginny thought. But what she'd never had, she'd never miss. 'Hasn't he threatened to cut you off without so much as a brass farthing at least half a dozen times since you left home? You know he doesn't mean it.'

'He does *this* time and it's all my sister's fault,' Sophie added.

'What's Kate done to deserve the blame?'

'She got married. To a wealthy barrister. A man who will, in the fullness of time, inherit a title and a country estate. It's put ideas into Daddy's head. He's compared the cost of a wedding against the cost of supporting me and decided a wedding makes more economic sense in the long term. He's actually got some chinless wonder lined up and panting to take me off his hands.'

'Does he have a title and country estate to look forward to?'

'Does it matter if he hasn't got a chin? I have three choices, Ginny. Marry him. Marry someone else. Or support myself.'

'Tough choice,' Ginny said.

But Sophie didn't get sarcasm. 'The worst!' she exclaimed. 'All that's saving me from a fate worse than death is this job...'

'He might not be a chinless wonder, Sophie. He might be, well, jolly nice.'

'Of course he'll be "nice". I don't want "nice", I want...' She stopped abruptly. 'I mean, really, Ginny, would you marry someone your father had picked out for you?' Then, 'Oh, damn! I'm sorry...I didn't mean...'

Oh, rats! Now Sophie felt guilty.

'It's okay,' Ginny said quickly. 'Don't fret.'

Despite the fact that they were total opposites in just about every respect, they'd bonded on their first day at school. It had been Sophie who, as the social queen of the class, had saved her from the fallout of being given the kind of name that no five-year-old should be saddled with.

As the solitary child of a feminist scholar—dismissive of playgroups and nursery schools—Ginny had little experience of mixing with children of her own age. She hadn't realised that her name *was* odd until she ran into the cruel ridicule of the classroom.

Sophie had recognised a born outsider and, for some reason neither of them had ever quite fathomed, had taken her under her wing. Maybe it was the attraction of opposites. She hadn't questioned it at the time, too grateful that since everyone wanted to be part of Sophie's charmed circle the teasing had instantly stopped.

While her odd background, a lack of interest in the latest fashion, boys or parties and an inclination for solitary study had meant that she'd never actually been part of the group, she'd never been an outsider after that, at least not at school.

And once out in the big wide world she'd quickly learned to deal with the rest of the world in her own way.

'Look, don't worry. I'll have another go, okay?'

'Will you? Thank goodness Philly talked her in-laws into letting you "sit" their apartment for the summer. I just wish you could have had my spare room. Only Aunt Cora has saddled me with visitors for the summer.'

'It is her apartment, Sophie.' And, much as she loved Sophie, she was in London to work. She'd get a lot more of that done in the quiet of the McBrides' apartment.

'I suppose. And jolly lucky in the circumstances.'

That, Ginny thought, rather depended upon your point of view.

But it would be okay, she reassured herself. By now Mallory would have left for his delayed weekend in the country. All she had to do was get past Mrs Figgis and her duster. Which actually might not be that difficult…

'Hector,' she said, as she dropped her cellphone into her bag. 'You're back on.'

'Richard?'

Richard Mallory looked up from the pad on which he'd been doodling a hamster. Wearing outsize spectacles. A slightly dishevelled hamster with a twig dangling over one ear and her cheeks aflame…

It suddenly occurred to him that everyone was waiting for him to say something.

He did a fast mental rewind, then, getting to his feet, he said, 'We're pushing a deadline here. I want this done today.'

Wendy, who'd been sitting beside him taking notes, followed him into his office, shutting the door behind her.

'So,' she said, holding up the notepad he'd left on the boardroom table. 'Tell me about the hamster.'

'Mesocricetus Auratus Auratus.' He'd taken the time to look it up. 'The golden hamster is a small nocturnal mammal discovered in the Syrian desert in the early twentieth century. Very popular as a children's pet although, since it's only awake during the hours of darkness, I don't see the attraction—'

'Believe me, if you were the small pet of a curious child you'd choose to be nocturnal.' Then, 'Okay, ten out of ten for doing your homework. Now, tell me about the one with the cute spectacles. Is that a blush?'

He took the pad from her, looked at the drawing for a moment, his body responding uncomfortably to the memory of the delicate pink flush that had heated Ginny Lautour's cheeks, the silky touch of her hair as he'd untangled a piece of shrubbery. A pair of grey-green eyes that had lit up from inside, overriding the 'ignore me' effect of unflattering clothes.

'She's apartment-sitting for my next-door neighbour,' he said, tossing it on his desk behind him. Where he couldn't see it.

'Excuse me? Are you telling me that she's a real, old-fashioned, honest to goodness girl next door?'

'She's real enough. And she lives next door.'

Further than that, he was not prepared to commit himself.

Wendy retrieved the notepad and took another look. 'I want to know everything. What's her name?'

He didn't immediately answer. His mind was too busy struggling with the image of her lower lip, full and luscious. The tip of her tongue cooling it…

Had it been an unconscious response to something that had crackled in the air between them? Or deliberate? A practised attempt to entice…

'Trouble,' he said abruptly.

Just how much trouble he'd know once he'd got the results of the security checks he was running on her.

CHAPTER THREE

Ginny rang Richard Mallory's doorbell.

She'd checked the basement car park—something that she'd have been well advised to do before she'd blundered in earlier—and his parking space was now empty. He'd finally left for his weekend in the country and the coast was clear.

Nevertheless, she'd be kidding herself if she pretended that her heart was beating at anything like a normal tempo. That her hands weren't horribly clammy. That she was feeling anything like as cool as she hoped she looked...

'Oh, Miss Lautour.' In an effort to impress Mrs Figgis, Ginny had changed from her boots, jeans and her purple shirt and was now wearing the kind of shoes that wouldn't harm the blond flooring, a long feminine skirt with a tank top and an expensive white linen shirt that hung to her thighs. The woman still didn't look particularly pleased to see her. 'Have you found your...pet?'

Her expression suggested that she did not have a very high opinion of young women who kept small furry creatures as pets. Worse. Allowed them to escape into other people's apartments.

'I'm afraid not. Which is why, since I realise how much extra work he's going to cause you until he's found, I hope you'll accept this.'

She offered the woman an apologetic smile—it wasn't difficult, she was very sorry she was doing this. Deeply sorry. But she couldn't abandon Sophie in her hour of need. Besides, she would gain a great deal of satisfaction from outwitting Richard Mallory. Once it was over and done with and she could enjoy her triumph in the quiet of her own living room.

'A small apology in advance.'

And she handed over the carrier she was holding.

'Work?' Mrs Figgis was distracted by the exotically flowering pot plant trailing out of the bag.

'Cleaning up after him. He'll tear up paper—' she gave a little shrug '—well, anything really to make a nest. And he'll leave, well, mess. Especially since he'll be frightened. I feel really bad about that and I just wanted to say that you must call me to deal with it.'

'Mess?' Mrs Figgis looked up, finally catching on to what Ginny was saying. 'You mean he'll leave droppings everywhere? Like a mouse?' Her face was a picture of outrage at the very idea.

'Pretty much,' she said. She'd never been allowed to keep any kind of pet, but one small rodent's droppings would be much like another, surely? And then, crossing her fingers behind her back, 'I just hope he doesn't chew through Mr Mallory's beautiful carpets.'

That did it. Mrs Figgis opened the door wide to admit her. 'Why don't you come in and have a thorough look round? Now. Before he can do any damage.'

Yes!

'Won't it hold you up? You must be leaving soon.

I can always come back later,' she offered. 'When Mr
Mallory's at home.'

'He's a busy man. I don't think we need to bother
him with this again.' Two women but with a single
thought... 'I've got some ironing I can be getting on
with.'

'If you're sure?' It really had been too much to hope
that Mallory's 'daily' would leave her to get on with
her search unsupervised, with nothing more than a reminder to set the alarm before she left. She stepped
inside. 'This is really kind of you. I'll be as quick as
I can.'

'Take your time, Miss Lautour. I'll go home a lot
happier if I know there's nothing running around in
here leaving messes.' And she shuddered.

Now Ginny felt *really* guilty. She'd think of some
way to make it up to the woman. Get her tickets for
some West End show, perhaps? Maybe she could take
the porter...

Her conscience partially salved by this opportunity
to encourage the course of true love, she followed Mrs
Figgis into the huge double storey living room where
all trace of Rich Mallory's dalliance with the wearer
of black silk stockings had been cleaned and polished
away.

'Why don't you start upstairs, Miss Lautour? Work
your way down.'

'What? Oh, right.' She looked at the spiral staircase.
Going back up there was the last thing in the world
she wanted to do, she discovered. But there was no
putting it off. Keys to find. Sophie's hide to save.
'Good idea,' she said, putting on a bright smile.

Actually, she thought it was probably the worst idea she'd ever heard.

He's not there, she reminded herself. He wasn't zonked out under the bedclothes after a night of passion. He was on his way to Gloucestershire. Presumably to try out the passion in a different bed.

Forget him!

She opened the door to his bedroom. It was now flooded with sunlight and the covers lay smooth on the vast bed with not so much as a speck of dust to disturb the lacquered finish of his bedside tables. Yet his presence was as strong as if he was in the room with her.

As if he was pinning her back against the door, the exciting scent of his skin doing unimaginable things to her inside.

She took a deep breath.

Nonsense.

Her nerves were on edge, that was all. They had every right to be on edge; she was putting them through the kind of experience that nerves could well do without.

And the sooner she got on with this, the sooner they would be able to relax. She quickly dealt with the drawer she'd missed earlier. An old wallet. Photographs of his family… What looked like recent holiday pictures of a young woman, enough like him to be his sister, with two young children. There was just one old picture. It was of Mallory himself at that gangling adolescent stage when hands and feet didn't fit the rest of him; he had an arm thrown about the neck of an equally uncoordinated mongrel pup.

She found herself battling with a lump in her throat. A man who kept a picture of his dog couldn't be a total monster, could he?

She swallowed hard. It didn't matter what he was, she told herself as she replaced the pictures and moved on to the bathroom. It had nothing to do with her. All she wanted was that disk.

As if anyone in their right mind would keep a spare key in the bathroom, she told herself as she went through the cupboards. It did give her the opportunity to check out his aftershave, though. She approved...

What was she doing? Lingering over nonsense when she should be in his dressing room. If there was a key, that was where it would be.

The cufflink drawers contained nothing but cufflinks. Dozens of pairs of cufflinks. Birthday...Christmas presents. Well, what else did a girl—girls—give a man who had everything?

She opened another drawer and had her answer. Ties. Pure silk, designer label ties. Every one of them with a touch of the same perfect blue as his eyes...

The remaining drawers contained nothing more exciting than neatly folded socks, beautifully ironed shirts, underwear. Her fingers lingered over a pair of soft grey shorts and she found her mind drifting back to the sight of him that morning. Exciting enough...

She snatched back her hand, slammed the drawer shut and, turning to the wardrobes that lined the opposite wall, began to work her way swiftly through the pockets of his clothes. But in her heart of hearts she knew it was pointless. Mrs Figgis was not a woman to hang up a jacket without first emptying the pockets.

She heard the bedroom door open behind her as Mrs Figgis came to hurry her along and she dived into the bottom of the wardrobe.

'Hector,' she cooed, picking up a hard worn walking boot and sticking her hand inside. 'Where are you, sweetheart...?' As her fingers encountered something soft and hairy she dropped it with a nervous shriek, backing swiftly out of the wardrobe. She'd thought her heart was beating fast... *Now* it was beating fast...

She swallowed, pulled herself together and picked up the boot to get a better look.

'It's a sock,' she said, and laughed with relief. 'Just an old woollen sock.' Not even Mrs Figgis was one hundred per cent perfect. She looked up, expecting to see her standing in the doorway with that disapproving look curling her upper lip.

'Drat' did not seem nearly strong enough to express her feelings as she discovered that it wasn't the housekeeper but Rich Mallory watching her with an expression that she couldn't begin to fathom. But he wasn't smiling.

'This is the second time I've found you in my bedroom. Are you trying to tell me something?' He spoke with the cool assurance of a man who'd been fending off eager women since puberty. Clearly convinced that this was simply another case of a pathetic woman flinging herself at him.

She *knew* he'd never believed in Hector...

Ginny, inwardly seething at being forced into such a position, swallowed her pride, dredged up a smile from the very depths of her soul and said, 'It looks bad, doesn't it?'

'The gossip columnists would have a field day,' he agreed. 'But if you don't tell them, I won't.'

He reached out a hand to help her to her feet.

Since her legs seemed incapable of managing this simple act for themselves, she took it. His fingers wrapped about her hand and for a moment neither of them moved. For a moment everything was so still that it felt as if time itself had stopped.

Then he pulled her up and, since he didn't step back, her nose finished up uncomfortably close to his shirt front. The scent of soft linen overlaying warm skin.

Not for the first time, she wished she was taller. Except then it would have been his throat, or his chin, or his mouth that she would have been no more than a breath away from.

She made a determined effort to look up. Say something intelligent…

'At least you're dressed this time.'

And looking totally fantastic in a cream linen suit and a band collar dark blue shirt.

'Stick around,' he offered.

'No need.' He was still clasping her hand, holding it against his chest so that she could feel the slow, steady thud of his heartbeat. 'I already know your taste in underwear.'

Oh, brilliant, Ginny! Why don't you just say what you're thinking…?

She cleared her throat. 'Actually, I'm here because Mrs Figgis wanted me to—'

'I know. She explained. You've had no luck yet?'

And once again Ginny had the disconcerting feeling that he wasn't talking about Hector.

'Um…'

His detached expression finally softened, the tiniest contraction of the lines fanning out from his eyes, his mouth widening into a slow, wide, oddly provoking smile that for a moment held her his captive. Then she snatched her hand away, as if by breaking the connection she could somehow get her brain back in gear.

She used it to push her spectacles up her nose.

Rich forgot all about the fact that Ginny Lautour was ransacking his wardrobe looking for a spare key to his desk and instead found himself wondering what she'd do with her hands if she didn't have her spectacles as a prop. If she didn't have them to hide behind. And what were they hiding?

There was only one way to find out.

He removed them—ignoring her gasp of outrage—and held them up out of her reach, checking them against the light, reassuring himself that they weren't just that—a prop, a disguise.

They were real enough, he discovered. The lady was, apparently, a touch short-sighted. But he wasn't surrendering them too soon. Instead, he opened a drawer, took out a clean handkerchief and began to polish them.

Her fingers twitched as if it was all she could do to stop herself from grabbing them back. He finished one lens, moved on to the next, taking his time about it so that he could get a good look at her eyes.

He hadn't been mistaken about them. Grey and green intermingled in a bewitching combination beneath a curtain of dark lashes that were all hers. No magic mascara to lengthen or curl them, they'd be soft to the touch, silk to his lips, he thought. And he wanted to touch.

Like Ginny, he restrained himself. For the moment. He continued to polish the lens. Here, in the artificial light of his dressing room, the silver-grey was dominant. But beneath the silver the green was shimmering dangerously.

He'd caught a glimpse of it that morning—a flash of recklessness, heat quickly damped down. Like the glimpse of curves offered by the clinging top she was wearing beneath the loose enfolding shirt, it had lingered with him, far more enticing than the most revealing gown.

More exciting than the most blatant of invitations, this veiled promise of hidden fire tugged at something deep inside him.

Or was it simply a mask to hide her true purpose? Hidden away beneath clothes chosen to conceal, behind the large spectacles, who was the real Ginny Lautour?

The name was uncommon. And yet familiar.

He would find out.

He took one final look at the spectacles. 'They were dusty,' he said, sliding them back into place. But as his thumbs brushed against the hot flush of her cheek, his fingers tangled with the silky hair that trailed over her ears, he'd have been hard pressed to say which of them was trembling. And with her face turned up her lips seemed to offer him the kind of temptation only a saint could be expected to refuse.

Well, he might not be quite such a sinner as his reputation implied, but any woman who strayed into his bedroom—twice—could hardly expect to escape without paying a penalty. And he lowered his lips to hers.

Soft, sweet, warm.

The heat was building fast and for a moment his palms cupped her cheeks, his fingers sliding through her hair and holding her his captive.

Not that she was offering any kind of resistance. No shocked outrage, the slap he almost certainly deserved. On the contrary, her mouth was clinging to his, her whole body softening against him in a seductive ambush that whispered enchantment in his ear. Stirring not just his body but his soul.

He lifted his head, easing back mere inches so that he could look at her, read her eyes. For a moment she did not move, but remained perfectly still as if moving would break some spell. Then she gave a little sigh and opened her eyes.

They were a clear, translucent green.

Yes! He knew it! He'd sensed the ambiguities in this woman's character, a secret core that she allowed no one to see. And he'd tapped right into it.

For a moment he felt exultant. As if he'd found the gold at the end of a rainbow. Captured the essence of this woman with a single kiss.

Then reality rushed back.

Could it be that he was the one who'd just been captured?

That her imperfect disguise had been deliberate. That he'd been meant to see through it.

Or was he, perhaps, losing his mind?

'It's not true, you know,' he said.

Her mouth moved as she tried to say something but no sound emerged. She cleared her throat and tried again. 'What?'

'They're no protection. Men do make passes at girls who wear glasses. Think about that next time you're tempted to spend any time in my bedroom.' Then, because it occurred to him that might be construed as an invitation, he let go of her, took a step back, putting clear air between them.

Ginny was floundering.

She should not have come back. The warning had been there when he'd touched her cheek before, in the unexpected yearning for him to touch her again, more intimately. In the way her body had delayed her even when her brain was telling her to get out of there while the going was good.

Now Richard Mallory had kissed her and it was as if her entire history was wiped clean. She had completely forgotten her determination to stay clear of involvement at all costs, knowing that her name brought with it baggage that she could never live down.

All it had taken was one little kiss to trigger off an emotional chain reaction that had her heading towards meltdown.

Well, *hello*, fool!

The urgent heat of desire was followed by an even swifter anger. She wanted to tell him exactly what she thought of him, that he should keep his hands to himself. Her brain warned her to keep quiet. That it was

always better to keep quiet. It was a near run thing but
the brain won.

That had never let her down.

But how had he known? About the glasses?

'Have you finished in here?' he asked abruptly.
'Checked all my shoes? Been through all the drawers?'

'Yes,' she said quickly, taking a step back herself,
putting herself out of his reach in case he could read
her mind. She really hoped he couldn't read her
mind… 'No!'

'Well, that was decisive.' It came out more harshly
than Rich had intended. He didn't want to scare her
away. He still needed to know all her secrets. He just
wasn't prepared to share his.

'You startled me. I didn't expect… Mrs Figgis said
you were going away. This morning…'

So that was why she was back. She'd thought he'd
gone. But what on earth did she expect to find in his
shoes? He doubted that she was looking for his old
socks.

'There was a change of plan. Maybe tomorrow,' he
said, cruelly holding out hope that she might yet find
herself with time and opportunity to search his apartment. Then, 'I do hope you went through everything.'
It wasn't as if there was anything for her to find. He'd
cleared out anything in the least bit useful to a com-
petitor. Left only a baited hook. With an invisible line
attached. 'I'd really hate to come back and discover
that Hector had taken up residence—' he glanced
pointedly at the sock she was still holding on to as if
her very life depended upon it '—in my sock drawer.'

'He's not in here,' she said, dropping it on the dressing table as if scalded. 'I'd better go—'

'No.' He reached out and caught her wrist as she made a move to pass him. 'Please carry on with what you're doing,' he demanded. 'Ignore me. Forget I'm here.'

'Easier said than done,' she declared, her chest rising and falling rapidly beneath the clinging top she was wearing under a long unbuttoned shirt. He made a determined effort to ignore it. 'You have a way of making your presence felt.'

'It's my apartment. And you invited yourself in.'

'Mrs Figgis invited me in,' she declared roundly.

'Did she have any choice?' No answer. 'If you want to look around, I suggest you get on with it. But, if you've finished in here, I'd like to change.'

He released her wrist, peeled off his jacket, tossed it aside. Carefully emptied his trouser pockets, tossing his wallet and keys on to the dressing table. Then began on the buttons of his shirt. He was tugging it out of his trousers when he realised that they were still standing eyeball to eyeball. That she hadn't moved a muscle.

'You're welcome to stay and watch,' he offered. 'But, as you've already reminded me, you won't be seeing anything new.'

Sophie was right, Ginny decided. The man was a bastard. She had started to check the lower levels of the bookshelves—just for show—while she tried to work out how she was going to use this unexpected turn of events to her advantage.

Rich Mallory turning up might have been her worst nightmare… But, despite the fact that he'd kissed her witless, it was not a total disaster. The taste of his mouth might be clinging to her lips, the flash of heat still burning in her veins, but just yards away from her his keys were lying on his dressing table.

All she had to do was get back into there and, well, if Bob wasn't exactly going to be her uncle, he was certainly going to be a second cousin.

Right at that moment she didn't know how she was going to manage it, but she did know that she wasn't giving up, because this was no longer just about saving Sophie's job.

It was personal.

It took a special kind of arrogance to assume that a woman only had to look at him for her to immediately want to fall into bed with him.

Even if it was probably true. She certainly hadn't done anything to disabuse him.

She stopped her angry poking at the bookshelves, lowered her head and banged it against the shelves.

He wasn't the only one who'd behaved badly. She hadn't exactly turned on the outrage, had she? Hadn't demanded to know what the devil he thought he was doing. Slapped his face.

She hadn't even stepped back, made it clear that she wasn't interested. He was the one who'd cut the connection.

She'd just let him kiss her. More than let him. She'd co-operated. Enthusiastically. It wasn't just Richard Mallory she was angry with. She was equally at fault.

After all, he was just living down to his reputation and she should have expected nothing better from him.

Well, maybe she was a bit surprised that he'd bother to flirt with someone like her. It wasn't as if she dressed provocatively or did anything to encourage flirtation. Quite the opposite.

And she didn't even own a pair of black silk stockings.

She got to her feet. Maybe it was the novelty of kissing someone who wasn't wearing lipstick that had tempted him. That had to be a whole new sensory experience for him.

She touched her upper lip with the tip of her tongue, tasting him. It had certainly been a new experience for her…

She snapped back to reality. Who was she kidding? She knew exactly what it was.

Poor girl, she looks like hell, probably hasn't had a pass made in her direction for so long she must be panting for it. He thought he was doing her a favour. Saw it as charity work.

Well, too bad. He was not as original as he thought.

Not that she cared one jot what he thought of her.

All she cared about was finding that disk and saving Sophie's job. And she was going to look him in the face and smile while she did it, no matter how hard that would be.

The fact that he would never know what she'd done, would always think of her as a slightly batty creature with a juvenile taste in pets, would make her victory all the sweeter.

She tried on the smile, just to practice, and she was

still wearing it when Mallory appeared in the doorway. He'd changed into a pair of jeans and a t-shirt and it didn't take an airport X-ray machine for her to see that he wasn't carrying anything in his pockets. And her smile became the real article.

If he was surprised to find her grinning like an idiot he made no comment.

'Any luck?' he asked, as if he'd been hoping she'd have made herself scarce.

Tough. He'd scared her off once, but no one had ever accused her of not learning from her mistakes.

'Not yet, but then you never actually believed he could manage your spiral staircase, did you?'

'You're the expert,' he said, heading straight for it. 'I'm making coffee. Would you like a cup?'

'Thank you. Coffee would be very welcome.'

'Come on down, then.' He glanced back at her, paused. 'That's if you've finished up here? Or could you do with some help to look on the higher shelves?'

No! 'No, thanks.' She mentally urged him down the stairs. He didn't move. 'I've just about run out of places to look, to be honest.' Then she glanced around.

'Lost something?'

She nudged her bag behind the nearest chair with her foot. 'My bag. I must have left it in your, um…'

'Bedroom?'

'Mmm.'

There was a long pause. Then, a touch irritably he said, 'Well, what are you waiting for? Go and get it. I'll wait for you.'

She didn't want to appear too eager. 'I wouldn't want there to be any misunderstandings.'

'Do you want me to get it for you?'

'No, I'll fetch it. Just—stay here. Okay?'

He shrugged and she made herself take her time, a prickle at her neck warning her that he was watching her. Wanting to turn around and check, but that would have looked so guilty. Or worse. A come-on…

Once out of sight, however, she dashed into his dressing room, snatched up his keys. He wasn't watching her, of course. He couldn't see her from where he'd been standing. He'd probably gone straight down to the kitchen. Please…

When she emerged—still minus her bag—she discovered that he hadn't gone anywhere. He hadn't moved from the top of the stairs. He'd actually meant it when he'd said he'd wait.

Wretch.

'Oh, there it is!' she exclaimed like an idiot, picking it up from behind the chair. 'I'll lose my head one of these days…' Well, he already thought she was stupid. He could be right…

'All you appear to be missing now is one small rodent,' he said, his face expressionless. 'Why don't you take a look around the kitchen while I get the coffee.'

'You really think he'd have survived a whole day in the kitchen with Mrs Figgis?'

Where was Mrs Figgis, anyway?

'She's gone now. He's quite safe.'

'Oh.' Then, because that sounded as if being alone with him bothered her, 'I was admiring it earlier. Your kitchen.' She made a vague gesture that suggested the brushed steel rack above the central island. 'The, um, utensils.'

'Well, that's what they're for. Show. The finest, um, utensils an interior designer could find.'

She ignored this attempt at teasing her. She knew where that led. 'You don't cook?' she asked.

'Not unless I absolutely have to.'

'Pathetic.'

'Women are such critics. You're a gourmet cook, I suppose.' He stood back so that she could precede him into the kitchen. 'A domestic goddess.'

'Perish the thought. Life's too short for stuffing mushrooms—'

'Is it? I'm of the view that one should do most things once. I've been saving that one up for a rainy day.'

'But unlike men—' she pressed on, refusing to play '—most men, anyway, women do have to make the effort if they want to eat. Let's face it, no man is going to do it for them.'

'That, if I may say so, is a highly sexist remark. Any time you want a fried egg sandwich, just say the word.'

'And which word would that be?'

'You get three guesses.'

'And if I don't guess right?'

'You have to cook one for me.'

It wasn't fair—he shouldn't be able to make her laugh. Fortunately, he turned abruptly to the sink and filled the kettle.

'Don't mind me,' he said. 'Help yourself.'

While she toured the kitchen he took coffee beans

from the state-of-the-art stainless steel American fridge.

She opened doors, making a pretence of looking for Hector, enjoying the chance to nose through his immaculate range of cookware, china, every kind of labour-saving electrical gadget a busy cook might dream of.

The only sound was of beans grinding.

She carried on looking. He had a food mixer that made her drool with envy. Maybe he'd let her borrow it. Just to test whether it actually worked.

No. Get the disk. Get out of there. Never return.

The silence lengthened. She knew he was watching her as he waited for the kettle. She moved a couple of boxes, thinking hard.

Now she had his keys, how on earth was she going to distract him long enough to get into his study? Go through his desk?

Opening the door to the cupboard beneath the sink, she was confronted with the answer to her prayers.

'Oh, good grief,' she said. She hadn't had to work on sounding surprised. How often did you get that kind of divine intervention?

CHAPTER FOUR

'PROBLEM?' Mallory asked.

Ginny knelt down, poking her head right inside the cupboard to get a better look and taking her time about replying.

'Maybe.' His silence assured her that she had his full attention. Only then did she back out, look up and say, 'You don't suppose he could have squeezed down through there, do you?'

Rich paused. Having watched her performance as she toured the kitchen, he'd awaited her next move with interest. He'd say one thing for Ginny Lautour, she never disappointed.

'Where?' he asked.

'There's this hole…'

'Hole?' Suddenly she had his full attention.

'Well, not so much a hole as a gap…'

He took a deep breath, carefully finished spooning the coffee into the cafetière, poured on hot water and covered it before he folded himself up beside Ginny. Her shoulder nudged distractingly against his as she turned.

'Show me,' he said.

She pointed wordlessly to where the pipe from the sink to the waste outlet disappeared through the floor of the cupboard and he leaned closer to get a better look, doing his best to ignore her hair brushing against his face.

Between the pipe and the wall was a space big enough for the tubbiest of rodents to have squeezed down.

It was what rodents did, after all. They lived down holes.

What he couldn't see was what she hoped to gain by having him rip his kitchen apart looking for this imaginary friend. Unless, of course, she'd been telling the truth all along and he was just a sad cynic who always assumed an ulterior motive.

Glancing sideways at Ginny, at the soft curve of her lips that had quickened so enticingly beneath his, he discovered that he wanted, more than anything, to believe her.

Even when he knew she was deceiving him, when he tried to keep a distance between them, he still found himself responding to her. Grinning like some big kid who had just discovered that girls are not just a pain in the butt.

Suckered by a single innocent kiss.

Innocent? Who was he trying to kid? His thoughts had been a long way from innocent. As for hers...

He turned back to the cupboard and reality. 'Please tell me,' he said, 'that you're winding me up. That you don't seriously believe Hector might be down there?'

Ginny knew that she shouldn't do this. Her conscience was waving red flags, warning her that this was a seriously bad thing to do. As if she didn't know that already.

But what about him? He'd kissed her. Not because she was some willowy beauty that he was seriously lusting after, had wooed with dinner in some expensive restaurant, plied with champagne. Two equals playing the same game. No. He'd done it because he thought he was irresistible. Because it pleased his male ego to prove it.

Bad enough. But then, when she'd responded with more enthusiasm than sense—and surely if a man kissed a girl he hoped for that reaction?—he'd backed off faster than a rabbit confronted by a fox.

Even short, seriously unwillowy girls merited a little more consideration than that. Not a quick step backwards and a don't-call-me-I'll-call-you about turn.

He deserved some pain.

And she needed a distraction. Something that would keep him occupied for long enough for her to save Sophie's bacon and get out of there.

So, although she knew her conscience would give her a hard time later, she crossed her fingers before looking straight into his dangerous blue eyes and before she could lose her nerve she said, 'Hector once got beneath the floorboards.'

'Here?'

'No, no. Not *here*. There are no loose floorboards in the McBrides' apartment.' His eyebrows invited— demanded—that she elaborate. 'It was in college,' she said.

This *had* actually happened, although not to her. Or Hector. Who Did Not Exist, she reminded herself. Her imaginary rodent was beginning to take on the heroic proportions of his namesake. She just hoped that Rich Mallory wouldn't prove to be his—or her—Achilles.

'They're old,' she explained. 'The college buildings. Gaps everywhere. The porters spent all day lifting

them—the floorboards—before he was finally cor-
nered.'

Rich Mallory stared at her for a moment, his expression warring between horror and disbelief.

Then he said one brief word that clearly expressed
everything he was feeling before he swept the contents
of the cupboard to one side to take a closer look.

'Now what?' Ginny asked, as Mallory regarded the
smooth white floor of the cupboard.

'Now I think I need someone who knows what he's
doing.'

For a moment Ginny stared at the back of his head.
Was he serious?

She realised, with something of a shock, that he
probably was. He'd made his first million before he
was dry behind the ears. How likely was it that he'd
ever had to struggle with the eccentricities of the carry
home flat-pack fitted-kitchen?

Okay, so his kitchen hadn't come from the local
DIY store on his roof rack. It had been assembled by
venerable craftsmen at vast expense. But beneath the
slate work surface and the state of the art joinery, the
principle was the same.

Probably.

So, the question was, should she tell him that the
plinth could be removed to get at the space beneath
the cupboard where a runaway hamster might hide?

She didn't think so. At least not yet.

It wouldn't be kind.

While it was perfectly acceptable to suggest a man
was a bit pathetic because he couldn't cook—hell,
most men were proud of the fact—it was quite another
thing to show him up in traditionally masculine skills.

It would be like fixing a car while he was busy calling the nearest garage.

It would make him feel inadequate.

Tempting though that was, she decided it would be wiser to leave it to the porter to tell him the good news.

Trying not to grin too widely, she got to her feet, leaving him to contemplate trouble, found some cups and poured out the coffee he'd made.

'Milk?' she offered.

He shook his head. An unruly cowlick of hair slid across his forehead.

'Sugar?'

The same response. The hair slid a little further and her fingers itched to push it back. She tightened them into a fist, forcing them to behave themselves. What was it about this man that made her want to touch him?

Magnetism.

Like gravity, it was an irresistible force and she shouldn't feel bad about it. He had same effect on all females, judging from the number of lovely women he'd dated.

She just didn't care to be that predictable.

Too late. He'd kissed her and the butterflies had not so much fluttered as stampeded around her stomach, while her knees had buckled pitifully. The only difference between her and all the other women being that she'd hated it.

In theory.

The kissing had been…spectacular.

What she had hated was feeling so vulnerable.

Being out of control in that way. A pawn to his knight…

'Maybe the porter could help,' she said, reminding herself that a clever pawn could win the game and dragging her mind back to the plan. 'Shall I go and ask him to come up?'

She could do with a little breathing space and once two big strong men started on something like this they'd forget all about her. All they'd want from the little woman would be an endless supply of tea or coffee. Which would leave her free to do what she'd come here for. And now she had his keys in her pocket it wouldn't take her any time at all.

A nervous *frisson* whispered through her body. It couldn't possibly be that easy.

'I'll speak to him,' he said, getting to his feet, taking the coffee from her.

Or maybe it could. That's the ticket, she encouraged mentally. This was men's stuff, after all. Off you go—

'In the meantime, maybe we should try to tempt him out with food?'

What?

'What do you think?'

She thought that was the worst idea in the history of the world, but while she was still trying to frame an answer that wouldn't send those expressive eyebrows of his right up to the ceiling, he said, 'Do you want to go and get some?'

Her smug superior mood evaporated as quickly as it had come. Where on earth was the nearest pet shop? And would it still be open…?

Then reality broke through. He wasn't asking her to

pop out to the shops. He was asking her to go next door and get some from her own supply.

Unfortunately, whilst Hector seemed to be achieving almost legendary status in his own right, it hadn't got to the point where she'd started buying jumbo packs of hamster food. Although, if this went on much longer, who could say what she'd do?

'You think something to eat might tempt him out of there?' she asked stupidly. Well, she was stupid. Only the most stupid person in the entire world would be having this conversation. But she needed a moment. She'd thought she had her wits well under control, but while she'd been remembering the way he'd kissed her, how she'd felt, they seemed to have wandered off somewhere and needed to be rounded up quickly.

'Few of us can resist temptation,' he replied.

And he should know, Ginny thought, looking at him as he leaned back against the cupboard, cup in hand, those heavy lids disguising his thoughts.

'What do they eat? Hamsters.'

When she didn't immediately answer he glanced up, regarding her over the rim of his cup.

Damn! She wished he wouldn't look at her like that. As if he knew every single thing inside her head. And then some.

'Anything that comes in a box with "hamster food" on the label,' she offered. It was the best she could do in the time available. 'I have to confess I've never read the list of ingredients.' Which was purely the truth. She'd never read the list of ingredients on any kind of pet food. Unfortunately, she didn't have a box with hamster food on the label. Then, inspired, 'Actually, I think he'd be more likely to respond to a treat.'

'Don't we all. I can't wait to discover what Hector's idea of food heaven might be,' he said. 'Chocolate?'

She pulled a face. That didn't take as much effort as thinking. Impaled on his unwavering blue gaze she was finding it a struggle to breathe, let alone think, remember…

'I've never given him chocolate. It would be terribly bad for him. A grape might do it,' she said, clutching at the straws of memory when the silence had gone on for way too long. Then, when he didn't leap to offer one, 'Or even a raisin.'

'In your own time.'

'I'm sorry?'

'Hamster food, grapes, raisins. I'm prepared to try anything if it means I don't have to start ripping my kitchen apart.'

He'd really do that?

Tempting as the idea was, she couldn't let him do it.

No. *Really.*

'Don't do anything too hasty,' she said.

'Always good advice. Why use a sledgehammer when you can use a nut?'

'A nut would be good,' she agreed. She was positive a hamster would enjoy a nut.

'So now all we have to do is bait the cupboard with something he can't resist and he'll fall right into the palm of your hand.'

He continued to hold her with nothing but the power of his eyes and something about the stillness of the man sent a tiny shiver of apprehension riffling up her spine. It was as if he was saying more, talking about something else.

She needed to move, break eye contact before she broke down and confessed…

'Right.' She turned quickly and stretched up to open one of the high level storage cupboards. There seemed to be a complete lack of the basic essentials. She glanced back at him. 'Where do you keep your dried fruit?'

He regarded her with a somewhat crooked smile. 'I thought we'd already established that I wouldn't know what to do with a raisin, Ginny.'

'What about a grape?' she snapped, losing it just a little as the tension got to her. 'Surely you keep in a plentiful supply of those to feed to visiting god-desses—' along with the champagne '—of the non-domestic variety.'

It was one thing to tell yourself that it would be easy to look this man in the face and tell him lies. It was quite another to do it. She had the feeling that he was toying with her, that she wasn't being nearly as clever as she thought she was. That he knew exactly what she was up to.

Nonsense of course. How could he?

It was just an over-active conscience giving her a hard time.

Well, she knew it would catch up with her sooner or later. She'd just hoped it would be later.

'Find me a goddess—any kind of goddess—and I'll feed her grapes,' he promised. 'Me, I prefer something to sink my teeth into.' He opened the fridge door and then turned to face her, a large red apple in his hand. And she had the strongest feeling that she was the one being tempted. 'How does Hector feel about apple?'

'Loves it!' she said brightly and reached out for it.

With his free hand he caught her wrist, prevented her from taking it. 'I don't want you taking any risks, Ginny.' His voice was soft, but the words sounded more like a warning than any deep concern for her personal safety. 'I don't want you getting hurt.'

'Hurt?'

'The knives are very sharp.' He let her go as suddenly as he'd seized her, turning away to take a knife from the block. With his back to her, she grabbed at her wrist, holding it as if burned. 'Now we wait,' he said as, having put a small piece of apple in the cupboard, he closed the doors.

Ginny realised that she was still rubbing at her wrist as if to remove the imprint of his fingers. Feeling foolish, she dropped it. More than foolish. She was an idiot.

She'd been within minutes of achieving her goal and she'd had the ball snatched out of her hand. Just because she was bothered about messing up Rich Mallory's kitchen. The man was a multi-millionaire, for heaven's sake. He could afford to have his kitchen put back together by the finest craftsmen money could buy.

He could start again from scratch if he wanted to. It was practically his duty, for heaven's sake. Weren't politicians always going on about how spending money kept the economy rolling...?

'How long?' she asked.

'Long enough to have something to eat.' He bit into the apple. 'I'm hungry. How about you?'

'Not hungry enough to contemplate one of your fried egg sandwiches,' she replied sharply.

'I'm not proud. I went out and earned the bacon. You can cook it.'

She was outraged. 'If you think you're just going to put your feet up like some Neanderthal, while I slave over a hot stove—'

He grinned. 'The woolly mammoth steaks are in the fridge.' Then, as he saw her face, 'But maybe you're right about putting my feet up. I've got plenty of work to do.'

Oh, great! Her and her feminist upbringing. If he used the study she wouldn't be able to get in there. Worse, he'd need his keys.

'Work?' she said, desperately trying to think of some way to retreat from her feminist stance.

'You know how it is. A caveman's work is never done. Spears to sharpen, arrow heads to make...'

He was still kidding? His eyes didn't look as if he was kidding. But she laughed anyway. She wasn't much good at the silvery tinkling kind of laugh that Sophie was so good at. It was more your ha ha ha sort of laugh and Mallory lifted his eyebrows.

Who could blame him?

'No,' she said. 'Don't do that. I'm sorry, I really should keep my sex equality rants for those that deserve them,' she said, with a mental note to practice the tinkly laughter in the privacy of her own home. You never knew when these skills would come in handy. 'You've been so—' So what? Kind? Considerate? Thoughtful? 'Sympathetic.' The words almost stuck in her throat she was smiling so hard. 'You go and put your feet up. Be as Neanderthal as you like,' she said, with about as much sincerity as a double-glazing salesman offering to do your windows for free as a 'demonstration'. 'To be honest, I'd love to have the run of your fabulous kitchen. A real treat…'

Unable to stand the I-really-don't-believe-this expression he was wearing for a moment longer, she opened the fridge door. The cool air was welcome on her hot cheeks. Apart from that it wasn't much use.

She cleared her throat. 'There's just one small problem. You've got milk, eggs—' she opened the box '—make that an egg, and some apples. You appear to have forgotten to bring home the bacon, after all.' She looked around the fridge door. 'Ditto the mammoth steaks.'

'They've all gone?'

He joined her at the fridge door, his chest nudging her shoulder as he leaned forward to check the meat drawer. She had the feeling he knew exactly what was in there. Nothing.

'A hunter's work is never done. So much for putting my feet up. Tell me what you need and I'll walk down to that deli on the corner.'

Rich forced a smile as he said this. He'd been enjoying the cut and thrust of the verbal fencing but suddenly he felt as if a huge weight had settled in his chest. He'd set his trap but deep down he'd been hoping, really hoping, that she wouldn't fall into it. That she'd pick up his warnings—plain enough to anyone with mischief in mind—and back off. Take the hint. Realise that she'd been rumbled and let it go.

He knew it was seriously stupid of him to even give her the chance. He should be giving her as much rope as she needed to lead him to whoever was behind this scam.

Ten years in a cut-throat business should have hardened him up, but the truth of the matter was that she had touched something in him. Something he'd thought he'd buried well out of reach of a pair of bewitching eyes.

His heart.

Of course, there was an alternative.

It was possible that she was as innocent as she looked. His subtle hints might have simply passed above her head unnoticed. In which case his keys would be lying on his dressing table. But how likely was that when she'd made such a transparent excuse to return to his bedroom?

He'd seen her nudge her bag behind the chair.

And it had to have been a key she'd been looking for this morning. Why else would she have been searching his bedside drawer? Why else would she have been so disappointed when she had picked up that earring? She could hardly have mistaken it for a hamster.

She'd jumped as if scalded when he'd caught her in his dressing room. She was smart, but she was too nervous to be innocent. Too nervous to be anything but a first time thief. It still wasn't too late…

'Actually—' he said abruptly, before she could gather her thoughts and provide him with a shopping list, get him out of the apartment '—scrub that. You were right first time. You wouldn't invite me to supper and then expect me to cook it.' He was a fool to himself, but he'd give her one more chance to change her mind. 'Besides, Hector is far more likely to emerge if it's quiet in here. I'll send out for something.'

'You don't have to do that,' she said. 'I've got a lasagne in my fridge.'

'You have?'

Now he was confused. She was supposed to want him out of the way. Wasn't she?

'My mother said she might visit.'

'Your mother the classical scholar?'

'I've only got one mother.'

'Of course.' Then, 'What about your father?' The more he knew about her, he reasoned, the easier it would be to find out why she was doing this.

'No, I haven't got one of those,' she said matter-of-factly.

The impassive response was a mask, he realised. Studied carelessness.

'I'm sorry,' he said, really wishing he'd never asked. He was in enough trouble already without adding a severe case of sympathy to the equation.

'It's no big deal. Single parenthood is practically the norm these days.' The merest suggestion of a shrug. 'My mother was always ahead of her time.'

He thought it was always a big deal, but she lifted her brows, daring him to contradict her.

'So?' she enquired. 'Are you going to risk it? The lasagne?'

'Why not?' Of all the risks he'd taken that day, he suspected her cooking would be the least to cause him grief. 'What's life without a little risk to leaven the mix?'

'Uncomplicated?' she offered. 'I'll go and fetch it.'

'What will you do if your mother turns up this evening?'

'It isn't very likely, to be honest. She's in London

for a conference. Women's issues stuff. She'll probably be talking half the night. Putting the world to rights.'

'For women?'

'Someone has to do it. But if she does turn up, I'll cook something else.'

There was the faintest suggestion of unspoken pain in those few simple words, he thought, impatient for the background check. He wanted to know everything about her...

'How practical you are,' he said. 'Do you need a hand? Carrying anything?'

'No, I can manage to carry one dish from my apartment to yours.' Then, 'Better make that two. I'll just be a minute or two while I sort out some salad and make a dressing.' Then, 'Oh.'

'Oh?'

'I haven't got a lemon—for the dressing,' she said. 'I don't suppose...?'

For a moment he'd thought—hoped—that maybe, just maybe, innocent had been right. Instead she'd been toying with him. His sympathy was misplaced.

'That I've got a lemon? If there isn't one in the fridge, then no.' He was sure she already knew the answer to that one.

'I'm afraid not.' She looked up at him, the faintest tinge of pink colouring her cheeks, her breasts rising just a little faster than normal. And those eyes were as green as new meadow grass... 'It'll have to be the deli after all, then. If you don't mind?'

'I can manage the walk to the corner,' he replied, keeping his anger under wraps. He knew what she was doing. Why should he be angry? 'Just a lemon?'

'Well, maybe some black olives, since you're going. And some crusty bread?'

'I think I can manage that. I won't be long.'

'Don't rush. The lasagne will take half an hour at least.'

Don't rush! He wanted to grab her and shake her and tell her not to be so damn stupid. Instead he said, 'We could eat outside if you'd like?'

'That would be great. I really like your garden. No pruning,' she said. 'And no pests.'

'There are always pests,' he said.

This was it. She quickly returned with the lasagne, put it in the oven and turned on the heat.

Now. Do it now.

Rich didn't hurry. He bought her lemon, some plump black olives, a crusty loaf. There were strawberries too and he bought some of those and clotted cream to go with them.

The condemned felon ate a hearty meal...

He'd tried, done all he could to divert her without actually telling her that he knew what she was up to. He could have dragged it out and declared an abhorrence of pasta, could have refused to be moved from his apartment even for the sake of what would undoubtedly be the perfect salad dressing. He could have insisted on sending out for food.

This morning the idea had seemed positively attractive. An amusing diversion while she thought she was luring him into a honey trap, and he used her to get to whoever was behind this raid.

But once he'd kissed her and diversion had morphed

into desire, he knew he couldn't do it. Already he was afraid that her green eyes would haunt him for ever.

He could simply have stopped her, of course. Made it impossible for her to get within a country mile of his disks. That was a temptation, too. But there would be someone else. There was always someone else. He wanted this over with. Most of all he wanted the man who'd sent Ginny to do his dirty work behind bars.

Piece of cake. She'd opened the drawer and there it was. Well, not exactly *there*, on top, just waiting to be picked up. There were half a dozen or so disks and she had to be sure she had the right one. But fortunately they were all clearly labelled.

If she'd really been up to no good, she'd have been very grateful to him for labelling his experimental software so clearly. She'd have expected it to be labelled with some totally innocuous title for security reasons.

Hadn't Sophie said he was security mad?

She shrugged, slapped the disk into her computer and left it to copy on to her hard disk while she took her time about collecting the green stuff for her salad from her fridge. Romaine, rocket…Her hand paused over a new pack of lemons. She could tell him she had found one after all, she supposed. Then she grinned. Bad Ginny. Don't push your luck. And she moved on. Watercress…

She piled it all into a basket with the rest of the ingredients for the dressing. Then, the disk safely copied, she emailed the document to Sophie before returning to Mallory's apartment and replacing the disk and his keys.

It had, in the end, been almost too easy, she thought.

Of course she still had the rest of the evening to get through.

By the time he returned the lasagne was bubbling in the oven and she was assembling the ingredients for the dressing.

'Perfect timing,' he said as he handed her the lemon and, while she squeezed it, he opened a bottle of wine, pouring a couple of glasses before going outside to contemplate his expensive view of the river while the little woman did her stuff in the kitchen.

She swallowed a mouthful of dark red wine.

Chauvinist.

She took another one and on a giddy high, fuelled by the adrenalin charge of the mad risks she had been taking all day, she was almost tempted to remove the piece of apple from the cupboard, let him think that Hector had emerged for his treat. It would serve him right.

Common sense suggested she would be better advised to leave well alone. Just be grateful that he had, in the end, made it so easy for her. On the point of finishing the glass, she stopped herself and instead began whisking the dressing.

All she had to do was get through the next couple of hours and then it would be over. Sophie was saved from the chinless wonder—at least for the time being. Mallory would, finally, be off for his delayed break in Gloucestershire. And her life would be back to normal.

Great.

So why wasn't she feeling happier?

'That smells good.'

Startled, she nearly upset the bowl, fumbling to hold on to it with trembling fingers.

It didn't help that he was watching her.

As if aware of her difficulty, he rescued her, seizing her wrist to steady it before moving the bowl out of danger.

'I didn't mean to startle you.'

He topped up her glass and taking her hand, pressed the wineglass into it, wrapping his long fingers around hers, holding it there until he was certain that she wouldn't drop it.

If he was trying to help he was going the wrong way about it, she thought as the trembling, if anything, became worse.

'Good for the nerves,' he assured her. 'Yours seem to be in need in fortification.' He didn't let go but continued to hold her, standing over her, not in any threatening way, but protectively, as if he would save her from herself.

Ridiculous. It was just because her hand continued to shake beneath his fingers, she told herself. He had no way of knowing that her nerves were in tatters because she'd been masquerading as an undercover agent all day. Double O three and a quarter.

Except that it wasn't just the risk of being caught with her hand in his desk drawer that was making her heart pound.

No, this came packaged with blue eyes capable of zapping the ability to reason right out of her brain, a mouth that made her forget all her long kept resolutions, a touch that would have melted permafrost...

He lifted the glass to her lips, tilted it, leaving her with no option but to swallow or dribble. She swallowed… Maybe he was right. The warmth of the liquid seemed to give her strength and finally she was able to take control of the glass.

'My n-nerves are f-fine. Thank you.'

He didn't argue with her, but his brows rose just far enough to suggest that he wasn't about to agree with her. She made an effort to pull herself together. The worst was over. Another hour or two and she could relax.

'Supper will be ready in about ten minutes,' she said.

'Then why don't you bring your glass, come outside and take a proper look at the garden? You couldn't have seen much of it when you were chasing Hector.'

The garden. Of course. Perfect. Such a very English topic of conversation.

So safe.

She seized it with relief. 'I'd love to.'

Except that his wasn't anything like the average English garden; there were no borders crammed with overheated colours, no tubs of vivid annuals, warm and familiar and safe. It was sophisticated, cool, masculine, only softened by a cluster of low growing maples set amongst the rocks that surrounded the pool.

She followed him out across the decking that jutted out over the pool and stood beside him watching the ghost carp drifting up to the surface now that the shadows were lengthening.

'It is lovely. Peaceful,' she said.

He glanced at her. Lovely. Peaceful. But not safe, she thought. Far from safe.

She looked around her, anywhere to avoid direct eye contact with him. A mistake. She simply drew attention to the disturbance of the perfectly raked gravel caused by her earlier intrusion. The scattered leaves broken off where she'd squeezed through Lady McBride's formal hedge.

'You must find the leaves from the McBrides' garden a nuisance in the autumn,' she said.

His smile was little more than a twitch of his lips at this attempt to keep the conversation on a garden party level.

Darling, the delphiniums are a picture…

Slugs have been such a problem this year…

Have you tried nemotodes…

'It's a box hedge, Ginny. It doesn't lose its leaves. Except when squeezed through by athletic hamsters. And their owners.'

'I made a bit of a mess…'

'Don't worry. It'll grow back.'

'Before the McBrides get home? I'm supposed to be taking care of the place, not wrecking it.'

'How long will they be gone?' He glanced at her. 'How long are you staying?'

'Oh, just until the end of September. I have to get back to Oxford before term begins.'

Rich returned his attention to the fish. 'Mrs Figgis said you're a student. Forgive me but you seem a little—'

'Mature?' she interrupted. 'I'm post grad. Working on my doctoral thesis. Doing a little lecturing to keep the wolf from the door.'

That explained a lot. Charity shop clothes. The desperate need for cash. Education was expensive and stealing his software had to be a lot more financially rewarding than stacking supermarket shelves.

'What's your subject?'

Before she could answer, the doorbell rang. He was inclined to ignore it; he was far more interested in what Ginny Lautour had to say, but seizing the opportunity to escape, she said, 'I'd better go and check on supper while you answer that.'

Damn!

His mood wasn't improved when he opened the door and Lilianne, without waiting for an invitation, flung herself into his arms.

'Darling! I'm so sorry! I was a total bitch last night. There you were working all night and I was, well...' She pouted. 'Disappointed.'

And then she kissed him.

CHAPTER FIVE

GINNY heard the woman's voice and she knew instantly that it wasn't Mrs Figgis coming back to ensure the apartment wasn't being overrun with rodents. It was low, throaty and oozing with sex appeal and there wasn't a thing on earth that could have stopped her from looking through the kitchen door.

One glance was all that she needed.

She retreated swiftly, opened the oven door again, determined to give the impression of applied concentration—a total lack of interest in whoever was calling.

Not that he would have noticed her even if she'd been standing next to him, tapping her foot impatiently and reminding him that he'd invited *her* to supper.

With his mouth glued to the scarlet lips of the tallest, thinnest, red-haired creature any man had ever dreamed about—a seven-denier black stocking woman if ever she'd seen one—he wasn't noticing anything.

It certainly put the kiss he'd given her into true, painful perspective. Forget all that outraged virtue. One minor, teasing kiss and she'd fallen for the Mallory charm just like every woman he'd ever glanced at.

Hook, line and sinker.

She hadn't been mad because he'd kissed her without so much as a by-your-leave. She'd just been mad that he'd left her wanting more.

Why else would witnessing the way he kissed a woman he truly desired—the serious effort he put into it—cause real physical hurt? Like being stabbed with a blunt knife. A few minutes ago she'd been congratulating herself that she would be out of his apartment in an hour or two.

How easy it was to fool yourself.

Well, she'd been saved by the bell and now she wouldn't even have to stick around another minute.

Lucky her.

She shut the oven door, glanced around the kitchen, her gaze lingering on the cupboard beneath the sink. She should do something about that...

Consign poor Hector to myth where he belonged.

But not right now. Right now she was out of here while he was too occupied to stop her. And she picked up her bag and headed for the door. Mallory's eyes swivelled in her direction as she passed them.

'Don't mind me. I'll come back when you're not so busy,' she said. Then, 'The lasagne's just about ready.' If he was still hungry after devouring his unexpected visitor... 'Don't let it spoil.'

It was the woman who spoke, breaking off the close quarter engagement to demand, 'Who's she?'

'I'm meals-on-wheels,' she snapped back before he could answer, twitching her shoulder out of Mallory's reach as he made a grab to stop her. Sheesh. She knew he liked variety, but surely one woman at a time was enough, even for him. 'Don't forget to put the dish to soak.'

He called out something as she let the door slam behind her. It might have been, 'Wait!'

That was the trouble with those heavy fire doors, she thought. You couldn't hear a thing through them. Not even the most peremptory of commands from an arrogant male.

Safely on the other side of the door, she muttered, 'No thanks. I'll come back when there isn't a queue.' Then, deciding that hanging around might not be such a bright idea, she took the lift down to Sophie's apartment in search of a little sanctuary and a large glass of something warm and steadying for her nerves.

Little enough in return for all the risks she'd been running in the last twenty-four hours.

Actually, it wouldn't hurt to check that the document had arrived safely. Ensure that Sophie didn't delete it again. Copy it on to a disk for her, even, so that she could take it into work tomorrow.

After that, all she had to do was 'find' Hector hiding out in one of her own cupboards, apologise to Rich Mallory for her stupidity—a note under the door should do it—then she could erase all thoughts of magnetic millionaires with electric blue eyes and seductive kisses from her mind and put the whole unnerving affair behind her.

Rich was beyond angry. He was furious. With Lilianne for turning up on his doorstep uninvited. With himself for allowing her to catch him off guard. Most of all with Ginny for taking the opportunity to waltz out of his apartment when he'd had serious plans for her.

He'd had her right in the palm of his hand. Well, if not the palm, somewhere pretty damn close and with a couple of glasses of wine and some of her own good cooking to relax her, she might have been coaxed, teased, wooed into indiscretion.

What kind of indiscretion scarcely mattered. One way or the other she'd be in his pocket rather than someone else's.

They'd both be using her but—whether she'd appreciate the fact or not—he would do her the least harm.

What kind of harm she might do him was something he didn't care to think about. He hadn't given a woman so much undivided attention since...

Since he'd been twenty years old and blindly in love with a fellow student who was as lovely as she was devious. She'd walked away with a software program he'd written and bought herself a job with it.

It had been a hard lesson. But well learned.

Until Ginny Lautour had looked up at him with a pair of bewitching green eyes.

Damn it, he didn't believe that Hector existed in anything but imagination—had never believed he existed—yet he'd still been prepared to pull apart his kitchen on the off-chance that she was telling the truth.

He'd really wanted her to be telling the truth.

Even when she'd been raiding his study and he knew for a fact she was lying, he'd found himself remembering the way her eyes had looked when he'd kissed her. And, like a small boy who'd been told by an older cousin that Santa Claus didn't exist and in his heart of hearts knew that it was the truth, he still wanted to believe...

But instead of Ginny, all dither and blush, he'd got Lilianne—clearly regretting her fit of pique and seizing the first opportunity that presented itself to put the clock back to midnight—flinging herself into his arms.

He didn't know what flowers Wendy had sent her, or the message that had accompanied them, but his secretary clearly knew her stuff because they had certainly worked.

He could scarcely complain. It wasn't her fault that the timing was off.

If Ginny hadn't seized the opportunity to escape before he'd managed to extricate himself from a truly vice-like hug, he could have eased Lilianne out with a regretful shrug. Okay, so he'd have looked like a complete heel. But a reputation for having a short attention span where women were concerned had its uses. No one expected any better from him.

As it was, she'd taken advantage of his slow reactions and while he was still caught between holding off Lilianne or going after Ginny and hauling her back, his unexpected guest had made herself at home in the kitchen and was now well into the domestic goddess routine.

And if she'd noticed that there were two used glasses she had clearly decided that discretion was the better part of…whatever.

Well, what had worked once, would undoubtedly work again. Only this time he would have the courtesy to warn her. That way he could dispense with the flowers. And any further misunderstanding.

Leaving him free to go after Ginny.

'Lilianne, I'm sorry—'

She'd tied a tea cloth around her clinging dress and had lifted the bubbling lasagne from the oven to the island. She licked the tip of her thumb then looked up at him.

'No more apologies,' she said. 'All forgotten. Gosh, this looks good. It could just do with a bit longer. Just long enough for a glass of that scrummy wine, perhaps?' Then, when he didn't immediately move to pour her a glass, 'How clever of you to have someone bring in home-made food. You must give me her number.'

'You should have telephoned,' he persisted, refusing to be distracted by the flutter of eyelashes. 'I'm busy.' He wasn't lying. He was working very hard to protect his interests and he'd always put work first, as she'd already discovered. But he'd never subscribed to the rule that you couldn't mix business with pleasure. 'That's why I've had to put off my weekend away.'

'I know. Your sister called me.' So, it was a conspiracy. He'd been right to avoid Gloucestershire. 'She told me you were up to your eyes in work.'

'She was right.'

'If you'd warned me last night...' She lifted her beautiful shoulders in the most elegant of shrugs. 'I'm sorry. I shouldn't have overreacted that way but I was mad because I'd planned something really special.' She lowered her lashes, moved closer and began to play with his shirt buttons. 'For us.'

He caught her hands. Stopped her.

She pouted. 'Darling, I promise you, I do understand that business has to come first. I won't run away again. We'll eat, then you can do whatever you have to and afterwards, well, I'll be waiting no matter how long it takes…'

He bit back the word that flew to the tip of his tongue. They'd been playing this game for a couple of weeks and it wasn't her fault that he'd suddenly lost interest. Confronted with an armful of beautiful and willing woman, he didn't understand it himself.

'I'm sorry, Lilianne, but I'm afraid that isn't an option.'

She smiled—it was the sultry, straight to hell smile that had snagged his attention in the first place. Practised, artful and so obvious compared with the startled innocence of Ginny's wide-eyed shock as he'd freed half of the McBrides' hedge from her hair.

As he'd kissed her.

Or maybe Ginny was a better actress.

Was it possible to blush on cue?

Lilianne, perhaps sensing that she didn't have his full attention, raised her hands to his shoulders and looked up at him from beneath lashes that owed as much to cosmetics as nature. 'Rich, please…'

'I'll call you a taxi,' he said. And disengaged himself.

Sophie wasn't sitting at home chewing her highly polished nails to the quick and worrying about her best friend—or her job—Ginny discovered. She wasn't home at all.

She was probably having a high old time in some club, or in an expensive restaurant having her hand held by some drooling male.

Nothing new there.

The only surprising thing about Sophie was that she hadn't been married to some rich minor aristocrat by the time she was nineteen. She had the kind of fragile beauty that was meant to be cosseted by a man who adored her. She was born to live surrounded by lush acres of parkland, with beautiful horses, decorative dogs and at least four adorable children. She would, of course, have a capable staff to deal with all the messy stuff.

Sophie herself had had it all planned out, with a shortlist of suitable candidates. It had been her sixth form project, receiving a lot more attention than her A-levels. Then, while Ginny had taken her four starred As and gone off to university, Sophie, with no intention of spending any more time cramming her head with useless knowledge, had taken a 'gap year' to work through her list and decide which of her prospective mates was going to be the lucky man. But somewhere along the way she'd taken her eye off the ball and been sidetracked by the serious business of having fun.

Sophie and Rich Mallory were made for each other, Ginny thought sourly. If she'd been truly cynical she might have thought that Sophie had got herself the job at Mallory's company in order to attract his attention.

Apparently not.

Maybe Sophie's father had a point. Ginny frowned as she took the stairs up to the McBrides' apartment. What had happened? Why…?

She got no further than the 'Why…?' before she spotted the man himself standing at her door. If she hadn't already mentally got him tucked up with the luscious female with the scarlet lipstick—and she'd been making a real effort not to think too much about that—she might have been paying more attention and been able to duck out of sight.

Too late. He'd heard the door, turned and spotted her while she was still trying to decide what to do. Short of dashing back down the stairs—and how would that help when she'd have to come back sooner or later?—she would appear to have no option but to smile and try to look pleased to see him.

She hoped she was more successful than he was. His expression suggested that he was torn between wishing he were somewhere else—preferably on a different continent—and, well, it was hard to say. He had more control of his facial expressions than she had. But maybe he was just a bit pleased to see her.

Or maybe that was wishful thinking.

Why on earth would he be pleased to see her? She was causing him nothing but trouble, for heaven's sake?

And why would her heartbeat lift a little—actually quite a lot—at the thought? What a ridiculous idea. He was the kiss-and-run type of man she most despised.

She'd got that charge from the mental challenge, but that was over, she reminded herself, even if he didn't know it yet. And her heart was pounding a little harder than usual because she'd run up the stairs. That was all.

Even so, the temptation to tell him, right now, that her little wanderer had returned and he could forget all about it was intense. But somehow she didn't think he'd be convinced. Not after the way she'd cut and run...

He would want to see for himself.

She had the feeling that he'd insist.

No. She'd let him off the hook tomorrow when he had other things to occupy him and he'd just be glad it was all over. Meanwhile, on with the performance...

'Have you found him?' she asked, making a real effort to look hopeful.

'Found him?'

'Hector. Why else would you be ringing my bell?'

'I'm ringing your bell because we were going to have supper.' He reached out, seized her elbow and, without bothering to check if she was still interested, he steered her firmly in the direction of his apartment. 'Your tactful withdrawal was beautifully done but quite unnecessary.'

'Oh, but it was necessary,' she said. 'There isn't enough for three.' Even if one of them looked as if she could survive for a week on a lettuce leaf.

'Lilianne isn't staying for supper. And, for future reference, I prefer to make my own arrangements in that department.'

'Oh.'

Bother.

Even as she thought it she was having to force down the corners of her mouth so that she wasn't grinning like a Cheshire cat.

'I'm so sorry. I didn't want her to think...' Well, no. Realistically, she wouldn't. 'What did she think?'

'That you were a caterer who produced home

cooked meals for single males incapable of doing it for themselves.'

The lines that bracketed his mouth deepened, the corners of his eyes creased in a sunset fan. He was clearly not the least bit worried about keeping his amusement to himself at this mistake.

'You know, there could be a major business opportunity there,' he continued. 'In fact, Lilianne wanted your telephone number. If you're interested, I'll pass it on.'

'Lilianne knows enough single men to make it worth while, does she?'

'Cat,' he said, but if anything his amusement increased.

Oh, drat. Jealousy was such a give-away. The last thing she wanted to do was give him the impression that she was keen to become yet another scalp on the crowded bedpost of his life.

'Yes, well, in that case I'll, um, dish up, shall I?'

'Good plan.'

He checked the cupboard while she removed the lasagne from the oven. Again. It was beginning to look decidedly crispy at the edges

'No sign of Hector,' he said.

She glanced at the open cupboard. 'It might be a good idea not to keep opening the door,' she advised. 'You wouldn't want to frighten him off, would you?'

She shouldn't do it, she knew, but Mallory just seemed to bring out the worst in her. A 'worst' she'd never encountered before. Since she couldn't admire the man for his heroic properties, the attraction just had to be pure lust. Although maybe 'pure' wasn't an entirely appropriate adjective. Since it was a first for her, she couldn't be certain.

Whatever, it offered a very good reason to keep her mouth shut and a safe distance between them. It also explained why she was finding it so difficult to do that.

'You think we should just leave it?' he asked. 'Wait and see if the apple goes?'

She was burning up with lust. He was just concerned about a hamster infestation. It figured.

'If it goes we'll know he's there,' she pointed out, confident in the knowledge that he wasn't. 'Then we can decide what to do.'

'You mean we can dismantle my kitchen?'

'That's it,' she said, quite prepared to do a little teasing of her own. But she was too quick with her smile.

'Perhaps we might try a humane trap before we do anything too drastic,' he suggested.

'You are no fun, Richard Mallory,' she said, as she divided the pasta between two dishes, sucking on the end of her thumb where hot sauce had bubbled on to it.

When he didn't immediately come back with some smart answer she looked up, prepared to laugh, but he wasn't smiling. Not one little bit. He'd shut the cupboard door and was just looking at her, his face unreadable.

For a long moment he was so still that her breath caught in her throat and couldn't find a way out.

Nothing moved. It was as if the world was on hold, waiting, so quiet that she could actually hear the blood pumping through her veins.

Then, when she thought that something explosive had to happen—would have welcomed something explosive, anything had to be safer than that dangerous silence—he reached out and took her wrist.

'Did you burn yourself?'

She couldn't say. His touch sizzled far more dangerously than hot pasta sauce, fizzing through her veins like a fuse, and she was beyond framing a coherent thought, let alone a straight answer. He didn't ask again, but simply looked for himself before lifting her thumb to his lips very briefly. Then he turned on the cold water and held it there so that it ran over both their hands.

Relief—or maybe it was the effect of cold water—released her from the breath-holding tension and she managed a choked, 'Thank you.'

He checked her hand then looked up, still not smiling. 'No problem,' he said.

On balance, she thought that he was less dangerous when he was smiling. Than not. She made a move to pull away, retrieve her hand, but he didn't let her go.

'No problem with your hand, anyway. However, if you think that taking a kitchen apart is fun, Ginny, you need some serious lessons in how to enjoy yourself.'

Only then did he release her, turn and pick up the plates. 'Can you bring the wine and the glasses?' he asked.

It wasn't an offer then.

What should surely have been relief felt rather more like regret; she was sure that if you needed coaching in fun he would be the man to get you through your finals with a starred first. The only kind of result she'd ever been willing to accept.

'I think I can handle that,' she replied, holding the glasses against her breast to stop them from rattling.

Rich carried the plates, kicking off his shoes as he stepped up into the little Japanese pavilion which had been built under the protection of the apartment wall, glad of a little cool air to clear his head.

Why was it that when Lilianne had sucked on her thumb he'd seen only the obvious sexual invitation? Something designed solely to tempt and as such—beyond instant gratification of the most basic kind—of very limited appeal? Or, in this instance, a complete turn off.

Whereas when Ginny had used the same gesture he'd known instinctively that it was an innocent reaction to a burned thumb rather than a seductive gesture contrived to turn him on.

And contrarily, the effect on him had been inflammatory.

He put the plates on the low table, then retraced his steps and rescued the glasses and bottle, which looked as if they were about to slip from her grasp. Shaking a little himself as their hands collided, fingers became entangled.

'Thanks,' she said, a smile wobbling briefly on her lips. 'I'll go and fetch the salad.'

'No, you sit down.' She looked ready to bolt and he wasn't giving her another chance to escape. 'I'll get it.'

'Oh, right. Don't forget the bread. And the dressing.

I should have put it in a jug. It'll need another whisk…'

He said nothing, just waited. She kicked off her shoes without embarrassment or making some stupid comment, then knelt gracefully on one of the cushions by the low table.

Her full figure would look wonderful in a kimono, he thought. Her hair in a knot, wisps escaping about her face. He imagined how it would be to pull loose the pins, have it tumble over his hands…

'Is that it?' he said.

'That's it,' she said. Then half-opened her mouth as if she wanted to say something else. But thought better of it and closed it again.

'I can do it,' he said. 'I may have caveman tendencies, but I'm not completely stupid.'

At least he hoped not. He'd given her the rope, but where had she run with it the second she'd escaped? Not back to her apartment, obviously. But not very far. There hadn't been time.

'Actually, I was going to say we need forks, too.'

He returned with the dressing properly whisked and in a jug and everything else they needed, then he too folded himself up on the cushions before pouring her a fresh glass of wine.

'We should be eating sushi,' she said. 'I should be whisking tea.'

'This will be fine. I just hope all your hard work hasn't been spoiled by the delay.'

'Just leave the crunchy bits round the edges.'

'Right.'

He offered her salad, took some himself. Taking his

time. Complimenting her on the food—well it *was* good—and keeping it impersonal. Not pushing for conversation.

Dusk was settling over the city, the sky was the soft violet of a late summer evening. 'I love this time of day.'

'It's better in the country. The air is fresher and you actually get to see the stars.'

'You live in the country? Whereabouts?'

'I live in Oxford. But I drive out to the country when I can. I can't wait to get back.'

'Then why are you flat-sitting in London?'

'I needed to use the British Library for some research. This is the only way I can afford to stay here. I'm really very lucky to have such a wonderful place rent-free.'

It was chance, then? That she was next door. Had she been targeted because of where she was staying? Or had it been planned that way from the beginning? She knew Philly McBride slightly. How had she met her?

'What's your subject?' he asked.

'The Hero: Myth or Reality?' There was not sufficient light to tell whether she was blushing. But he was almost certain she was.

'And have you come to any conclusions?'

'I'm still working on it.'

'What else do you do?'

'Sorry?'

'You study, lecture, drive into the country, keep a pet hamster. I'm trying to round out the picture here. See the whole woman. Where do you live? Have you got anyone important in your life? Do you like the movies?'

'That sounds more like an inquisition. What about you?'

'My life is an open book. My business world is regularly featured in the financial pages, my personal life a constant fascination for the diary columnists. But I'll concede the point. You answer a question, you get to ask one. Is that fair?'

She shrugged. 'Okay. I live in rooms in college.'

'Do you enjoy that?' She raised her eyebrows. 'You get to ask me a supplementary.'

'Yes, I like it. And it's convenient.' Then, 'How do you feel about having your life under the microscope? Being the object of endless speculation.' She sounded as if she really wanted to know. As if…

Lautour. The name finally clicked.

Her mother was Judith Lautour, the militant feminist who had chosen some brilliant scholar as the father for her baby. An early experiment in genetic engineering. Could two geniuses raise an infant prodigy…?

The outrage in the press that had sent the woman's books into the best-seller charts for weeks.

'The truth?' he said, when the silence had gone on too long. 'It used to incense me, but really, what's the point? It's mostly fiction, after all, a daily soap opera, a little excitement over the morning coffee. You know how it is—a single man with a fortune has to be married for the amusement of the masses, preferably more than once. Or outed as gay.'

'You seem to have done pretty well in avoiding both those fates.'

'The first is a question of time. Or rather a lack of it. Women require a certain amount of attention. To feel needed. If they're neglected they tend to wander off and look for someone more attentive.'

'You're telling me that you're not the one who loses interest?'

'Work it out for yourself, Ginny. If I was sufficiently interested, I'd make more effort to ensure they didn't feel neglected. Last night I got involved in work and forgot Lilianne existed.'

'She appears to have forgiven you.'

'She left me a very rude note. She deserved an apology but that's it. End of story.'

'Oh.'

'As for the second… Well, when you've been photographed with enough lovely women, no one bothers to ask the question.'

She lifted her eyebrows. 'Is that *all* you do? Have your photograph taken?'

'You've had your supplementary, Ginny. It's my turn.'

'Have I got anyone important in my life?' she prompted.

'No one who cares enough to put a ring on your finger,' he answered for her, unable to resist the opportunity to provoke something more than a yes or no answer.

'Marriage is such an outdated institution, don't you think?'

'You follow your mother in more than scholarship, then?'

She hesitated. 'Not entirely,' she said. 'I wouldn't make her choices.'

'To be a single parent?'

'Out of passion, maybe. But she used a sperm donor, you see? She is gay, you see.'

Forget one question—there were a dozen forming on his lips. Who? Why? What kind of childhood had that been? How she'd lived with the curiosity, the inevitable intrusion. He kept them to himself.

'Actually, I don't,' he said, finally.

'Don't see?'

He saw, felt for her, wanted to reach out and wrap her in his arms and hold her, protect her...

He shook his head. 'I don't take the view that marriage is an outdated institution. No matter what the relationship. I believe that a lifetime commitment should be honoured with due ceremony and the total understanding of the contractual obligations of both parties.' He'd been unexpectedly moved at the solemnity of the undertaking between his sister and her husband as he'd witnessed their signatures in the register. Ginny looked doubtful and he shrugged. 'Like any business undertaking,' he added. He did, after all, have a reputation to live down to. 'The wedding ceremony, no matter how simple or extravagant, provides all that.'

'With a jolly good party afterwards, with the pick of the bridesmaids for dessert.'

And he found himself wishing he hadn't made that comment about business. Marriage, if it was done well—and there was no point in doing it any other way—was a lot more important than any business undertaking.

'Maybe I'm old-fashioned, but I believe in order.' Then, 'No, my question is—'

'You've had your question!'

'On the contrary. You suggested one, I discounted it and then you sneaked in another one. It's definitely my turn.' And he found a grin from somewhere. 'Twice.'

He was a lot better at this kind of stuff than she was, Ginny realised. She'd laid down the rules of this engagement, but too late she realised that he wasn't the kind of man to play by anyone's rules other than his own.

He'd always bend them to his convenience, taking complete advantage of her lack of any experience in this kind of double-edged banter to draw out the kind of information that she normally kept under lock and key.

She never told strangers about her mother. She left the tittle-tattle to other people and they'd never let her down yet.

But she was learning.

This time she didn't leap in, even though he paused, like the gentleman he wasn't—gentlemen didn't kiss girls they'd only just met—offering her the opportunity to contradict him. Instead she kept a wary silence, clamping her jaw shut and refusing to break it even when it stretched to snapping point.

Refusing to give him the satisfaction.

Refusing to… 'What?' she demanded, unable to bear it a moment longer. 'What do you want to know?'

His eyes creased in a smile—dammit, she knew he'd smile—and he said, 'I want to know what you're doing tomorrow.'

CHAPTER SIX

HER caution had been well placed.

Ginny, for just a few tantalising moments, had been remembering how it felt to be back in control. Well, almost. Her heart rate had still been a little rapid, but the tremor that had been as unpredictable as the aftershock of an earthquake since Rich had kissed her thumb had begun to subside to manageable proportions. Now she was right back where she'd started.

Doing? Tomorrow?

Using extreme care—so that it wouldn't clatter against the china—she placed her fork on the side of her plate. A sip of wine would have helped the sudden dryness in her mouth, but she didn't dare pick up her glass, certain it would shatter between her fingers.

Like Richard Mallory she believed in order, had determinedly avoided the turmoil and mayhem with which her brilliant but unconventional mother had so carelessly blighted her childhood, her adolescence.

She never wanted to be out of control, ever again.

She'd tripped once, fooled by the easy treachery of a warm smile and kind words, betrayed by a yearning to be wanted, needed, not as some experiment but just for herself.

She had the emotionally bloodied knees to show for it when the object of her affections had sold his story to a tabloid newspaper.

Now she would only ever step out of line, take risks, for Sophie; despite her friend's shallow 'playgirl' exterior she'd always been there with an outstretched hand whenever the world had seemed a black and lonely place. If the tables were turned, Sophie would do this for her. Without question.

So she determinedly ignored the excited hammering of a heart that should have, did know better and hunted out one of the stock answers that she kept about her for just such occasions.

It took rather longer than it should. But it had been a long time since she had actually needed to use one of them.

If she didn't come up with one soon, he'd know it was just an excuse…

Except she didn't need an excuse. The truth would do perfectly well. 'I'm working tomorrow,' she said. Then, because, she also had an unconquerable curiosity—the kind that had always taken her to the top of the class, won her academic scholarships—she couldn't quite stop herself from adding, 'Why?'

Rich had been expecting an excuse. Had been interested to know what she'd come up with on the spur of the moment. The length of time she'd taken to answer suggested that, put on the spot, she hadn't found it easy. Then, before he could congratulate himself on his cleverness, she'd turned the tables, waylaying him with a question to which he had no answer. Or, at least, not an answer he was prepared to confront. Or admit, even to himself.

'Oh, nothing.'

Nothing? If it was nothing why ask? He could see

that was what she was thinking, and he was wondering the same thing himself.

There he was all lined up to ask her thoughtful, probing little questions, encouraging her to reveal her innermost thoughts, secrets, desires and without warning he'd been asking her what she was doing tomorrow. Not as part of some well-thought-out strategy, but as if he was going to ask her out on a date, for heaven's sake.

As if he was desperate to spend more time with her.

Bed, sex…well, yes. No problem. He didn't need any emotional commitment for that. But this felt… emotional…

Not that it mattered. He was safe enough. He'd known she would come back with some feint and he was right. She'd got what she wanted. She had no reason to spend any more time with him.

So why ask 'why'?

To gain a little thinking time he struck a match, and lit the candles inside a simple glass candleholder so that the garden retreated into the darkness and only her face reflected back the soft light.

There was, he would be the first to admit, nothing about her to make him look twice under normal circumstances. She didn't make the slightest effort with her appearance. She'd clung to spectacles when most girls would have abandoned them for contact lenses. She wore no make-up. There were no artificially applied sunshine streaks to draw attention to her mousy hair. No clothes cleverly cut to display her body to advantage.

There was not a thing about her to shout to the world, 'Look at me, I'm beautiful...'

If she was trying to look invisible—and of course she was—she couldn't have done a better job.

Maybe that was what made him keep looking. The contradiction between the fact that there was, apparently, nothing hidden, nothing false about her coupled with the powerful conviction that her lack of artifice was, in itself, a disguise. Whatever it was, it worked for him.

With nothing more than the soft luminescence of her skin in the twilight and green eyes full of secrets, she had his full attention.

She also, he was almost certain, had a disk containing his newest software project. Or at least, she thought she did, which amounted to the same thing.

She had a disk. One she'd stolen from him. And the minute she used it he'd have her. At which point she could speak to the police, or tell him everything he wanted to know.

In the meantime, he told himself, spending time with her would be no hardship. And whether it was the head of Mallory plc or Rich Mallory the man who was driving that thought he wasn't going to argue with it.

'If I have to dismantle my kitchen,' he said, finally answering both her questions—the one she'd asked and the unspoken one he'd read in her eyes—'I'm going to need an assistant.' He paused just long enough for her to think about that. 'Someone to hand me a screwdriver when I need one,' he added provokingly, because he loved the way she never failed to rise to a little provocation. 'But of course if you're too busy…'

Of course she'd be too busy. Hector was pure invention. How apt, he thought, that someone familiar with the Homeric myths should adapt the 'Trojan Horse' scenario to get inside his security 'fortress'.

How clever.

And the slightest shiver rippled down his spine, a *frisson* of excitement.

Was that the attraction? The knowledge that this was a lot more than the usual kiss-chase, played out on a purely physical level. It was a game of wits.

Right now she thought she'd won, that she'd got what she was looking for. Why would she waste any more time on him?

There wasn't a reason in the world. Tonight her little runaway would be 'found' and in the morning he'd find a polite little note under the door informing him of that fact, apologising for all the trouble she'd caused him. She'd probably even make a point of thanking him again for being such a good neighbour. And do her level best to avoid him for the rest of her stay. It shouldn't be that difficult. Their paths would never have crossed if she hadn't discovered, somewhat belatedly, that the bedroom she was searching was occupied…

And with a jolt he realised what that meant. Someone he trusted must have told her that he would be away.

Ginny was finding it harder and harder to remember that she was in Rich Mallory's home under false pretences. Talking, sharing a meal, a bottle of wine—and she'd better not have any more of that!—she'd begun to relax. He was so easy to be with. To laugh with.

Now she was being given the chance to spend the morning cosied up with the darling of the diary columns, babe magnet of the month—any month—all-round hunk and multi-millionaire. Okay, so the cosying would be in the kitchen. Screwdrivers and spanners rather than smoked salmon and champagne. But it was Rich Mallory's kitchen and anyone would tell her that she'd be a fool to say no.

Except Sophie, of course.

But while some hitherto unknown, untapped feminine need was urging her to let the work go hang—she could work any time but this was a once in a lifetime opportunity that should not be missed—the responsible, prudent part of her brain, the part that had never let her down, counselled instant retreat.

She found herself stalling.

Okay, so he was flirting with her. Big deal. Clearly the man couldn't help himself. Or was it that he felt it was expected of him, that she'd be disappointed if he didn't make an effort? On neither account should she feel particularly flattered.

Even if she was foolish enough to succumb to Mr Ever Ready's charm on the kitchen floor it obviously wouldn't mean a thing to him. While she…

She'd be an even bigger fool to fall for it.

Prudent was right. She did not need this.

'Richard,' she said, and feeling the power of his name on her tongue her concentration wavered and common sense went walkabout. But then he did one of those is-this-actually-going-anywhere-soon? things with his eyebrows and she dragged her wandering wits back into line. 'You do not have to rip apart your kitchen,' she said. 'Really. I'll go out first thing tomorrow and buy one of those humane traps. It'll be kinder all round.'

The minute the words had left her mouth she knew she'd made a mistake. He shifted slightly—it wasn't anything as positive as a shrug—and she had the uneasy feeling that he'd been waiting for her to say something of the sort.

'You're very relaxed about this,' he said, confirming her suspicions. 'In your place most women would be frantic by now.'

Clearly he believed men were made of sterner stuff. Remembering how her room-mate at college had panicked, running around like an idiot in a similar situation... No forget similar—nothing in the history of the world had ever come close to this.

'I don't see how getting frantic will help,' she replied. That was supposed to sound calm, the wise words of a woman in total control of her world. It just sounded defensive.

'It won't,' he agreed, 'but it's a natural reaction. Nothing to be ashamed of. Aren't you afraid the poor little thing will starve?'

Now she knew he was going out of his way to provoke her. Make her feel unnatural and cold-hearted. She knew she was neither of those things. That if Hector were real he would have grapes and the fattest nuts and whatever else his little heart desired. And that, curiously, made his accusation easier to deal with.

'Not imminently,' she replied. 'He's the best fed

hamster in London. Probably.' He couldn't refute it.
'Glossy of coat, bright of eye—'

'And with a turn of speed that wouldn't disgrace an Olympic hurdler.'

'You've got it.'

'Doesn't that kind of energy require constant feeding?'

She was getting seriously irritated with him. 'The hungrier he is, the more likely it is that he'll take your bait,' she said, through teeth that weren't totally gritted, but it was a close run thing.

'He hasn't shown any interest in that apple.' And she had the feeling that she was the one being baited.

'Well,' she said doubtfully. 'It is a red apple. He prefers the hard, green ones.' Oh, good grief...

'Is that right?'

His eyes glittered in the candlelight, as if ransacking every word, every inflection for...something. And again she had the feeling she was treading on ice so thin that a warm breath would melt it.

'How old is he?'

'Two,' she said, saying the first number that came into her head. 'And a bit.'

'Isn't that quite old for a hamster?'

'It's not young,' she agreed with rather more hope than conviction since she had no idea how long a hamster might be expected to live. She should have done some serious homework before embarking on this foolishness, she realised. It had just never occurred to her that she'd be drawn into an in-depth discussion on the subject. In fact, the whole thing had got way out of control. Then, with a jolt, as she saw where he might be going with this, 'You think he's dead, don't you?'

She didn't have to look horrified. She was. She kept her teeth clamped tight shut to avoid the groan escaping. How on earth could she have said something that stupid?

Before she knew it they'd be into the second verse of All Things Bright and Beautiful and raising a little plaque in Hector's memory…

She had to get away from him before this nonsense went any further. She'd put a note under his door first thing. Panic over. Hector found. It was perfectly possible that he'd doubled back while she was fighting her way through the hedge… Found home and food and then curled up and taken a very long nap after his exertions…

'This has been great,' she said. 'Good food, good wine, good company, but I really have to go.' She didn't wait for him to go through the motions of encouraging her to stay, but quickly got to her feet. Then she said, 'Ouch!'

She was a sofa person. The bigger and squashier the sofa, the better. Sitting on the floor oriental-style had given her a dead-leg and, as it failed to support her, she went back down as fast as she'd risen. But with considerably less grace and upsetting a glass as she tried to save herself.

He was beside her before she could blink. 'Are you hurt?'

'Not unless you count my dignity,' she said, biting back a groan and forcing a smile. 'Just give me a minute for the circulation to get going and I'll try that again.'

She rubbed her leg in an attempt to speed up the process, but Rich stopped her. 'Keep still and lie back.'

What?

'I'll be fine,' she said quickly, determined to do nothing of the sort. She would hop if necessary. Even as she sent the message to her legs to stop behaving like a pair of wet hens and do as they were told he ran his hands gently over her foot.

'You'll be fine quicker if you'll lie back and leave it to me to get the circulation going.'

Of course she would. It was foolish and stupid to make such a pathetic fuss. He was being kind, that was all. Just because he'd kissed her once didn't mean a thing.

If he'd enjoyed the experience he'd have done it again.

And it wasn't as if she could even feel anything very much, she protested when 'prudent' and 'common sense' waved the caution flag from their corner. Her leg was numb. But she shivered, nonetheless, as he propped her foot against his chest and began to work on her ankle, his fingers searching out the pressure points.

'I tend to forget that sitting like that for any length of time is an acquired skill,' he said matter-of-factly and glancing up at her.

So matter-of-factly that she realised just how foolish she was being. He wasn't going to leap on her the minute she was out flat. He had Miss Scarlet Lipstick for that kind of thing. Ready, willing and…

She blocked out the thought. And started breathing again.

'Okay?' he asked after a moment or two.

'Umm,' was about all she could manage as he slowly kneaded the life back into her ankle, her calf.

More than okay, actually.

In fact, her only coherent thought at that moment was one of gratitude for a seriously painful evening of mutual leg waxing that Sophie had inflicted upon her earlier in the week. At the time—between screams of pain—she'd protested that she didn't need smooth legs, that no one ever saw her legs.

Sophie—taking advantage of the fact that she was living upstairs to put her through one of her 'it's-time-you-made-more-of-an-effort-with-your-appearance' evenings—had just grinned and carried on, saying that it was one of the things you did, '…like wearing sexy underwear. Just in case.'

Her response, that it was *clean* underwear you were supposed to wear 'just in case' only brought an enigmatic smile from Sophie. But the next day a courier had arrived at her apartment bearing an elegant box containing a set of underwear that defined the word 'sexy'. The handwritten note had simply said:

This beats 'clean' any day, wouldn't you say?

And right now she was really, really wishing that instead of her plain, sensible underwear she'd put on one of those black lacy thongs and the matching bra, a miracle of engineering that would do spectacular stuff to her cleavage…

Stupid. As if he'd notice…

But anything more rational was impossible just at that moment because there was a war going on inside her head.

The bit of her brain where all the sensible stuff happened was tut-tutting furiously and telling her to forget about sexy underwear. What she should be wearing, it warned, was that good solid pair of jeans.

A skirt, it continued with finger-wagging persistence—even a long skirt—was no protection against the infiltration of masculine fingers intent on the sensuous kneading of her flesh.

He'd reached her knee now and the bit of her brain that seemed to frizzle whenever Rich came close, the bit that sent warm flushes to her cheeks, buckled her knees and made her breasts leap and send out 'touch me' signals, went into overdrive. It was saying lie back and enjoy this, Ginny.

Umm. Enjoying it was definitely the more attractive option.

He glanced up. 'Am I hurting you?' he asked.

She blinked. Had she actually 'ummed' out loud? Maybe she was letting herself get a little bit *too* relaxed. 'Er, no.' Then, in case she had, and because she didn't want him to think she'd 'ummed' with pleasure, she qualified it. 'Not much, anyway. You're doing a good job.'

A glint in those blue eyes, a tiny tuck in the corner of his mouth, suggested he knew exactly what he was doing.

'Is the feeling coming back? Are you getting pins and needles?'

She was getting something, but it wasn't the torture of pins and needles. More like a tingling warmth that was seeping through her veins, licking over her skin as he held her calf in his palm, stroking her leg from knee to ankle, hand over hand in long smooth strokes.

A tingling warmth that was pooling and settling low in her belly.

'It's not unbearable,' she managed.

Far from unbearable. His touch was gently probing, tender, setting light to nerve-endings in a seductive caressing of her skin...

Then he shifted his attention to her thigh and somewhere deep within her a panic button was pressed. This was too intimate... Too dangerous...

Too late; the warm pool at the centre of her being heated up, spreading slowly through her until her entire body was liquefying with pleasure at his touch. She didn't care how far he went. It wasn't just her breasts that were begging to be touched...

A moan of longing slipped past the guard of her lips. Rich looked up, his face all shadows, unreadable.

In the silence, a question.

One to which her body's answer was a resounding 'yes'. But to which 'prudent', slipping through unnoticed in the confused turmoil of her brain, was already slamming the doors, putting up the shutters, refusing to listen.

'Oo...ch,' she said. A sound somewhere between a moan and an ouch.

It was unbearably loud in the quiet of the small

circle of candlelight and when he looked up again his eyes were no longer glittering. They were more grey than blue now—soft and smoky… It was probably the effect of the candles. Except they were burning still and clean…

'The feeling is back?'

'Absolutely,' she said. And because she had to do something, say something to shatter the tension, 'How did you learn a skill like that?'

'Like what?' He sounded vaguely confused too. 'Oh, sitting on the floor. I spent some time in Japan,' he said, and stopped what he was doing. She immediately wished she'd kept quiet. 'How's the other leg?' he asked.

Oh, terrific. Now he could read her mind. That would never do. It was definitely time to make a move.

'Fine,' she said quickly. This time he apparently believed her and she was instantly sorry. Confused— it was what she'd wanted, wasn't it?—but sorry.

She'd had both legs waxed and it seemed a shame to waste all that pain…

'I'm sorry, Ginny.'

'No, it's fine,' she said quickly, feeling guilty about that 'oo-ch'. Pretending that he'd hurt her. 'I love your pavilion, the whole thing—'

'I didn't mean to upset you. About Hector,' he added, because she hadn't got the faintest idea what he was talking about. And clearly it showed.

Who? Oh, *Hector*.

Oh, drat. He wasn't apologising for the unconventional seating arrangements. And he hadn't been fooled by her 'oo-ch'. She had to face it, he'd probably done this dozens of times. Hundreds of times. He'd clearly known exactly what he was doing and it certainly didn't deserve an ouch. Or even an 'oo-ch'.

It rated nothing less than an X-certificate moan.

'No. No, really, I'm fine,' she said with forced brightness, pushing her skirt modestly back into place with hands that were visibly shaking, sitting up, backing off a little. 'He'll be back tomorrow, you just wait and see. Hungry, sorry for himself and worn out.'

She could almost see the little bedraggled creature. Another minute and she was going to be in tears. She sniffed. She was already close…

'Thanks for the first aid,' she said.

'I should be thanking you,' he said, rising to his feet, offering a hand to help her up. But not denying the nuisance bit, she noticed.

That, somehow, made it easier to place her hand in his but, as he pulled her up in one smooth movement, in a *déjà vu* moment she was once again confronting his shirt buttons; it was the dressing room all over again.

The scent of well-laundered clothes, good soap, warm skin. The closeness of man she desired. Shockingly.

It was an anything-could-happen moment when he might have swept her into his arms and kissed her senseless. And she, shockingly, knew that she just might let him.

It wouldn't take a lot.

She wasn't far from senseless already.

Just far enough to take a step back before the scene went into re-run, before Rich took off her spectacles again and, without so much as a by-your-leave ma'am, he was kissing her again. She forced herself to let go of his hand.

It shouldn't be this difficult...

'How is it?' he said.

Dazed, confused, she said, 'What?' Then, 'Oh, the leg. Fine. Good as new.'

His hand was still there, an offer of support should she need it, as she slipped into her shoes. But she wasn't about to play the helpless female just for the pleasure of his touch. Instead, she made a move to go.

'Do you have to go?' His hand, resting on an upright beam, cut off her escape. 'Can't I tempt you to a little brandy?'

'Yes... No...'

He smiled, making her confusion worse. 'I think I understand that. But you see my problem?'

He had a problem? 'What problem?'

'What am I going to do with that bowl of strawberries?'

About to suggest he tried them on Hector, she restrained herself. She was in enough trouble already.

'That's not a problem, Rich. If you can't eat them I'll be happy to give them a good home.'

'That wasn't the right answer,' he said, his voice a little ragged, his eyes suggesting that he had plans along the lines of one bowl of strawberries, one bowl of cream and some slow indulgent dipping.

She was clearly going mad.

'I'm sorry. It's the only one you're going to get. I've got a pile of work to do.'

He let his hand drop but didn't immediately move to let her pass.

'Someone reminded me today that work never goes away. That you shouldn't let it rule your life.'

'That is true and when I've got time I'll give it some thought. But right now I've got a very tight schedule and a limited amount of time.' The truth at last. 'Thanks for being such a great neighbour,' she said and, rather to her surprise, meaning it. 'I've been a total nuisance.'

Actually, when he wasn't morphing into serial lover mode, he *was* a great neighbour. She quite liked him. Really. In fact, she couldn't see what Sophie's problem was with him. If she needed a husband he had all the necessary qualities…

Money.

Good looks.

A short attention span.

No, Sophie knew what she was about.

And so did she. Clearly that showed in her face, too, because this time when she made a move towards the open French windows he stood aside, but she hadn't taken a step before his hand was at her back as he fell into step beside her.

It felt possessive, as if now that he'd touched her, kissed her, she was in some way his. Which was plainly ridiculous. Why would he even want her, when he had a fabulous redhead at his beck and call?

It wasn't personal, she reminded herself. It was just something he did.

Or maybe it was simply her overheated imagination beginning to hallucinate. She could hardly blame it after the day she'd put it through. She collected her bag from the kitchen, momentarily escaping his touch as he took her at her word and got out the strawberries and the carton of cream, before walking her across the hall to her own door, placing them into her hands.

She felt awkward taking them. As if she should invite him in to share them. Make coffee.

But he was probably counting on that. How many times had he used that routine before? Get real, Ginny. Why would he have to bother? Anyone but you would be at his feet by now.

Anyone but her. Right. She was a one-off. An original. A failed experiment.

'Thank you,' she said. 'These will go down well with a couple of chapters from Homer.'

'No, Ginny, thank you for the great food. Should you decide to go into business, I'll place a regular order.'

'Maybe I will. It probably pays a lot better than ancient history.'

'People always need to eat.'

It was that kind of clear vision that had made him a millionaire. Probably. 'I'll bring your dishes back tomorrow,' he said.

Maybe it was the thought of him turning up unannounced on her doorstep, but her hands, a moment ago quite steady, were suddenly incapable of juggling the bowl and the cream and inserting the key into the lock. Not without inviting catastrophe.

Seeing her problem, he took the key from her and unlocked the door before dropping it back into her palm, just the way he had with the earring that morning.

Had it only been that morning?

It seemed light years ago.

'Don't worry about Hector, okay? We'll find him.' And then he held her shoulders lightly and kissed her. On the cheek. A brush of lips, nothing more, and before she could say anything smart, or stupid, he was on the far side of the hall at his own door. He turned, looked back. 'Don't work too late, Ginny. Try and get some sleep.'

Since he was waiting for her to go inside, shut her door, she did just that, leaning back against it and letting out a long, slow breath.

'Get some sleep,' she muttered to herself, rubbing the flat of her palm over her cheek to smooth the down that seemed to be standing on end. Her fingers lingering on the place where his lips had brushed her skin. 'Oh, that'll be easy...'

Forget orange juice and scrambled eggs. That man just tapped straight into the National Grid every morning and powered up. That could be the only possible explanation why he only had to touch her for every cell in her body to light up and fizzle like an overloaded power line.

Rich leaned back against the door. Groaned. What on earth was the matter with him? His body was throbbing. Hard and aching. But not just for sex. If he'd just wanted sex he'd have been in bed with Lilianne right now. She couldn't have made it plainer that the 'chase' was over. She'd been hot for it.

It was something of a shock to his libido to be told to lie down, forget it, he wasn't interested. But it was suddenly and blindingly obvious to him that he hadn't been doing anything more than going through the motions for a long time. What had Wendy said about an endless parade of women out of the same mould?

She'd exaggerated. It hadn't been endless. But there had been too many women and not nearly enough relationship.

Ginny Lautour wasn't out of any mould. She was an original.

He'd known it the minute he'd opened his eyes and seen her, one moment covered with blushing confusion, the next as cool and collected as a duchess at a garden party. Known it when he'd looked into her eyes and she'd lost it again...

How many women could invent a hamster—would have the imagination to invent a hamster—and then make him seem so real that he wanted to believe...? Almost did believe...

How many women could attract him with nothing but a ridiculous propensity to blush and the power of her eyes?

Only one.

It was time to stop fooling himself.

He wanted sex, but he wanted a lot more than that. And he wanted it with Ginny Lautour.

He'd had enough of the who-can-pretend-best verbal fencing. With his hands on her ankle, her leg, on the sweetest dimpled knee that it had been a crime to hide beneath jeans or a long skirt; it was her he wanted. And he wanted her now.

He wanted to undress her, taking his time about it, exposing the reality of her body in the slow, sensuous dance of love. He wanted her naked, her pale skin gleaming in candlelight. He wanted to see her blush as he kissed her, touched her. He wanted to see her eyes blazing like emeralds as, with his hands, his mouth, his tongue, he stripped away all her deepest secrets and lay bare the reality of her soul.

He shook his head.

There had been a moment, the stillness between one heartbeat and the next, when he'd thought it would be possible. But something, the smallest movement, a retreat from intimacy, if not the longing for it, had warned him that it would be a mistake.

And when he'd looked into her eyes, no longer a bright pellucid green but a swirling cloudy grey, he'd seen something more.

Her body might have been willing, her head might be urging her to do it—it was the most reliable weapon in the arsenal of the female spy—but her heart would not have been along for the ride. And that told him more about Ginny Lautour that any dossier from a security consultant.

Someone had hurt her. Made her afraid to let go, no matter how loudly her body was clamouring for her to go for it. He didn't care that she'd stolen from him, what the cost in thwarted desire or financial loss, he wanted every part of her. Total meltdown.

He wanted her sure and certain of her power. Demanding, assertive, taking what she needed, living up to the hidden fire he'd glimpsed in her eyes.

Deep inside him, deeper than he'd ever gone, he

knew that if he could take away the fear and give her the courage to let go, to leap off the edge rather than fall or be pushed, then he wouldn't have to ask for anything in return. She'd give him everything he'd ever wanted.

And he was way beyond the name of a software pirate.

At that moment he wanted Ginny Lautour with a bone deep need, with a hunger that had stirred not just his body but his soul. It was a feeling so new, so unexpected, so disturbing, that he knew he should be thankful that she hadn't fallen for his tricky little ruse to get inside her apartment. Grateful that she'd sent him packing, given him a chance to get his head straight and his body under control.

Grateful, hell.

She was already so deep inside him that he doubted he would ever be rid of her. He wouldn't be human if he didn't want her in his bed. Now. This minute.

What he was going to get was a long cold shower and another night alone with his computer. And Wendy was right; it was no substitute.

CHAPTER SEVEN

GINNY had told Richard Mallory that she was going
to work and she'd meant it. She wasn't the kind of
girl who swooned when a man looked at her as if he
wanted to undress her slowly, and then do unimaginable things to her...

She pressed the cold glass bowl to her cheeks.

Not her. No way. Not that she'd had much experience of men doing anything of the kind. And what she
did have served only to warn her against being foolish
enough to fall for it ever again.

Not that he'd sell the story to the tabloids. At least
they had that in common. Too much publicity, too
little truth.

Even so, it took a minute to insert a little meta-
phorical steel into backbone before she managed to
lever herself away from the door, dump the strawberries and cream in the fridge well out of the way of
temptation, and head for the safe harbour of her desk.

Work was the answer. It always had been.

Once she immersed herself in Homer she would forget all about his long fingers caressing her legs. No
problem. She could do it. Piece of cake.

She booted up the laptop. Called up the file she'd
been working on. It would anchor her mind, stop it
from wandering off on little side trips of its own, day-
dreaming about the totally delicious way Richard's

dark hair curled around his ears, for instance. Or that little crease that appeared at the corner of his mouth just before he smiled...

And she refused to indulge herself in those little tingle-in-the-pit-of-the-stomach moments that happened whenever she looked at him. Whenever he looked at her. Whenever she thought about him...

'Stop that!'

Talking to herself wasn't good either....

She took a deep breath and began to read the notes she'd made the day before so that she could put them into some kind of order. Order was good.

Okay. She began to read.

Her eyes moved across the words. Individually they were good words. Probably. Collectively they weren't actually making it past the disturbing sensory stimulus that still lingered, despite all her best efforts to banish them from her thoughts.

Nipples tingling as they brushed against her shirt. The disturbing ache low in her abdomen. Her mouth full and soft...

When she'd read the same paragraph three times and still had no idea of what it said, when her notes disappeared and the screen-saver began to dance across the screen, the words 'piece of cake' seemed to beat out a mocking rhythm to her heartbeat.

Furious with herself, she went into her bathroom and splashed cold water on her face. Then her neck. At which point she understood why people took cold showers...

She was not going to take a cold shower. What she was going to do was make a cup of tea. Herb tea.

Raspberry and echinacea, which according to the label helped with alertness.

Staring at the pretty pink tea, she was confronted with the fact that she was already alert. Very, very alert. Positively zinging with alertness in places that were doing absolutely nothing to help her concentration on mythic Greek heroes. The only man she was concentrating on was not a myth, nor was he Greek. And he certainly wasn't a hero.

Okay. Change of strategy. She'd call Sophie, who could—when she put her mind to it—distract for Britain. Her ditzy friend could also confirm that the document had arrived safely, that her job was saved. Then she could put Richard Mallory, computer disks and hamsters right out of her mind.

There was no answer. Of course there wasn't. It was Friday night and Sophie would be out partying as always. For once in her life Ginny wished she'd gone with her.

She left her a message, asking her to check her email and call her in the morning.

Then she poured away the herb tea, which did not taste anywhere near as good as it looked and smelled, and decided what she really needed was not a cold shower, but a warm bath—this time with a few drops of lavender oil to counteract the stresses of the day. That would deal—once and for all—with any lingering alertness.

The warm, sweet-scented cocoon of water did its job. Lying back in the big tub she felt totally relaxed, almost weightless. The gentle pressure of water against her breasts, her abdomen, thighs, eased away

the tension until her entire body felt soft and blissfully
yielding. Then she closed her eyes and let her mind
drift. And it wandered right back to Richard Mallory
and the way his hands had stroked the life back into
her leg. Only this time he didn't stop at her leg...

She leapt out of the bath, mindless of the water
pouring off her body and on to the floor. Enough.

She did not desire Richard Mallory.

Any more than he desired her.

Beyond the fact that she was female and therefore
a target for masculine vanity. The extra I-am-
irresistible gene that men seemed to get packaged with
the Y chromosome. Along with an innate urge to
prove it to the world.

That he could have, almost certainly would have,
sweet-talked her into his bed she did not doubt. He
was, physically, a man with enormous personal appeal.
He was also a man of infinite experience and her almost instant response to him—almost!—left her in no
doubt that if he'd turned up the sexual volume he
could have drowned out all her rational arguments.
Her own traitorous body, with its built-in programming to reproduce—programming that even her
mother had been unable to resist—would have been
his biggest ally.

But it would have meant nothing to him. Less than
nothing.

If, a week later, he remembered her at all it would
be because she was a bit odd. The flaky girl with the
hamster. Not much to look at but, what the heck, he
hadn't been doing anything else that evening...

Bastard.

She pulled on a pair of washed soft baggy cotton pyjamas, shook loose her hair, brushing it until her scalp tingled, stimulating the blood supply, getting the oxygen circulating around her brain.

Then she gathered up all her clothes and dumped them in the wash basket, methodically going through the pockets.

In the purple shirt she found a shrivelled up piece of hedge. And the earring. Her hand closed over it and she smiled. Wrong. He could have been doing something else.

She put the earring in a safe place and then she went back to work. The Hero: Myth or Reality.

And suddenly she wasn't so sure.

Rich had two things clamouring for his urgent attention.

The report from the security people who were running a check on Ginny stacked up on the in-tray of his fax machine.

And the need to check the mail waiting icon on his computer.

Of the two, the mail waiting was the most important. And the one he least wanted to look at. If the disk she'd taken had been accessed without an authorisation code it would prompt a scan on the computer running the program and then, using the latest wireless technology it would, like ET, 'phone home' and download the results into his laptop.

It would deliver a list of the documents on the rogue computer. All the names in its address book. He would know who she'd emailed and when. More importantly, he would also know to whom she had copied his disk.

She'd had the time, while he was shopping for her lemon, to send it to half the world.

And suddenly he didn't need a cold shower.

Ginny Lautour was not some innocent young woman, he reminded himself. She was the enemy. No, not 'the' enemy. *His* enemy. She was intent on stealing from him, laughing at him with those dangerous green eyes while she was doing it. Bewitching him with those dangerous green eyes.

His mind hadn't been his own since he'd switched on the light this morning and caught her—like a rabbit momentarily frozen in the headlights of a car—guilt written all over her face.

The speed with which she'd recovered herself should have been enough to warn him that she was no innocent. That the blushing confusion was all an act.

The only thing about her that hadn't been fake was that moment when she'd backed away from intimacy. Or was he fooling himself again? She already had everything she wanted; she didn't need to do the whole Mata Hari bit.

Except that if she'd been that good an actress she wouldn't need to steal software to finance her studies. She wouldn't need to do that anyway. Judith Lautour might be a single mother but she was hardly poverty-stricken. She was never off the television or out of the best-seller charts.

He made a pot of strong coffee and carried a mug, black and sweet, through to his study where he checked his laptop for the telltale email.

Nothing.

He sat down. Double-checked. There was no problem with his connection. Mail had been dropping into his inbox all evening—some of it from his Chief Software Engineer, marked urgent. But there was no download from his doctored software, nothing to suggest unauthorised access to his secrets.

He ignored the mail from Marcus—it was Friday evening, for heaven's sake, and there was nothing so urgent that it couldn't wait until Monday morning—took a mouthful of coffee and considered the options.

Maybe she hadn't used the internet to pass it on. She'd been out somewhere. Not far, though. There hadn't been time. Could she have met someone outside? Or used the regular mail? There was a post box on the corner...

He picked up the internal phone and called the porter. 'Mike, have you seen Ginny Lautour go out this evening? The girl who's flat-sitting for the McBrides?'

'I haven't seen her since I came on duty at six. Is there a problem upstairs?'

'No, nothing for you to worry about.' He picked up the sheaf of papers from the fax machine and began to flick through them. 'It's just that she was looking for something earlier. I thought she was at home but she isn't answering.'

'If it's urgent I'd normally suggest trying Sophie Harrington's apartment. They're good friends—'

'Really?'

She had a friend who lived in the building?

'Well, yes, they are a bit of an unlikely pair, but

they were at school together according to Miss Harrington.'

'What number is her apartment?'

'Seventy—'

Next door to Cal and Philly McBride? Ginny had said she knew Philly slightly.

'But Miss Harrington hasn't come in yet. Do you want me to ring through to Miss Lautour?'

'No. Don't disturb her. She's probably working. It'll do tomorrow.'

Harrington? He replaced the receiver, trying to recall why the name was familiar. He was sure he'd seen it recently. Then he shrugged. It would be listed in the entrance lobby. He'd have seen it dozens of times...

Then he stopped thinking at all as he saw the newspaper article that had been attached to the report. She wasn't hiding behind spectacles but looking up into the camera and laughing. Relaxed, happy, in love and full of the joy of life. Eighteen, nineteen...

The headline read An Experiment That Failed...

There was a brief rehash of the circumstances of her birth, the endless speculation at the time about who her father might be, every crazy thing her mother had ever done. But then it got down to explaining how Judith Lautour's much vaunted experiment in genetic manipulation had been a total failure. That, far from being a superwoman, her daughter was just another undergraduate going through the university mill. According to her current boyfriend, the one who'd obviously supplied the photographs, she was more interested in going to parties, getting drunk and making up for lost time now she was allowed to mix with the opposite sex than working for her degree...

That it wasn't true, any of it, was clear from the very thorough job the security agency had done.

She'd only had one boyfriend as an undergraduate. One had probably been enough. Rich was pleased to note that he hadn't made it to the second year, despite his early promise. Someone had cared enough to make sure he'd paid for his betrayal and his lies.

But then the newspaper wasn't interested in the truth, only in giving Judith Lautour a sandbagging; it didn't matter who got hurt in the process.

And he had thought he knew what it was to be done over by a diary columnist with nothing to fill his page.

He continued to read. No father. Well, he already knew that. A mother who gave her all to her causes and who'd switched her daughter from day school pupil to boarder at her expensive public school when she herself had taken to camping out with her fellow protesters.

She hadn't been well served by those who should have loved her, he thought, and he called the agency, widened the area of enquiry, stressing the urgency, before giving up on the coffee and pouring himself a glass of Scotch.

He crossed to the open French windows and looked out over the lights of the city, attempting to make sense of what he'd learned. There was, apparently, no man in her life. She was quiet, studious, hard-working. No one had a bad word to say about her.

So what the devil was she doing searching his apartment?

He wandered outside and breathed in the scent of...lavender.

*   *   *

Ginny tried a few breathing exercises to focus her mind and block out the distracting presence of Richard Mallory a few yards away from her on the other side of the wall.

Work. That had always been the answer. It would answer now…

She stared at the screen, typed a few words, deleted them, started again. After ten minutes she stopped. Okay. It was going to take more than breathing exercises.

She picked up the latest Lyndsey Davis novel. A treat she'd been saving as a reward for work well done. If she could lose herself in that…

She couldn't.

Realising that she was in deep trouble, she flicked on the television and found that instead of the film she saw only a pair of blue eyes, creased in laughter. Blue eyes, still and watchful. Blue eyes heating up as he'd taken off her spectacles and then, slowly and deliberately, kissed her.

She leapt to her feet, prowling the apartment. This was ridiculous. How dare this man invade her head and, ignoring the 'no trespassing' sign, evade all efforts to evict him, set up camp and make himself at home?

No. That wasn't right.

This wasn't his fault. Nothing that had happened today was his fault. She couldn't even blame Sophie. If she'd said no, absolutely not, no way, that would have been that. But Sophie was her friend and knew she could count on her when she was in trouble.

Except this time it wasn't only Sophie who was in trouble.

She'd been asking for it from the moment she'd stepped over Rich Mallory's threshold. From the moment she'd been caught and hadn't immediately owned up, confessed, told the truth instead of coming out with that nonsense about a missing hamster.

She was in the wrong and she deserved everything she'd got...

And boy, had she got it.

She ran her fingers across the keyboard of her laptop. But it was hopeless to even think of work and she pulled off her spectacles and tossed them on to her desk, pinching the bridge of her nose between finger and thumb.

Sleep would be an equally hopeless endeavour and unfortunately it was way too late to put on a pair of jogging pants, go out into the streets and run the man out of her thoughts. Instead, she flung back the French windows to let in fresh air and stood looking out at the lights of the city spread before her, but the sounds coming off the river—music, people having fun—just made her even more restless.

Warm milk? Would that dull the senses?

She opened the fridge door but, confronted by the bowl of strawberries, ripe, red, luscious, her senses revolted. They didn't want to be dulled down, they wanted excitement...

She tore open the carton and, taking a strawberry, she dipped it into the thick yellow cream. Then bit into it.

Not exciting enough, but good. Very good.

She nestled the cream carton in the centre of the strawberries and wandered barefoot out into the gar-

den. She didn't have a Japanese pavilion like her dis-
quieting neighbour, nowhere to sit cross-legged and
meditate, quietly recover her equilibrium.

Tough. Her equilibrium had been having everything
its own way for far too long.

She padded across to an elegant white painted love-
seat, sat down, put up her feet and stretched out her
legs.

If she was going to be disturbed, she decided, might
as well be *thoroughly* disturbed and enjoy the experience.

She picked up a huge strawberry by the hull, dipped
it into the carton of cream, then, tilting her head back,
she lowered it to her mouth, biting it off at the stem.
Cream and juice dribbled out of the corner of her
mouth and she laughed, catching it with the tip of her
tongue.

From beyond the hedge she heard a faint sound.

More than a sigh, less than a groan.

Richard Mallory. All the danger, excitement a girl
could ever want…

Heart hammering, she lifted her head, sucking her
fingers clean, using the time to gather self-possession
about her like a blanket before she turned to look at
him.

It was a waste of time.

Nothing could prepare her for the sight of his dark
figure backlit by the soft light spilling out of the open
windows. His face was all shadows that were only
deepened, intensified by the pale glimmer of cheek-
bone, the hard edge of his jaw, the halo effect around
his dark curls.

Then he lifted his hand and the light caught the
heavy cut-glass tumbler as he lifted it to his lips.

In her head she tasted the Scotch on his lips and her body dissolved at the thought.

'Want to share?'

Had he said that or had she? Or were the words locked in her head where only she could hear them?

There was a long moment when he didn't move. When she couldn't decide whether she was supposed to answer him or whether she was waiting for him to answer her.

Then he moved slowly towards her, pushing his way through the box hedge. Somewhere in her throat a protest formed—she was supposed to be taking care of the McBrides' apartment, not wrecking it—and then died. The hedge would grow back. It was what hedges did…

Rich said nothing, just placed his glass into her hand before lifting her feet to make room for himself on the bench. Once beside her he dropped her legs across his lap. He had the thighs of an athlete, firm and strong, the denim slightly rough beneath her ankles. His hands were cool against her instep as he absently stroked her feet, regarding her with a level penetrating gaze that offered no clues to his thoughts.

If they echoed her own she was going to get all the excitement she could handle.

His eyes never leaving hers, he reached out and helped himself to a strawberry from the bowl on her lap, dipped it in the cream, once, twice, before carrying it to his lips. For a moment he held it there and she watched the cream move slowly over the green frill of the hull and spill on to his thumb. Then he bit into it. Ginny, who'd been holding her breath, let out a little squeak, then buried her face in the glass and took a mouthful of Scotch.

It was a mistake.

For a moment she thought she'd choke as air and spirit hit the back of her throat simultaneously, but somehow her epiglottis managed to sort out what went where. The air filled her lungs and the Scotch found and warmed her stomach before spreading out through the rest of her body like wildfire.

'That's a fine single malt,' Rich said after watching her silent efforts not to splutter and cough. 'You're supposed to sip it, savour it. Slowly.'

Her throat was still trying to disentangle her vocal cords and she didn't even attempt to reply.

It was okay. He hadn't finished.

'I should be cross with you.'

'I'll sip in future,' she said quickly. Then, apparently driven by some centuries deep feminine need to disturb this man in the same way he profoundly disturbed her, she slowly drew her fingers across her left breast in a large cross. 'I promise.'

There was something deeply satisfying about the fact that he too seemed to be having some difficulty with the simple mechanics of breathing. She wanted him breathless. She wanted him lost for words, unable to reason, at her feet, an open book that she alone could read.

She was, quite clearly, losing her mind.

He eventually managed a slightly hoarse, 'I'm delighted to hear it.' His face, though, betrayed nothing of his thoughts. 'But I wasn't referring to the whisky. I was referring to the fact that you lied to me.'

Oh…*Hector!*

He'd found out what she was up to. Forget excitement. Forget Rich Mallory at her feet. What she was about to get was trouble. With a capital T. In fact, she was up to her neck in the deepest dunghill—

'You told me you had to rush off to catch up on important work—'

What?

'And yet here you are, sitting in the moonlight, indulging yourself in nothing more taxing than eating strawberries.'

He was talking about supper? About the fact that she'd rushed of, scared out of her wits by her own burgeoning desires?

'I meant to work,' she said quickly. Any belief that she was off the hook was mitigated by his stillness, by the soft, slightly ragged quality of his voice. She suspected that, if anything, she was in deeper trouble.

This was simply picking up the scene where they'd left off. As if there had been no interruption. The air was as loaded with expectation, the connection between them as intense as that moment when he had looked up, his eyes asking a question to which she had had no answer. Except run.

She hadn't run far enough.

'I tried to work,' she said. 'Honestly.' Then, 'I was seduced away from Ancient Greece by a sinfully delicious bowl of strawberries and cream.'

'Now that I know what it takes I'll put in a regular order. But you still misunderstand me. I have no problem with the indulgence.' He picked up another strawberry by the frilly green hull, dipped it into the cream. 'My only objection is that you are alone.'

And he it offered it up to her lips.

It was an age-old gesture and Ginny recognised it for what it was, understood that to accept the fruit from his hand bore a deeper, more primal significance.

Every inherited female instinct warned her that, in taking the food the hunter had brought her, she was accepting the hunter. It was ancient and primitive and had no place in the equal opportunities twenty-first century.

But in the soft light of a gibbous moon it cried out to everything that was female within her, kindling elemental needs, yearnings; bypassing all the barriers she had so carefully erected against hurt. It stirred her damped down sensuality and sent it licking hotly along her limbs, seeping through her body and into her soul, blotting out all memory of hurt or pain.

Filled with a desire she scarcely understood but recognised as something unexpected, something powerful, a force that if she were bold enough she could take and use for herself, rather than something fearful to be held in check, she leaned into him and, taking hold of his wrist, her eyes never leaving his, she bit into the strawberry.

The explosion of taste, texture, pure pleasure filled her mouth. The animal warmth of his skin, the pure male scent of him overriding the sweetness of the fruit, the ragged sound of his breathing, reached out and grabbed her remaining senses and shook them into shocking Technicolor awareness.

And this time the soft, low sound that wasn't quite a moan, but was definitely more than a sigh, came from her.

She was suddenly hungry, starving, ravenous for life and, guided purely by instinct, she bent her head and licked up the trickle of juice and cream that was running down his thumb.

He dropped the half-eaten fruit and, his hand open, he reached out and cradled her cheek in the palm of his hand, his thumb brushing against her temple. For a moment neither of them moved, spoke.

Below them in the darkness the city rumbled and roared and went, unheeding, about its business. Ten storeys above the river the only sound was that of her heart beating, the only light came from the heat in Rich Mallory's eyes.

His fingers slid through her hair, tangled in it, wrapping it over his fist until he had her his willing prisoner. Then he lowered his mouth to hers. She expected a fierce and hungry passion. Anticipated it. Craved it.

He touched the corner of her lips in a butterfly light kiss. Gentle, sweet, yet her intense awareness of him magnified his touch a thousand times. Every inch of her skin flushed with pleasure, felt as if it were reaching out to be caressed, wantonly inviting the most intimate of kisses.

It was shocking, thrilling, a sensory experience beyond anything she had experienced, could ever have dreamed of.

Then he licked along her lower lip, his tongue dipping into her mouth to taste her, taste the sweet fruit she'd eaten, and in return she confronted the reality of that bone-melting moment of her imagination as she tasted the whisky on his tongue.

CHAPTER EIGHT

RICH was losing it.

He was losing it in the scent of warm skin, silky hair that owed nothing to artifice, a womanly body naked beneath the thin cotton of her pyjamas.

His mouth moved over the yielding sweetness of Ginny's lips, and the detached part of his mind—the part that never quite switched off from whatever project he was working on—couldn't compete with the overload of sensations and it shut down.

Losing it...

Who was he kidding? He'd lost it—lost himself—the moment he'd set eyes on her stretched out on the garden seat, a ripe strawberry poised above her lips. It had been a private moment of pure indulgence and her unconscious sensuality had left him breathless.

He didn't care who she was, what she wanted from him. He knew only that he desired her, craved her, wanted her in some way that was so different, so unfamiliar, that he was floundering like a boy who'd just discovered that girls were not an entirely bad thing, but hadn't worked out quite what to do about it.

And similarly afraid.

Ginny Lautour was different and this was a step into the unknown. A step from which, once taken, there would be no turning back.

She did not come wrapped up as a glittery parcel,

scented, made-up, dressed by some expensive couturier—a gift to be opened and enjoyed at leisure in a mutual pact where both parties knew exactly what they were getting. He doubted she'd ever been than cynical.

It shocked him just how cynical he'd become...

She was not just another woman, a passing attraction that temporarily snagged the small—very small—part of whatever attention he could spare from work. A little arm candy to keep his company profile high in the media.

Her clothes were awful, her hair was a mess, she wore no make-up and yet she made every other woman he'd ever met seem dull, monochrome, totally forgettable.

Confused, he drew back. What exactly was it about this woman that set his senses alight? Not her hair, surely? He opened his hand, let its silky length slide through his fingers and she nuzzled her head against his palm like a contented cat. He almost thought he could hear her purring.

Not even her clear, translucent skin innocent of anything more seductive than a smear of strawberry-stained cream on her cheek, although that was surely different enough...

He rubbed his thumb over the pink smudge, let it wander over her neck, her throat.

And it couldn't be her body. Her clothes were chosen to conceal rather than tempt. Even now she was wearing what looked like a pair of kid's cotton pyjamas...

Thin cotton pyjamas.

His hand, with a mind of its own, brushed lightly over her breast, his palm grazing a hard, jutting nipple.

That was all she was wearing. There was nothing between them but a few buttons and a cast iron certainty that he had not intended to go beyond a teasing kiss.

He wanted her to trust him. He wanted her to know that he would never do anything to hurt her.

His fingers, with a life of their own, slipped the first button.

'Ginny...?'

Her name was a question. This was going faster and further than he had ever intended and he needed to see her eyes, to know what she was feeling, what she wanted. He wanted all of her, not just her body, but something more that would be just for him...

'Look at me.'

Somewhere, a long way away, a telephone began to ring and, with the tiniest of sighs, she obeyed him and opened her eyes. In the moonlight they were liquid, seductively dark. He'd thought his body could not be more aware, more responsive. He had been wrong...

'You were right,' she said.

'Right?'

'Strawberries definitely improve with sharing.'

...more wrong than he could ever have imagined.

'Or maybe it's the Scotch and the kisses that make them taste so good,' she said. She handed him the glass, which dealt with the wandering fingers, then lay back against the arm of the seat, smiling dreamily. 'Do you hear bells?'

He set the glass down at his feet. He didn't need

whisky. He was getting all the stimulus he needed just looking at her.

'Bells?' Yes, he'd heard bells. The whole of the earth was ringing with the sound... 'I'd like to take the credit, Ginny, but I think you'll find that the ringing in your ears is the telephone.'

She looked momentarily startled, then grinned. 'I knew that.'

'Sure you did,' he said, and felt like grinning himself. Ear to ear like a big kid. 'Do you want to go and see who it is?'

'I'd rather sit here, sharing strawberries and looking at the moon.'

It was a good plan, except that if they stayed there the strawberries were not going to be playing much part in the proceedings... As for the moon, all he had to do was look into her eyes.

Deep, dark with hidden depths, he'd been going down for the third time with no possibility of ever coming up again when he'd been saved by the bell. Not that she seemed in any great hurry to see who was calling.

He understood that.

He didn't want to go anywhere, either. It took an enormous effort of will to remind himself that this was not something to be rushed, lift her legs from his lap and get to his feet, trusting in the dark to hide just how stimulated he was.

'The moon isn't going anywhere.'

Cool air rushed into the empty spaces where Richard's body, his hand, his mouth, had moments earlier been stoking up her personal central heating system, warming her from the inside out. And Ginny shivered.

'Clearly you have a very poor grasp of astronomy,' she said. 'The moon, let me tell you—' about to confound him with astrophysics, she discovered that she was fairly shaky on what, exactly, the moon did '—isn't about to stay put for our convenience.'

'Neither is whoever's calling you.'

No. She willed the telephone to stop, but it continued to ring and ring and he offered her his hand to help her up.

'It's probably your mother hoping for some of your excellent lasagne,' he reminded her. 'And a bed for the night.'

Damn. She'd forgotten she'd told him that. How like her mother it would be to turn up on the one occasion she wasn't wanted. Especially when the alternative had been so much more enticing. But, wherever the evening had been going, the journey had been interrupted for the second time.

Once by her out of fear. Fear of being hurt, of making a fool of herself, being made a fool of…

And now by him. She couldn't begin to guess why, except that it must have been a conscious decision. Maybe she was misjudging him, but she didn't believe he was the kind of man to put anything important on hold simply to answer the telephone.

Clearly she wasn't that important.

It was probably just as well. Losing her head over a man who wouldn't remember her name a week from now wasn't smart.

And she had always been smart.

Mostly.

She needed no help to get up but she took his hand anyway, just for the pleasure of touching him one more time. For the life affirming warmth of his fingers as they gripped hers before pulling her to her feet. And she wouldn't have been human if she hadn't been hoping for a repeat of what had happened in his dressing room.

He did seem to take every opportunity that offered itself, the slightest excuse, to kiss her.

The phone stopped ringing but he didn't pull her into his arms. It seemed a pity when she was getting to enjoy it so much. If she were bolder, she could kiss him…

He took a step backwards before the thought could take hold, almost, she thought, as if he wanted to avoid any possibility of a close encounter with the front of her pyjamas. And there was the expensive crunch of Waterford glass being crushed beneath his feet.

He glanced down, not at the glass but at her feet, and before she could blink he bent and caught her behind the knees, scooping her up into his arms. With one hand she clutched at the bowl. With the other she made a grab for his shirt collar as he carried her inside, her fingers curled against his collarbone, her cheek against the straining sinews of his neck.

He held her for longer than seemed strictly necessary considering the thickness of the carpet, the total lack of glass, the sheer effort involved—she was not one of those stick insect girls he favoured.

Not that she was complaining.

And the thought crossed her mind that he wasn't

going to put her down, that having swept her off her feet, literally, he was going to carry her straight through to her bedroom. That he was going to finish what he'd started with her buttons, continue his raid on her senses, make love to her with the kind of passion that would sweep away any thought of protest, absolving her of the responsibility of making the decision...

Then he let go of her legs, held her steady as she slid down his chest, his washboard flat stomach, his thighs.

And confronted the reason why he'd stepped back, put some distance between them...

He grinned and said, 'Strawberries always do that to me.'

'Ditto,' she managed through a throat apparently stuffed with cobwebs. 'At least, I didn't mean *that* exactly...'

Not that at all, but an opposite and answering need. A hollow ache that was as natural as breathing and ensured the perpetuation of the human race...

The grin faded, his blue eyes darkened and for a moment anything might have happened. Even as she longed for it to happen, willed it to happen, he took a long shuddering breath that shivered through her and said, 'Promise me that you won't wander out there in your bare feet again.'

It occurred to her that unless she promised he was going to keep her locked in the circle of his arms. For a moment she considered testing the idea.

'I'll clear up the glass—' he said, taking her answer

as read and releasing her '—but you know how it is. One piece always gets missed.'

'Always,' she agreed. Then, because she couldn't think of another thing to say, she offered up the strawberries and said, 'Do you want to take these home with you?'

'I thought we'd already decided they were for sharing.' Then, releasing her, he glanced at the phone. 'Why don't you try 1471 to see who called?'

She stirred. 'If it was my mother she'll assume she got the number wrong and ring again in a minute or two.'

'And if it wasn't your mother?'

'A double-glazing salesman having a hard night?' she offered.

Or Sophie, returning her call. And, feeling suddenly horribly guilty, she shivered.

'You're cold.'

About to say that it wasn't the temperature that was the problem, she thought better of it. 'I'm fine, really.' But that was a lie. She wasn't fine. She was fairly sure she wouldn't be fine for a very long time.

'Pity about the Scotch,' he said.

No, the pity was that he didn't still have his arms around her, that someone had chosen that moment to telephone, that she was a coward and had cut and run earlier…

Except, of course, it had to be that way. How could she possibly make love with a man to whom she'd lied? And she couldn't possibly tell him the truth, not without talking to Sophie first.

'I'd better go and put these in a couple of dishes,'

she said, backing towards the kitchen. Then, with a shrug, 'The other way is a bit messy for Lady McBride's sofa.'

It would, however, be absolutely perfect in bed…

She turned and fled to the kitchen, found a couple of bowls and shared out the remainder of the straw-berries and cream between them with trembling hands, reminding herself that she didn't have thoughts like that.

At least she hadn't.

She couldn't believe how boring her life had been until she'd met Richard Mallory.

And it got more exciting by the minute. When she returned, Rich was looking at the screen of her laptop.

This time the shiver was something quite different. It wasn't borne out of excitement, or anticipation, or an edgy fear of risk. It was a response to the queasy apprehension of discovery.

She'd left it on and all he had needed to do was touch the mouse for it to come out of sleep mode. How long had she been in the kitchen? Long enough for him to find the email she'd sent to Sophie with his document attached?

'You weren't fooling, you really did try to work,' he said.

She swallowed, glanced at the screen. He was look-ing at her notes. 'Oh, yes.'

'Fascinating stuff.'

That was it? No outraged accusation?

Of course not. There was no way he could know what she'd done without checking her server and he hadn't had time for that—had he? How long had she been wool-gathering in the kitchen? No. It was okay. He'd be demanding explanations, retribution, the long arm of the law...

And he wasn't doing any of those things. Why would he look, anyway? There was no reason for the judder of nerves that made the bowls rattle against the low table as she put them down. Only a bad conscience.

She realised he was waiting for some response.

'Not that fascinating,' she said. 'I couldn't seem to, um, concentrate.'

'No,' he said. 'Concentration eluded me, too.' He glanced at her. 'I wonder why?'

Now, Ginny told herself. Get it over with. Own up and tell him...

'It's been a difficult day,' she said. That, at least, was the truth. As much of it as she could part with while Sophie was depending on her, anyway, she told herself as she back-pedalled away from the chasm of mendacity yawning at her feet.

She might be short of experience on this kind of thing, but she knew that deception was a bad start to any kind of relationship. And a bad end, too.

But the truth wasn't hers to tell.

In an attempt to change the subject, she opened the McBrides' well-stocked drinks cabinet. 'Would you like another drink?' she asked brightly.

Madness. She should be feigning tiredness, her heavy workload, anything that would persuade him to take his disturbing presence back to his own apartment. And this time she would shut the French windows. Lock them. Never open them again...

The fact that she didn't want him to go, ever, was an awfully good reason to make sure they never met again.

He was a danger to her peace of mind. Had been from the moment she had first set eyes on him. The phrase 'lust at first sight' hovered just out of sight, on the edge of reason…

Richard turned from the laptop and looked at her. 'House-sitter's perks?' he said, but with a smile that sent the lust factor up a couple of notches.

Never had 'peace of mind' looked so unattractive.

'I'll replace it,' she said.

'No, I will. But only if you'll join me.'

'Then I'll never get any work done tonight.'

'No.' The silence could have lasted no more than a heartbeat. It felt like for ever. 'Tell me that you really want to work and I'll leave you to it.'

There was only one possible answer to that. She knew it and she was certain that he did, too.

'I really want to work, Richard.'

He crossed to her, took her hand. 'In that case, I'll take a rain check on the drink.' He bent to kiss her gently on the cheek. 'I'll clear up the glass in the morning, when it's light enough to make sure I get it all. Don't work too late.'

And, before she could even think of a reply, he was striding out through the windows. There was a rustle as he took the short cut through the hedge, the dull clunk as he shut his French windows and then nothing.

She stood there for a moment, scarcely able to believe that he'd taken her at her word. Men weren't supposed to do that! They were supposed to tease a little, use their powers of persuasion to get a girl to change her mind. Weren't they?

How come she'd got so lucky?

Was he really not interested?

Once, twice even, he might have kissed her out of curiosity, or because the opportunity presented itself, or because…well, just because. Three times suggested something more.

It wasn't as if she'd fallen into his lap this time. She'd been on the other side of the hedge and he'd made all the moves. Her hand strayed to the button he had undone. She would never forget the way he'd been looking at her when she'd opened her eyes…

Never forget the moment she'd been sure that he was as interested as a man could get.

Yet he'd walked away because she'd told him that was what she wanted.

Could it be that simple? That he was actually a lot nicer than anyone, including Sophie, had given him credit for? Or could it be that he was a really old-fashioned guy who didn't believe in taking things too far on a first date…?

For a minute the idea appeared funny. Then she sat down abruptly, her hands over her mouth.

She'd met him just that morning, for heaven's sake! And there had been no 'date'. Just a series of encounters, none of them arranged. None of them intended or looked for. Quite the opposite.

And all of them ending, or beginning, in exactly the same way. With the kind of intimacy that she avoided at all costs. Except that she hadn't been avoiding it just now. She'd been rushing headlong towards it until he'd made all the right noises and given her the breathing room she clearly needed.

The shattering noise of the telephone made her jump. This time she scrambled to answer it. Anything—even a night of her mother's radical political opinions—would be better than dealing with the uncomfortable realisation that she had been willing, eager, absolutely panting to spend the night with her next-door neighbour on the most minimal acquaintance.

Rich closed his French windows and locked them. Locking himself in rather than the world out. Not quite trusting himself to stay on his side of the hedge. Never had walking away from a woman been quite that difficult.

Or quite so wise.

Except, of course, he wasn't walking away. He'd be there tomorrow, clearing up the broken glass as he'd promised…

And it was quite possible that Ginny might ask him in for breakfast.

He might even say yes. But then he'd have to ask her what she was doing with the draft for Mallory plc's annual company report on her computer. It was hardly a state secret since it had been published a couple of months ago, but even so it was clear evidence that she'd been up to no good the minute he'd left the apartment.

But why had she stolen it? And, even weirder, why had she emailed it to Sophie Harrington? All either of them had to do was phone the PR department and they'd have been sent a copy.

It could hardly have been a mistake…

The program disk couldn't have been more clearly labelled. It would have taken an idiot to overlook it. And Ginny Lautour, whatever else she might be, was no idiot.

He was reserving that role for himself, apparently.

Right now though the light was flashing on his answering machine, reminding him that he, too, had a reputation for putting work before pleasure. At least amongst those who knew him well. Perhaps he should try living up to it.

There were two messages, the first from Marcus, asking him to call back. Remembering the emails he hadn't bothered to open, he hit the fast dial to the computer lab, hoping he wouldn't get an answer.

The phone rang twice and was picked up. 'What the hell are you doing in the office at this time of night?' he demanded.

'You're a fine one to talk, Rich. But thanks to your all night stint, the program is now up and running like a dream so we're just off to the pub to get some grub and a pint by way of celebration. You can join us if you've got nothing more exciting to do.'

'Us?'

'Me and Sophie. She's a hopeless secretary but she makes great coffee.'

From somewhere in the background he heard a yell of anguish.

Sophie?

'Sophie?'

'Sophie Harrington. New girl. Very decorative. Every office should have one. Ouch!'

'So why haven't I met her?'

'Because I've been doing my best to keep her out of your way. I've got the looks but not the money to compete with you. Not that it's made any difference. She's only interested in one thing. Work.'

'Don't go to the pub, Marcus. Bring Miss Harrington here and we'll celebrate in style.'

'Well, actually...'

'It's on her way home. Take a taxi. Now.'

The other call was from his sister, thanking him for the flowers, trying to get him to change his mind about coming down for the weekend. 'Bring a girl,' she said. 'The more the merrier.'

Now there was a temptation. What would his sister make of Ginny? Rather a lot, he thought.

Marcus was right. Sophie Harrington was very decorative. And he was probably right about money, too. Tall, slender, blonde, her hair had been cut by someone who would charge telephone numbers and her clothes had the understated elegance that went with designer labels; she screamed high maintenance and unless he made Marcus a director he wouldn't be able to afford her.

And he was inclined to agree with the porter. She didn't look as if she'd have a thing in common with Ginny.

'Sophie, do come in.' He blocked the way as Marcus attempted to follow her. 'There's an excellent pizzeria just across the square,' he told him.

'What?'

'Take your time.'

He ignored the well-deserved glare and closed the door, guiding Sophie through to the living room.

'I understand that we're neighbours,' he said. Her eyes widened nervously. 'Please, make yourself comfortable.' She looked anything but comfortable as she folded herself up into one of his armchairs. 'Can I get you a drink?'

'Just water. Please.'

He fetched her a glass, considered reacquainting himself with the single malt but thought better of it, and instead sat opposite her. 'We haven't got long.' If he was Marcus he'd bribe the pizza guy to jump the queue and make it snappy. 'Do you want to do this the hard way or are you just going to tell me what's going on?'

Unlike Ginny she didn't flush. She went white and said, 'Oh, knickers.' He made no comment. 'Look, whatever happened, Ginny isn't to blame, okay?'

'I rather suspected that. Why don't you tell me exactly what she's supposed to have done?'

'Nothing!'

'You're going to have to do better than ''nothing'',' he said. 'If you don't want me to call the police.'

'You wouldn't!' She groaned, put her face in her lap. 'Ginny's going to kill me.'

'I doubt it.' He thought of the way her lower lip had trembled when she had seen him at her computer and had to fight down a smile. 'She didn't strike me as having the killer instinct.'

She looked up. 'You've met her already? She didn't say. When?'

'The way we do this, Sophie, is I ask the questions. You answer them. And I'd really like to have the whole story before Marcus gets back with your supper.' If he attempted to send him out on some other pretext he was likely to get a black eye. 'That way you can take your supper, and a rather fine bottle of wine, downstairs to number seventy and continue your celebration in private.'

Sophie looked at him for a moment and decided to talk.

'I was in Wendy's office the day your sister phoned. Inviting you for the weekend? Her wedding anniversary?'

Rich said nothing.

'Wendy said you wouldn't go. She said that you weren't into happy families.' Then, apparently unnerved by his continued silence, 'She said it, not me…'

Since silence was working so well, he kept it up.

'She said that you only dated women who presented no risk. Women you would never fall in love with because they were all exactly like some girl who'd given you a hard time once.'

Tall, thin, self-obsessed. Only the hair colour changed.

'What else did she say?'

'Look, I don't want to get her into trouble. She was really sad about it, okay?'

'And?'

'And nothing. She said what you really needed was

a good old-fashioned girl next door. Someone a bit, well, less like your average supermodel. And I thought, well, Ginny fits that description.'

'Good. Old-fashioned. And next door.'

'Umm.'

'And by no stretch of the imagination average.'

She swallowed. 'Yes.' Then, 'No.' And then he saw her relax. 'How clever of you to realise that so quickly. And she's had a pretty ropey time of it too, with her crazy mother. I mean, who would ever call their daughter…?'

She stopped.

'Iphegenia?' he offered, filling in the gap.

'She told you.' And Sophie Harrington's face lit up in the sweetest of smiles. 'She told you her ridiculous name.'

'I believe she was attempting to impress me with her, um, probity. Since I'd just caught her going through my drawers. Looking for a key to my desk. So that she could steal a computer disk.'

'No! I mean, there wasn't a disk to steal. I made all that up, for heaven's sake. I mean, come on, you're Mr Security…' Then, 'She didn't manage it, did she?'

'Not without a little pointing in the right direction. I wanted to know what she was up to. Who was behind it all.'

'Guilty as charged, guv. I just wanted her to meet you, talk to you.'

'Wouldn't it have been wiser to wait until we met in the lift?'

'Oh, please! She'd have hidden behind those hideous spectacles she insists on wearing.' Then, with rather more perception, 'And, since she's not some willowy babe, you'd have let her.'

'Probably,' he admitted.

'Definitely,' she replied. 'You have to talk to Ginny... Why didn't she tell me you'd met this morning?' She frowned. 'What happened?'

Good question. What had happened? He'd met a girl with green eyes and hadn't been able to get her out of his mind since.

He answered her question with one of his own. 'Tell me, Sophie, does Ginny have a pet hamster?'

'A hamster?'

Which was answer enough, but he watched her trying to work out what she should say for the best. 'Only the truth will save you.'

'From what?' He raised his eyebrows. 'No,' she said quickly. 'She doesn't have a pet hamster.'

'Thank you.' He got up then. 'How did you persuade her to do it?'

'Once, at school, I had my diary confiscated in class. If the Head had read it I would have been expelled so Ginny volunteered to climb in through the school secretary's window and get it back for me while I was in full view of the entire school on the tennis court. Losing my house singles match.' She lifted her lovely shoulders and said, 'For diary, insert computer disk.'

'And, instead of expulsion, this time she would be saving you from the sack? Is your job that important to you?'

'Oh, please! No job is that important. If I'd really messed up I'd have confessed to Marcus. Not that he'd have trusted me with anything important...' She stopped, aware perhaps that she wasn't doing Marcus any favours. 'Ginny was volunteering almost before she knew it. Telling me how easy it would be, how your cleaning lady always left the French windows open to air the place...' She stopped before she dropped someone else in it. 'Of course, she thought *I'd* do it. I'm afraid I had to lay it on a bit thick. I told her you were a bit of a bastard.' She pulled an embarrassed grin. 'Sorry about that.'

'Don't apologise. You were nearly right. I'm a *total* bastard, which is why, if you value your job, you won't tell Ginny we've had this conversation.'

There was a sharp ring at the doorbell and she got up, put her hands on his shoulders and kissed his cheek. 'I won't tell on you, Rich Mallory. As long as you don't do a thing to hurt my dearest friend, I won't tell a soul that you're really an old softie.'

Which was fine. All he had to do now was to think of some way to get Ginny to tell him what she'd done. Of her own volition.

CHAPTER NINE

GINNY'S mother rattled on about her latest crusade while she made her some supper. It was an easy conversation. All she had to do was drop in the 'Really?' and 'That's shocking' and 'Absolutely' prompts whenever a pause suggested it was necessary, while letting her own thoughts wander where they would.

Apparently she'd been doing it too well. 'I'm glad you're so enthused about this, Ginny. I'm putting together a committee to run this new campaign and I want you on board.'

What?

'I'm a bit busy for committee work, Mother. My thesis—'

'Your thesis won't make a whit of difference to the world. With your genetic inheritance it's time you were out there, moving mountains…' She stopped so suddenly that Ginny's thoughts were jerked clean out of her daydream about the lingering pleasures of strawberries and cream and right back to reality.

'And what exactly is my genetic inheritance?'

'Scholarship, a vision of equality—' she began. Her stock answer.

'I got those from you,' Ginny said. She was no longer prepared to accept her mother's evasions. She needed to know the truth. 'I'd like to know, exactly, what my father brought to the turkey baster.'

169

'Don't be vulgar, Ginny,' she said, looking at her wrist-watch, getting to her feet. 'I'd better get some sleep. I'm catching the early flight to Brussels. I won't wake you.'

But there was a tinge of pink to her cheeks that hadn't been there a moment before. She'd got her fatal blush from her mother, too.

'There wasn't a turkey baster, was there?' she said, standing to block her mother's escape.

For a moment they confronted one another and then Judith Lautour sank back into the chair. 'No, Ginny. You were conceived the old-fashioned way with an excess of passion and too little thought for the consequences. That came later.'

Covered with confusion, Ginny said, 'But why hide it, why pretend…?' And then reality bit. 'Oh, I see. He was married.' Her mother's silence was confirmation enough. 'You made up the experiment story to protect him.'

'No, Ginny, not him. He wasn't that selfish. Far from it… His wife was, is, an invalid. In a wheelchair. He loved us both, but she needed him more.'

And the truth hit her like a sandbag so that she sat down suddenly as if winded. She was winded. 'Sir George Bellingham.' An eminent physicist, his young wife had been mown down by joyriders, lost the baby she was carrying, and had been in a wheelchair ever since. They had both always treated her with special affection. Always been there when her mother had been away on some crusade or other. Sublimating her passion in support of her 'causes'.

He was her father?

Oh, yes. How obvious it was when you knew. And his wife, she realised, with the twenty-twenty vision of hindsight, must have known too.

Her mother pulled a wry smile. 'Actually, it was a great career move for me. There wasn't a lot of mileage in being a radical feminist if you fell in love at first sight back then.'

'At first sight?'

'Eyes across a crowded room, fireworks, a full-scale orchestra in the head, an instant rip your clothes off moment in the first empty room you can find.'

Ginny swallowed. 'Oh.'

'The sex was okay. Totally permissible in what was, after all, the permissive society. But only as a recreational activity. And only once you equipped yourself with every method of birth control known to woman.'

'Right.' Then, because she didn't actually want to think about that too clearly, 'Even my name was chosen to suggest a loathing for the male species, wasn't it?'

'I'm sorry, Ginny.'

Sorry? She looked at her mother. 'I've never heard you say that before. Never heard you apologise for anything you've done.'

'I realised my mistake when the interest didn't die down. Go away. You'll never know how much it hurt me to send you away to school, get you out of sight so that the whole "experimental child" thing would drop. I tried to make you invisible but journalists have long memories and endless patience. These things always come back to haunt you. I should have told you the truth when that hideous piece appeared in the papers. Told everyone. George said it would only make things worse.'

'He would say that.' Then, 'No, I'm sorry, of course he was right. Do you still love him?' Stupid question. Of course she did. 'Do you still...?' She stopped, really didn't want to know the answer to that question.

Her mother answered anyway. 'No. He wanted to be part of your life. Be there for you. He couldn't—not if we were...' She faltered. Swallowed hard. 'I...we couldn't do that to Lucy. She was generous, understanding, so good... She deserved our consideration. It was the least I...we...could give her. I'm sorry, Ginny,' she said again.

She got up, hugged her mother. 'Don't be sorry. I'm glad you had someone, even if it was just for a little while.'

'Ginny? Are you awake?'

She hadn't slept. She'd spent the night going over her childhood, remembering all the times that George had been there. Coming with his wife to open days at school when her mother had been away so that she'd have someone. The gifts they'd bought her. Her first bicycle. A strand of pearls for her eighteenth birthday. Special things.

She'd watched the dark rectangle of the window turn from the dull red-tinged black that was the best the city could offer, to purple, then lilac. Remembering.

She'd always felt like a freak. But now she knew she'd just been well, like everyone else. And it felt wonderful. She turned to her mother with a smile. 'I was just going to get up and make you some coffee.'

'No, I'll get breakfast at the airport.' She dismissed the offer with an impatient gesture, back to her usual brisk self this morning, although she looked dark around the eyes as if she hadn't slept much either. 'I just thought you should know that there's a man outside in the garden.'

Richard.

And suddenly she was wide awake, her whole body tingling with expectation.

'He appears to be doing something with a dustpan and brush.'

'He must be a new man, then,' she said, hiding a smile. Her mother, as a first wave feminist would certainly appreciate that.

'Who is he? And what's he doing out there at six in the morning?'

She let her head fall back on to the pillow, tingling and expectation dissipating in harsh reality as she realised exactly what he was doing. Richard Mallory was clearing up the broken glass at the crack of dawn to avoid an early morning reprise of kiss and run. She could hardly blame him. How many times could you back away from saying, showing what you were feeling before the question stopped being asked?

Maybe she should ask her mother.

'It'll be the gardener,' she said.

'He doesn't look like a gardener.'

She knew what he looked like. The exact colour of his eyes. The way his mouth lifted at one corner just before he smiled. The way his chin…

'This is the city. Gardeners don't chew stalks of grass and wear smocks in London.'

'Don't be facetious, Ginny.'

At six o'clock in the morning? Perish the thought.

'No, Mother. Hadn't you better be going? You don't want to miss your plane.'

'Yes, I'll give you a call as soon as I get back. We'll talk about that committee.'

Ginny groaned as the bedroom door closed behind her and she let her head fall back on the pillow. But it was no use. Richard Mallory was in her garden and she was wide awake, listening for a tap on the window. Hoping for a tap on the window. Fooling herself into believing that he would tap on the window…

Idiot. It wasn't going to happen. If he'd wanted to see her he would have left it until later so that they could have shared breakfast. She'd dumped the strawberries down the waste disposal but she could always go and get some more…

She flung back the covers, pulled on her sweats and a pair of well past their use by date trainers and went out for a run in the nearby park before the traffic fumes began to clog up the air.

That way, if he did knock, she wouldn't be waiting like the pathetic female she was, for the man of her dreams—any girl's dream—to invite himself for breakfast.

Her run was long and punishing and, feeling virtuous, she stopped on the way home for coffee and doughnuts.

She had the bag between her teeth and was juggling precariously with the double *latte* as she fiddled with the zip on her change pocket trying to get at her door key, when she heard the unmistakable sound of a door opening on the other side of the elegant lobby.

No! Not now! It wasn't fair!

She'd lived in this apartment for a whole week without so much as a glimpse of her next-door neighbour. Today, when she looked like a limp rag—a limp, steaming rag—and her hair was clinging damply to puce cheeks, fate chose to play the unkindest trick on her.

She closed her eyes, hoping, praying that he would take the hint that this was Not A Good Moment and go wherever it was he was going without stopping to speak.

Or failing that, because he probably wouldn't be that rude, keep conversation to a brisk, 'Hi!' in passing.

'Can I help?'

No such luck. She opened her eyes and there he was standing beside her, a small cardboard box in his hands. Apparently going nowhere.

Her mouth stuffed with paper bag, the best she could manage was, 'Ungst.'

She assumed he would take the coffee and doughnuts to leave her hands—and mouth—free. She should have known better. He hooked his fingers inside the waistband of her jogging pants and tugged her closer.

A tiny squeal escaped her lips. Shock, surprise, pure pleasure at the feel of his fingers against her bare flesh.

'Cold,' she said when he looked up, straight into her eyes. Well, that was what her brain said. The sound that emerged from around the paper bag sounded more like an anguished yelp.

'On the contrary, I think you'll find that you're hot,' he replied as, without taking his eyes off her face, he hooked out the pocket, unzipped it and extracted the key, then tucked it back out of sight. Taking his time about it.

It wasn't fair. He only had to look at her, touch her, to reduce her to quivering jelly. He, on the other hand, looked utterly cool and collected.

'All that running,' he said. And something about the way he said it suggested that he wasn't talking about the last hour she'd spent pounding the asphalt but something else entirely. And that it was no longer an option.

'My mother saw you clearing up the glass at what seemed like the crack of dawn,' she said crossly, as it occurred to her that there was absolutely no need to continue holding the bag between her teeth and removed it. And, determined to remove the smug grin from his face, added, 'I told her that you were the gardener.'

'I know. She told me that the hedge was a disgrace and that I should get it tidied up.'

She felt her mouth drop open. 'She didn't! She wouldn't…' Of course she had. 'She's absolutely impossible. I hope you told her to get lost.'

'On the contrary, I assured her that I'd get right on to it—' he sketched a salute '—ma'am.' He took the baker's bag and looked into it. 'Just in case you'd rather she didn't know exactly what did happen last night. Which I think deserves a doughnut for restraint under pressure. Apple doughnuts. My favourite. So…healthy.'

'Nothing happened,' she declared, ignoring his teasing.

He glanced up and there was nothing teasing about his expression. 'If that was nothing, Ginny, you must lead a very exciting life.'

Running again. With her mouth, if not with her legs. She'd been running all her life. The only time she'd ever stopped she'd been betrayed. But Richard Mallory wasn't going to take her to bed and then sell the story to the tabloids. And it wasn't because he didn't need the money...

'Actually,' she said, keeping her feet fixed firmly to the floor, 'last night was about as exciting as it's been for me in a very long time.'

'For me too.' She stared at him. 'So, do I get a doughnut?'

'H-help yourself,' she said, then because she couldn't quite take in what she thought he was saying, she turned quickly and headed for the kitchen. He stopped to pick up the box he'd been carrying and then followed her. 'It's a good job I decided on an extra large coffee,' she said, with what she hoped was the most casual manner.

'Me, too...'

Could that possibly mean what she thought it meant? 'Can you find a couple of mugs and share it out while I make myself fit for company?'

'Don't take too long, Ginny.'

She turned back, looked at him, looked at the box he was holding and then up at him again and suddenly the excited butterflies took a nosedive. What was in the box?

'You didn't have to rush to bring my dishes back,' she said. It had to be her dishes...

'I didn't.'

'Oh.'

'The coffee will get cold,' he reminded her.

She was not convinced that he had the temperature of the coffee on his mind and took her time over the shower, washing her hair with the shampoo guaranteed to make her hair shine like silk—well, it worked for the woman in the ad—and blowing it dry while she tried to decide what he did have on his mind.

And what was in that box.

Whatever it was, she intended to be ready for it. With the sexy underwear. Just in case. Then she pulled on a pair of black matador pants that Sophie had talked her into buying and a pale green linen shirt that hung loosely to her hips.

Somehow she knew, just knew, that the next half hour would be a lot more bearable if she was looking her best. She even considered the application of a little make-up, but decided that would be a dead giveaway.

Oh, and the underwear wouldn't be?

She smiled at her reflection. If he'd got as far as the underwear it wouldn't matter.

Richard was sitting at the kitchen table, licking the sugar off his fingers. 'I was just coming to check that you hadn't been—' he looked up and for a moment seemed to forget what he was saying '—washed away.' Then he smiled. 'Come and have one of these before I eat them all.'

'I think I'll just stick with the coffee, thanks.' The

box was sitting on the table with all the menace of an unexploded bomb. 'What is that?'

'It's not a "that" but a "who". Take a look.'

She opened the lid a crack. There was a rustle from inside the box and she gave a little shriek as the bad feeling in the pit of her stomach came up and hit her in the throat. Then it went down again like a high-speed lift.

She'd caught the briefest glimpse of bright, button-black eyes and a flash of buff fur. 'Is that what I think it is?'

'One small and impossibly heroic golden hamster. Like Odysseus, he was lost and wandering. But now he's home in time for a feast.' He broke off a small piece of doughnut and offered it to her. 'Does Hector like doughnuts?'

She swallowed. He knew. He knew she'd been lying and this was his way of showing her. 'It's not Hector,' she said.

'It's not?' He held her pinned in her seat with the force of his eyes. 'What are the chances of two hamsters running loose in my apartment, I wonder?'

Rather than answer, she opened the lid of the box again. The little black eyes gleamed up at her from a nest of straw. Then blinked. Then disappeared.

'Oh… Sugar lumps.' She risked a look at Richard Mallory. 'Where did he come from, Rich?'

'The truth?'

'The truth,' she agreed.

'The local pet shop. And, actually, they were all out of male hamsters so he's a she. Your turn.'

'Yes. My turn. I'm sorry, Richard.' He didn't say a

word. 'I'll tell you the whole story, but first I have to make a phone call.' She made a move to stand up, go through to the living room so that she could call Sophie and warn her that the game was up.

He reached across and put his hand on her arm. 'Don't go.' He extracted a tiny cellphone from his breast pocket and handed it to her. 'No more secrets.'

'No.' Her fingers were shaking as she punched in Sophie's number. It seemed for ever before her sleepy voice answered.

'Sophie, I've got a problem. In fact, we've both got a problem.' Never taking her eyes from Richard's face, she said, 'I think I'm about to be arrested for breaking and entering.'

'What? No... Is Richard Mallory with you?'

'Yes, look, I've made a total—'

'You've done fine. Now, just listen very carefully—'

'Sophie, please, this is important.' She was listening to Sophie but all her attention was on Richard, trying to read his expression. 'Really important—'

'When I hang up I want you to reach across the table, put your hands on either side of his face and then apply your lips to his and kiss him. Thoroughly. Have you got that?'

'What?'

'Trust me, darling. You're the academic, but where men are concerned I'm the expert.'

'Sophie, you don't understand—'

'Yes, I do. Perfectly. Which is why I know you shouldn't be wasting time talking to me.' Then, 'But when you come up for air, I want to hear all about the hamster.'

And, about to ask what she knew about Hector, Ginny realised she was listening to the dialling tone.

There was the briefest pause while she digested her conversation with Sophie and while Richard waited, his face giving her not the slightest clue to his feelings.

'You know, don't you? That I made the whole thing up? That Hector is about as mythical as his namesake.'

'I wanted to hear it from you, Ginny.'

'And you will,' she said, her heart beating so hard against her ribs that he must surely hear it. 'But not right now.'

It was an awfully long way across the kitchen table. Instead of leaning across the table she put the phone down and walked around it until she was standing in front of him.

A few grains of sugar clung enticingly to the corner of his mouth and she reached out, brushed them away with her finger.

A small sound escaped his lips and, reaching out, he caught her about the waist, pulled her on to his knee and kissed her. For a long moment she surrendered to the sweetness of his mouth as it plundered hers, wrapping her arms around his neck, leaving herself open to him, trusting him not to hurt her. After what seemed like for ever, she leaned back a little to look at him and, fighting a smile, said, 'Have you noticed that doughnuts seem to have the same effect on you as strawberries?'

'The only thing in the world that affects me like

that, Ginny, is you,' he said, his voice soft, thick, like velvet tearing.

'Ditto,' she whispered.

'Then there's only one thing left to ask you.'

She waited. She wasn't going anywhere and neither, apparently, was he.

'How do you feel about spending this weekend with me in Gloucestershire? It's my sister's wedding anniversary. My whole family will be there and I want them to meet you.'

'Me?' she asked and, remembering the champagne bottle... 'Won't I be a bit of a letdown? Surely they're expecting someone a little more glamorous?'

'They're not expecting anyone. I don't take women home with me. I'm breaking the habit of a lifetime with you, Ginny. I only intend to do it once. Will you come with me?'

'Later,' she said. 'Ask me again later. We've got some unfinished business right here...'

And after that she didn't need Sophie to tell her what to do. It all just came naturally as she showed him exactly what she wanted. It was a world away from being swept off her feet. This was what her mother had been banging on about for as long as she could remember.

Total equality.

And what she had finally admitted to last night. Total love.

The marriage of a millionaire was always news. That Richard Mallory was marrying a girl whose own curious background had aroused so much interest in the press at the time of her birth made it the kind of story that was a gift to the tabloids. And the newsmen were out in droves when Iphegenia Lautour married Richard Mallory three short months after they met.

Inside the college chapel, however, it was like any other family wedding. Richard's sister, sitting near the front and fidgeting about her two small girls who, as bridesmaids, were in pole position to cause chaos, was brimming with delight that her brother was finally settling down. She clutched her own beloved's hand and said, 'It's wonderful, isn't it? She's so wonderfully… ordinary.'

'Richard doesn't think so.' He grinned. 'But then, as everyone said when I married you, love does tend to be a bit short-sighted…' And got his ankle kicked for his cheek.

Wendy looked smug, as if she'd known exactly how it would happen. She'd even agreed to hamster-sit while the pair of them were away on honeymoon.

Marcus, newly appointed to the board of Mallory plc, and now given total responsibility for new product development was there only because he was best man. As he kept telling Richard, he was much too busy to have any kind of a social life…

Judith Lautour was torn between two absolutes—the absolute certainty that her daughter could have done anything in the world she wanted—and the absolute certainty that she was about to do just that.

'Sophie, please go now or I'm going to be late.'

'You're supposed to be late.' She twitched Ginny's

veil into place. 'He has to actually sweat that you're not going to turn up.'

'He knows that I'd never do that to him.'

'This wasn't meant to happen, you know. You were just supposed to have an affair, a bunch of fun. Everyone knew that Richard Mallory was never going to settle down…'

Ginny grinned. 'Sorry to disappoint you.'

Sophie hugged her. 'I'm not disappointed. I couldn't be happier for you. All I ask in return for this piece of stunning, if unexpected, match-making is to be godmother to your first child.'

'You've got it. Sophie…'

'Goodness, look at the time. I've got to fly—'

'Richard said you'd resigned from your job.'

'Darling, I tried, honestly, but I'm not cut out to be a secretary. I can't type two words in a row without messing up. Marcus needs someone he can rely on. I'm not that person.'

'He fell for you like a ton of bricks.'

'Yes, well, there's that, too. He's sweet, but not someone I could imagine waking up beside even occasionally. Let alone for the rest of my life.'

Ginny didn't press it. 'What are you going to do?'

'Sophie, if you don't go now we'll be there before you.' She turned to where George Bellingham, distinguished in grey morning suit, waited to do his duty as an old family friend and give away the bride.

'I'm gone,' she said and exited in a flurry of rich burgundy silk.

'You look stunning, Ginny,' he said, once they were alone. Then, before she could answer. 'I have something for you. A gift to a bride from her father.' It was the first time he'd said the word and Ginny felt a lump forming in her throat as he opened the box he was carrying and produced a pearl choker set with diamonds. 'It belonged to my mother. Lucy and I want you to have it. She knows, Ginny. She's always known. She loves you as I do.'

'I…um…' She couldn't speak, but waved soundlessly in the direction of her throat, indicating that he should fasten it there.

Richard thought he would die waiting for her, turning at every sound, checking his watch surreptitiously every few seconds and then at some unseen signal the music changed and she was there, walking towards him.

His breath caught in his throat as she lifted her veil, looked up at him, and he saw her eyes shining with something that he knew was there just for him, something that no one else could see, and as she placed her hand in his he raised it to his lips and said, so that only she could hear, 'I love you.'

And she murmured back, 'Ditto.'

THE BILLIONAIRE'S PASSION

by

Robyn Donald

Robyn Donald has always lived in Northland in New Zealand, initially on her father's stud dairy farm at Warkworth, then in the Bay of Islands, an area of great natural beauty, where she lives today with her husband and an ebullient and mostly Labrador dog. She resigned her teaching position when she found she enjoyed writing romances more, and now spends any time not writing in reading, gardening, travelling and writing letters to keep up with her two adult children and her friends.

Don't miss Robyn Donald's exciting new novel, *His Majesty's Mistress,* out in March 2008 from Mills & Boon® Modern™.

CHAPTER ONE

ALLI PIERCE wove another frangipani blossom into the lei. After an appreciative sniff of the perfume from its shameless golden throat, she said, 'I'm completely determined to get to New Zealand, but I won't sell myself for the fare!'

'I know that,' her friend Sisilu said peaceably in the local variation of the language the Polynesians had carried across the immense reaches of the Pacific Ocean. 'Calm down. It was just a comment Fili made.'

'What's the matter with her lately? She's turned into a nasty little witch.'

Sisilu grinned. 'You're so naïve! She's mad with you because she's got a serious crush on Tama, but he's got a serious crush on you. And she still reckons it's unfair that just because you've got a New Zealand passport Barry pays you New Zealand wages and not island ones. After all, you've been living on Valanu since you were a couple of months old.'

Alli anchored a lock of damp red-brown hair away from her hot face with a carved shell comb. 'Actually, I agree with her,' she said honestly. 'It makes me feel guilty, but Barry says it's company policy.'

'He'd know. Have you seen the new owner yet?'

'New owner?' She stared at her friend. 'Sea Winds's new owner? Here?'

Sisilu's dark eyes gleamed with sly amusement. 'Right here in throbbing, downtown Valanu.'

Alli laughed. 'Big deal.' But she sobered immediately. 'No, I haven't seen him—you know Monday's my day off. When did he get here?'

'Last night—arrived out of the blue on a private plane.'

A frown drew Alli's winged brows together. 'I thought Sea Winds was sold to a huge worldwide organisation. The head guy wouldn't come here—too busy being a tycoon. This man is probably just some suit from management. What's he like?'

'Big,' Sisilu told her, with a sensuous intonation that told Alli the new owner was tall, not fat. She sighed with purely feminine appreciation. 'And he's got presence—he's the owner all right. Not that I've seen much of him. He's been shut up with Barry all day, but he did a quick tour of the resort while we were rehearsing this morning.'

Alli's frown deepened. 'If he's the owner,' she said forthrightly, deft hands weaving more flowers into the lei, 'I'll bet that as well as being tall he's middle-aged, paunchy and going bald.'

Sisilu rolled bold dark eyes. 'I should take you up on that—it would be easy money! You couldn't be more wrong. He's got wide shoulders and long, strong legs—not a clumsy bone in his body and a stomach as flat as mine or yours. Flatter, probably.' Sisilu counted off his assets with frank relish. 'Slade Hawkings walks like a chief, looks like a chief, talks like a chief—he's already got the girls buzzing.'

Hawkings? Surprise scuttled on chilly feet down

Alli's spine, but it was a common enough name in the English-speaking world.

Don't go imagining bogeymen, she warned herself. 'If he is the owner—or even an executive with power—he won't be interested in us islanders.' And to banish the cold needle of alarm she added briskly, 'So the girls might as well stop buzzing. Apart from the fact that he probably lives in America or England or Switzerland, men like him go for women who are sophisticated and knowledgeable.'

'If he's a day over twenty-eight I'll eat this lei,' Sisilu said cheerfully. Her tone altered when she said with a sideways look, 'As for that crack about middle-aged men—it just shows what a baby you are; the middle-aged ones are the ones to watch. Which is why you should be keeping an eye on Barry.'

'Barry?' Alli stared at her in astonishment. When her companion nodded, she went on with heavy sarcasm, 'You mean Barry Simcox? The hotel manager who was utterly broken-hearted when his wife ran back to Australia with their little boy because she couldn't stand living in this "godforsaken island in the middle of the Pacific Ocean"? I quote, of course. *That* Barry—who has never even looked sideways at me?'

'*That* very same Barry,' Sisilu said with a toss of her head. 'You might not have seen him looking at you, but others have.'

Alli snorted.

'Well, don't say I didn't warn you.' Her friend went on. 'The new owner would be a much better lover. He looks like a film star, only tougher.' After an elaborate sigh she added, 'And you can tell by looking at him that he knows what he's doing when it comes to making love—he's got that aura, you know?'

'Well, no, I don't know.'

Sisilu eyed a hibiscus flower with a critical frown before discarding it. It fell with a soft plop onto the floor. 'Oh, yes, you do.' She added slyly, 'Tama has it too.'

Tama was the second son of the island chief, and Sisilu's cousin. Alli flushed. 'I wish he hadn't decided he is in love with me.'

'It's because you're not in love with him,' Sisilu said wisely, choosing another bloom. 'And because you're different—you don't want him when every other girl in Valanu would happily take him for a lover. As well, of course, virgins are special in our culture. Don't worry about him; he'll get over it once you leave.'

Both worked in silence for a few minutes before Sisilu ruthlessly dragged the conversation back to the topic foremost in her mind. 'And the new owner does not live in Switzerland or England or America—he lives in New Zealand.'

'So do about four million other people.'

'As for the sort of women he likes—when he saw you walk across the foyer five minutes ago he looked as though he'd been hit in the face with a dead shark. I know *that* look too,' Sisilu finished smugly.

In her driest voice Alli said, 'I'm sure you do—but are you certain it wasn't you he was watching? After all, you're the most beautiful girl in Valanu.'

Sisilu said prosaically, 'He didn't even see me.'

'Wait 'til he does.' Busy fingers pausing, Alli watched her friend thread several more hibiscus flowers into a head lei. Dark as blood, rich as passion, they glowed with silken light. 'Anyway, if he's that gorgeous he's probably gay.'

Sisilu's laugh demolished that idea. 'Far from it. When he looked at you he liked what he saw. He might be interested in helping a countrywoman, especially if you gave him an incentive.'

'Not that sort of incentive, thank you very much,' Alli returned with robust forthrightness, threading in several long pointed leaves to give the effect of a ruff. 'If he wants to help me he can keep the resort going.'

It was the only chance she had to save enough for her fare to New Zealand.

Her friend ignored her. 'Making love with him would not be difficult. He has the kind of sexuality that sets off fires. I wish he'd forget he's the boss and look my way.'

Alli closed her eyes against the shimmer of the sun on the lagoon. Beneath the high-pitched shriek of a gull she could hear the slow, deep roar of the Pacific combers smashing onto the coral reef.

The girls she'd grown up with on Valanu had a forthright, honest appreciation of their sexuality. Once married they'd stay faithful, but until then they enjoyed the pleasures of the flesh without shame.

Alli's father had seen to it that she didn't follow suit.

'Why are you so keen to leave Valanu?' Sisilu asked unexpectedly. 'It's your home.'

Alli shrugged, slender golden fingers still for a second before she picked up another flower from the fragrant heap beside her. Her generous mouth hardened. 'I want to know why my mother left us, and what drove my father to hide himself away here.'

'You know why. He went to school with the chief in Auckland. Naturally, when the tribal corporation wanted someone to run the system, they thought of him.'

Golden-brown eyes sombre, Alli nodded. 'But there are too many questions. Dad wouldn't say a word about any family. I don't even know who my grandparents were.'

Her friend made a clucking noise. To be deprived of family in Polynesia meant much the same as being an outcast. 'Your father was a good man,' she said quickly.

Two years previously, after Ian Pierce's death, Alli had gone through his papers and found the one thing she'd longed to know—the name of her mother. That find had encouraged her to save the money she needed to pay an investigator to find Marian Hawkings. Three months previously the dossier had arrived. Now she was saving desperately to meet the woman who'd borne her, only to abandon her.

She said steadily, 'My mother was an Englishwoman who married Dad in England and came to New Zealand with him. After they divorced she married another man, but she's a widow now, still living in Auckland. I don't want to intrude into her life—I just want to know a few things. Then I'll have some sort of closure.' She concentrated on weaving the final flower into the lei.

Her friend's shoulders lifted. 'But you'll come back, won't you? We are your family now.'

Alli smiled mistily, deft fingers flying as they tied off the lei with long strings of *tii* leaf. 'And I couldn't have a kinder one. It's just that the need to know gnaws at my heart.'

'I understand.' Sisilu grinned. 'Anyway, you'll hate New Zealand. It's big and cold and different—no place for someone who loves Valanu as much as you.'

She looked up as a woman strode towards them. 'Uh-oh, here's trouble,' she said beneath her breath. 'Look at her face!'

Without preamble the trainer of the dance troupe said, 'Alli, you'll be dancing tonight—Fili's sick. And we need to make a good impression because the owner of the hotel is deciding whether to keep Sea Winds open or close it down.'

Both girls stared at her. 'He can't do that,' Alli blurted.

'Of course he can, and from what I'm hearing he'd do it without thinking twice. When it was first built it paid its way, but the war in Sant'Rosa cut off the supply of tourists, and for the past five years it's been losing more and more each year,' the older woman said bluntly.

Alli frowned. 'If things are that bad, why did the new owner buy it?'

'Who knows?' She picked up one of the lei and examined it, then dropped it and turned away. 'Perhaps he was cheated. Although he doesn't look like a man who'd allow that to happen to him. It isn't any of our business, anyway, but make sure you dance well tonight.'

Aware that she was a widow, whose job at the resort paid for the schooling of her three sons, both girls watched her go.

Soberly Alli said, 'If the resort closes it will be a disaster for Valanu.'

Sisilu said with a wry smile, 'So perhaps if the owner likes what he sees when he looks at you it will help all of us if you are nice to him. You might be able to influence him into keeping the hotel open.'

As she dressed for the dancing that night, Alli remembered the hidden worry in her friend's voice. The man who'd caused this fear hadn't eaten in the restaurant, but he'd be there for the floorshow, watching from somewhere in the darkness of the wide terrace. The women getting ready in the staff cloakroom were more silent than usual; already everyone knew that the resort was threatened.

'He's there, so no giggling,' the organiser said sternly as excited yells and applause from the audience indicated that the men's posture dance had reached its climax. She cast an eye over Alli and her face softened. 'You look good—those cream frangipani suit your skin and your red hair.'

That was about the only thing she'd inherited from her mother. Shortly after her father's death Alli had found his wedding certificate, and with it a photograph—her father, looking so proud of himself she almost hadn't recognised him, and a laughing woman. Apart from hair colour, Alli didn't look at all like her mother, but the wedding certificate attached to the photograph implied that this woman had borne her.

And then left her. With the marriage certificate and the photograph had been a legal notification of divorce, and a newspaper clipping about her mother's marriage a couple of years later to another man.

The staccato rhythm of the drums settled into a sultry beat, and she and the other dancers took their places in the line. Alli adjusted the uncomfortable bra and began singing an old island love song. The dancers filed out from behind the woven screen that shielded the door from the audience, voices blending in harmony, mobile hands eloquently conveying the story.

From the darkness behind the diners, Slade watched them with a critical eye; amateurs they might be, but they were good. Unfortunately the hokey bras made of half-coconuts detracted from the effect. If he decided to keep the place open they'd go.

Not that the audience cared. His mouth curved in a cynical smile as he surveyed the enthusiastic group of diners.

Give them erotically charged lyrics and lithe bodies polished by the light of flares, dark eyes that beckoned from beneath garlands of perfumed flowers, white teeth flashing in come-hither smiles, and they were more than happy.

He examined the dancers again, realising with sardonic derision that his gaze kept drifting back to Alli Pierce. His chief troubleshooter had come back with photographs of her, but none had done her justice. In them she'd looked young and enthusiastic, whereas in the flesh the overwhelming impression was of glowing, sensuous freshness emphasised by tilted lion-coloured eyes, a laughing provocative mouth, and dramatic cheekbones.

Although she danced with tantalising grace, and managed to look both innocent and seductive festooned with wreaths of flowers and green leaves, her hands fluttering in stylised, exquisite movements, that sensual, enticing surface was a lie.

Beautiful, sexy and twenty years old, it seemed that Alli Pierce had decided on a career as a con artist.

Ignoring an unwelcome itch of desire, he focused on her with the keen brain and ferocious concentration that had propelled his father's thriving local organisation onto the world stage. The investigator he'd dispatched to the island had learned that her father had brought her there as a baby, and that the locals didn't believe she had Polynesian ancestry.

'Not,' the investigator had told him wearily, 'that they were at all forthcoming about her or her father.'

Slade's brows shot up. 'I thought places like Valanu were hotbeds of gossip.'

'But not to outsiders.' The middle-aged woman shrugged. 'They were extremely protective of her. I did manage to find out that the hotel manager's wife left him because of Ms Pierce, but the next person I talked to about it said that that was a lie.'

'What do you think?'

The older woman's expression turned cynical. 'The people there have a pretty liberated attitude to pre-marital sex, and she certainly seems like the other girls—flirtatious and light-hearted. I saw her several times with the manager and he's certainly hot for her. But so is one of the local boys—the chief's second son. She could be running them both, of course.'

Indeed she could, Slade thought as he watched the way the torches summoned mahogany flames from her long, flower-studded hair. Only slightly taller than the other women, she was built on more racy lines, and her skin gleamed gold rather than bronze.

And he shouldn't be eyeing her like some old lecher in an oriental slave market; he was supposed to be grading the show. Ruthlessly he bent his attention to the other dancers, the ambience, the effect of the whole package on the audience.

Song and dance finished on a sweetly melancholy note; after a moment's silence the audience erupted in exuberant applause, and the dancers, laughing, swung into a fast, upbeat Valanuan version of a hula.

Slade watched hips swinging suggestively, hands sinuously alluring and smiles that tempted every man in the audience—including him, he realised with disgust. Exasperated by the pagan appetite stirring into awareness, he sensed someone's arrival beside him.

'For amateurs, we think they're pretty good,' the manager said, his voice too easy and confident for a man who knew his job was on the line.

'Of their sort, excellent,' Slade said casually. 'Who are they?'

'Oh, just local girls—most of them are staff. The one on the far left teaches at the local school, and second from right is Alli Pierce, whose father was a

New Zealander, like you. She's not a regular, but one of the girls is ill tonight so she's taken her place.'

'The girl who works in the souvenir shop?'

And possibly the mistress of the man beside him; there had been a far from fatherly intonation in the manager's voice when he spoke of her, and he certainly paid her three times the local wage. As she conveniently lived in a house next door to Simcox's, the accusation was probably correct.

Eyes fixed on the dancers, the man beside him nodded. 'Ian Pierce brought Alli to Vanalu when she was a baby; apparently her mother died in an accident when she was only a couple of weeks old.' His voice altered fractionally. 'She's a lovely girl, and she deserves more than Valanu can offer her.'

And you'd like to provide it, Slade thought grimly. His narrowed eyes followed Alli Pierce as the line of dancers swayed off into the darkness, his body tightening when she turned just before she stepped out of the light of the flares and looked directly at him.

Transfixed by a feral response to that swift glance, he barely noticed the three men who leapt out with a wild yell above a sudden clamour of drums.

Angrily he summoned the ragged remnants of his self-control; in his relationships he required much more than lust, the lowest common denominator. Hell, it had been years since his hormones had driven him along that bleak path.

Droning like a distant engine, the manager's voice intruded into his thoughts. Slade forced his mind away from an inviting, enticing face.

'Bright too,' the man was saying. 'But her father

wouldn't hear of her going to a better high school in New Zealand. It's a shame she's stuck here—she'd do well if she had more opportunity.'

Slade thought cynically that she hoped to force that opportunity by extracting money from a total stranger.

Marian wasn't going to be her ticket to a newer, better life. Shocked and bewildered by the letter Alli Pierce had sent her, his stepmother had done what she did whenever she was faced by something she couldn't handle—turned to Slade.

An image of the girl's face flashed with teasing seductiveness against his eyelids. He'd see her tomorrow and he'd scare the hell out of her—and enjoy doing it. Of all forms of crime, blackmail came close to being the most despicable.

And while he was doing it he'd find out why she'd targeted his stepmother.

In the small room where the dancers were getting out of their uncomfortable bras and the pareus swathed tightly around their hips, Sisilu said gleefully, 'He was staring at you. See, I told you he was interested! And so are you.'

'I am not!'

'Then why did you turn around to stare at him?' her friend demanded unanswerably.

Alli rubbed her palms over her cold upper arms and muttered, 'I just wanted to see what he looked like.'

'You felt him watching you.' Sisilu nodded wisely and quoted a local proverb about eyes being the arrows of love.

'Oh, rubbish,' Alli said, knotting her own pareu above her breasts.

In fact, she didn't know why she'd acted on that compelling impulse, but she could see him now as if he stood in front of her—a tall man, broad-shouldered and formidable, the starkly moulded framework of his face picked out by a spurt of flame from the torches. He exuded authority and a compelling magnetism that still kept her pulse soaring.

'Well, what did you think of him?' Sisilu asked.

'He has presence,' Alli admitted grudgingly, pushing her hair back off her damp cheeks.

Sisilu laughed, but to Alli's relief left the subject alone.

An hour or so later, at home in the small house she'd shared with her father, she recalled the swift, hot contraction in the pit of her stomach when her gaze had clashed with that of the new owner. For a stretched moment the laughter and applause had faded into a thick, tense silence. Although it was sheer fantasy, she felt as though they'd duelled across the hot, crowded space, like old enemies—or old lovers.

'You're just imagining things,' she scoffed. 'You could barely see him.'

On an impulse she went to the safe and took out the folder containing all that she had of her family— the photograph of her father and mother, the legal certificates with their alien names, the newspaper cutting.

Why had her father changed his name when he came to Valanu? And hers too. It made her feel as though she'd been living a lie for twenty years.

Carefully she unfolded the newspaper clipping.

Dated three years after her birth, a year after her parents' divorce, it told of the wedding between Marian Carter and David Hawkings.

If there'd been a photograph of the newlyweds she'd have been able to judge whether Slade Hawkings looked anything like David Hawkings.

'No, it's too far-fetched; coincidences like that don't happen,' she reassured herself, and went to bed, where she lay awake for hours before sinking into a restless, dream-disturbed sleep.

Of course in the morning she woke too late to swim in the lagoon. As it was, she'd opened the doors of the shop only seconds before the first influx of customers arrived—a group of young men from America on a diving holiday.

They swarmed around her, teasing, laughing, flirting enthusiastically, but without any sign of seriousness. Because there was no harm in any of them, she laughed, teased and flirted back.

However, there was always one who pushed his luck; smiling, she eluded his hands, turning him off with a quip that made him yell with laughter.

He was saying with an overdone leer, 'Same time tonight, honey?' when Barry Simcox arrived.

Previously she'd have thought nothing of Barry's frown, and the way he watched the young man, but Sisilu's comment the previous day had put an uneasy dent in her easygoing friendship with the manager.

Once the divers left the shop, Barry came in. And with him came the new owner.

Alli's heart jumped so strongly she had to stop herself from pressing her hand over it to keep it in place.

In the soft, bewitching clarity of morning Slade Hawkings looked even more forbidding than he had in the dramatic light of the flares.

Fussily, Barry performed the introductions. 'Mr Hawkings is here to check us over,' he said with a smile that just missed its mark. He turned to Slade and informed him, 'As you've seen from the figures, Alli has done well with the souvenir shop.'

Alli held out her hand and said quietly, 'How do you do?'

Green eyes, translucent and emotionless as glass, examined her—almost, she thought, as though she'd surprised him. His hand was warm, but not unpleasantly so, and dry, yet she sensed latent power in the lean fingers and brief grip. He didn't wring her fingers painfully together as many men did.

Colour heated her skin at the memory of Sisilu's summing up—this was definitely a man who knew women.

'How do you do?' Slade Hawkings returned in a deep, cool voice, dismissing her with his tone and the flick of a humourless smile.

Stung, Alli stiffened her spine. OK, so he was the boss, and the powerful angles and planes of his face were both compelling and daunting, but he had no reason to look at her as though she were rubbish underneath his shoes.

She turned to put out more stock, but Slade Hawkings said levelly, 'I'd like you to stay, please.'

So she waited in outwardly respectful silence while the two men discussed the shop at length.

Slade Hawkings commented, 'Stone carving isn't an

art that Pacific Islanders are noted for. Why are you selling this stuff here?'

Barry opened his mouth to answer, but in a voice that stopped the other man's words before they could be uttered, Slade said, 'Alli.'

'We used to stock woven bags,' she told him, bristling, 'but the customs officers in New Zealand and Australia thought they might hide insects. Since fumigation doesn't do much for a bag, I looked around for something else.'

Slade nodded. 'And imported this cheap product to take their place?'

In a tone so courteous it skidded dangerously close to insolence, she said, 'They are not imported—there's always been carving on Valanu. Because there were no large trees on the atoll, the islanders worked coral instead. These are god figures—not the most sacred, of course, but they're carved with skill and all the correct ceremonies.' She indicated an eye-catching quilt on the wall. 'These are not imports, either. A woman whose mother was a Cook Islander showed the Valanuans how to make them. They're hugely popular, but I do make sure the buyers know they aren't a traditional craft on Valanu.'

She expected him to blench at the pattern of bold scarlet and white lilies, but he startled her by saying, 'I hope you're paying enough for them—they take years to finish.'

In answer she flicked the tag around so that he could see the price. He leaned over her shoulder to look, and she breathed in a hint of elusive scent.

Undiluted essence of male, she thought wildly—no

hint of cologne or soap, just a faint whisper of fragrance, clean and salty and intensely personal. Astonished, she felt her mouth dry and her skin tighten unbearably. His closeness beat against her like a dark force of nature.

Appalled by her reaction, she dropped her hand and clenched it at her side, not daring to move in case she touched him. The only sound she could hear was the uneven thudding of her heart.

Then he stepped back, snapping the invisible bonds that had locked her into a trance.

Alli forced her face to register a bland lack of interest before turning to face him. Eyes as cold as polar ice and every bit as hard met hers.

'Do you sell many?' he asked laconically.

Alli's chin tilted. 'At least one a month. We'd sell more if we could get them. They're popular.'

'You look very young to be managing this shop,' he observed.

Barry jumped in. 'Since Alli's been here she's increased turnover considerably. She speaks the local language as well as English so she's an excellent liaison with the craftspeople on the island. And she has great taste, as you can see.'

Slade Hawkings's eyes turned colder, if that was possible. Ignoring the other man, he asked her about the turnover, about her ordering, relentlessly making her justify everything she'd done.

When he left half an hour later she felt as though he'd wrung every scrap of information from her. Shaking inside, she watched him stride beside the manager

across the foyer, tall and lithe—a true chief, wearing
his inborn authority with panache.

Or, considering him from another angle, a shark,
right at the top of the food chain!

CHAPTER TWO

HER mouth parched from Slade Hawkings's grilling, Alli poured herself a glass of pineapple juice, but had only swallowed a little when the after-breakfast customers arrived.

It turned out to be one of those days—hot, busy, with more than its fair share of irritating and irritated people. When she closed the doors at seven that night she was tired and hungry and badly in need of a swim. At least Fili had recovered enough to dance, so she didn't have to don the outrageously uncomfortable coconut bra!

The new owner of the resort had passed through the foyer a couple of times, cool and utterly sure of himself—the consummate predator. Beside him, Barry's fraying composure marked him as prey.

'Like the rest of us,' Sisilu said forthrightly when Alli hurried in to say hello before the show. 'Everyone's walking around as though they might tread on a stonefish.'

'Surely he wouldn't just close Sea Winds down and walk away from it—apart from anything else, the buildings are worth a lot of money.'

'He's a very rich man—someone said he's a billionaire now.' Sisilu shrugged as though that explained everything. 'You don't get where he is by not making hard decisions. And he's not here to lie on the beach

24

and work on his tan; he came here to do something. It's like he's electrified the whole place.'

'With the sheer force of his personality?' Alli jeered. 'No matter what he was like everyone would be jumpy; people tend to get stressed when their jobs are at stake.'

'But this feels personal,' her friend said abruptly. 'He's got it in for someone. All right, you laugh—but he's a man who makes things happen, and something's going to happen now. I can feel it.'

Strolling towards the lagoon across sand still warm from the day's heat, Alli pondered Sisilu's words. In the distance she could hear the feverish drumming that heralded the fire dancers, and said a silent prayer for them all.

At the water's edge she dropped her pareu into a heap and walked out into the lukewarm water, sinking into it with a long sigh of relief.

Personal? No, how could it be? Sisilu was reacting morbidly to the situation.

But as Alli struck out parallel to the beach she wondered in selfish frustration why Slade Hawkings couldn't have waited another six months to buy the resort. By then she'd have saved enough to pay her passage to New Zealand—first the several days' trip to Fiji on a copra boat, then a flight to Auckland.

Her jaw tightened. She'd find a way to get there; no arrogant hotel owner was going to stop her. She had a mission, and she'd see it through.

Buoyed by the silken water, she floated on her back and stared at the stars, huge and white and aloof, their lovely, liquid Polynesian names more real to her than the ones her father had given them. They'd be different in New Zealand. And she'd be leaving behind her all her friends, a familiar, comfortable way of life...

She fought back a nascent shiver of homesickness. Much as she'd miss the island and her friends, she wanted more than Valanu could offer. And, judging by Slade Hawkings's attitude, even if he didn't close down Sea Winds she had no future there.

Diving as easily as the dolphins that sometimes visited the lagoon, she breathed out slowly and swam through a silvery wonderland towards the beach. Eventually her toes found the sand; frowning, she stood and wiped the water from her eyes, because someone waited for her beside the small pile of her pareu.

Tama.

Oh, not now, Alli thought wearily, and then felt mean. He didn't *want* to suffer from unrequited love!

She twisted her hair onto the top of her head and waded towards the beach. 'Good evening,' she said in English, deliberately using that language to distance herself from him.

He answered in the same tongue. 'Fili said you're going back to New Zealand with the new owner.'

'Where on earth did she get that idea?' Alli answered contemptuously, stooping to pick up her pareu.

'From Sisilu, I suppose.' His eyes were hot, but his voice revealed his pain. 'She said you'd talked about sleeping with him so he'd keep the resort open.'

Furious, Alli knotted her pareu over her scanty swimsuit. 'Slade Hawkings has the coldest eyes of anyone I've ever seen. I don't think he's open to negotiation.'

Tama gazed at her hungrily, his eyes sliding the length of the wet pareu. 'You want to go to New Zealand. He might take you.'

She drew a deep breath. 'Tama, be sensible.'

'Alli, marry me.' When she shook her head and started off up the beach he caught her up. 'I can change my father's mind. He knows you and loves you—he'll come around soon enough.'

The cluster of coconut palms beside the house was only a few metres away. Gently she said, 'Your father will never change his mind. The last thing he wants for you is marriage to a woman with no background, no family, no nothing. He is an aristocrat of the old school, and I'm a nobody. It simply won't happen.'

He grabbed her by the arm and swung her to face him. 'It could if you agreed.'

She said firmly, 'No. I'm going to New Zealand.'

'Why?'

She looked around at the glimmering expanse of the lagoon, the elegant statement of the coconut palms, the combination of soft sweetness and astringent salty scent that spelt Valanu to her—the sheer magical beauty of it all. Reverting to the local Polynesian tongue for emphasis, she said quietly, 'Because it's where I belong. Just as you belong here.'

He made a sound in his throat and pulled her against him. Startled, Alli stiffened, and when he began to press kisses over her face she mumbled, 'Let me go. Now!'

'Alli, you're driving me mad,' he said in a low, passionate voice. 'I need you—'

'No, you don't.' Instinctively repelled by his arousal, she had to remind herself that this was Tama, who'd teased her all through school, who'd laughed and picked her up when she'd fallen over, who'd been so like a brother that she hadn't even realised when he'd decided to fall in love with her.

He rested his cheek on her head. 'You don't know how I feel,' he muttered.

She freed her arms and cupped his face with both her hands, staring into his eyes and trying to convince him. He seemed older and harder, as though he'd made up his mind to do something.

'I know I don't feel the same way!' she said sadly.

'Because you won't let yourself—you think it's wrong because my parents are so old-fashioned. I can make you feel it.'

He pressed an urgent kiss on her mouth, and this time she pushed at his chest, her hand tightening over his solar plexus as she clenched her jaw. When she could speak she said, 'Tama, no!'

Something in her tone got to him, because he dragged in a deep breath and stepped back, dropping his arms. Tears stung her eyes as she watched him struggle for control.

Why on earth did this business between the sexes have to be so complicated?

He said thickly, 'I love you.'

'Tama, I think of you as my brother. Your mother is the only mother I've ever had,' she said gently. 'I love you too, but not like that.'

He looked away. 'We could make it impossible for them to say no,' he said unevenly. 'If there was a child my mother wouldn't turn it away.'

Alli sucked in her breath, but said steadily, 'You'd have to rape me, and you wouldn't do that.'

'No,' he said, and the hungry, determined man disappeared, replaced by the beloved companion of her childhood.

'And we couldn't do that to your parents,' she said, aching for him. 'They trust you—and they trust me too.'

He gathered his dignity around him to kiss her forehead softly. 'Then there is nothing more to be said. I hope your voyage brings you happiness, little sister.'

And he turned and strode away down the beach, leaving Alli shaken and forlorn, wrenched by the loss of her last security as she watched him disappear into the darkness. Slowly she turned and walked towards the house she'd grown up in, no longer a sanctuary for her.

Two steps away from the clump of coconut palms her every sense suddenly woke to full alert, pulling her skin tight in primal fear. She stopped and stared into the shadows. Tall and dark and dominating, a broad shoulder propped against a sinuous trunk, someone waited for her there, silent and still as some sleekly dangerous night predator.

Foreboding knotted her stomach, and her pulse ricocheted. In her most matter-of-fact tone, she said, 'Good evening, Mr Hawkings.'

He straightened, but stayed where he was. Illuminated by the gathering radiance of a rising moon, she felt exposed and vulnerable.

'Good evening, Alli.' There was a subtle insult in his use of her first name. 'I thought for a moment I might have to come to your rescue.'

'No,' she said curtly. 'Have you lost your way?'

'On the contrary. I came looking for you.'

A flash of fear hollowed out her stomach. Acutely aware of the way her pareu clung to her wet body, she asked huskily, 'Why?'

He paused. 'To see what a con artist looks like.'

The cold, implicit threat in his words silenced her until she produced enough composure to say, 'I don't know what you mean.'

'You wrote a letter to Marian Hawkings informing her you were her long-lost daughter and asking her why she abandoned you and your father.'

Sweat sheened her forehead and temples. Her heart skidded to a halt in her chest, then started up double time. She could only just discern the arrogant framework of his face, and what she saw there terrified her—icy distaste and a ruthless warning.

Alli swallowed to ease a throat suddenly dry. 'How—how did you know?'

'I'm glad you don't deny it. She told me.'

'Are you related to her?' she asked breathlessly.

'In a way.'

Frustration ate into her, but she rallied. 'I don't remember saying anything in my letter that could be construed as a con.'

'Perhaps blackmail would be a better word. I read your letter; it was aggressive, and there was a clear intimation that you were coming to New Zealand to meet her.' His voice was hard and uncompromising.

'I didn't intend it to be aggressive, but, yes, I said that. She owes me one meeting, surely?' Alli fought back a bewildering mixture of emotions. 'So she's not going to meet me?'

'Why should she? She has no daughter called Alli—'

'Alison,' she said raggedly.

'Or Alison.'

'Actually, it's Alison Marian.'

'Is it?' He couldn't have made his disbelief more obvious. Without bothering to comment, he went on, 'On the date you gave for your birth she was in Thailand on holiday with friends. I don't know where you got your information, Alli—always providing it wasn't just a stab in the dark—but she rejects it entirely.'

Pain squeezed Alli's heart in a vice so ferocious she thought she might never be able to take a breath again. She fought it with every ounce of will. 'I see,' she said, each word deep and deliberate and steady. 'In that case there's nothing more to be said. Goodbye, Mr Hawkings.'

'Not so fast. Where did you hear about her?'

It couldn't hurt to tell him. Perhaps it might even rock his confident self-possession a little. She'd like that—it might ease the pain that gripped her.

'I saw her name on my father's marriage certificate.'

He moved so quickly she gasped and took a stumbling step backwards. In the moonlight his face was a mask, superbly carved to reveal no emotion, but she saw the glitter of his eyes and knew with a bitter satisfaction that she had startled him.

'You're lying,' he said, and covered the ground between them in two quick strides.

Head held high and eyes glittering, she stood her ground. 'She was Marian Carter, born in Hampshire, England. She met my father there, married him a year later, and emigrated to New Zealand with him. I was born roughly two years afterwards. Not that it's any of your business.'

'I don't believe you,' he said icily.

'So?' Humiliated, she felt her wet hair tumble around her shoulders in a clammy mass. 'I'm not interested in what you believe. If Mrs Hawkings doesn't want to acknowledge me, I'm certainly not going to press the issue.' She gave him a brittle smile. 'Harassing one's own mother is not polite, after all.'

A lean, implacable hand clamped around the fine bones of her wrist. He didn't hurt her, but she felt like a bird caught in a trap.

'You're a cool one,' he said levelly.

It wasn't a compliment. Every cell in her body shrieked an alarm. 'Let me go.'

Moonlight gleamed on his face, lighting up a smile that chilled her with its cynicism. 'Who was the boy on the beach?' he enquired in a tone that combined both indolence and steel.

'An old friend.' She twisted away and stepped past him, aware that he chose to let her go. Although he hadn't marked her skin, his touch had scorched through her like lightning on a hilltop.

His smile narrowed. 'A pity your touching renunciation wasn't necessary.'

Alli looked up at him with apprehension tinged by fear. In spite of the fact that she disliked him intensely, he made her overwhelmingly conscious of the hard muscle under the superbly cut casual clothes, of the cutting edge of his intellect.

'Is eavesdropping a hobby of yours?' she asked, not trying to soften the scathing words.

She'd have said it was impossible, but the autocratic mask of his face hardened even further. 'Only when I can't avoid it. You should check that no one's around before you turn a man down,' he shot back, a raw note in his voice scuffing her nerves into shocking sensitivity.

They were quarrelling—yet she didn't know him enough to quarrel. 'I don't need to—the islanders are too courteous to intrude.'

'Or too accustomed to seeing you with a man to be interested?' he enquired pleasantly.

Her breathing became shallow; instinct warned her to get the hell out of there, but she couldn't move. Eyes widening, she stared up into his formidable face.

He lifted her chin with one forefinger and smiled as he examined her—feature by feature—with unsparing calculation.

Not a nice smile. Yet she couldn't move, couldn't do anything except suffer that inspection as though she was an object being examined with a view to purchase.

'It's no use casting your spells on me.' Each word was delivered with a flat lack of expression, although a contemptuous undertone sent wariness shivering down Alli's spine. 'Your mouth is slightly swollen from another man's kisses and I've always been foolishly fastidious. I'm also immune to the enchantment of a tropical moon and a pretty face.'

Ripples of feverish sensation threatening to carry her away, Alli gritted her teeth until she could say evenly, 'Goodnight.'

She straightened her shoulders and strode up the shell path towards the house without a backward glance. Yet she knew the exact second Slade Hawkings turned away and headed back down the beach towards the resort.

Because it hurt too much to think of her mother's rejection, she spent the hours until she slept vengefully imagining what she should have done when Slade touched her. Unfortunately imagining him sprawled on the sand clasping his midriff and gasping for breath proved to be an unsatisfactory substitute for the real thing. Why hadn't she let him know bluntly that she resented strangers pawing her?

Instead of hitting him, she'd noticed the tiny pulse beating in his jaw, registered the elusive fragrance that was Slade Hawkings's alone, and felt the fierce demand of his will-power battering her defences.

She found some relief in punching her pillow before turning over to listen to the waves on the reef. Always before their pounding had soothed her, but tonight unwilling excitement still throbbed like a drug through her veins and, later, through her dreams.

Alli made sure she arrived at work ahead of time the next morning. After restocking the shelves she arranged a cluster of brazenly gold hibiscus on the counter, their elaborate frills reminding her of the frothy confections Edwardian society women had worn on their proudly poised heads.

'Good morning,' Barry Simcox said from behind her.

Pulse hammering, she straightened and whirled in one smooth movement.

He stared at her in bewilderment. 'Are you all right?'

Feeling an idiot, she muttered, 'I'm fine, thank you. You surprised me.'

'I didn't realise you were the nervous type.'

'I'm not!' she said truthfully, smiling to show him that she was completely in control of her erratic responses.

He nodded, and looked around the shop. 'You do have a knack with design,' he said absently. 'Hawkings mentioned it yesterday.'

'Did he?' She wanted to ask him what else the new owner had said, but of course she didn't. Instead she probed tentatively, 'Has he told you anything about his plans for Sea Winds?'

His pleasant mouth turned down at the corners. 'Nothing. He's playing his cards damned close to his chest.'

Like her and the rest of the staff, Barry stood to lose his job if the resort was abandoned. However, he could go back to Australia and resume his career.

She summoned a bright smile. 'A woman yesterday said we ought to mass-produce the quilts. She thought we should import some sewing machines and set up a little factory.' Her laughter blended with his startled guffaw. 'I didn't tell her that most of the islanders have sewing machines, or explain that the reason the quilts are so valuable is that they're handmade.'

A cold voice said, 'If you're ready, Simcox, I'll see you now.'

Poor Barry almost choked. 'Yes, sure, certainly,' he said, turning away from Alli so quickly he had to grab the nearest thing, which happened to be her bare shoulder.

'Sorry,' he babbled, letting her go as though her skin had burnt his fingers.

Keeping her eyes away from Slade Hawkings, Alli retired behind the counter and opened the till.

'Good morning, Alli,' he said, the thread of mockery through his words telling her that he understood her reaction and found it amusing.

Her eyes glinted beneath her lashes. 'Good morning, Mr Hawkings,' she returned with every ounce of sweetness she could summon, ignoring Barry's alarmed stare.

'You're looking a little tired,' Slade said, adding, 'Perhaps you should try to get to bed earlier?'

Although she read the warning in the manager's expression, she showed her teeth anyway. 'You needn't worry. I won't let anything I do at night affect my work.'

She heard the hiss of Barry's breath whistling past his teeth. Far too heartily, he leapt in with, 'Slade, I've got those figures ready for you now.'

Slade Hawkings looked at him as though he was an irritating insect. 'Let's see them, then.'

Watching them walk back across the foyer in the direction of the one suite the resort boasted—which Slade had claimed—Alli wondered how two men, from the back rather similar in size and height, could look so different. Barry walked straight enough, and his clothes were good, yet beside the other man he looked…well, spectacularly insignificant.

Everything about Slade Hawkings proclaimed that he was completely in command of himself, his surroundings and his life. He looked, Alli thought with a sudden clutch of panic, exactly like a man who'd close down a poorly performing resort without a hint of compassion for the people who worked there.

So why did her body respond with swift, forbidden excitement whenever she saw him?

For the next two days rumours buzzed around the resort, growing wilder and more depressing each hour. Alli was kept busy with a new wave of tourists, most of whom wandered into the souvenir shop at some time to stock up on T-shirts, bright cotton pareus, or a hat for protection from the fierce sun. Excited children raced past the shop on their way to the lagoon, and each night the troupe danced and sang as though their lives depended on it.

'Barry's looking pretty sick, and the waiter who delivers the meals says the Big Man is getting grimmer and grimmer,' Sisilu said from the depths of an elderly cane chair on the second night.

She'd called in on her way home after the floor-show, joining Alli on the verandah.

'What's Hawkings doing?'

'Going over figures.' Sisilu could never be serious

for long, and almost immediately she started to laugh. 'Hey, did anyone tell you about the girl who thought Mr Hawkings was part of the package that first night?'

Alli's brows shot up. 'No! What happened?'

'She saw him at the show and really came on to him.'

'What did he do?'

Sisilu grinned. 'He joined her group, and half an hour later he'd fixed her up with a good-looking American. Fili said she looked like a stunned fish, trying to work out what had happened! He's clever, that man.' She sent Alli a laughing sideways glance. 'So what's with you and him?'

'Nothing,' Alli shot back.

'Fili said the Big Man saw you and Barry laughing together in the shop and didn't like it.'

'Fili must spend all her time dodging round looking for scandal,' Alli said, resigned to the fact that on an island the size of Valanu nothing was secret. 'And when she doesn't find it she makes it up. If Slade Hawkings looked angry it's because he doesn't like me and I don't like him.'

Sisilu chuckled. 'So why doesn't he like you?'

'Oh—we just rub each other up the wrong way.' Alli wished she'd kept her mouth shut.

'Which usually means that there's something going on underneath. I think he wants you, and men like that are used to taking what they want.'

A hot little thrill ran through Alli, but she said, 'You've got an over-active imagination.'

'I saw him watch you walk across the beach yesterday.' Sisilu fanned herself and rolled her eyes. 'His face didn't change, but I could feel his attention like laser beams. I'm surprised you didn't.'

Alli moved uncomfortably and Sisilu started to laugh. 'You did, didn't you? I can tell you did! You going to do something about it?'

CHAPTER THREE

ALLI shook her head so swiftly the orchid behind her left ear went flying into the scented night. 'Even if he does, I don't know anything about…well, about anything. You know what my father was like.'

'He didn't do you any favours,' Sisilu said, wrinkling her forehead as she recalled Ian Pierce's strictness. 'Making love's nothing much—I mean, it's great, and I like doing it, but the world doesn't revolve around it. The longer you put it off the bigger and bigger it gets, I suppose. Are you scared?'

'Not exactly,' Alli said thoughtfully.

When Tama had kissed her she'd felt nothing beyond regret that she couldn't feel as he so obviously did. But Slade's touch had charged her with forbidden excitement. She could still feel it like fireworks inside, all flash and fire and heat.

Hastily she finished, 'But I feel that if my father thought it was so important then I shouldn't do it just for fun.'

Sisilu understood respect for one's elders. She shrugged, then cocked her head and got to her feet as laughter floated through the sultry air. 'Sounds like Fili and the others going home; I'll go with them.'

After she'd left Alli got ready for bed, but an unusual restlessness drove her outside again. She stood on the edge of the verandah and gazed around, won-

dering if she'd hate New Zealand, as Sisilu so confi-
dently expected.

She'd certainly miss the moonlight glimmering on
the still surface of the lagoon, and the breeze rustling
the palm fronds, carrying the tang of salt and the tropical ripeness of flowers and fruit. And she'd miss her
friends.

But she was going, whatever she missed.

She sat down on the old swing seat and rocked
rhythmically. What exactly was Slade up to? Why had
he bought the resort in the first place? It seemed an
odd thing for a hard-nosed businessman to do. Surely
he'd checked the figures before he'd paid a cent for
it? He must have known that it was perilously close
to failure.

Her mouth curved cynically. And he certainly didn't
strike her as a philanthropist, ready to sink his own
money into a dying enterprise just to help the islanders!

If he did close Sea Winds she didn't know what
she'd do. She'd have nothing—no future, no present,
no chance or choice. The island had a policy of jobs
for native Valanuans, and she didn't want to take any
work from them. In fact, she'd been training someone
to take over in the souvenir shop.

Her father's income had died with him; even the
house was hers only because the tribal council let her
stay there as a mark of respect to her father.

Besides, there was Tama...

The crunch of shells beneath shoes brought her to
her feet; heart beating feverishly, she peered into the
darkness. Even before her eyes made out the man

strolling up the shell path from the beach she knew who he was.

Fighting back a heady excitement that blasted out of nowhere, she blurted, 'What do you want?'

'To talk to you,' Slade Hawkings said coolly, taking the steps. He stopped at the edge of the verandah, his silhouette blocking out stars and the moonpath over the lagoon.

Dwarfed by his formidable presence, Alli asked abruptly, 'What about?' Oh, Lord, she sounded like a belligerent teenager.

'The resort.'

'Why?' she said warily, brain racing. 'I don't know anything about its financial affairs.'

'Simcox tells me that you're very well integrated into Valanuan life.'

She stiffened. Where was this going? 'I can't remember any other home.'

'But it's not your home,' he pointed out. 'You have a New Zealand passport.'

'What has that got to do with Sea Winds?'

He turned to examine the garden. 'I believe your father leased the house from his local tribal council.'

Chills chased each other across her skin. She said pleasantly, 'You've been doing some research. Why?'

'I make it my policy to learn as much as I can about my enemies,' he said calmly, turning back to look at her.

To cover her shocked gasp she rushed into speech. 'I suppose I should be terrified to be an enemy of the great Slade Hawkings? If I'd known that was a possibility I might not have written to my mother—'

'She isn't your mother,' he interrupted in a flat, uncompromising tone. 'And you're right. I make a bad enemy.' He paused to let that sink in. 'However, I can be a good friend.'

But not to me, she thought, suspicion snaking through her.

'Above all, I'm a businessman.' Another deliberate pause.

As a technique for unsettling people, Alli thought, trying to hide her growing unease with flippancy, it worked brilliantly. She didn't know whether he was trying to provoke her into speech, but common sense warned her that silence was by far the best option.

He said matter-of-factly, 'You know that Sea Winds is losing money hand over fist; I'd be a lousy businessman if I let such a bad investment drag my profits down year after year.'

This time Alli couldn't hold back her biting comment. 'I'm surprised a businessman of your reputation bought the place.'

'I had reasons,' he said shortly, a note of warning in the deep voice.

What reasons? The whisper of an implication smoked across her brain, only to be dismissed. Sinking though it was, Sea Winds would have cost him a lot of money—far more than he'd have needed to spend if he wanted to gain power over her.

Alli lifted her gaze to his dark silhouette. Against the radiance of the moon she saw a profile etched from steel, and shivered inwardly. Something Sisilu had said to her came back again—something like *be nice to him—for all of us...*

Her teeth worried her lip before she said neutrally, 'If you spent money on it—'

'Surprisingly enough, money isn't always the answer. It should never have been built here. There isn't room for a decent airport so everything has to come through Sant'Rosa, and the civil war there has made tourists extremely wary of this part of the world.'

Everything he said in that aloof, dispassionate voice was the truth, yet the conversation rang oddly false. Alli swallowed. 'Why are you telling me this?'

'I want your opinion on what closing the resort will do to the islanders.'

'Why me?' She didn't try to hide her incredulity.

He shrugged. 'I'm not stupid. You know these people, and I'm willing to accept that you want to do your best for your friends.'

'Even though I'm a blackmailer?' she flashed back.

'I assume that even blackmailers have friends.' His tone could have cut ice. 'You seem to.'

It had been stupid to let him see how his opinion of her stung. Compared to the welfare of the islanders, her hurt feelings were totally unimportant.

She drew in a deep breath and said frankly, 'Most of them will go back to working copra, planting and fishing and village life. The tribal council won't have as much money for schooling, because copra is not hugely profitable, so the secondary school will almost certainly close. Bright children won't be able to go to university. The health clinic will probably close too, except for tours by visiting doctors.' She couldn't see his expression, but he could see hers when she finished bluntly, 'Some people will certainly die.'

His silence lifted the hairs on the back of her neck. Should she have pleaded? Did he have any sort of social conscience at all, or was this a trick?

Eventually he said, 'So what would *you* do to keep the resort open?'

Panic kicked her in the stomach. 'I—what? What could I do?'

He walked across the verandah, stopping so close to her she could see the white flash of his narrow smile.

'Keeping Sea Winds going would be a sacrifice for me—I'm asking what you're prepared to sacrifice for your friends.'

Blood pumped through her, awakening her body to urgent life, but her brain seemed to have been overwhelmed by lethargy. She moistened her lips and croaked, 'If you mean what I think you're meaning...'

'That's exactly what I mean,' he said, that note of ironic amusement more pronounced. 'I want you, Alli. You must have guessed—it's not as though you're a sweet little innocent.'

Stunned, she licked her lips and swallowed. 'You're going to have to be clearer than that.'

Boredom descended like a mask over his face. 'Really?' he mocked, his mouth twisting. 'Then perhaps I should demonstrate.'

And he kissed her.

Alli had read books, she'd listened to friends discussing their love life—and she'd been kissed often enough to know what it was all about. But until Slade's mouth took hers she'd had no idea that a man's kiss could drive every sensible thought ahead of it like leaves in a hurricane, robbing her of breath and common sense until she was left witless and shaking in his arms.

His mouth was cool and masterful, and potent as lightning, she thought vaguely, before a rush of sensation blotted out everything but wildly primitive need.

When he broke the kiss her hands tightened on the fine cotton of his shirt and she pressed closer with an instinctively sinuous movement, afraid that he'd walk away and leave her.

'Sweet,' he said, his voice raw with sensual arousal. 'Open your mouth for me...'

Sighing, she said his name, and he laughed beneath his breath and kissed her again. And this time there was nothing cool about it at all.

Locked against his hardening body, she shuddered as her passionate response rocketed her into another universe. Desire merged inevitably into hunger, then blossomed into a desperate craving. This, she thought dimly as he explored the soft inner parts of her mouth, as she savoured the exotic taste of him, as she melted into surrender—this was what she had been waiting for...

Slade lifted his head, but only to kiss her eyelids. Strong arms tightened across her back, pulling her against him. Shudders of pleasure ran like rills through her. She moved languorously against him, and shivered at the fierce delight the heat and pressure of his taut body kindled in the pit of her stomach.

She felt his chest expand, and was filled with excitement because she was doing this to him.

No wonder her father had kept such a close watch on her—this was dangerously addictive, a reckless abandonment to sensuous thrills.

And then Slade's arms dropped and he stepped back, leaving her shivering in the warm night air, her body filled with frustrated longing for something she'd never experienced.

'Just so we don't get this wrong,' he said evenly, as though nothing at all had happened, 'are you offering me yourself in return for my keeping Sea Winds open?'

Humiliation doused every last bit of arousal. Cold and furious, Alli clenched her hands by her sides to stop herself from shaking. 'Is that what you want?'

'I'm always prepared to deal,' he said, watching her with half-closed eyes.

'No,' she said when she could speak again. 'I'm no prostitute.'

He wielded silence like a weapon, but two could play at that game. Fighting back tears of shock, she refused to let loose the bitter words that trembled on her tongue.

'I wasn't thinking of prostitution,' he said obliquely. 'More an exchange of benefits.'

'A business deal?' She didn't have to summon the scorn in her voice—it came without warning. 'But that's what prostitution is, surely? There's certainly no emotion in it.'

He smiled without humour and touched the corner of her mouth with a knuckle. 'Really?' he drawled, tracing its lush, tender contours. 'You could have fooled me. Shall I kiss you again?'

Something unravelled deep inside her. Aching with desolation, she stepped back, away from his knowledgeable, tormenting caress, and said stonily, 'There's a difference between sensation and emotion.'

'I think we could probably forget about semantics while we made love.'

The best way to finish this would be to prove how utterly stupid she'd been. 'So let's deal. How often would you expect me to sleep with you in return for the continuation of the resort? Just once? Or would you expect me to be available whenever you came to Valanu? How often would that be?'

'Whenever I wanted,' he said with a silky lack of emphasis. 'I don't think just once would slake either of us.'

'And how long would it last?'

'Until I got tired of you,' he said coolly. 'Of course I'd expect you to be faithful in between visits.'

'And would you be faithful?' When he paused she looked straight up into his face and said, in a voice that shook with scorn, 'Nothing would persuade me to sleep with you for money, or benefits, or any other reason. In fact, I don't ever want to see you again.'

'That can certainly be arranged,' he said.

She was wincing at the sheer off-hand brutality of his reply when he began again, and this time the sexual edge was gone from his tone.

Brisk, businesslike, without inflection, he said, 'Get down off your high horse, Alli—I don't want you in my bed. However, I'll keep the resort going if you stay here on the island and work in the souvenir shop.'

'What?' she whispered incredulously.

'You heard.' His voice hardened. 'If you agree, your friends will keep their jobs, children will go on to university, and people will live.'

'Why?' But she knew why.

'It's a simple transaction. I don't want you contacting or trying to see Marian Hawkings ever again.'

Hearing it like that—a bald statement delivered in a tone that brooked no compromise—sent equal parts of anger and desolation surging through her.

'And you have the nerve to call me a blackmailer,' she said flatly.

'So we each use the weapons we have to hand,' he retorted with bland indifference.

Even as she admitted to herself that she had no choice, she looked for a way out. 'And do I have to stay here for the rest of my life—or Marian Hawkings's life?'

He paused, then said, 'You'll leave Valanu when I agree you can.'

Fear and frustration almost made her burst into a furious outburst, but if she lost control he might renege on the deal. She said wearily, 'Why are you doing this?'

He misunderstood her, perhaps deliberately. 'Because I want you kept well away from Marian.'

'If I promise not to contact her—'

He lifted a hand, but when she shrank back he dropped it again, saying incredulously, 'I wasn't going to hit you!'

'I know.' She'd realised that the second she'd jumped back.

'Did your father beat you?' he asked in a soft, lethal tone that scared her more than anything else.

'No—never!' Anger drove her to say, 'He was a gentleman—literally!' She let the word sizzle through the air before finishing woodenly, 'All right, I'll accept your offer—but I want it in writing first.'

She was shocked when he laughed, apparently with real amusement. Mortified, she heard him say, 'You'll hear from my lawyers within a week.'

'If I don't, the deal's off,' she said rashly. 'And for your—and Marian Hawkings's—information, I had no intention of forcing myself onto the woman. I just wanted to ask her some questions.'

'Then learn to couch your letters in more diplomatic language,' he returned curtly, turning to go. 'As for your questions—she has no answers. If this whole business about looking for your mother is true, you've been searching up the wrong street.'

It took a real effort, but Alli kept her silence. She knew that Marian Hawkings was her mother, but the lies the woman must have told Slade fitted in with the profile she'd built in her mind—a woman who had never wanted anything to do with the daughter she'd borne.

She said, 'Before you go, tell me one thing.'

In a voice that conveyed both a warning and a threat, he said, 'I don't have to tell you anything.' But he stopped at the foot of the steps and turned to look at her.

Refusing to be denied, Alli ploughed on. 'This is going to cost you a huge amount of money, so what is Marian Hawkings to you? I know she's not your mother—unless you were the result of an affair before she married your father. I assume she's your step-mother.'

For a moment she thought he was going to refuse to answer, until he said, 'She is my stepmother. Now I want an answer from you—you said that you saw her name on your father's marriage certificate. She was married before she married my father, but her first husband's name was not Ian Pierce.'

'I know,' she said quietly. 'It was Hugo Greville. Hugo Ian Greville—Pierce was my father's mother's maiden name. He changed his name by deed poll when your stepmother left him. After he died, I found the papers with their marriage certificate, the divorce papers, and a clipping about her marriage to your father.'

Moonlight lovingly delineated his features, the silver flood dwelling on the strength and cold determination that stamped his face. 'So you knew who I was before I got here?'

'No,' she said acidly. 'You weren't mentioned in the newspaper clipping. And I had no idea the new owner of Sea Winds was another Hawkings.' She looked at him to see if he believed her, but his expression revealed nothing. 'Even when you got here I didn't make the connection. It is a reasonably common name.'

'I see.' He was silent for several seconds. 'I'm on my way out of Valanu in half an hour. Keep your nose clean and you might win some time off for good behaviour.'

Bewildered, furious and exhausted, Alli watched him stride towards the beach until the shadows swallowed him up.

CHAPTER FOUR

ALLI swung a long leg over the horse's back and dropped gracefully from the saddle. 'Good girl,' she said, chirruping in a way the grey understood. It gave a soft whicker when she flipped the reins and stood looking along the beach, north, to where Valanu lay, thousands of kilometres away across the lonely Pacific.

Eighteen months after she'd made that bargain with Slade Hawkings she'd waved the island a tear-drenched farewell. Although she still missed her friends there, after six months in New Zealand she was becoming accustomed to its temperate climate, was enjoying the play of seasons and the new life she'd made for herself.

And, although today was chilly, the Maori celebration of Matariki had long passed, with the rising of the Pleiades in the northern sky. Spring was almost over and summer was on its way.

'Hey, Alli!'

She turned to wave to the middle-aged man loping across the short grass of the paddock, bald head gleaming.

'Hi, Joe! Trouble?'

'Might be. You've got a visitor.' He extended his hand for the reins. 'I'll deal with Lady and you go on

down to the Lodge; the guy doesn't look as though
he's used to being kept waiting.'

Alli frowned, keeping hold of the reins. 'Who is it?'

'Come on, hand 'em over. He didn't say who he
was, just that he wanted to see you.' He grinned. 'Perhaps he saw your photo in the paper when you helped
rescue those yachties, and realised that under all that
salt and sand there was a pretty face.'

'I hope not,' she said involuntarily.

She'd been desperate to keep out of the limelight,
but a persistent journalist had managed to get one shot
of her hauling on the line that had brought the crew
of the yacht to safety through the huge surf.

At least her face had been barely recognisable. The
other staff at the Lodge had joked that the only reason
the shot had appeared in the paper was because she'd
dumped her wet jeans when they'd dragged her down
in the surf, and the tights beneath showed her legs to
perfection.

When she still hadn't moved, Joe jerked his head
towards the backpackers' lodge and said, 'Go on. If
he gets stroppy yell for Tui.'

She laughed. Joe's wife was built on sturdy lines, a
woman with a tongue that could slice skin, yet sing
tenderly haunting lullabies to her grandchildren.
Sometimes she joked that she needed to do both with
the backpackers who came to this stretch of coastline
to surf the massive waves.

'Thanks,' Alli said, and set off along the narrow
metalled race that led through the dunes to the Lodge.

Who on earth could her visitor be? The friends

she'd made all lived around the Lodge, yet if Joe didn't know who he was the man couldn't be a local.

Perhaps it was someone from Valanu?

She stepped through the door into the reception area and said, 'Sorry I took so long to get—'

Shock drove the breath from her lungs and the words froze on her tongue.

'I'm a patient man,' Slade Hawkings said calmly, turning around from his scrutiny of the scenic calendar on the wall.

Two years faded into nothingness and she felt as defenceless against his powerful male magnetism as she had when they'd first met. He was watching her with the aloof, unreadable expression she recalled so well.

She swallowed and asked thinly, 'What do you want?'

He cocked an arrogant black brow. 'Perhaps to see why you reneged on our deal.'

'I haven't contacted m—Marian Hawkings,' she shot back. 'Which is what the deal was really about.'

'That's a matter of opinion.' But he spoke without rancour and some of her apprehension faded.

'And the Valanu resort is no longer losing money,' she finished.

'Thanks, I believe, largely to you.' Lashes drooped over the hard green eyes, so startling in his tanned face. 'Who'd have thought that a little South Seas siren would turn into a hot publicist?'

'How did you know—?' She stopped abruptly. *'Siren?'*

'If it fits,' Slade drawled. 'When ideas for improving the hotel's publicity started to percolate through, the new manager had to admit they came from you. Targeting the upper end of the market and laying on a flying boat to get the guests in from Sant'Rosa was an inspired move. The nostalgia angle is working very well, and lunch on an uninhabited island seems to be appealing to plenty of would-be Robinson Crusoes out there.'

She shrugged. 'Well, those who are filthy rich, anyway. I was surprised your organisation ran with my ideas.'

'They were fresh,' he said indifferently, 'and it was clear that you had the backing of the chief.'

She had to stop herself from looking as uncomfortable as she felt. Tama's father had packed his son off to Auckland, ostensibly to take a degree but really to get him away from his unsuitable crush on Alli, who had, as the chief said, behaved properly. In return, he'd pragmatically thrown his considerable prestige and authority behind her plans for the resort.

And the new manager, who'd arrived two days after Slade left, and a week before Barry Simcox went back to Australia, had let her have her head.

Slade continued smoothly, 'Tell me, did Barry get back together with his wife once he landed in Australia?'

Something in his tone made her narrow her eyes, but he met her enquiring look with an opaque, unreadable gaze.

Alli shrugged. 'How would I know?'

He looked amused, but said easily, 'How did you get off Valanu? The manager said no one seemed to

know where you were until they got a postcard from
Fiji a week or so later.'

She said stiffly, 'If he'd thought to ask the chief
he'd have found out. I worked my passage on a yacht.'

'I suspected so.' His smile showed a few too many
teeth. 'The one with the group of young Australians?'

'The one with the middle-aged Alaskan couple,' she
snapped.

His brows rose in a manner she found infuriating,
but he said blandly, 'I suppose I should be grateful
that before you left you trained someone to take your
place in the souvenir shop.'

'I don't want your gratitude,' she returned. 'What
are you doing here? And don't tell me you're going
to force me back to Valanu. I didn't know how to deal
with that sort of blackmail before—but I do now.'

'I'm pleased to hear it. No, I'm not ordering you
back. I have no power to make you go, and I rarely
repeat myself. And, as you said, the whole idea was
to keep you away from Marian.' His demeanour
changed from indolent assurance to one of decisive-
ness. 'But now she wants to see you.'

She said quietly, 'I don't want to see her.'

Slade waited for a long moment, his expression intimidating. When he spoke his voice was a lethal purr.
'A little revenge, Alli?'

'Alison,' she told him. 'I call myself Alison now—
more adult, don't you think?' She still hadn't got used
to it, though.

'Your employer called you Alli.'

She said curtly, 'He shortens everyone's name. And,
no, it's not revenge.'

'Then what is it?'

Alli paused, trying to work out how she felt. Longing to see her mother vied with another instinct. 'Self-defence. I can only take so much rejection. And so far that's all she's done to me.'

In the intimidating, angular set of his face she saw the man who'd expanded the thriving firm he'd inherited from his father to a pre-eminent position on the world stage.

He said smoothly, 'I don't think rejection is what she has in mind.'

The desire to meet Marian Hawkings tempted Alli so strongly it almost overwhelmed her common sense. If she didn't take this opportunity she might never have another. And eventually she'd despise herself for sheltering behind the cowardly fear of being hurt. But caution drove her to probe, 'Then what *does* she have in mind?' Acceptance would be too much to hope for.

Slade wondered what was going on behind her guarded face. 'I don't know,' he said abruptly.

She looked at him with those exotic lion eyes. 'How did you find me?'

'The newspaper photograph.'

Her dark brows lifted in irony. 'That was a month or so ago.'

'Marian's been ill,' he said shortly.

Once he'd given Marian the dossier his investigator had put together she'd avoided the subject for several weeks. Then a bout of flu had laid her low, just after he'd seen the photograph of Alli in the newspaper.

It still irritated the hell out of him that, in spite of

the grainy photograph, her face had leapt out at him from the page.

Not that she was classically beautiful, he thought critically, angered by the weakness that tested his self-control. But something about her challenging eyes and inviting, sensuous mouth stirred his sexuality into prowling appreciation, aided by the rare combination of dark, rich hair and glowing golden skin, and the body her lovers had woken to lush, svelte femininity.

When Marian had decided she wanted to find Alli he'd had to admit that he knew where she was, although he'd refused to contact her until the doctor had agreed that Marian was fit enough to cope.

He said abruptly, 'She wants to tell you something.'

Hope, so long repressed, flickered like a spark inside her. 'If it's just that she's not my mother she's already told me that, remember?'

His broad shoulders moved in a slight shrug. 'It's not that.'

'Then what?'

He walked across to the window and looked beyond the garden to the regenerating sand dunes, replanted with the native grass that had been the original vegetation. 'It isn't mine to tell,' he said curtly.

'I can't just leave the Lodge.' Her quiet tone hid a desperate hunger to see the woman who'd given her life.

'I've already talked to your boss.'

'Joe?'

He smiled. 'His wife. She's giving you the rest of the afternoon off, and I believe you're not working tomorrow. I'll drive you down and make sure you get back.'

Alli fought a brief, vicious battle with herself before yielding to temptation. 'All right, I'll get changed.'

'Take enough clothes for the night.'

Her incredulous glance met eyes as cool and unyielding as jade. 'I won't need them, surely?'

'Nevertheless, bring them.' When she looked mutinous he said matter-of-factly, 'I always believe in being prepared for any eventuality.'

Alli bit her lip, but when she came down twenty minutes later she carried a bag packed with a change of clothes.

She followed the sound of laughter to the kitchen, where Slade was drinking coffee and talking to Tui as she kneaded a batch of bread.

He seemed perfectly at home, and her employer was certainly enjoying his company, although that didn't stop her from saying firmly, 'Better give me your address and phone number in case I need to ring Alli up.'

Slade took out a slim black case and scribbled something on a business card. 'I've put my e-mail address there as well,' he said, anchoring the card to the table with a sugar bowl. 'Sometimes it's the quickest way to get in touch with me.'

A look of sheer horror settled on Tui's face. 'I'm not touching any computer,' she said robustly, dividing the dough into loaves. 'Alli keeps trying to make me use it, but it's just like magic to me, and I've always been a bit wary of magic.'

'According to you the telephone is magic too,' Alli teased, 'and so is electricity.'

'I understand those,' her boss told her, 'because I learnt about them at school. You young things can deal with the latest technology—I'll stick to my generation's.'

Insensibly warmed by the older woman's cheerfulness, Alli dropped a kiss on her cheek and went out with Slade Hawkings into the unknown.

Once in the large car, she sat back in a divinely comfortable seat, with the scent of leather in her nostrils, and watched the green landscape sweep by until apprehension seeped in to replace the lingering warmth of Tui's presence.

If she turned her head a little she could see Slade's hands on the wheel; for some stupid reason the sight of his lean, competent fingers made her heart quiver, so she kept her eyes on the lush countryside.

As though he understood her wariness, he began to talk—at first about the rescue of the yacht. When they'd exhausted that subject, somehow they segued onto the subject of books. He had definite views, some of which she agreed with and some she didn't. Alli discovered that he was that rare thing, a person who didn't take disagreement personally, and halfway to Auckland she realised that she was in the middle of a vigorous debate about a film she had enjoyed.

'Weak in both plot and acting,' he condemned, 'and with a dubious moral base.'

'Moral base?' she spluttered.

He shrugged. 'I subscribe to the usual moral values.'

Astonished, she lost the thread of her rejoinder and stared at his profile, the strong framework of his face providing a potent authority that would last him a lifetime. Heat smouldered in the pit of her stomach. The two years since she'd seen him had only increased her susceptibility to his disturbing magnetism.

Her silence brought a slanting ice-green glance. 'Cat got your tongue?' he asked politely, before returning his gaze to the road ahead.

She plunged back into the argument, but tension more complex than the merely sexual plucked at her nerves. She didn't want to like him; she certainly didn't want to feel this reluctant respect. It was far too dangerous.

The conversation lapsed as they approached Auckland and the traffic got heavier. Alli knew the route to the airport, and a few other necessary addresses, but once he left the motorway on one of the inner-city interchanges she lost all sense of where they were going.

It turned out to be one of Auckland's expensive eastern suburbs. Slade drove into the grounds of a modern block of apartments, parked in the visitors' car park and killed the engine, his face set in forbidding lines.

'She's expecting us,' he said.

Bewildering fear hollowed out Alli's stomach. Her mouth dry, she walked past camellia bushes and a graceful maple tree to the door, waiting while he pressed a button that activated a hidden microphone.

'Slade,' he said, adding, 'With a visitor.'

A woman—surely too young to be Marian Hawkings?—answered, 'Come on up.'

He opened the security door and said without expression, 'Marian's goddaughter is staying with her.'

Inside was discreetly luxurious—a bronze statue of vaguely Greek ancestry, a sea of carpet and marble, landscapes on the walls, a huge vase of flowers that only the closest observation revealed to be real.

'The lift is over here,' Slade said, his fingers resting for one searing moment on her elbow as he indicated the elevator.

It delivered them too swiftly to the fourth floor, and more carpet that clung to Alli's shoes, more statuary, more flowers.

Trying to inject some stiffness into her backbone, she told herself grimly that Marian had landed on her feet after she left the man who'd changed his name to Ian Pierce.

The woman who opened the door was a few years older than Alli, elegant and beautiful. And every black hair of her head, every inch of white skin, radiated disapproval when she looked at Alli.

'Caroline, this is Alison Pierce,' Slade said. 'Alli, Caroline Forsythe, who has given up her holidays to stay with Marian while she's convalescing.'

'How do you do?' Caroline Forsythe didn't offer her hand. Her blue eyes skimmed Alli's face with a kind of wonder. 'It's no hardship to stay with Marian. Come on in—she's expecting you both.' She directed a brief, conspiratorial smile at Slade that spoke volumes. 'She's in the sitting room.'

Masochist, Alli thought fiercely, letting her anger overcome a faint, cold whisper of danger.

In the sitting room Alli vaguely registered light streaming in through large windows, gleaming on polished furniture, on more pictures in sophisticated colours, on flowers that blended with the décor.

A woman in a chair stood up. Her eyes met Alli's and the colour vanished from her skin, leaving it paper-white.

Horrified, Alli saw her crumple. She cried out, barely aware of Slade's swift, silent rush to catch Marian Hawkings's fragile figure before she hit the floor.

As he lifted her in his arms Caroline hissed at Alli, 'Get out of here—*now*. Before she comes to, I want you out of this building.'

Blindly Alli turned away, but the whiplash of Slade's voice froze her. 'Caroline, get a glass of water with a splash of brandy in it,' he commanded, laying his burden down on the sofa, 'and make tea. Alli, stay where you are! She asked to meet you.'

Alli felt Caroline's dislike scorch through her. She didn't blame her; horrifying scenarios of her conception were blasting through her mind. The one thing she hadn't thought of was rape—but even now she simply couldn't conceive of her father doing that. After all, they'd been married…

'Sit down,' Slade went on, examining her with merciless eyes. 'I don't want you fainting too—you're as white as paper.'

She dropped into a chair, watching her mother's colourless face until Caroline came in with a glass and stood between them.

'It's all right, Marian,' Slade said gently. 'You fainted, that's all. You're fine now.'

'What—? Oh…' Marian Hawkings tried to struggle up.

'Lift your head a bit and drink this,' he said. 'I wouldn't have brought her if I'd known you were going to scare the hell out of us like that.'

'Let me see her.' But her voice was filled with dread.

'After you've had some of this.' He held the glass to her lips, only straightening when she'd taken several sips. He turned and with unyielding composure said to Alli, 'Come here.'

When Caroline started to object, Slade overrode her with one brief, intimidating glance.

'Alli?'

Slowly, skirting the furniture with extreme care, Alli made her way to the sofa, concern almost overriding her shock. The woman who lay there was still beautiful, with fine features and blue, blue eyes.

And after one swift, shaken glance Marian Hawkings went even whiter, and closed her eyes as though she'd seen something hideous.

With obvious effort she opened them again. 'Yes, I see. Caroline, my dear, do you mind leaving us? I'm sorry, but I need to speak to Alli and Slade alone.'

'Of course I don't mind,' the other woman said pleasantly, 'but do take care, Marian. You're not well yet.'

When she'd gone, Marian said weakly, 'Flu, that's all it was. Slade, would you help me up, please?'

He lifted her, propping her against the side and back of the sofa.

She looked at Alli, her eyes darkening. 'I wish I could say I was your mother, Alison, but I'm not.'

It was almost a relief. 'Then who was?' Alli asked in a cracked voice.

Marian swallowed, her face inexpressibly sad, and tried to speak. She whispered, 'I can't. Slade—please…'

Lying her back against the sofa, Slade said harshly, 'Your mother was Marian's sister.'

Nausea clutched Alli as the implication struck home. She sprang to her feet, saying contemptuously, 'I don't believe it.'

'It happens,' he said briefly. He lifted a photograph from the side table and handed it to her. 'Your mother. And a copy of your birth certificate.' He paused before adding, 'Which you must have seen, as you have a passport.'

'My father organised it when I was sixteen,' she said absently. Now that she was faced with the proof she'd sought with such angry tenacity she didn't dare open the envelope.

Slowly, her fingers trembling, she slid the photograph free. Yes, there was her father, his expression almost anguished as he looked into a face—oh, God—into a face so like hers it gave her gooseflesh.

The woman in her father's arms was shorter than she was, but she had the same features—the same tilted eyes, the same exotic cheekbones, the same full mouth. She was laughing and her confidence blazed forth like a beacon, defiantly provocative.

A piece of paper beneath the photograph rustled in Alli's hand. She looked at it and swallowed. For the first time she saw her birth certificate, and on it her mother's name: Alison Carter. She had been twenty-four when she'd borne her lover's child.

Cold ripples of shock ran across Alli's skin. Whatever sins Alison had committed, she must have loved Marian to give her child her sister's name.

But to betray her like that! Sickened, she stared at the betraying document. Oh, God, her demands for acknowledgement must have opened up bitter humiliation and pain in this woman who was her aunt.

'What happened to her?' she asked in a raw voice.

Marian Hawkings looked at Slade. He said levelly, 'When Marian discovered that her sister was pregnant she told Hugo to leave. He did so, and the guilty lovers disappeared to Australia. A month later Alison rang from Australia to tell Marian that she had aborted her child.'

Alli sucked in a ragged breath. 'Why?'

He shrugged. 'Apparently she was tired of Hugo and thought Marian might want him back. Then, a year or so after that, Marian was informed that she'd been killed in Bangkok. She'd flown into Thailand alone.'

Trying to sort this incredible story out, Alli looked down at her mother's photograph, then glanced at Slade's arrogant, unreadable face. 'So who am I?' she asked in a voice that shook.

'When Marian got your first letter I instigated a

search. It's taken this long to find out that her sister lied about the abortion. You are the child she had. And, no, we have no idea why she lied, or why she left you with Hugo a few days after you were born and simply disappeared.'

Alli felt as though she'd taken the first step over a precipice—too late to go back.

As though he sensed her emotions, Slade poured a small amount of brandy into a glass and handed it to her. 'Drink some.'

She obeyed, shuddering as the liquid burned down her throat. It did help, though; when the alcohol hit her empty stomach, warmth eased the chill.

Leaning back against the cushions, Marian said weakly, 'Slade, finish it, please.'

'There's not much left. Hugo Greville changed his name and took you to Valanu because he'd been at school with the chief and could presume on their friendship to ask for sanctuary.'

Sick at heart, Alli got to her feet and addressed Marian Hawkings for the first time. 'I'm so sorry I brought all this back to you.'

The older woman leaned forward. 'This has been a shock for you too.'

'Not, perhaps, as much as you think. I've always known my mother abandoned me at birth, or very soon afterwards, so nothing much has altered.' She said steadily, 'Thank you for telling me. I'll go now.'

She'd got halfway across the room when Slade joined her. 'I'll take you home,' he said deliberately.

'It's all right—'

'Don't be an idiot.'

She paused, then nodded and went docilely with him, waiting in numb silence while he spoke to Caroline in the hall. Down by the car the sun still caressed the waxen glory of the last camellia flowers, and the harbour scintillated blue and silver, but inside Alli was cold, so cold she thought she'd never get warm again.

Slade said nothing as he drove away, and Alli stared unseeingly ahead, only focusing when the car slowed down outside a sturdy Victorian building.

'Where are we? Why aren't we going back to the Lodge?'

'I live here,' he said, manoeuvring the big vehicle into a parking spot in a basement car park.

She turned a belligerent face to him. 'So? I don't.'

He killed the engine. 'I don't think you should be alone tonight,' he said calmly. 'You're in shock, and I doubt very much whether you'd care to confide to anyone else what you've heard today, so you might as well stay here.'

'No,' she said dully, struggling to overcome the impact of the appalling story. She couldn't cope with the fact that the woman who'd wreaked such havoc had been her mother.

'Come on,' he said, and leaned over to open her door.

She caught a trace of the subtle scent that was his alone; that purely male scent, she thought confusedly, stamped him as definitely as a scar. 'I don't want to,' she said, a little more strongly.

He sat back and looked at her. 'You'll be perfectly

safe,' he said pleasantly enough, although she registered the note of steel through the words.

'Aren't you afraid I might be like my mother?'

He lifted an ironic eyebrow. 'Promiscuous?'

She bit her lip and he said, 'It doesn't matter what
you are. I'm not like Marian. I know how to deal with
people who annoy me.'

She shivered. 'I need a cup of tea,' she said. 'After
that I want to go home.'

'All right.' He hooked an arm into the back and
brought out her case. 'You also need a shower to wash
the slime off,' he said unexpectedly, and she looked
at him in wonder, because that was exactly how she
felt—unclean, as though her mother's actions had
tainted her from the bones out.

Tiredness overcame her, sapping her courage and
determination. She knew she should refuse to go with
him, but it was so much easier to allow herself to be
carried along on the force of his will.

Without speaking, she walked with Slade across the
concrete floor and waited docilely while the lift
whisked them upwards.

CHAPTER FIVE

LIKE the man who owned it, Slade's apartment was large and compelling, so close to the harbour that reflected light played over the palette of stone and sand and clay. He showed Alli into a bathroom tiled in marble and left her there after explaining the shower controls.

Taking in its luxury, and the vast glossy leaves of a plant that belonged in some tropical jungle, Alli realised instantly that the room was a purely male domain. No toiletries marred the smooth perfection of the counter, and there was no faint, evocative perfume to hint at a woman's presence.

And she should *not* have felt a swift pang of relief. She stripped and turned on the shower; once in, she bewildered herself by sniffing gingerly at the soap in the shower.

Not even a touch of pine or citrus, so the faint fragrance she noticed whenever she was close to Slade was entirely natural.

'Pheromones,' she muttered. Years ago she'd read an article that suggested people unwittingly used subliminal scent to choose a genetically suitable mate.

If that were so, Slade would produce magnificent babies with her.

Tamping down the hot spurt of sensation somewhere deep in the base of her stomach, she thought stringently, and with Caroline.

Probably with every other woman on the planet too. Part of his magnetism was the impact of all that superb male physicality.

Oddly embarrassed, she got out her soap from its container and lathered up.

No wonder Marian Hawkings hadn't wanted to meet her! She must be a living reminder of humiliation and misery. Although logic told her it was ridiculous to take her parents' sins onto herself, she felt smirched. Her emotions were raw, and so painful she had to concentrate on the small things, like rinsing her hair until it squeaked, and wiping out the shower when at last she left it.

When she eventually emerged from the bathroom, every inch of skin scrubbed to just this side of pain, teeth newly cleaned and hair towel-dried, Slade met her at the door.

'I should have told you there's a hairdryer in the cupboard,' he said, examining her with formidable detachment.

Although she tried for polite gratitude, his nearness produced a stilted, ungracious tone. 'Thank you, but if you don't mind my hair wet, I'm fine.' She'd never used one before, and now was not the occasion to try something new.

'Why should I mind? The first time I saw it wet— when you walked out of the lagoon like Venus unveiled—I noticed that it looked like a river of fire,' he said silkily.

Alli's heart jumped. He'd changed too, into a cotton

shirt the green of his eyes that moulded his shoulders.
His trousers did the same to narrow hips and muscled
thighs. Although she now wore her smartest jeans and
a camel-coloured jersey that had cost her almost a
week's wages, his effortless sophistication made Alli
feel she should check for hay in her hair.

The sitting room overlooked the harbour and the
long peninsula of the North Shore that ended in the
rounded humps of two ancient, tiny volcanoes. Behind
loomed the bush-clad triple cone of Rangitoto Island,
thrust up from the seabed only a few hundred years
ago.

Searching for a neutral topic, Alli commented, 'I'm
always surprised when I'm reminded that Auckland is
a volcanic field. I wonder when the next explosion will
be.'

'I feel as though it happened this afternoon,' he said
grimly. 'Come and pour the tea.'

Though he refused a cup.

'I need something a bit stronger.' He added dryly,
'Perhaps I should have asked if you'd like that too?'

'No, thanks.' So far she'd managed to behave with
dignity; she wasn't going to jeopardise her control. It
was, she thought desperately, about all she had left.

He splashed a small amount of whisky into a glass,
half filled it with water, then came to sit opposite her
on a huge sofa. She set the teapot down and picked
up her cup.

'Put in some sugar,' he said abruptly.

'I don't like—'

'Think of it as medicine.' When she didn't move he
leaned over and dropped in a couple of lumps before

settling back to survey her through half-closed eyes. 'You're in shock.'

Shock? Oh, yes; when he looked at her like that, a smile curving his hard mouth, his eyes glimmering like jade lit by stars of gold, her throat closed and her heart sped up so much it hammered in her ears. Probably this was what had happened to Victorian maidens when they swooned.

Well, she wasn't going to be ridiculous. She'd seen the sort of woman he liked: sophisticated and elegant. Caroline Forsythe was about as different from her as anyone could be.

She sipped the tea tentatively, making a face at its sweetness, but its comforting heat persuaded her to drink it. Her father had considered coffee only suitable as a way to end dinner.

Glass in hand, Slade leaned back in the leather sofa and surveyed her. 'What do you plan to do now?'

'Do?'

'Do,' he repeated in a pleasant tone, adding with an edge, 'Beyond drinking two cups of tea.'

'Go back to the Lodge,' she said warily. 'Why?'

He was watching her with detached interest, as though she were a rare specimen of insect life. 'It seems strange that someone with a degree in English should be content with a job in the office of a back-packers' lodge frequented mainly by surfers.'

'How did you know—?' She stopped and glared at him. 'Why should I be surprised? You kept tabs on me, didn't you!'

'I always knew exactly what you were doing until you left Valanu,' he said calmly. 'I know you took an extra-mural degree from a New Zealand university and passed with A grades.'

'Was it part of the new manager's job to send you reports on me?' she asked, reining in her anger with an effort that almost chipped her teeth. 'I hope you paid him extra.'

When he spoke his voice was as careless as his shrug. 'I protect my own.'

'It makes my skin crawl to think you've been spying on me,' she retorted passionately.

'I don't take chances. As you can see, Marian is fragile. When I first went to Valanu the only thing I knew about you was that you were Simcox's lover and that you wrote an aggressive letter.'

Outraged, she stared at him. 'I was not his lover! Never!'

'My informant seemed sure of the facts.' He spoke with a calm assurance that made her want to throw the teapot at him. 'And he certainly felt more for you than the care an employer owes to an employee.'

'If you've got a dirty mind and listen to stupid gossip it might have seemed like that,' she returned with relish. 'That doesn't mean it was the truth.'

His ironic smile hid whatever he was thinking. 'It doesn't matter now.'

Alli wanted it to matter. She wanted, she discovered with something very close to horror, him to be furiously jealous. Alarmed, she steered the subject in a different direction. 'Given your opinion, what made you change your mind about contacting me?'

'Facts,' he said laconically.

When she directed a blank look at him he elaborated, 'Once I realised you looked like Marian's sister I got one of my information people to find the truth. It took her a while, for various reasons.'

'The name change?'

He nodded. 'Alison told everyone that she and Hugo were going back to Britain. Quite a lot of time was wasted trying to track them down there. The logical thing for them to have done was cross the Tasman Sea—in those days you didn't need passports to travel between Australia and New Zealand. It took a while for the researcher to find them.'

'Do you think my—Alison tried to put them off the scent?' She held her breath while he drank a little of the whisky.

'It seems a logical assumption. Then, of course, your father changed his name and yours when he went to Valanu, but eventually we pieced together a sequence of events, backed by legal documents. The records proved you were Marian's niece. But by then you'd left Valanu.'

'I'm surprised you bothered looking,' she snapped.

'Ah, there's a difference between an opportunist and a relative.' His mouth twisted in a smile that held equal amounts of wryness and mockery. 'Then the television news shortened the search by showing you hauling shipwrecked yachtsmen through the surf.'

'And you recognised me?' she said, before she could stop the words.

'I never forget a good pair of legs.' His smile was hard and cynical.

He was baiting her. Ignoring it, she said, 'Why did Marian decide to see me? Unless she wants to prove once and for all that I'm not her daughter. She doesn't have to—I won't insist on a DNA test. The photograph and my birth certificate are proof enough for me.'

When Slade didn't answer, she looked up and saw that he was swirling the liquid in his glass with an expression she couldn't interpret. Eyes enigmatic, he parried her enquiring gaze.

Something in her heart tightened unbearably. She said with stiff pride, 'If she wants to establish once and for all that I have no claim on her I'm perfectly willing to sign a disclaimer.'

His dark lashes came down to hide his eyes. In a level voice he said, 'It's not so easy. In certain cases signing a disclaimer might not be enough. New Zealand law can be tricky.'

Which meant that he, at least, had considered and researched the options. Alli swallowed more of the tea, shuddering at its cloying sweetness. 'So why did she want to see me?'

'I suspect that she felt you deserved to know your own parentage.'

'That's—kind of her,' she said reluctantly.

'And perhaps because you are her only living relative.'

Alli pointed out, 'She's got you.'

Slade watched her covertly as he drank some of the whisky and set his glass down on the table. 'But there's no blood relationship.'

Some years after his own mother had died Marian had come into his life like summer, bringing laughter and life and love into a silent, grieving house. That childhood adoration had matured into a protective love that still held.

'In Valanu,' Alli said quietly, 'a child can live with another family and he'll consider everyone in both his birth family and his adoptive family to be his kin.'

'In New Zealand the same thing happens amongst Maori families. But Marian grew up in England,' he said briefly, 'and things are different there.'

When she said brusquely, 'I know that,' he examined her tantalising face from beneath his lashes, wondering about her life on the island.

'Were you fostered by another family?'

'No.' She tempered her abrupt reply by adding more mildly, 'I did spend a lot of time with the family next door.'

'Ah, the home of the lovelorn Tama,' he observed blandly.

He was almost sorry when Alli ignored the taunt. 'I don't think you can be right about Marian; after all, she must have hated my—my mother. Why would she want anything to do with me?'

He shrugged. 'You know why—she now has the information she needs to convince her that you are her niece. You have a certain look of her father, apparently.'

This clearly didn't satisfy her, but it was all he was going to tell her. He watched her pick up her teacup again, her lovely face absorbed, the exquisite curve of her cheekbones stirring something feral into smouldering life inside him.

When he saw tears gather on her lashes he was astonished at the swift knot of tension in his groin.

Even when she was distressed and unsure of herself, her glowing golden sensuousness reached out and grabbed him, angering him with an awareness of his vulnerability. He had to exert all his will not to pick her up and let her cry out her disillusionment and pain on his shoulder.

Any excuse to get her in your arms again, he thought savagely, despising himself. After two years he should have been able to kill this mindless, degrading lust. His lovers were chosen for more than their sexuality; it infuriated him that this woman's face and body had lodged in his brain for years, stripping away his prized control.

Deliberately, he sat back and decided to let her cry. She'd been unnaturally composed after listening to the real story of her life; weeping would help ease her shock.

'Sorry,' she muttered, getting to her feet and striding to the window with less than her usual grace.

Slade found himself following her. This, he thought grimly as he walked across to stand behind her, must have been how her father had felt—helpless in the face of an overwhelming hunger.

He, however, wouldn't allow himself to be dazzled by a face and a seductive body.

Or the unusual urge to protect her. His lovers were independent women, more than capable of looking after themselves. Nothing he'd seen or heard of Alli Pierce made him think she was any different, and too much hung on her character for him to lower his guard.

She was staring out of the window; when he came

up behind her, her shoulders went rigid, but she didn't move. Gently he turned her around.

'It will probably leave you with a headache,' he said, gut-punched by the tears spilling from her great lion-gold eyes onto the tragic mask of her face, 'but I've read somewhere that crying is the best way to deal with stress.'

She gulped. 'Screaming and th-throwing a t-tantrum is a lot more positive,' she muttered, and suddenly her defences were breached and she began to cry, great silent sobs that tore through her slender body.

In a way she had been alone all her life, but she had never before been faced with her utter isolation; when her father had died she'd had friends, the time-honoured rituals of island life to console her.

Marian Hawkings might be her aunt, but she wanted nothing to do with her, and who could blame her? The mother she'd fantasised about and the father she'd never really known had taken the secrets of their guilty love to the grave.

But even as she shivered she was enfolded in warmth. Slade Hawkings pulled her against his big body and held her while she wept into his shoulder, his cheek on the top of her head, his heart thudding into hers.

He even thrust a handkerchief into her hand as though she were a lost child; the simple gesture made her cry even more.

Eventually the sobs subsided into hiccups, and she blew her nose and stepped back, wiping her eyes so that he couldn't see how embarrassed she was.

'Feeling better?' he asked, his deep voice so detached she knew he was wondering how to get rid of her.

'Not at the moment,' she mumbled. 'But at least I haven't got a full-blown headache.'

'Go and wash your face and I'll pour you a brandy,' he said.

'I don't need one, thanks.' She fled into the bathroom and stared, horrified, at her face, puffy and mottled and tear-stained.

Cold water ruthlessly splashed on helped, and so did a brisk mental talking-to, and the swift application of lipstick.

But it took every shred of will-power she possessed to close the door behind her and walk into that elegant sitting room with her head held high and her chin angled just the right side of defiance.

'Brandy,' Slade said with an enigmatic smile, handing her a large glass with a minuscule amount of liquid in it. 'Drink it down and then I think we should go for a walk.'

She stared at him as though he was crazy. 'A walk? Here?'

'There are places.' When she didn't move he said more gently, 'I know you don't like it, but it does help.'

So he'd noticed her involuntary grimace at Marian's apartment. The taste hadn't improved, but it must have had some effect on her because after she'd drained it she said, 'All right, let's go for a walk.'

He parked the car at the foot of one of the little volcanic cones that dotted the isthmus. Silently they walked up the steep side, terraced by sheep tracks as well as trenches built centuries ago to defend the huge fort that had been the local Maoris refuge against enemies.

Although she considered herself fit, by halfway Alli was puffing, her mind fixed on one thing only—getting there. Pride forbade her to suggest a few moments' rest.

Slade's long, powerful legs covered the ground with ease, and when they reached the top he stood with the wind teasing his black hair and glanced at her searchingly.

She knew what she looked like—red-faced and gasping. Yet one green look from him made adrenalin pump through her, banishing tiredness in a flash of acute awareness. When he smiled, she was mesmerised.

'Auckland,' he said, and gestured around them.

What's happening to me? she thought, unbearably stimulated. Instinct gave her the answer: you're attracted to him.

No, she thought feverishly. *Attracted* is not the way to describe this overwhelming response.

Struggling to reclaim some scraps of poise, she stared at the panorama below them—a leafy city between two harbours, the dark lines of hills forming other boundaries, islands in a sea turned pink by the light of the setting sun.

It's quite simple and uncomplicated, she thought despairingly. You want Slade desperately and dangerously, on some hidden, primeval level you didn't even know existed until you met him.

It terrified her, this hot, sweet flood of desire, as

limitless as the ocean, as fierce as a cyclone in the wide Pacific, as tempting as a mango on a hot day...

And hard on that discovery came another. Was this what had driven her parents to betray Marian?

'Alison—'

'Don't call me that,' she said, shuddering. 'Grown up or not, I've decided I prefer Alli.'

'I can't say I blame you,' he said unexpectedly.

'If it's the truth—'

'It is.' He spoke with such utter conviction that she believed him. 'I've never heard Marian tell a lie.'

'So my parents were sleazes of the highest degree. I don't want to be linked with them, not even by name.'

'Sometimes the truth has many facets. Your father was hugely respected in Valanu.'

Unsurprised that he knew this, she nodded. Ian Pierce had organised the accounts for the tribal corporation, helping them deal with trade and bureaucracy.

Slade resumed, 'You can't deny the link, no matter how much you disapprove of what they did. You set this process in motion. All right, so you've found out a few facts that you don't like, but they were your parents. I have no idea what your mother was like, but part of her is in you. And I presume you loved your father?'

Eyes filled with the glowing pink-mauve sky over a distant range of hills, Alli said, 'I don't know. I suppose I took him for granted. He didn't neglect me—he was firm and he made sure I ate properly and that I knew right from wrong.'

But he'd never cuddled her, or told her he loved her, or kissed her; although parcels of books had arrived several times a year he'd never read a bedtime story to her. When she'd been happy or sad or hurt she'd taken herself to Tama's family along the road. From them she'd learned about love and laughter and how to quarrel—all the subtle intricacies of relationships.

'He wouldn't be the first man to love not wisely but too well.' A cynical inflection coloured Slade's comment.

'If it *was* love.'

'If it wasn't, he certainly wouldn't be the first man to lust unwisely and too much.' A note of derision ran through his voice.

But not you, she thought, humiliated afresh. Slade wouldn't think the world well lost for passion. He had too much self-control.

'Now that you know the circumstances of your birth,' he said, 'do you intend to take this further? Do you want to track down your father's family?'

She shuddered inwardly. 'Right now, no. I feel dreadful for bringing it all back to Marian—and I feel tainted.'

'An over-reaction. Of them all, you were the innocent one.'

'Marian and me,' she said, thinking that although his pragmatism was as sharply aggressive as a cold bucket of water in the face, it was also oddly comforting.

'As I pointed out before, you have only Marian's side of the story. Your mother might have had another

one. If their behaviour disgusts you, make sure you
don't follow their example.'

Was he referring to her supposed affair with Barry
Simcox? She gave a sardonic smile. 'That's easy
enough. As far as I know I have no sisters to betray.'

A car drove up to the parking area and disgorged a
group of boisterous, laughing adolescents who
swarmed up to the obelisk with much yelled banter.
Someone produced a camera; Alli flinched at the flash,
envying them their noisy, cheerful ease.

'You know what I mean.' Slade watched the young
people with an alertness that reminded her of a warrior. 'If anything about your behaviour worries you,
fight it. There is nothing will-power can't overcome.'

Probably the tenet he lived by! She blinked when
the sun dipped behind the hills. 'It'll be dark soon—
shouldn't we be heading back down?'

'We'll walk down the road.' He took her elbow and
urged her onto the sealed surface. 'It's well lit.'

Keeping her eyes rigidly on the black bitumen
ahead, she pulled away from him. He dropped her arm,
but strode beside her.

Of all the shocks this day had brought, the knowledge that from tomorrow she'd never see him again
was the one that hurt the most.

Surreptitiously she straightened her shoulders.
When she'd first fought his disturbing, dangerous cha-
risma, she'd been able to overwhelm it with construc-
tive and vigorous resentment because he'd forced her
to stay on Valanu.

Unfortunately, this time he'd been aloofly kind. Dislike and outrage weren't going to rescue her; she'd have to fall back on will-power.

So he was gorgeous? So he made her stomach quiver and her bones melt and turned her brain to soup? Get over it, she told herself with tough common sense. After all, she'd been totally unmoved by other gorgeous men.

But none of them had had Slade's combination of compelling physical appeal and inherent strength and authority.

And then there was Caroline Forsythe, who was probably in love with him.

Night fell softly around them, and the lights of the city shone out to combat the increasing depth of darkness.

Slade didn't give anything away, but his beloved stepmother's goddaughter had to be a better partner for him than a woman who'd be a constant reminder to Marian Hawkings of shame and treachery.

A better partner? Listen to yourself, she thought with harsh scorn; what sort of fantasy are you spinning? Stop being so stupidly, wilfully, madly ridiculous.

Slade neither trusted nor liked her, and, although his potent sexuality made her too aware of her own femininity, she didn't know what she really thought of him.

Yells from behind and the sound of car doors slamming amidst gales of laughter swivelled her head around.

'Stay well on the side,' Slade commanded.

At the first squeal of brakes he swore beneath his

breath and pushed her across the road onto the downward side, locking her against him as he dived over
the edge into the darkness.

He twisted so that he landed beneath her, his hard
body cushioning her fall. Gasping, she lay sprawled
across him, wincing as a harsh, grating noise from the
other side of the road was followed by a heavy thump
and the sound of metal crumpling and tearing.

'Are you all right?' Slade demanded fiercely, his
arms tightening around her.

'Yes,' she croaked. 'Are you?'

'I'm fine.' Apparently not convinced by her answer,
he ran his hands over her arms and down her legs.
Only then did he push her into a sitting position and
say, 'Do you know anything about first aid?'

Alli scrambled to her feet, heart chilling as a scream
sawed through the mild air. 'I've done a course,' she
said, trying to remember one thing—anything—she'd
learned. 'Check the breathing first,' she said aloud.

'OK.' He hauled her up the steep grassy bank and
onto the road, where he thrust a mobile phone into her
hands. 'Ring 111 and then SND. When they ask what
service you want, tell them it's an accident on the
Summit Road on One Tree Hill.'

'Be careful,' she blurted when he turned away. 'The
car might explode.'

He gave her an odd glance and said ironically, 'And
people might die. Don't worry—it's not on fire.'

He disappeared over the far edge of the road as Alli
fumbled with the numbers before following him.

A few seconds later she told the woman who answered, 'At least five are hurt—one's on her feet, help-

ing get the driver out, and one's sitting on the grass. She looks as though she's broken her arm. One's screaming, but she doesn't seem badly hurt.'

'And the others?'

'Two have been thrown out—they don't seem to be moving.'

'All right, we'll get ambulances there as soon as we can,' the woman said calmly. 'Check those on the ground—airways first, then breathing, then circulation. If they're a safe distance from the car don't move them.'

Alli went to each in turn, hugely relieved to discover that both men were breathing regularly. One had blood on his face, but when she touched his cheek he opened his eyes and frowned at her. The other didn't move.

She stood up, intending to head for the girl with the broken arm, when the one who'd been screaming came rushing across and tried to fling herself onto the unconscious man.

'No!'

Alli managed to stop her, but the girl turned on her, lashing out and sobbing, 'He's dead. I know he's dead!'

Slade grabbed her and pinned her arms, commanding harshly, 'Stop that, or I'll slap you.'

For a second she stared into his face, until his ruthless determination cut through her shock. Blinking, choking on her tears, she whimpered, 'He's dead.'

'He's not dead,' Slade told her.

The sound of a siren wailed up from below. 'OK, that's the ambulance,' Slade said. Releasing the girl, he said to the one who'd helped him assess the driver, 'Take her round the next corner and wave it down.'

'Come on, Lissa.' Her friend touched the girl's arm and together they walked down the road.

Slade asked, 'How are the others?'

'One is conscious; he's breathing freely.' She indicated the girl with the broken arm. 'I haven't had a chance to see how she is.'

She was white and in pain, but she said, 'I'm all right. They made us girls put the seat belts on. And Simon had one too, of course.' She bit her lip and looked across at the car. 'He's the driver. Is he all right?'

'He seems to be.'

'What about the others? H-how are they?'

Alli said quietly, 'They're breathing, and they look pretty good to me. I'm sorry, but I won't touch your arm—I think it's best to wait for the ambulance staff to deal with it.'

An hour later, after they'd both given their accounts of the accident to an efficient young constable and been given a lift down the hill, Slade slid behind the wheel of his car and said briefly, 'Come on, let's go home.'

'Home?' Alli said on a slight quaver.

'I'm not taking you back to the Lodge now,' he said brusquely, backing the car out of the parking space. 'I've got a spare bedroom—you can spend the night there.'

When she opened her mouth to protest, he cut in, 'You'll be quite safe.'

'What about Caroline?'

Slade looked left and right, then eased out into the stream of traffic. 'What,' he said pleasantly, 'about her?'

The words like bricks in her mouth, Alli said, 'I thought she might have some reason to mind.'

'No reason,' he said.

Silently they drove beneath the streetlights until they reached his apartment.

CHAPTER SIX

SLADE'S spare bedroom intimidated Alli with its excellent taste.

He smiled ironically at her quick glance around, and said, 'Spare rooms do have a tendency to look like hotel rooms. A quilt from Valanu would make it more exciting.'

Dangerously cheered because he'd remembered such a minor thing, she said, 'But much less elegant. The decorator would have a fit. Anyway, I think it suits you.'

She flushed when he eyed her with an amused gleam in his green eyes. 'I'm not sure how to take that,' he observed. 'Cold and unwelcoming?'

'Restrained,' she said firmly.

The amusement vanished from his gaze, leaving it unreadable. 'The bathroom is through that door over there. Do you need anything?'

'No, thank you.' What had she said to be so completely rebuffed?

Up until then he'd been the perfect host; he'd persuaded her to eat, and been concerned when she'd only been able to manage two slices of toast. Because the edge of challenge in his tone had muted she'd let herself relax.

Now it was like standing next to a glacier.

90

Thick lashes veiling his gaze, Slade nodded. 'In that case, goodnight, Alli.'

After he'd left the room she showered, startled to discover blood on her skin and clothes. One of the men who'd been thrown from the car was in a dangerous coma; another, with the casual beneficence of fate, had suffered nothing more than mild concussion and a cut arm. The driver apparently would be all right too.

Once in bed, she felt her thoughts buzz around her mind in wild confusion; the adrenalin crash made sleep seem an unattainable nirvana. She listened to the alien sounds of the city, trying to block out the wail of a distant siren with the remembered roar of waves pounding the reef in Valanu.

Restlessly she turned on her back and stared at the ceiling, trying to push an unwelcome truth away. Valanu was her past; she couldn't go back. Besides, she wanted to be here—just through the wall from Slade...

When the dream began she recognised it, but as always, although she knew what was coming, she couldn't snap free from the prison of her mind.

She was cold, so cold the ice in her veins crackled when she moved. It stabbed her mercilessly with a thousand tiny knives, yet she had to keep going, had to find a warm place before the ice reached her heart. Panting, mindlessly terrified, she forced herself to run through the empty, echoing corridors of an immense house, hammering on every door she came to. Most of the rooms were empty, but occasionally she'd come to one and see light through the keyhole, hear laughing voices.

Then she'd call out, but entry was always refused, even after she begged to be allowed in. All she wanted was a few seconds in front of the fires she could hear crackling behind each obdurate door.

Eventually, all tears frozen, she found herself out in a bleak forest, with snow falling in soft drifts. She forced herself on until the drifts caught her feet and she fell. Shivering, she had to crawl…

But this time she didn't feel the terrifying ice creep through her veins. This time someone came and picked her up and carried her into the warmth. And when at last sleep claimed her she was in sheltering arms that melted the snow and kept the howling winds at bay…

She woke to heat, the gold of sunlight through her eyelids, and a subtle, teasing scent…

Lashes flying up, Alli jerked sideways, body pumping with adrenalin. Beside her Slade stirred, muscles flexing under far too much sleek bronze skin. He didn't appear to be wearing any clothes.

'Stop wriggling,' he murmured, his voice rich and slightly slurred.

When she gasped he woke instantly, without moving. Recognition narrowed his eyes into metallic green shards. Obeying instinct, Alli jack-knifed out of the bed.

Slade rolled over to link his hands behind his head and survey her with formidable self-possession. Alli suffered it a second before realising that while her T-shirt covered the essentials the briefs she wore beneath it revealed every inch of her long legs—inches he was now assessing with a heavy-lidded gaze and a hard smile.

She didn't have the self-assurance to walk away from him looking like some good-time girl from a men's magazine, but neither was she going to reveal her embarrassment by scuttling across to her clothes.

Abruptly she sat down on the edge of the bed, as far away from him as she could, and hauled the sheet over her legs. His dark brows rose.

Alli swallowed, but her parched throat made the words gritty and indistinct. 'What the hell is going on?'

'Perhaps you could tell me that?' he suggested, subtle menace running through the words like silk.

She wanted desperately to lick her dry lips, but something stopped her. Instead she demanded childishly, 'What are you doing in my bed?'

'Before you start accusing me of rape—'

Her blood ran cold. 'Rape?' she croaked.

'Relax. Nothing happened.' The flinty speculation in his eyes belied his mocking tone. 'Unless crawling down the hall making pathetic whimpering noises could be called an event.'

Humiliation flooded through her. *'What?'*

He stretched and sat up, exposing far more skin than she could deal with. 'You appear to be a sleepwalker.'

Vague scraps of the dream swirled around her. She shut her eyes against both it and the effect his sleek bronze chest was having on her already strained nerves. 'Oh, God. What did I do?'

'You huddled dramatically on all fours outside my

door, muttering that you were frozen, that you had to get close to the fire before the snow killed you.'

Rigid with mortification, she said, 'I—I haven't had that dream for years. And I haven't walked in my sleep since I was a kid. I'm sorry I inflicted it on you.'

'I imagine yesterday was traumatic enough to wake any number of old devils,' he said objectively.

Something struck her, and she opened her eyes to glare at him, trying to ignore the way the mellow light through the curtains burnished his broad shoulders and tangled in the male pattern of hair across his chest. He was utterly breathtaking in his potent male confidence. 'But—why are you here?'

'I carried you back, put you between the sheets and endeavoured to leave. You had other ideas,' he told her, the laconic irony in his tone lacerating her pride even more. 'Besides, your feet and hands were frozen. I planned to wait until you were warmed up and safely asleep, but every time I started to get out you woke crying and pleading, and in the end staying here seemed the easiest solution.'

Shamed colour swept across her face, then drained away. 'You could have woken me up,' she said lamely.

He shrugged, muscles coiled beneath his skin. Hastily Alli looked down at the floor, using every ounce of energy to resist the hot, untamed need that roared into life in the pit of her stomach.

Slade told her, 'I tried that too, but you didn't respond. Not even when I called your name.'

Desperately she said, 'I'm sorry.'

'Don't worry about it.'

There was no sophisticated way she could get out
of this. Closing her eyes a second, she said, 'I—well,
thank you.'

'At least we both got some sleep,' he said dryly.
'And now, if you don't mind, I'll leave you.' When
she stared at him, he added in a tone that could have
dried up a large river, 'I normally sleep naked, but I
did have the sense to drag on a pair of briefs. If it
doesn't embarrass you...' He started to fling back the
covers.

Alli clamped her eyes shut and sat stiffly, longing
for him to go and leave her to collapse into a puddle
of raw chagrin.

He'd reached the door when she heard him drawl,
'I hope I don't have to tell you that if this was a ploy
it didn't work.'

Her eyes flew open. Like some bronze god, from
the arrogant carriage of his head to the set of his wide
shoulders, he hadn't turned fully to face her, so the
twist of his spine outlined the pattern and swell of
muscles across his back.

Never before, she thought dazedly, had she appre-
ciated the male triangle of wide shoulders and narrow
hips, barely concealed by briefs. Sensation scorching
through her, she dragged her gaze away from the long,
powerful legs.

'A ploy?' she snarled. 'You must be joking.'

One black brow lifted. 'I've never been more serious. I don't let anyone blackmail me, and I don't fight
fair.'

His level words sent a chill through her. Keeping
her gaze level and composed, she retorted, 'So it's just

as well I don't want to fight and I'm not a black-mailer.'

Her stomach churned when he gave her an edged smile and walked out, closing the door firmly behind him and leaving behind an impression of streamlined strength and ruthless, formidable power.

And a compelling male sexuality so potent Alli's pulse was still racing half an hour later, when she emerged from her bedroom, showered and dressed in the clothes she'd worn to see Marian Hawkings.

Following distant sounds, she arrived at the kitchen, where Slade was dealing efficiently with an impressive espresso machine.

'What do you want done with the sheets and tow-els?' she asked, hoping that the curtness of her voice concealed the jolt of arousal spiking through her.

'Leave them.'

'I've stripped the bed.'

He pushed a cup of black coffee towards her. 'Leave them, Alli. I have a housekeeper who'll deal with them.'

'Lucky you,' she said, and turned on her heel.

'Alli?'

She kept going.

'Don't put me to the bother of coming after you,' he said, his cool words underpinned by inflexible de-termination. 'You may not have had a mother, but from the little I've heard about your father he'd have made sure you were taught manners.'

'And I'm sure you know it's not polite to order around your guests—however unwelcome, seedy and suspect—as though they were your servants,' she returned.

His wry laugh shocked her.

'*Touché*,' he said. 'Except that I should point out that good servants are far too rare nowadays to treat badly. Come and have some breakfast. Tui told me you're pretty impossible in the morning until you've eaten.'

Alli turned slowly. 'Nonsense. I just don't like being accused—'

'I can't remember accusing you of anything,' he stated grimly. 'Especially of being seedy and suspect.' He paused, then added, 'Or unwelcome.'

Slade watched her glorious eyes darken into mystery. She said, 'I *know* I'm unwelcome, and you implied the rest when you told me you didn't blackmail easily.'

She was an enigma. Last night a weeping bundle of terror, this morning incandescent with indignation until he mentioned her sleepwalking—if that was what it was.

Courted since he'd grown into his shoulders in his mid-teens, experience had taught Slade that he could act like an ancient despot and some women would still pursue him.

Money, he thought cynically as Alli hovered in the doorway, talked very loudly.

'You are not unwelcome,' he said curtly. 'I'm sorry if I made you feel that you were. Do you want this coffee or not?'

'It certainly sounded as though you thought that—

that I'd tried to set you up,' she said, but she came back warily into the kitchen.

She lifted the mug to her mouth, hiding behind it, but when she drank her lips moved in a slight, sensuous movement that made him glad he had a counter between them.

Last night had been endless. He'd lain in her bed in the darkness, so aroused by her soft curves and satiny skin that it had taken all his control to leash his hunger. It served him right for telling her so pompously that will-power could do anything!

Even now he desired her with a desperation that came too close to clouding his brain. In spite of the promptings of caution he wanted to believe it had been a nightmare that had driven her in search of some human warmth during the night. Although she'd clung to him she'd made no overt indication of wanting sex, seeming content to snuggle in his arms like a bird sheltering from a storm.

But he'd learned in a hard school not to take things at face value, and lust guaranteed poor decisions. He didn't know enough about Alli to risk trusting her.

Too much depended on not screwing up—and that, he thought, clamping down on memories of her body against him in bed, was not the most felicitous word to use!

'Tell me about the dream.' He poured himself a cup of coffee.

She hesitated, then shrugged. 'It's always the same—one of those self-repeating sagas. I'm looking for shelter, but no one will let me in.'

'Orphan in the storm? You kept muttering about

being cold.' He watched as she took another mouthful of the hot liquid, noting the catspaws rippling its surface. Her hand was trembling.

'Yes—well, that's part of it. I know that if I don't get warm I'll die.'

She hadn't been shivering when he'd found her outside his door. In fact she'd been locked in stasis, her body rigid, not even moving when he'd searched for the pulse in her throat.

He could still feel the silken skin beneath his fingertips.

Ruthlessly he forced his mind back to the straighter path of logic. Her hands and feet, however, had been cold. 'No wonder you were terrified.'

Her shoulders lifted a fraction and she drank some more coffee, holding the mug as though she still needed to warm her hands. 'Children often have that sort of recurring dream, but mostly they grow out of it.'

'I'm surprised you dream of the cold when you couldn't have ever experienced it on Valanu.'

She stared at him for a time, golden-brown eyes thoughtful. 'Until now I've never thought of that. Interesting, isn't it?' she finally said. 'Although I had *Grimms' Fairy Tales*, so I knew there was such a thing.'

The peal of a doorbell made her jump; when she looked suspiciously at him he said, 'I'll be back in a minute.'

Alli watched him go, her taut nerves wound even more tightly. Who could this be—friends? A quick glance at her watch dispelled that idea; only very intimate friends would turn up before eight in the morning. Caroline Forsythe?

The opening of the kitchen door brought her upright, her armour tightly fastened around her.

'Breakfast,' Slade said, carrying a couple of takeaway packages. 'Bring your coffee and we'll eat it in the next room.'

She followed him into a combination dining and living room, less formal than the room she'd seen yesterday. Comfortable and expansive, it channelled the morning sun through a wall of glass doors. Outside, lounging furniture looked over the water from a wide, long terrace.

Slade unloaded the boxes onto a table and proceeded to set out the food. Noting her swift glance at the harbour, decorated with its colourful weekend bunting of sails, he said, 'It's still chilly outside—too cold to eat there in comfort.'

'I'm getting acclimatised to New Zealand's climate.' She gave a soft laugh. 'At first I thought I'd never get warm again.'

'Cereal?' he asked.

Another hungry growl from her stomach reminded her she'd had no dinner the previous night. 'Yes, please,' she said simply.

Incredibly, sharing the first meal of the day with him brought a wary happiness. As she ate her cereal, and the splendid Eggs Benedict that he'd unpacked, they discussed Valanu and the resort, and the people Slade had dealt with there.

'How is the chief?' he asked idly.

She swallowed the last of the delectable eggs and

smiled. 'Very well. He's talking about a joint fishing venture with the Sant'Rosans.'

'And his son? Second son,' he amended blandly.

'Tama? He's fine,' she said stiffly. 'He's doing an administrative degree here in Auckland, and otherwise he spends a lot of his time, I'm told, nagging his father and the tribal council for more and more money for health issues.'

Slade's black brows quirked. 'Is he married?'

'Yes, to a charming Auckland girl.'

'Did you mind?'

'Not in the least.' She smiled with sunny nonchalance. 'His father has finally forgiven him, and the last photo Sisilu sent me was of the chief at a meeting with a small blonde girl perched on his knee.'

'And Barry Simcox?' When she looked blank he said lazily, 'I assumed you'd keep in touch?'

'No. Isn't he working for you now?'

'Not for a couple of years.' He offered her a bowl of fresh fruit. 'Try the cherimoya—it's like eating tangy custard. How about the dragon lady who ran the dancing troupe?'

Alli laughed. 'She's fine too. Still terrifying the manager into doing whatever she wants him to.'

He was, she thought after breakfast, when she went to get her bag, a good companion. His keen mind stimulated her, like his somewhat cynical sense of humour, and to her surprise she'd discovered that they shared some favourite writers and singers.

When he wanted to be he was utterly charming, but his charm masked a dangerously compelling strength. Skin tightening, she tried to banish the memory of waking up next to him. Had his hand been curved around her waist, or had that been another dream?

A nice one this time…

'He was asleep until you did your outraged virgin bit. He probably thought you were one of his girl-friends,' she said severely to her reflection, and carried her pack out into the hall.

He was waiting by the front door, but as she came towards him the telephone rang. 'Excuse me,' he said without hurry. 'I'll take it in the office.'

Alli lowered her pack to the floor and examined a magnificent, almost abstract landscape that was defi-nitely New Zealand. It was a bush scene, sombre yet vibrant. With a myriad of greens and browns the artist had conveyed the sense of peril and hidden mystery she'd noticed in the New Zealand forest.

She thought nostalgically of the waters of the la-goon at Valanu—every shade of blue melding into glowing turquoise beneath a brilliant sky. Sometimes she dreamed of the soft hush of trade winds in the coconut palms, and the crunch of blazing white sand beneath her feet.

Safer than dreaming about snow, she thought sar-donically.

Yet she was learning to love New Zealand. The parts of it she'd seen were beautiful in a wild, aloof way.

On a table beneath the bush picture a nude bronze art deco dancer postured with sinuous abandon. Ab-sorbed in its mannered, erotic grace, Alli jumped when Slade spoke from behind her.

'That was Marian.'

Composing her face so that he wouldn't read the sudden wild hope there, she turned around slowly. 'Oh?'

'She wants to see you before I take you home,' he said briefly. 'It won't be much of a delay.'

Alli could read nothing in his face. 'Did she say why?'

'No.' He opened the front door, holding it to let her through in front of him.

They drove along Auckland's streets, busy with tourists and those who'd decided to eat brunch beside the harbour on this sunny Sunday morning.

Alli tried to rein in her seething thoughts, glad when Slade said abruptly, 'I rang the hospital this morning to find out how those kids were.'

'I meant to ask you at breakfast,' she said remorsefully. It had fled her mind because she'd been enjoying herself so much.

'They've all been discharged except the boy in the coma and the girl with the broken arm. She'll be discharged this morning, and the boy is critical but stable.'

'I do hope he recovers without any damage. The boys insisted that the girls wear the seat belts,' she said. 'They were so boisterous I wondered if they'd been drinking, but it didn't seem as though they had.'

'High on youth,' he commented dispassionately.

Alli glanced at him, her stomach tightening at the arrogant symmetry of line and angle that was his profile. How did he do it? she thought desperately. Being with him sharpened all her senses; today the sky was brighter, the perfume of jasmine through the window more musky and evocative, the texture of her clothes against her skin supple and fine and erotically charged.

Once more they took the silent lift up to the fourth floor. This time it was Marian who opened the door— a Marian much more composed than on the previous day. She accepted Slade's kiss, and then asked Alli, 'My dear, how did you sleep?'

'Fine, thank you,' Alli said mundanely, relaxing only when their hostess waved them into the room where she'd received them the previous day.

'Do sit down,' she said, and settled into her chair, examining Alli with a small frown between her exquisitely plucked brows. 'I was shocked when Caroline told me that Slade had rung to say you'd had to deal with an accident—what a ghastly thing! I'd have nightmares for a week!'

Without looking at Slade, Alli replied, 'At least only one person was badly hurt.'

'Do you know how he is?'

Concisely Slade explained what he'd learned.

Marian sighed. 'I feel for his poor parents.'

A slight pause stretched Alli's nerves to breaking point. She felt completely alien in this luxurious room—and that was odd, because she hadn't felt like that in Slade's apartment.

Marian picked up an envelope from the table beside her chair and held it out. 'I asked you here this morning because I want to give you something.'

Alli tensed. If she's offering me money, she thought disjointedly, I'll—I'll throw it at her!

Fingers trembling, she opened it. But there was no money. Intensely relieved, she took out a photograph and examined it, her heart contracting; this time the woman was in full face, eyeing the camera with a half-smile. In colouring and features she was almost identical to the face Alli saw in her mirror every morning.

She looked across at the older woman.

'Yes,' Marian said, 'it's your mother.'

Blindly, Alli turned it over. Her mother's handwriting was a bold scrawl. *To my sister Marian,* she'd written. *So you don't forget me.*

Well, running away with her sister's husband had made sure of that!

'Thank you.' Then she suddenly remembered something, and scrabbled in her bag until she found an envelope. 'I don't know whether you want this, but it's a—it's yours, anyway.'

She held it out. Automatically Marian accepted it, but she didn't open it. 'What is it?'

'It's a wedding photograph I found in my father's things,' Alli said uncomfortably.

Another awkward pause followed, broken by Marian's quick reply. 'No, I don't want it, I'm afraid.' She handed it back. 'Do you know anything about your mother at all?'

Alli tucked the photograph of her mother into the envelope and put it in her bag. 'Nothing. My father never spoke of her.'

For a moment the older woman looked inexpressibly sad, but the fleeting expression vanished under the mask of a good hostess. 'Were you happy as a child?'

Alli gave her a brilliant smile and stood up, Slade following suit. 'In lots of ways I had a super childhood. Children are very resilient, you know. They accept things.'

Marian's glance tangled with Slade's. 'Yes, I know. I'm glad you were happy.' She got to her feet and led the way to the door.

But before they reached it she stopped and turned to Alli. 'Thank you for coming to see me,' she said unexpectedly. 'You must have felt like telling me to go to hell when I rejected your approach so comprehensively two years ago. But your existence came as a...' she hesitated, as though discarding the word that came naturally to her tongue and substituting another '...a huge shock. I thought you'd—never been born, you see.'

It was, Alli could see, all the excuse she was going to give. And it was also a definite goodbye. She didn't blame the older woman; each sight of her niece had to be an exercise in remembered bitterness.

'It's all right,' she said swiftly. 'I do understand. Thank you for giving me this photograph—I'll treasure it.'

Marian's smile was a mere sketch, and before she could speak Slade said, 'It's time we went, Alli.'

'Caroline will be so sorry to have missed you,' Marian said.

But Caroline must have come in while they were talking, because she was in the hall when they came out. Alli felt the other woman's resentment, cloaked though it was with a gracious smile, when Caroline asked, 'Are you going to be at the Thorpes' tonight, Slade?'

'Yes,' he said, smiling at her.

'Oh, good. I'll see you there, then.' Her look at Alli held a flicker of smugness. 'Lovely to have met you, Alison. Goodbye.'

Less subtle than Marian's farewell, but no less definite. Alli nodded and said goodbye, and went out with Slade into a blue and gold and crystal day, warm as a welcome and heady as champagne.

Its beauty was almost wasted. As they drove north they spoke little. A few hours ago she'd woken up in this man's arms; by the time they reached the Lodge she felt as though he'd withdrawn to the other side of the moon.

Sadness almost closed her throat.

'Who was it,' Slade remarked as they swung off the road onto the rutted track that led to the Lodge, 'that said to be careful what you wish for because you might get it?'

'Bluebeard, probably,' Alli returned jauntily. 'Don't worry, I'm not shattered. I was surprised to discover that my upright father was an adulterer—and with his wife's sister—but I suppose I always suspected there was something odd about the situation. Men who find refuge at the back of the trade winds usually have something to hide from.'

'Indeed,' he said dryly. 'A very philosophical attitude.'

Outside the Lodge she held out her hand for her pack and said formally, 'Thank you very much for—for everything. Goodbye.'

But her plans to get rid of him quickly were countered by Tui, who marched out through the door and said, 'Are you coming in for lunch, Slade?'

He shook his head with an appreciative smile. 'No, I have to get back to town.'

'You're missing hot scones,' Tui said, adding slyly, 'With whipped cream and home-made tamarillo jam.'

'You know how to tempt a man; unfortunately I have an appointment in Auckland. Thank you for the offer—can I take you up on it another time?'

'Any time,' Tui told him.

He looked at Alli, green eyes gleaming. 'Take care,' he said, and turned and strode lithely back to the big car.

Left to herself, Alli would have gone inside, but Tui stayed and waved, so she did too, because anything other would have produced questions.

'What we used to call a real dish,' her boss said with pleasure. 'He's got presence, that one. I'll bet the women chase him.'

'He might have made up his mind which one he'll have,' Alli said, thinking of Caroline's eminent worthiness to be Slade Hawkings's wife. He'd said she had no right to object to anything he did, but he was meeting her that night at the Thorpes', whoever they were.

And Caroline Forsythe struck Alli as being quietly determined.

'Ah, well, better get back to work,' Tui said with a last wave that was answered by a short toot as Slade's car took the cattlestop. 'You're looking a bit tired. Have a nap, and then take Lady out for a gallop along the beach.' She waited until Alli hefted her bag before asking, 'When are you going to see him again?'

'Not ever,' Alli said, the words resounding heavily inside her head.

Tui laughed. 'It's not like you to be coy.'

'I'm not!'

Her employer said cheerfully, 'Well, let me tell you something, girl—that man wants you. He'll be back, you'll see.'

Don't do this, Alli said silently. 'I didn't know you were a mind-reader.'

'Can't do minds, but I'm pretty good at body language,' Tui returned smartly. 'He's tracking, Alli. If you don't want him, you'd better start running.'

TUI bustled into the kitchen, her expression a mixture of sly humour and surprise. 'You're a close-mouthed one,' she accused, slapping a newspaper down on the table in front of Alli. 'You haven't said a word about last weekend in town with the handsome hunk. Not even about being hounded by the paparazzi!'

Swallowing the final mouthful of delectable chicken pie, Alli turned a startled face to her. 'What?'

Tui flattened the paper out and pointed triumphantly. 'There you are—and it's easy to see it's you! Not like the other one on the beach.'

Sure enough, someone had taken a photograph of Slade's car as he'd driven out of the car park under his apartment building. Stomach roiling, Alli noticed a smile on her photographed face. She couldn't remember smiling—especially not a satisfied smirk like that, hinting at a long night of well-sated passion.

Beneath the photograph the gossip columnist had written, *Who is the woman leaving Slade Hawkings's apartment early—very early—one morning?*

'Didn't you see the photographer?' Tui asked, her curiosity palpable.

'No.'

'Can't say I blame you—if I were sitting beside Slade Hawkings I wouldn't be looking for paparazzi.' Tui pushed the newspaper closer. 'Go on, take it.

That's the second time you've hit the headlines—you'd better start a scrapbook.'

'I don't want it,' Alli said defiantly, averting her eyes from the photograph.

'Well, want it or not, you'd better get ready to go out, because that's Slade Hawkings's car coming up the drive right now.'

A bewildering mixture of apprehension and awareness churned through Alli. Leaping to her feet, she muttered, 'Damn! Oh, damn!' and cast a hunted look through the window.

'Probably the first time a woman's reacted like that to his arrival,' Tui said knowledgeably. 'I'll go and meet him—you change into something that looks a bit more upmarket. Those jeans fit nicely, but your sweatshirt isn't ageing gracefully.'

'He won't notice.' Not true, she knew.

Her employer knew it too. 'That one notices everything. Go on. What about your nice mossy green jersey? It looks great with your skin. And put some lipstick on.'

Alli cast another harried glance through the window before fleeing. Once in her small bedroom she shrugged into the jersey, but rebelled at lipstick.

He'd come about the photograph, of course. No doubt he was angry. Well, so was she. Who the heck had staked out his apartment so early in the morning? And why? They wouldn't have done it for plain Alli Pierce, so they must have been tracking Slade.

Head erect and shoulders painfully squared, she walked back to the Lodge, flinching when a wood pigeon swooped across her path at eye level about two feet in front of her, its white breast gleaming in the sun.

Her pulse raced from flutter to jungle beat when she saw Slade in the office. Her first involuntary thought was that lipstick wouldn't have helped anyway. Darkly dominant, he turned to examine her, his displeasure like an icy cloud.

'Come for a drive,' he said, and forestalled her automatic refusal by saying, 'Tui says she can manage without you for half an hour.'

'Longer than that if it's necessary,' Tui said with a stern glance at Alli. 'See if you can persuade her to take her holidays, will you? She's got about ten days in lieu.'

Tui, not now! Self-preservation goaded Alli into terse speech. 'I don't need holidays, and I'd rather walk along the beach.'

No way was she going to let herself be locked in the car with him for half an hour.

Equally crisply, Slade returned, 'Fine. Show me the way.'

Once outside the Lodge she asked, 'Have you heard how the boy in a coma is?'

'Recovering well,' he said. 'No brain damage, apparently.'

'Thank God,' she breathed.

'He was lucky; if he's got any sense he'll learn from it.' Slade looked around as she indicated the board-walk between the dunes. 'This is very different from Valanu.'

'Much colder,' she said with a half-smile, then swung into tourist mode. 'Tui and Joe and the local conservation society are doing their best to reclaim the dunes. They've got them fenced off so no one can ride through them, and, as you can see, it's working.'

Out on the beach, the sun smiled down on rows of waves sweeping onto the beach in perfect formation. Lithe black forms played amongst them—surfers. The water was warming, and very soon they'd be able to discard their wetsuits.

'Why are you here?' Alli asked.

'Partly to discuss the photograph in the paper today.'

'We can't do anything about that,' she said with a casual shrug. 'No one knows who I am, so any gossip will die. What I'd like to know is why the photographer was so conveniently there. Do you usually have paparazzi staking you out?'

'Occasionally.'

'Why that day?'

'I doubt if it was anything to do with you,' he said shortly.

She glowered at him. 'Of course it wasn't. You're the celebrity, not me.'

'I'm not a celebrity, and gossip doesn't worry me.'

'I'm afraid I don't have your lofty attitude to it. Finding myself in the newspaper made my skin crawl. What I can't work out is where the photographer was. I didn't see anyone.' Probably because she'd been too busy sending Slade sideways glances through her lashes. The thought of people all over New Zealand drawing conclusions from that smile rankled.

'It was taken with a telephoto lens from the park across the street.' Slade stooped and picked up a length of driftwood, hefting it a moment to test its weight before hurling it into the surf. Watching it sink below the waves, he said, 'Don't worry about it—you won't appear in any other photographs.'

'I'm glad to hear it.' Keeping her eyes on the distant place where the beach receded into a soft salt-haze, Alli frowned against the sun. A painful needle of hope pricked her heart, tormenting her with its persistence. To get rid of it once and for all, she said briskly, 'It's very kind of you to come and tell me this, but really I didn't expect it. A phone call would have been enough, although that wouldn't have been necessary either. After all, we've already said our goodbyes.'

Stone-faced, Slade scrutinised her. 'You surely don't believe that Marian would just hand over a photograph of your mother and send you on your way without another word?'

She'd believed just that—after all, Marian's farewell had seemed more than definite.

'I see you do.' His voice was dry. 'You're her only relative.'

'For which she's probably devoutly thankful.'

'You were certainly a shock to her,' he admitted. 'However, she doesn't want to lose sight of you.'

Alli didn't know what to say to this. In the end she contented herself with a cautious, 'That's very kind of her, but I don't want her to feel any sort of obligation to me.'

'It comes with the territory,' he said shortly. 'Families work like that. She's asked me to tell you that she'd like you to stay with her so you can get to know each other.'

His expression didn't alter, but she knew he disapproved of this latest development. Alli fought a brief, bitter battle with herself. Marian was offering what she'd always wanted—a family. Yet a deep-seated wariness held her back. 'Caroline—'

Slade cut in with abrupt authority. 'Caroline won't be there.'

Meanly relieved, she said slowly, 'How long does Marian want me to stay?'

'A couple of weeks.' He smiled briefly and without humour. 'I suggested that she and you spend time together at the bach.'

Alli knew that northern New Zealanders used that word to refer to a small, unpretentious holiday house by the beach, but she had a pretty fair idea that Slade's bach would be neither modest nor unsophisticated.

'I don't think that's a good idea,' she said quickly, before she could change her mind.

'Why?'

'I can't believe that she'd want to know me. I must bring back some pretty shattering memories.'

'That won't wash,' he returned instantly. 'She had a very happy marriage with my father—happy enough to rob the fiasco of her first marriage of its sting.'

'I suspect she feels sorry for me. Well, I don't need to be rescued—I've made a good life for myself, with friends and a job I enjoy. I'm not a charity case.'

She angled her chin up at him, the feline enticement of her face temporarily overwhelmed by a cold, still pride. The wind snatched up a handful of dry sand and hurled it at them, making her blink and turn away.

Coolly he said, 'I don't recollect either Marian or I insinuating that you were some orphan in the storm.'

She flushed at the memory that phrase brought back, and he said something under his breath before resuming on an impatient note, 'And since Tui says you're overdue for holidays I can't see why this is such a big deal.'

That, she thought wearily, was the problem—for him it wasn't a big deal. For her it was becoming increasingly so. His suggestion came wrapped with such tempting possibilities—a family, and a man she was starting to dream about whenever she loosened the reins on her will-power...

If only Tui had kept her mouth shut!

'Thank you very much,' she told him firmly, 'but it's not necessary. I wanted to meet my mother and find out why she abandoned me. OK, meeting her is impossible now, but I do know what happened. I have no claim on either of you, so it's probably better that we leave it at that.'

He said calmly, 'You prised the cat out of the bag, Alli; it's too late to thrust it back in again. If you turn Marian down she'll keep trying. She doesn't give up easily.' He looked around at the beach and the surf, the wild exuberance of the gulls whirling over the surf like scraps of white paper, and said dispassionately, 'It wouldn't surprise me if she turned up at the Lodge.'

Alli tightened her lips to hide an odd feeling of being driven discreetly but inevitably into a decision she wasn't ready for. 'She'd hate it. It's very casual and laid-back, and most of our clientele are surfers or fishermen or naturalists.'

'She's adaptable.'

Alli turned her face to the sea. While they'd been talking the wind had dropped away, and the breeze that feathered across her face now was soft with the promise of summer.

Indecision kept her silent. She longed to forge some links, however casual and fragile, with the only relative she had; it was, she thought with a touch of bitterness, ironic that if she let herself be drawn into the family she faced real danger from Slade.

Well, not from Slade—from her reckless feelings for him. Prudence counselled her to refuse; the heady thrill of being close to him weakened her resolve.

And from what Slade had said he didn't plan to be at the bach.

In the end she licked the salt from her lips and surrendered. 'All right, then. I'll go to the bach for ten days if Poppy, Tui's daughter-in-law, can take my place at the Lodge.'

Within half an hour she was staring at the road twisting away in front of them.

'Your employer still doesn't entirely trust me,' Slade observed, uncannily echoing her thoughts. 'She wasn't going to let you go unless I gave her the address and phone number of the bach.'

'I don't think Tui trusts anyone but her family.'

He nodded. 'Probably a good maxim to live by.' He didn't add, *And sometimes you can't even trust them,* but no doubt he was thinking it.

Alli certainly was.

Slade's bach turned out to be the only house on a hillside above a melon-slice of champagne-coloured sand. The building *was* far from modest; backed by the dark luxuriance of coastal forest, the double-storeyed colonial gem stood four-square and proud, surrounded by a columned verandah with balconies above.

'It looks like a doll's house!' Alli exclaimed, leaning forward as they negotiated the steep drive. 'A very large doll's house.'

'It used to be the original homestead for the area.' With the skill of familiarity Slade steered around a hairpin bend shaded by the thick, feathery canopy of kanuka trees.

Just north of Auckland they'd left the main road and driven through fertile valleys where dairy farms, vineyards and orchards mingled in harmony beneath a range of high hills sombre with a thick, tangled cloak of New Zealand bush.

'I don't see any farm,' she said, beating back a giddy mixture of foreboding and anticipation.

'We've been coming through it for the past fifteen minutes—it started at the first cattlestop. When my father decided he wasn't made for country life he put in a manager's house closer to the road and replanted this hillside in native trees.'

The drive swung around the back of the house onto a wide gravel forecourt. Slade stopped the vehicle and turned off the engine. 'Welcome to my home.'

Alli froze. 'I thought you lived in Auckland.'

'I spend about half my time there. Why? Does it make a difference?'

'No,' she denied, because what else could she say?

Nothing would have persuaded me to come if I'd known you intended to be here too. Not likely.

He saw through her, of course. Steel edging his words, he drawled, 'Don't worry, I'm off to Tahiti tomorrow.'

Her relief must have shown too clearly, because he smiled—not a nice smile. 'You could come with me,' he suggested, in a tone that was a subtle insult.

Alli scrambled out of the car, her nerves twanging. 'No, thanks.'

He climbed out and reached in the boot for her pack, straightening up with a strap over one shoulder. 'Scared, Alli?'

The direct challenge made her seethe. 'I came to see Marian.'

Tall and dark and compelling, he slung her pack onto his shoulder and walked across the forecourt to a door. It opened as he got there, and Marian beamed at him.

Feeling awkward, Alli followed him and was greeted with a more restrained smile. 'Come in,' the older woman said. 'How are you, Alli?'

'Fine, thank you,' Alli replied automatically.

'I'm so glad you could come. Slade, I've put Alli in the middle bedroom.' Chatting lightly about the journey, she led Alli up the stairs to the top storey and into a room decorated in shades of ivory and soft cream.

Acutely aware of Slade following them with the pack, Alli said, 'Oh, this is lovely. So restful.'

'It has a pretty view out over the bay.' Her hostess gestured towards the glass doors that led out onto the balcony, then indicated another door. 'Your bathroom is through there. We'll leave you to refresh yourself, and when you come on down we'll have afternoon tea. Turn left at the bottom of the stairs and follow the voices!'

The room had been decorated with a deft hand—an old-fashioned iron-framed bed looked as though it had always been there, and long curtains puffed gently in the breeze. Instead of unpacking, Alli went out onto the balcony and discovered with delight that it was a private one.

She took a deep breath, inhaling the delicious spicy scent of kanuka trees and the ever-present tang of salt.

Time enough to admire the view later, she thought, turning reluctantly away. Swiftly she sorted her clothes into the wardrobe, then picked up her sponge bag and walked into the bathroom.

After washing her face and combing her hair, she tracked the other two to a room that opened out onto the same magnificent view of the sea.

'Slade tells me you drink tea,' Marian said cheerfully. She patted the white sofa beside her and said, 'Come and tell me how you like it. So many young things don't drink tea or coffee nowadays, I find. It's almost a relief to find someone who does!'

After ten minutes Alli decided her hostess's exquisite manners were a mask. But then, she thought with a fleeting glance at Slade's angular face, they were all wearing masks. The time she'd agreed to spend in this lovely house stretched before her like a small taste of eternity.

After she'd drunk her tea Marian commanded,

'Slade, why don't you show Alli around? I'm sure she'd like to see the beach.'

With his trademark lithe grace Slade rose from the chair. 'Come along, Alli,' he said, with a smile as burnished and bland as sheet metal. 'Let me introduce you to Kawau Bay.'

He took her out onto a wide deck, overlooking the beach, and led her down a couple of steps and across a lawn.

'I love pohutukawas,' Alli said, stopping by one huge tree. 'They symbolise Northland's summers, with their crimson and scarlet flowers like millions of tiny tassels, but they don't grow by the Lodge.'

'They like it rocky,' Slade told her as they went down another two steps to the beach, 'but they can't stand the cold west and southerly winds that sweep over the west coast. Give them a cliff overlooking an island-sheltered bay and they're happy.'

'This is charming.' Smiling, she took in the small curve of sand, the smooth waters of the wide inlet and the shapes of islands to the east. Loyally she added, 'But I do love the west coast. It's so wild and free and dangerous.'

'This can be dangerous too,' he said. 'Don't swim on your own. It's not like the lagoon at Valanu, where you might as well be in a bath.'

'That had its dangers too,' she said quietly, thinking of a friend who had been taken by a shark.

'Life's full of danger.' Slade sounded sardonic. 'The Maori say that the west coast is like a man, strong and virile and warlike, whereas the east coast resembles a woman, beautiful and soft. I'm sure they'd be the first to admit that women can be just as dangerous as men in their own way.'

The sand crunched beneath Alli's feet when they reached the tideline. She stopped there and looked around, her expression grave and considering. To one side, under the low headland that separated this bay from the next, a wharf ran out into deep water. Two boats were tied up to it: a large cruiser, with swept-up bow and all the flashy mod cons, and an elegant dowager from the thirties, solid, dignified and restrained.

'I used to jump off the end of the wharf,' Slade told her. He looked down at her. 'I suppose like me you learned to swim before you could walk?'

'Literally,' she agreed. 'The lagoon was an ideal place to learn, of course.'

'Do you miss Valanu?'

She said thoughtfully, 'Yes, but I always knew I'd have to leave one day. Living there was like living in a fairy story.'

'How long was your father ill before he died?'

'I'm surprised you don't know,' she said, the acid in her voice tempered by irony. 'A year.'

'He didn't think to come back to New Zealand for medical care?'

She looked at the pink-gold sand and said desolately, 'He wouldn't go anywhere, not even to the clinic until it was far too late. I think he wanted to die.'

It was the first time she'd admitted it to herself.

To her astonishment Slade's warm hand enclosed hers. Sensation ran up her arm, quick and shocking as electricity, and somehow transmuted into ripples of slow, wondrous sensuality that gave her a tantalising glimpse of what it might be like to be loved by Slade Hawkings…

Except that it wouldn't be love. So, although the comfort he offered was powerfully seductive, she pulled her hand from his. 'I think he really loved Marian all the time.'

'I won't say forget it, because the past casts long shadows, but mulling it over and wondering what really happened is a waste of time and mental energy,' Slade said in a voice that lacked any emotion. 'Not only are you never going to know, but I'm sure your father would have wanted you to make your own life without dwelling on his mistakes. Let your parents sleep in peace, Alli.'

She was touched by his understanding, and surprised at the slight abrasiveness of his tone in the latter part of it. 'Yes, sir,' she said meekly.

He laughed, a deep sound that twisted her heart. 'Did I sound like a grandfather? I can pontificate with the best of them.'

'I don't think you were pontificating,' she said, trying hard to be objective. 'It's just that—well, my father was difficult to love because he never unbent, but he was always *there*, and he was reliable. And he was a man of honour. He was respected. When he died they buried him with the chiefs.' She looked up and said simply, 'And he made sure I didn't lie, or steal. He had very strong moral principles, so I suppose I want to know how a man like that could betray someone as comprehensively as he did Marian.'

'He may never have had a grand passion before he met your mother, and been totally unable to deal with it. The thing you have to remember is that he didn't betray you,' Slade said austerely.

She nodded, thinking that this was a strangely intimate conversation to be having with him—one she should not have embarked on. It would, she thought warily, be dangerous to reveal too much of herself to Slade.

She stopped beneath a pohutukawa branch overspreading the beach. A large tyre had been tied to it. 'Your swing?' she said brightly.

'I believe my father was the original user, but this is not the original tyre, or even the original chain. We often have visitors here, and their children love swinging as much as I did.'

The thought of him as a child did something odd to her heart. He'd have been a handful—bold and determined and intelligent...

Banishing such subversive thoughts, she said even more brightly, 'This is a wonderful place for children.'

And almost winced at the banality of her words.

'Indeed,' he said gravely. 'But I hope you will enjoy it too. As soon as I'm gone you'll be able to relax.'

'You don't make me nervous!'

The moment she said it she knew she should have kept her lips firmly buttoned. He looked at her with a gleam of something very like amusement in his green eyes, but as she glared at him it died, to be replaced by a piercing intensity. Alli's mouth went dry. She heard some bird calling, the clear notes dropping into a spreading silence.

He said quietly, 'Then why do your eyes go dark on the rare occasions when you look at me—?'

'I look at you quite often!' Too much—but usually when he couldn't see.

'Mostly you concentrate on an ear, or my hair, or the pocket of my shirt,' he said blandly. 'And did you know that tiny pulse in the base of your throat speeds up whenever I come near?'

Mesmerised, she shook her head. 'I—no.'

By then her mouth was so arid she almost croaked the words. He lifted a lean, tanned hand and touched the hollow in her throat, and any further attempt at speaking was doomed.

How could a fingertip do so much damage? It drained her of will-power until all she could do was stare into his narrowed eyes as though they were her one hope of salvation.

He laughed softly, and then his face came nearer. Alli closed her eyes against the fires in his, but by the time he kissed her mute, imploring mouth she could no longer think. Lost in a rush of heat, she swayed, and he pulled her against his strong body.

It was so familiar, as though she'd done this thousands of times, and she relaxed into him and let his kiss wreak devastation on her already shaken defences.

Her skin tightened deliciously. She shivered as his hand slid down her back to find the curve of her hips, but she didn't pull away.

Whenever she'd kissed other men their arousal had always faintly repelled her, but now, with Slade, she relished the evidence of his desire. Response, white-hot and elemental, scorched through her, washing away inhibitions and fear.

He lifted his mouth, but before disappointment struck he pressed a series of kisses along the line of her jaw. Delight leapt from nerve-end to nerve-end in a tornado of sensation, a delight that turned fierce and wild when his mouth found the soft lobe of her ear and he nipped it, using his teeth with exquisite precision.

That tender nip made her acutely, deliciously aware of the weight of her breasts, of over-sensitive tips against his hard chest. From her breasts, that wildfire sensation homed in on the place deep inside her, a place that ached with desperate hunger.

His hand swept from her hip to cup the side of her breast; while she dived further into the wilder seas of sensation his thumb played with tormenting slowness over the pleading tip.

Alli's groan was torn from her innermost feelings—a sound, she dimly realised far too late, of surrender.

And then his mouth left hers and he said in a voice entirely empty of any emotion, 'Still positive you don't want to come to Tahiti with me, Alli?'

Stunned, she met coldly calculating eyes, green and cold as crystals. Shame flooded her as she understood that he'd been testing her.

She wanted to slap his arrogant face, and then, humiliatingly, she wanted to burst into tears!

CHAPTER EIGHT

PRIDE gave Alli the strength to pull herself together. She stepped back and said, in a voice she prayed was composed enough to fool him, 'I came here at Marian's invitation, so going to Tahiti would be rude.'

Slade smiled cynically. 'More entertaining, though.'

She shrugged. 'What's fun got to do with it?' She hoped she'd managed to prick his pride with her scorn.

If she had he didn't show it. Instead he stood back courteously to let her walk ahead of him up the steps to the lawn. 'You are, of course, entirely correct,' he said evenly. 'Security is always important.'

She stopped. 'What exactly do you mean by that?'

The gold rays in his eyes glinted. 'What do you think I meant by it?'

'Listen to me,' she said fiercely. 'I don't want money from Marian.'

If she'd thought her directness might throw him she had misjudged the man. He said, 'I'm glad to hear that.'

But she could tell he didn't believe her.

Clenching her jaw to hold back a bitter disillusionment, she said, 'I'm not going to try and justify myself—people with prejudices are rarely able to change them even when confronted by the truth. And this *is* the truth. I've managed my life so far without asking for money from anyone; I don't intend to start now.

Besides, if you think I'm here to feather my nest why did you bring me?'

'So you didn't *ask* Barry Simcox on Valanu to pay you three times the rate everyone else was paid?' he observed, taking her elbow and turning her towards the house.

Even that brief touch shortened her breath. 'He said that because I was a New Zealander that's what I should be paid...'

Her voice faded under Slade's sardonic glance. How stupid she'd been! Of course she hadn't been entitled to the extra money; Barry had made the decision after her father died, no doubt thinking she needed extra income.

'It seemed logical at the time. I just didn't think,' she said lamely. She dragged air into her lungs and spoke into the disbelieving silence. 'I'll pay back every cent I owe you, and you can stop testing me. It's harassment and it's demeaning.'

He said on note of mockery, 'Indeed? I don't want your money—you've more than repaid it with your excellent ideas about getting Sea Winds back on its feet. As for harassment—while it was happening I could have sworn you enjoyed it just as much as I enjoy kissing you.'

Stunned, she risked a glance at him, and met a coolly watchful scrutiny. Pleasure it might have been, but he'd been in complete control of the situation—unlike her, weakly melting in a puddle at his feet!

He added, 'And making love to you would be pleasure also.'

Colour stained her skin. 'Lovemaking as a test of integrity? The thought makes my flesh crawl.'

'If we made love,' he said silkily, 'I suspect that by the second kiss everything but carnal appetite would fly out of the window.' He watched more colour roil up through her skin, and went on, 'I had reason to distrust you. You must admit that your first letter to Marian was aggressive enough to make her very wary.'

Alli flushed. 'I was—angry, I suppose,' she said reluctantly. 'I wanted to know why she—why my mother had abandoned me.'

She still didn't know that, and now she never would. But it no longer overshadowed her life. Somehow Slade had redirected her energies.

I am not in love with him, she thought, sudden panic kicking her stomach.

Slade said, 'It's the primal fear of children, isn't it— abandonment by the mother? I was barely four when my mother died. I remember the shock and the bewilderment and the terror.'

Heart-wrung for the small, heartbroken boy whose mother had left him in the most final of ways, she said quietly, 'At least I didn't know what I was missing.'

At the bottom of the steps leading onto the deck, he said, 'Just to set the record straight, if it *is* money you're interested in you should know that Marian's income is derived from a trust fund. She can't touch the principal.'

Alli went white. 'I find you utterly disgusting,' she retorted, and ran ahead, across the deck and into the house.

Once in her room she paced the floor until she regained control over her seething emotions. That final cut from Slade had been calculated to wound.

Why did he dislike her so much?

Because their kiss had affected him as much as it had her?

She dismissed the thought immediately. Slade had probably been born with an innate knowledge of how to please a woman, a skill honed by practice.

So kissing her hadn't been a big deal for him. Oh, he'd wanted her—but lust came easily and meant very little.

After all, she wanted him...

She walked out onto the balcony. While she'd been pacing the sun had dipped low in the west, its long rays gilding the bush behind the house and edging the clouds with gold. Slade was strolling towards the beach, tall and confident, his gait as smooth as the silent, killing lope of a predator.

A knock at the door made her jump.

It was Marian, smiling and pleasant. 'I thought you might like to come down and have a drink with us. A fax has just come through for poor Slade—he has to leave tonight instead of tomorrow morning, so we'll have dinner early.'

Alli glanced down at her clothes. 'Should I change?'

'Oh, no—you look lovely.'

Something in Marian's tone made her look up sharply, but the other woman had already turned away. 'See you in a few minutes,' she said brightly, and disappeared down the stairs.

Slowly Alli tidied up before following her hostess.

It was an odd evening, with hidden tensions prowling beneath the relaxed, sophisticated surface. As always, Marian was the epitome of a gracious hostess, and Slade was amiable enough—in the fashion of a well-fed tiger.

Apart from the lazy appreciation in his tone when he spoke to her, Alli thought savagely, you'd never know that he'd kissed her senseless.

At last she could bear it no longer. 'Do you mind if I go up now? I'm a little tired.'

Slade's gaze rested thoughtfully on her face as Marian said, 'Not at all. Do let me know if there's anything you need, won't you?'

'Thank you.' Pinning a smile onto her mouth, she turned to Slade. 'Have a safe journey,' she said quietly.

'Thank you.' His eyes were more golden than green, and unease brushed like a feather across her skin.

Back in her room, she sat down in the darkness and tried to work out what had set her intuition jangling.

Something about this situation didn't ring true. Slade warning her off was logical. She suspected he trusted very few people, and only after they'd earned it. And he was hugely protective of his stepmother.

Frowning, she struggled to make sense of a jumble of hunches and faint impressions.

Marian had asked her to come here, supposedly so that they could get to know each other, but beneath the older woman's superb manners lay something else, something so tenuous it was only visible in swiftly concealed flashes.

Not dislike, she thought carefully, not even caution.

If she hád to pin it down to one thing, she'd say that Marian was in the grip of tightly controlled fear.

'No,' she said aloud, shaking her head.

She had to be over-dramatising, because why should Marian be afraid of her? And if she was, or if that emotion she sensed wasn't fear but something else— say, repugnance—why had the older woman asked her to stay?

It simply didn't make sense. 'So you're wrong,' she said slowly.

The hands in her lap suddenly clenched. She didn't know what Slade thought or felt or wanted, but he'd made no secret of the fact that he didn't trust her.

Perhaps he'd seconded his stepmother's invitation in the hope that Alli would reveal herself in her true colours, whatever they were?

That made sense. Marian might not be able to spend more than the interest from her trust fund, but in comparison to most people she was rich. And Slade was well on the way to becoming a billionaire, if he wasn't already. So when a relation showed up out of the blue naturally they'd want to know what sort of person she was.

Especially as her parents seemed to have had very low moral standards!

'In other words,' she murmured to the distant sound of an outboard motor puttering quietly around a nearby headland, 'you're on trial because they think you might be like Alison.'

As a child, when she'd imagined finding her family she'd always assumed they'd accept her freely and lovingly. Maturity had tempered that first innocent belief, of course, but it still hurt to know that any hope of acceptance lay in convincing Slade she hadn't come to prey on Marian.

She woke to a silent house and a breathless dawn shimmering across the bay; the trees on the hillside were cloaked in mist that streamed upwards in transparent tendrils.

It was an exquisite beginning to a time that was an odd mixture of laughter and tension. Marian had a keen sense of humour that often bubbled over into wit. She never asked personal questions, but she wanted to know about Alli's life in Valanu, and Alli was happy to tell her.

But gradually, while they walked along the beach and beneath the canopy of the forest Slade's father had planted, while they ate meals at charming vineyard cafés and explored the lovely countryside around, visiting a marine reserve to watch fish that approached them without fear, Alli realised two things.

One was that whenever someone approached Marian she introduced Alli as a friend, chatted briefly, and then moved on within a few minutes.

The other was that Marian revealed very little of herself. She didn't speak of her family, and she never talked about the sister who had borne her husband's child—she didn't even mention Slade often.

While the sunny days passed in golden serenity, Alli's resolve hardened. Once this was over she'd go back to the Lodge and pick up her own life. She might even, she thought, go to Australia. And although that felt like running away, it also seemed eminently sen-

sible, because she didn't want her presence to upset
this woman she was learning to like.

Once she asked, 'Did my father have any relatives?'

Marian looked at her with quick sympathy. 'He was
an only child, and his parents died young. He never
spoke of cousins or any family.'

'And you?' Alli ventured.

Marian's face closed down. 'A few distant cousins in
England—I've long lost touch with them.' Smoothly
she moved onto another subject, cutting off any further
questions.

Not that Alli would have asked them.

Almost a week after Slade had left, she was walking
down the stairs when she heard what sounded like a
soft groan from behind her. Every sense alert, she
swung around. The housekeeper usually spent the couple of hours after lunch at her cottage in the next bay,
so Marian was the only other person in the house.

The silence suddenly turned oppressive, weighing
Alli down. It had to be Marian, who always rested for
a short time after lunch. But it hadn't been a snore...

Oh, well, she could only make a fool of herself.
Biting her lip, she turned and ran lightly up the staircase. Outside the door to Marian's room she stopped
and listened, but heard nothing else.

Her swift, tentative knock seemed to echo, but she
heard a faint noise from inside the room. She drew in
a deep breath and said, 'Marian? Are you all right?'

No answer. By now worried, she said, 'I'm going
to open the door.'

Carefully she turned the handle and peeked in. The
curtains were drawn, but through the dimness she

could see the older woman in an armchair; she seemed to be asleep, but something about her stillness alarmed Alli.

'I'll just check that you're all right,' she said quietly, and approached the chair.

Halfway across the room she realised that Marian's eyes were open and fixed on her. Was she enduring some sort of waking dream?

Tensely, Alli said, 'Are you not well?'

No answer, although the muscles in the older woman's throat moved as if she tried to speak. Panic punched Alli in the stomach; she took Marian's hand and said steadily, trying to fill her voice with reassurance, 'Marian, wake up. It's all right, you're at home and in your bedroom…'

Silently Marian continued to stare at her—no, Alli thought with a shiver, *through* her. Something was seriously wrong. She said, 'I'll ring Mrs Hopkins and get her to call an ambulance and your doctor. Don't worry—you'll be fine.'

She lifted the telephone by the bed and punched the housekeeper's number through, only to get no answer. Mrs Hopkins had been going out to lunch, she suddenly remembered.

For the second time in too few weeks she dialled 111 and, when an impersonal voice answered, explained exactly what had happened.

'Just talk gently to her,' the voice at the other end said, before the connection was cut.

Alli picked up the older woman's flaccid hand and said quietly, 'An ambulance is coming. It won't take long—you'll soon be in hospital, where they can find out what the problem is.'

The housekeeper arrived back from lunch just before the ambulance, and packed her employer's bag while the medics stabilised her. Feeling like an extra leg, Alli hung around, desperately concerned. Gone was Marian's smiling charm; she'd suddenly become old and desperately fragile.

'Should we ring Slade?' Mrs Hopkins worried as the stretcher carried Marian down the stairs. 'It looks like a stroke to me.'

'He's in Tahiti, but I don't have an address.'

'Neither do I.'

They looked at each other, the housekeeper clearly seeking guidance.

Alli said, 'I'm going to the hospital with Marian— I'll drive her car down. Can you ring Slade's office and tell his PA or secretary or whatever he has what's happened, and where Marian is?' She hesitated, then said, 'I'll ring you as soon as I can and tell you what's happening.'

Clearly relieved to have something to do, the housekeeper nodded. 'All right.'

Torn by fear and compassion for the woman in the ambulance ahead, Alli drove Marian's powder-blue Mercedes down, wondering if this attack had been her doing.

And things got worse at the hospital. She didn't know the simplest things about Marian beyond her name; she had no idea what other illnesses she'd had, what the address of her Auckland residence was, or even how old she was.

But at last a very small, pale Marian was in bed, hooked up to an array of instruments. She still hadn't moved. Her helplessness shocked Alli. For the first time she felt some sort of kinship with the older woman.

'I'll stay with you,' she told her, touching her hand. 'But first I need to ring Mrs Hopkins and reassure her that you're in good hands.'

Marian looked gravely at her, not a flicker of comprehension in the blue eyes. Sick with worry, Alli took herself off to the payphone.

The housekeeper asked urgently, 'How is she?'

'She hasn't changed, and no one's told me anything, but she's comfortable. Have you heard from Slade?'

'Yes, he's on his way home and expects to be here later tonight. He's going straight to the hospital as soon as he gets in.' Mrs Hopkins sighed. 'It must be a stroke. It doesn't seem possible—she's not a day over fifty-five!'

'If it is a stroke, it's not a death sentence,' Alli said crisply, hoping she was right.

'Of course it's not, and they can do such wonderful things now, can't they?' She sounded too emphatic, as though trying to convince herself.

On the way back, Alli discovered she was trying to convince herself too. Refusing to accept any possibility but a full recovery, she sat down by the bed, taking Marian's lax hand in hers. It seemed ridiculous to feel as though her touch helped, but in this world of beeping, gurgling machines it was at least human. Some distance away a baby cried—thin, exhausted wails that made her ache.

She never had any idea how long she sat there, holding her aunt's hand and talking quietly to her; as night closed down outside she dozed, and was more than half asleep when a subtle scent brought her to full alertness. Twisting in the chair, she looked up at Slade's face, its strong framework sharply prominent. Her heart leapt and she scrambled up awkwardly, so relieved to see him that she almost burst into tears.

He said quietly, 'How is she?'

Marian's eyelids flickered. 'Better now you're here,' Alli said, her voice wavering. 'Look, she knows you've come.'

He leaned over the bed, kissing his stepmother's forehead. 'It's all right,' he said in a deep voice. 'It's all right, Marian, I'm here.'

And, to Alli's astonishment, Marian's mouth moved a little and she sighed.

Slade straightened. 'Alli, there's no need for you to stay now. Sally Hopkins says you've got Marian's car?'

'Yes.'

He tossed her a swipe card. 'It's the key to my apartment. I've ordered a driver to take you back there.'

She caught the card and said, 'But how will you get in?'

'I have a spare.' He looked keenly at her. 'And, Alli—thank you.'

CHAPTER NINE

ALLI woke with heart thudding and ears on full alert. Darkness pressed heavily on her until a subdued noise from the kitchen indicated that someone had just closed the fridge door.

She drew a sharp breath and swung her long legs over the side of the bed, hooked her thin cotton dressing gown over her shoulders and padded warily out into the hall. More homely sounds reassured her—the clink of a glass on the granite bench, the sound of a tap being turned off—but it was a muttered swear-word that told her who was there.

Slade couldn't have heard her, but before the door was more than a few centimetres open he'd swivelled around to face her. She froze, because in his face she saw a cold anger that stopped her mind.

Something had gone very wrong.

'It's all right,' she said quickly.

He put his glass of water down on the bench and said politely, 'I'm sorry—I thought I was being quiet.'

'How—how is Marian?' she asked, aching for him.

'She's recovering. It wasn't a stroke.'

So what was wrong? Alli said tentatively, 'That's wonderful—isn't it?'

He drained the glass and set it back on the bench with controlled care. 'Indeed it is.'

The discipline of his expression and tone sent shivers scudding down her spine. 'Do they know what the problem is?'

He shrugged and leaned back against the bench. Hooded eyes dispassionate yet intent, he said, 'So far they don't know, but the general conclusion seems to be that she's exhausted and needs to conserve her strength, so her body just shut down. They expect her to revive when her unconscious decides it's safe to do so.'

She asked quietly, 'Was it me?'

Unreadable eyes searched her face with icy detachment. 'I don't know.'

The words came without conscious thought. 'Why is she afraid of me?'

'She's not afraid of you,' he said with sharp emphasis.

'I'll leave tomorrow.' Her voice was flat and completely determined.

'It's too late for that.'

Her skin tightened. She thought she could feel the tension like an electrical force around them, a dark turbulence shot by lightning.

Desperate to get away, she turned and fumbled for the door handle, her heart blocking her throat when he said something explosive beneath his breath and reached past her to wrench open the door as though he'd like to tear it off its hinges.

Startled by the silent ferocity of his arrival, she flinched.

For several seconds they stood facing each other. Alli's breath came faster as her heart sped up; she saw the colour in his eyes swallowed up by darkness, and knew that her own were widening endlessly...

Afterwards she could never remember who broke first—whether the hand she held out to ward him off found his muscled forearm, or whether his hand lifted to touch her face.

Whatever, when he cupped her cheek and said her name in a low, raw tone excited anticipation prickled through her in a response as elemental as it was dangerous.

Some hidden part of her brain warned that she'd be sorry, but it was swamped by an intense, entirely carnal desire. 'Yes,' she said simply, knowing exactly what she was agreeing to and unable to think of any good reason why she should deny herself this.

For her own protection she wouldn't dare stay in contact with Slade, but before she disappeared from his life she'd know what it was like to make love with him.

Freed at last from fear, she opened her mouth beneath his hard demand to give him what he wanted— what they both wanted. His arms tightened around her, and she gasped when he picked her up and shouldered his way through the door, carried her down the hall and into a bedroom. Once inside, he set her down on her feet, supporting her by the shoulders. His scrutiny was so intense she could feel the gold and green flames licking around her.

'I've wanted this since I first saw you in Valanu,' he said harshly.

Passionate anticipation bubbled up through her. Eyes enormous, she nodded.

As his lips found the spot where her neck joined her shoulders he pushed her dressing gown from her shoulders, his hands sliding on down her back to the hem of her T-shirt. They were warm and strong, and instead of whipping the shirt over her head they slid up beneath it.

Alli shivered, and he said, 'Are you cold?'

'No,' she whispered, on fire from her skin to the aching centre of her being.

This time he kissed her lips, tormenting her with the teasing lightness. A hungry little noise escaped from her throat and she looped her arms around his neck, trying to bring his mouth closer to hers.

One lean hand cupped her breast. Alli shuddered, and dragged an impeded breath into famished lungs. Electricity arced from her breast to the pit of her stomach, relaying the torrid effect of his touch through every cell in her body. Her breasts felt heavy, so responsive to his caresses that she was sure they throbbed.

'You can touch me if you want to,' he murmured, and gently bit the lobe of her ear.

Excitement whipped up higher through her body. Swiftly she unbuttoned his shirt. The heat from his taut skin seared her fingertips, and when she looked up the gold lights in his eyes scorched through the ragged remnants of her self-control.

The soft material of her T-shirt became an unbearable barrier; she fumbled for it, hungering for the feel of his skin against hers.

'What is it?' His voice was a sexy rumble. 'What do you want?'

'I want—I want—' Unable to formulate the words, she pushed the sides of his shirt further apart. Finally, she muttered angrily, 'I want you.'

Black lashes almost shaded the green and gold glitter of his eyes. 'Good, because I want you too,' he said, the words such a blatant act of possession that they stopped the breath in her throat.

She stared at him, meeting his narrowed eyes with a hot shiver of urgency that exploded like a fireburst inside her. 'Then take off your shirt,' she said raggedly, unable to dissemble.

Her whole body longed for him, craved him, demanded him—if she didn't get what she wanted she thought she might die of need.

He dropped his hands, stepping back in silent invitation.

Dry-mouthed, she pushed his shirt from his shoulders and down over the corded muscles of his arms, letting it fall to the floor.

The impact of his bare torso hit her like a shockwave. Lamplight burnished the powerful shoulders and chest to bronze, sheened the sleek skin of his flat abdomen.

Any more, she thought feverishly, and I'm going to swoon at his feet!

Slowly, her heart beating a tattoo in her ears, Alli pressed the flat of her hand over his heart, reassured when she felt its uneven beat driving into her palm. Against his formidable masculinity her hand looked pale and fragile, but at her touch his chest rose sharply.

Acute, gratified pleasure pierced her. She wasn't the only one lost to this overwhelming desire. Although she couldn't make herself look into his face, his silence and his stillness reassured her; with tentative strokes she examined the texture of hair and skin until her questing fingers reached a small dark nub.

Again that sudden rise of his chest startled her, and she whipped back her fingers, only to have them clamped beneath his. He said, 'Surely you know that men and women aren't very different? We like to be pleasured, and your touch pleasures me.'

At last Alli gathered enough courage to look into his face.

What she saw there shocked her; raw need hardened his features and gleamed in his eyes, so concentrated she could feel it blasting into her. A rising tide of passion almost blocked her thoughts.

'Take off your T-shirt,' he said, the words soft and rough.

For a second she hesitated, tempted to demand that he do it, but something about removing her own clothes appealed to her pride. Head held high, she met his eyes as she slid the material over her head, lowering it to stand before him in nothing but narrow cotton briefs.

Silently he reached for her, and some part of herself was comforted because his hand shook slightly when it mimicked hers, his thumb lightly stroking the pink centre of her breast.

Sensation arrowed through her, white-hot and elemental. Slade pulled her into the heat and strength of his body, and she sighed and linked her arms around his neck and mutely offered herself to him.

He kissed the hollow at the base of her throat, and

then his mouth slid slower, tasting, teasing, exploring each gentle curve with slow, erotic finesse.

And when he reached one pouting, pleading centre he drew it inside his mouth. Her knees buckled and she cried his name in a voice that betrayed every molten, reckless sensation bursting through her.

Slade lifted his head and surveyed her with narrowed, glittering eyes. Wonderingly, she touched his mouth, so uncompromising, yet capable of delivering such intense delight. He kissed the tip of her finger, and when she slid it into the moisture inside he bit the skin tenderly, his sharp teeth sending a thrill of desire though her.

'I can think of a better place for us to be,' he said, and he picked her up.

The coolness of the sheet beneath her back and legs provided an intriguing contrast to the urgency that sizzled through her; she relaxed onto the pillows, only noticing then that he had taken her into his bedroom.

When he'd finished undressing she forgot everything in the wonder of watching him with complete absorption, every cell in her body throbbing in desperate anticipation.

On Valanu she'd seen male tourists in bathing suits so minuscule they might as well have been naked. Now she realised that the scrap of material swathed around hips had made a huge difference; without it, Slade was magnificent.

She swallowed, wondering feverishly if this was going to work...and if she should perhaps tell him that she'd never made love before.

He came to the edge of the bed with the silent,

powerful grace that marked him out from other men. Alli held herself still while he eased down beside her, and for the first time she felt the shock of nakedness— skin flexing against heated skin, the slow play of muscles, the feeling of being overwhelmed by sheer masculinity.

Utterly exposed, her skin colouring under his gaze, she buried her shy face in his shoulder and nuzzled him, and his faint, tantalising scent filled her nostrils, replacing the nervousness and fear with a quiet, lovely certainty. She kissed his shoulder, and then sank her teeth delicately into the skin before licking it.

Big body shuddering, he said harshly, 'For this once, let me do the work, all right?'

Surely he didn't expect his lovers to lie there and do nothing? Puzzled, she glanced up and met his eyes, almost flinching back at their heat.

He finished, 'Otherwise it might well be over before we start.'

Perhaps it had been a while since he'd made love.

That thought excited and pleased her, as did the suggestion that he wasn't in full control when he was with her.

She touched the taut skin over his solar plexus. 'I can do this, though?'

'Only if I say the times tables aloud while you do,' he said, and kissed the throbbing little hollow in her throat, and then the curve of her breast.

This time when he took the tight little bud into his mouth and began to suckle she thought she knew what was coming, but the exquisite sensation wrested what was left of her control from her and sent it whistling down the wind. Alli groaned, her hips rising instinctively against him.

'Not yet,' he said softly, moving to the other breast while one hand discovered the small hollow of her navel and the curve of her hip.

Ravished by delight, she made an incoherent little noise in her throat and ran her hands up his back, relishing the way the muscles bunched beneath her palms.

His hand moved further down. She wanted him to continue more than life itself, yet she stiffened in instinctive fear.

'It's all right,' he said softly. 'I just want to see if you're ready.'

Ready? Oh, she thought longingly, she was so ready—couldn't he sense it? But, although she arched upwards again in silent plea, he sat up and reached for something on the bedside table.

She watched as he donned the condom, and wondered at her pang of sadness.

Slade looked at her. 'The first time I saw you I thought of the golden pearls of the Pacific, because your skin glows like them. You seem to radiate light and heat and passion.'

And he kissed her again, and this time when his hand reached the cleft between her legs she relaxed, most of her apprehension vanishing like mist in sunlight, and groaned harshly when he stroked her there before easing a finger inside.

Torn by unbearable anticipation, she didn't know whether to obey the urge to pull him over and into her, or the equally strong one that insisted she lie there and let this voluptuous lethargy carry her wherever it wanted her to go.

Slade took the decision from her. He moved over her and pressed against the slick entrance. Slowly, carefully, he eased a little way into her.

Her breath locking in her throat, Alli stared up into his face, a savagely carved mask of primal appetite.

'Am I too heavy?' he asked.

'No.' She swallowed and tried again. 'I like it.'

And, indeed, lying like this beneath him was probably the closest to heaven she was ever likely to get.

He frowned, but pushed a little further, focusing entirely on her, his face clamped in severe lines as he controlled the hunger she sensed in him.

And control it he did, tormenting her with his restraint until pleasure burned through her and she whimpered with the need for more than this slow, cautious progress. Driven by wild desire, she gripped his hips, holding him against her. He thrust deeper, and again even deeper, releasing a hunger that smashed through her final barriers.

Alli twisted recklessly against him, clasping him with inner muscles she'd never used before until he gasped, 'No!'

Too late. Slade's mouth came down on hers and somewhere in the fire and passion of that kiss, his control shattered.

Joined with him in ecstatic union, Alli closed her eyes and welcomed each movement of his powerful body, her every sense so acute it was almost painful to feel his heat and the coiled steel of his body as he took her with him into unknown regions of the heart.

No wonder desire brought down kingdoms!

Nothing could be more wonderful—but then a cresting wave of sensation flung her up, up, up into a storm of sensuality, holding her on a knife-edge of intolerable rapture.

Slade, she thought with what was left of her mind. Slade...

Somehow she forced her eyes open, filling her vision with his darkly drawn face, the fire in his half-closed eyes and the gleam of sweat on his body. Her lips formed his name as, overwhelmed by unbearable ecstasy, she cried out and convulsed beneath him.

Slade went with her on that incredible journey into the heart of the storm, eventually collapsing on the distant shores of satiation, his chest heaving as she cradled him in her arms and let ebbing passion lull her into dreamy bliss.

When he moved, her arms tightened around him in the instinctive need to keep him so close that nothing could ever come between them. But he used his great strength against her, rolling so that he lay beneath her.

He lay there for long moments, her slim, lax body light on him, her flushed, languid face half turned on his chest and her eyes already closing, and swore silently and at length.

How the hell had it got to this? You blew it, he told himself grimly. You knew it was dangerous, but you couldn't bloody well control yourself.

When he was seven Marian had come like sunlight into his life. Slowly, suspiciously, he had trusted her enough to let himself love her.

And now, only a few miles from here, she lay in a

fugue of exhaustion caused by the girl who slept on him in sensual exhaustion. He tensed as Alli yawned and rubbed her cheek against his chest in a gesture as artless as it was seductive. His body stirred beneath her, and mentally he cursed his total lack of will-power where she was concerned, each cold, biting word reeking of disgusted derision.

Yet he watched her while she slept, storing up every moment, every second, with the eager greed of a miner hoarding gems.

Alli woke to silence. Dazed by unremembered satisfaction, she stretched and yawned, wondering sleepily why her body felt different—and then she remembered and shot upwards, searching the room for a man who wasn't there.

She was alone, and in her own bed. Well, Slade's spare bed, she thought, feverish colour scorching her cheekbones. He must have carried her there after they'd made love and she'd gone to sleep in his arms.

Jumbled images of the previous night circled her brain. She might have been a virgin but she could recognise expertise when she came across it. Making love was no novelty to him.

So, while it had been a slow, incandescent trip to heaven for her, for him it had just been fun as usual.

She listened, but the apartment was silent. Biting her lip, she got out of bed, flushing again when she realised that she was still naked. A neat pile on a chair indicated that Slade had returned her discarded clothes too. Hastily she made for the bathroom.

After a shower she dried herself down and examined her gleaming, naked body for sombre moments in the mirror. Apart from lips that were fuller than usual—and more tender—she looked the same. Several marks, too slight to be called bruises, startled her. His beard, she thought confusedly, must have been just long enough to abrade the delicate skin of her breasts. At the time she hadn't noticed.

'But then you probably wouldn't have noticed a firework display on the end of the bed,' she muttered, and hid her face by towelling her hair dry.

He had left a note outside her door. Stupid dread constricting her heart, she stared at it for a second before stooping to pick it up. Without salutation, his bold writing informed her that he had gone to the hospital, where he would see her when she was ready. He'd signed it with a formal signature, *S T Hawkings*, and added a postscript. Marian had been transferred to a private hospital; he'd sketched a map showing her how to get there.

'I wonder what the T stands for,' she said, folding the paper and putting it in her pocket. 'Thunderbolt, perhaps?'

But although her tone was wry, silly tears stung her eyes, and she found she couldn't manage anything for breakfast beyond a cup of coffee.

That downed, she left the apartment and drove sedately across town, stifling her nervousness at the traffic with the hope that Marian had recovered consciousness.

The new hospital was considerably more upmarket than the public one Marian had been taken to the previous day. She was shown into a kind of ante-chamber to Marian's room, and while the nurse went in to check that the patient could see her Alli absently noted bowls of flowers and a couple of pretty, unassuming landscapes on the walls.

When the door clicked open again she looked up, startled when she met Caroline Forsythe's eyes.

'She's not up to seeing you just now,' Caroline said calmly. 'Slade is with her, so I'll wait with you.' She glanced out of the window. 'In fact, I'd like to go for a walk, and they have lovely gardens here. Would you like to come with me?'

'I think I'll wait here, thanks,' Alli said. The other woman, she saw, wore an engagement ring.

Caroline shrugged. 'It'll be a while.' She surveyed Alli. 'You look as though you've spent a sleepless night too. Come on, some fresh air will do you good.'

'How is she?'

'Conscious,' Caroline said readily, holding open the door to the hallway. 'Which is wonderful. But she says she feels very tired. What on earth happened?'

Caroline's voice had softened when she spoke of her godmother, so Alli got to her feet, feeling mean for refusing to accompany her when the other woman was so clearly worried. Together they went down in the lift, and, while they walked in gardens sweet with the first roses, she told Caroline what had happened.

'It must have been terrifying,' Caroline said sympathetically. 'Oh, look! That glorious Graham Thomas rose is out in the arbour. Let's sit down here for a moment, shall we?'

She waited until they were both seated, then asked, 'What happened to give Marian a heart attack?'

Alli stopped abruptly. 'A heart attack! But Slade said it was something else!'

'Did he?' Unsmiling, Caroline examined her. 'Why did you agree to stay with her when you must have known that the mere sight of you brought back the most hideous memories?'

Her words shocked Alli into rising, but Caroline's hand shot out swiftly as a snake and fastened around her wrist.

'Listen to me,' she said flatly. 'I don't know whether you've been told what happened with your parents, but if you haven't, it's time you were.'

CHAPTER TEN

DISCONNECTED thoughts tumbled in jerky confusion around Alli's mind. She said, 'I don't think—'

'Normally I wouldn't intrude,' Caroline interrupted with pleasant firmness, 'and I owe you an apology for what I said to you the first time you came to see Marian, but I was awfully worried about that meeting.'

Alli couldn't hide her shock, but Caroline went on smoothly, 'Yes, I know all about it. I did mention that Marian and I were very close, which is why I'm telling you that your presence is so utterly traumatic for her. It's not personal, believe me. Your mother—'

Interrupting in her turn, Alli said shortly, 'I know what my mother did.'

'It must have been a terrible thing to hear.' Caroline glanced at her engagement ring. 'When we were in Tahiti Slade thought that perhaps the best thing to do was get Marian to go to counselling.'

She paused and turned the ring so that it caught the light. Alli's fragile composure fractured into splinters.

Frowning, Caroline looked up. 'Now he's worried she might have a complete nervous breakdown, and he feels responsible because he agreed to let you meet her.'

Nausea roiled in Alli's stomach; so he had taken Caroline to Tahiti—and did that ring mean an engagement?

Caroline explained, 'He is very protective of Marian. But then, strong men usually are protective of their women.'

Fortunately she didn't seem to need an answer, because Alli couldn't think of a word to say.

'She was so good to him as a child. His father was away so much that he'd sent Slade to boarding school when he was only six, but Marian insisted that Slade come home. She was a real mother to him, so you can see why he's so worried about her now.'

Ungracefully Alli stood up. 'I've always seen that. Neither of them need worry about my presence any more.' The words felt thick, clumsy on her tongue.

'I'm so sorry.' Caroline scrambled to her feet. 'It's an impossible situation for you all.'

'So impossible that the simplest and quickest way to resolve it is for me to leave,' Alli said with a twisted smile.

'Yes, that would probably be the best thing. Only— Marian will feel obliged to keep in touch.'

Alli shrugged. 'If she doesn't know where I am she won't be able to,' she said briskly. 'Give her my love, won't you? And tell her I never meant to hurt her.'

'Of course I'll do that.' She asked, 'Do you have money?'

'Enough.' The thought of borrowing money from this woman, however kind she was trying to be, stung.

Caroline nodded. 'Good luck, then.'

Three months later Alli slung her bag onto the Valanu wharf and turned to wave to the Californian couple who'd let her work her passage from Sant'Rosa. 'I'll be back in a couple of days,' she called.

They waved, and she walked into the port.

Heat settled onto her like a steamy blanket, in spite of the soft caress of the trade wind. She looked about, wondering how she could feel so little for the place she'd called home. Now, home was wherever Slade was.

Because she didn't dare think about him, she pushed the memories into the furthest recesses of her mind. Tui at the Lodge had overcome her fear of computers and e-mailed that Marian was fine, and that Slade had come looking for her in a towering rage the day after she'd grabbed her clothes, offered a garbled explanation for her departure, and run.

Her instinct to take refuge in Valanu like a wounded animal, hadn't been the most sensible decision, but then she hadn't been thinking sensibly when she'd left New Zealand.

Staying at the resort was out. Not, she knew, that Slade would come looking for her now; no doubt he and Marian were only too glad to see the back of her. If he was engaged to the lovely, oh-so-helpful Caroline, the last thing he'd want was a one-night stand hanging around!

Grimly she headed for a small, somewhat sleazy motel close to the port. This was only a respite, anyway. During the long, lovely nights when she'd kept her lonely watch on the vast Pacific, she'd worked out a plan of campaign.

First a pilgrimage to her father's grave and a visit to Sisilu.

Then she'd sail with her nice Californians to Australia, find a job there, and make a life for herself without Slade, without Marian, without emotional complications.

Just like her father.

Of course, she thought with wintry resignation, you could call a broken heart an emotional complication. Hers didn't seem to want to heal; so far time hadn't eased the intense ache of loneliness and longing at all. Instead of outrunning her pain, she'd carried it with her.

At the motel the receptionist took an impression of her credit card, showed her a small room overlooking the swimming pool, and with mechanical courtesy wished her a good stay on Valanu. Alli didn't know her, which was a relief.

A weary lethargy imprisoned her in the room for the rest of the afternoon; she lay on the surprisingly comfortable bed and watched the ceiling fan whirr around, only stirring at sundown to shower and change into a pareu. Tomorrow she'd contact Sisilu, but right now she needed air.

The decision made, she was locking the door when a prickle of danger lifted the hairs on the nape of her neck; she froze, then glanced over her shoulder. Slade was striding towards her through the purple dusk like a silent, lethal force of nature. Heart jolting into a pounding, uneven rhythm, she fumbled the key into the lock again. But before she could take refuge inside a hand closed over hers and pulled the key out of her fingers.

'You took your damned time getting here,' Slade said icily.

She was shaking, her vision dim and her mouth dry, the faint, essential scent of him swamping her senses. 'What—is it Marian?' she finally managed to ask huskily, refusing to look any higher than his throat.

'She's fine,' he bit out. 'She is, however, worried sick about you.'

Possessed by fragile joy, she didn't move, couldn't speak.

'Aren't you going to ask what I'm doing here?'

'So tell me,' she said thinly.

His fingers on her elbow brooked no resistance. 'We'll go back to the resort. This place is about as unsavoury as Valanu gets.' He opened the door of a waiting cab and ushered her in.

She should have resisted, but running away hadn't helped; this meeting might provide some sort of closure, free her from the intolerable weight of lost expectations and forlorn hope. They sat for the short trip in silence; Alli knew she should be shoring up her defences, but it was too late for that.

Was this, she'd wondered on those long night watches while she'd gazed at the familiar impersonal stars wheeling in their grand patterns, how Alison had felt about her father—so in love that anything, even betraying a sister, had meant little?

In that case, why had she abandoned him and their child? Why had she told Marian that she'd aborted the baby? Nothing made sense—but then, loving Slade didn't make sense either.

He took her to the private entrance of the honeymoon suite; once inside she stared around, avoiding the part of the room where Slade stood watching her. 'It's been redecorated,' she commented jerkily, trying to impose some sort of normality onto this meeting.

'The whole resort's been refurbished.' He sounded completely fed up. 'Alli, look at me.'

His will forced her to obey. 'Is Marian fully recovered?' she asked.

'Once she got over the shock of your flight,' he said caustically. 'What the hell drove you away? Caroline said you were fine when you two walked in the garden together.'

Presumably Caroline had done her best to save Marian worry. 'I left because my presence stressed Marian so much she couldn't cope. I know she tries to think of me as an ordinary human being, but every time she looks at me she must see my mother.'

'Possibly,' he said bluntly, 'although she certainly doesn't blame you for your mother's behaviour. I thought I'd convinced you of that.'

'She suspects I might be like Alison, amoral and greedy.' When he frowned, she persisted, 'So do you. That's why you assumed I was sleeping with every man who came near me, wasn't it?'

'Is that what you believe?' He came across the room to her, and when she took a step back he stopped. In a voice she didn't recognise he said, 'I have never lifted my hand to a woman, and I will never hurt you, Alli. But I need to know something.'

Her lips formed the word. 'What?'

His hard, beautiful mouth tightened. 'Whether you were a virgin when we made love.'

Astonished, she blinked. 'Why does it matter?'

'It does. I had you targeted as a thoroughly relaxed young woman, taking sex lightly and without angst.'

'Promiscuous, in other words.'

He hesitated, then said, 'No. You grew up here, where sex is considered a recreation.'

'Only,' she said tartly, 'for those who aren't married, or promised in marriage. My father didn't seem to worry about the islanders' attitude to sex, but he certainly didn't approve of liaisons when it came to his daughter.' She smiled bitterly. 'Amusing, isn't it? I just thought he was old-fashioned.'

'He knew—none better, I imagine—what damage it can do,' Slade said. 'You haven't answered me.'

Admitting that she'd been a virgin would be giving too much away; only a woman in love would risk so much for a man who wasn't in love with her. 'I don't think it's any of your business. I haven't asked you how many women you've made love to. Where did you get the idea that I was Barry Simcox's girlfriend?'

He shrugged. 'His attitude, which backed up what I was told—that you had broken up his marriage.'

'Who told you that?'

'It doesn't matter,' he said briefly. 'Is it true?'

'No. His wife hated Valanu, but she wouldn't admit it because she'd pushed him to take the position. I think she'd imagined living some sort of colonial life, sipping gin slings and flirting with the unmarried men while servants did all the work.'

At his snort, she said with a bleak smile, 'She was a romantic, I suppose. The reality—a failing resort with precious little social life of the sort she'd expected—was a huge shock, and she didn't try to hide how miserable she was. So she looked around for something to give her a reason to leave.'

'You don't think finding you naked with her husband was reason enough?' He spoke neutrally, but she saw the flicker of a muscle in the angular line of his jaw.

She said curtly, 'I'll bet whoever told you that didn't say that I was screaming at the top of my lungs at the time.'

'What the hell was he doing?' An intimidating, ice-cold combination of steel and fire, Slade's voice sliced through her words.

'He was rescuing me from a cockroach,' she told him with acid precision. 'I was changing in the staff bathroom for the evening show when it jumped me.' She shuddered. 'Have you ever seen one? They're huge and black, and this one dropped from the ceiling and ran down my back. I freaked. Barry was on his way to the men's room, and when he heard me yelling he thought I was being attacked. He came tearing in and saved me. I was hauling my pareu on when his wife came racing in and called us every foul word under the sun. She left on the next plane with their little boy.'

'He wanted you,' Slade said harshly. 'Everyone knew it.'

'Possibly, but I didn't want him.' She stared at him with flat defiance. 'Why is this important—or even interesting—to you? I might be my mother's daughter, but I don't sleep with married men. Or engaged ones.'

He said abruptly, 'Are you insinuating that I'm engaged?'

Her conversation with the other woman suddenly took a new twist. Caroline hadn't said she and Slade were engaged, though she'd certainly implied it. Had she set Alli up?

'Are you?'

'No.' His mouth closed like a clamp. 'I have never been engaged. And you still haven't answered my question.'

He might not be engaged, but that didn't mean he was interested in Alli as anything more than a convenient outlet for his sexual needs.

Pain burning like fire through her, she walked across to the window and looked into the garden, barely noticing the lush greenery starred with flamboyant hibiscuses and the pure, sculpted blooms of frangipani.

'Yes, I was a virgin,' she said quietly, uneasily aware of anticipation running through her like an underground river.

'I thought as much,' he said remotely. 'I'll take you back to the motel and you can pack; we're leaving in half an hour.'

Anticipation died a swift, brutal death. She reached out and clutched a curtain. 'Why?'

'I don't seduce virgins,' he said savagely.

'So if I hadn't been a virgin you'd leave me here?'

He stared at her as though she'd suddenly gone mad. 'Don't be an idiot.'

Outraged, she snapped, 'And you didn't seduce me—I wanted to make love to you! So don't go thinking that because you had your wicked way with me you owe me something! You don't. As an introduction to making love it was pretty damned good, but women nowadays don't feel any obligation to marry the first man they sleep with.'

She could have bitten her tongue out once she realised what that final sentence indicated. Sickly she waited for a put-down.

He said levelly, 'Marian asked me to bring you back.'

Bewildered, Alli shook her head. 'Why? My presence brought about her collapse—'

'It didn't.' He spoke with such assurance she turned to search his hard face for some indication of what was going on. Without any success. The mask was back in place, hard and unreadable and totally ruthless. He finished, 'She has something to tell you.'

'More secrets?' she asked wearily, shoulders slumping. 'I've had enough of them. In fact, I've had enough of this whole situation.'

'Tough. You don't have the choice. You've tried running away, but wherever you go I'll be one step behind until you've heard what Marian has to say. After that no one will follow you if you want to go. But she's not going to rest until she's told you what she has to say. And I'm not going to leave you until you've heard it.'

Alli dithered, but in the end she said with grim resignation, 'All right, then. I'll come back—but after that I'm going.'

At Auckland airport, the luxurious private jet was met by a car that dropped them off at Marian's apartment.

Outside her aunt's door Alli took a deep, jagged breath, astounded when Slade's hand covered hers, its warmth and strength offering support.

She didn't dare look at him, and before the door opened he let her go, but she carried his touch inside her like a fire in the depths of winter.

Marian stood there, the anxiety in her blue eyes fading to relief. 'My dear,' she said, putting out a hand to draw Alli inside. 'Oh, my dear, I've been so *worried* about you!'

'I've been worrying about you too,' Alli said on a half-laugh, 'but you look great!'

'Such a silly thing to have happened! Exhaustion, the doctor said, and the aftermath of the flu, and I seem to have developed a propensity for fainting now and then—as you know only too well, poor girl. But it won't happen again; I've promised Slade and my doctor that I'll eat regularly and sleep eight hours a night, and take iron pills every day! Come through and tell me what you've been doing.'

Slade allowed them ten minutes of catching up before saying, 'Marian, you're procrastinating. Tell Alli what you told me.'

Marian sighed. 'You were such a dear little boy— what happened to turn you into a despot? Very well, then.' She sipped water from a glass, but instead of returning it to the table beside her she clutched the tumbler. In a level, almost conversational tone she said, 'First of all, Alli, your mother and I were half-sisters.'

'Half-sisters?'

'Yes. We had different mothers. I think my father

loved Alison's mother, but he was a snob, and she wasn't the sort of person who satisfied his rigid ideas of suitability, so after Alison was born he married my mother, who came from a good family.'

She looked past them both, seeing other faces, other events. Stunned, Alli said, 'He abandoned his first family?'

Marian looked tired. 'Oh, no.'

But she didn't continue straight away. Instead she took another sip of water, replaced the tumbler on the table and gazed down at the large diamonds winking in her engagement ring and gold wedding ring as though seeking strength from them.

Alli almost screamed with the tension, starting slightly when Marian began again in a tightly controlled tone.

'He kept them in a nice house in the nearest city. We lived in the country. I knew nothing about it, of course, and neither did my mother. My first intimation of the situation came when I was seventeen and had newly left school. Alison tracked me down and told me everything.'

She stopped again, her expression blank. Swallowing to ease a dry throat, Alli thought desperately, *Please, finish it quickly!*

'Keep going.' Slade's voice was calm and steady.

Marian took a deep breath. 'She wanted to tell me that she resented being supplanted by me. Even more, she resented the fact that she was a bastard. She called herself my father's dirty little secret, and it was obvious that she despised both her parents—but especially her mother. She told me that everything I had, everything I'd been given—a good school, social standing, legitimacy—had been stolen from her.'

She hesitated before adding, 'She told me she wanted it back.'

When Alli shivered the older woman nodded sadly. 'She meant it. I didn't know what to say to her—to be truthful she frightened me—but after that she stalked me. I didn't realise that's what it was, of course—in those days we had no word for such a thing. But wherever I went, there she was too. Sometimes it would be several weeks before I'd see her, but she always came back. She sent me birthday cards and Christmas cards.'

'Why didn't you tell your father?' Alli asked, horrified.

'I couldn't bring myself to.' Marian seemed to have retreated into herself. 'My mother might have found out, and I knew how dreadful that would be for her. Marrying Hugo was such a relief. I loved him very much, and he lived on the opposite side of the world. But Alison was in the crowd outside the church when we were married.'

She swallowed and sipped more water.

Slade frowned, hard gaze fixed onto his stepmother's beautiful face. 'Go on,' he said gently.

'So we came to New Zealand, and it was as though a weight fell off my shoulders. For a year I was happy. When I discovered I was pregnant Hugo and I were so delighted and life was wonderful—and then she knocked on my door.'

Alli sat frozen, her hands clasped so tightly in her lap that her knuckles shone white.

'To cut a long story short,' Marian said tiredly, 'she was obviously pregnant.'

Any remaining colour drained from Alli's skin, taking all warmth, all joy with it. It was like standing on the brink of a precipice, unable to stop herself from taking the fatal next step.

Marian said, 'She boasted that she'd seduced Hugo and that the baby was his. Her next step, she said, was to stake a claim to my inheritance. My mother had died shortly after my wedding, and Alison was certain she could persuade our father to change his will so that she was the only beneficiary of the trust fund he'd planned to set up for us both. It was the first I'd heard of that, and it meant, of course, that he acknowledged her legally as his daughter.'

With the blood drumming in her ears, Alli heard Marian say, 'Of course I asked Hugo if it was true. He was desperately ashamed, but he admitted it. She had sought him out and dazzled him—he said that he loved me, but he hadn't known what passion was like until he met her.'

Alli swallowed.

Remorselessly Marian's soft voice went on, 'I sent him away, and then I lost my baby—it was born premature and died within minutes. Then I had a telephone call from Alison—as soon as she'd heard that my child was dead she'd aborted hers. She said—she said—' She shuddered.

'I don't want to hear anything more.' Alli's voice grated on the words.

Marian looked at her with eyes filled with tears. 'I know. But—it's almost over.' She waited until Alli gave an almost imperceptible nod. 'She said I could have Hugo back if I was desperate, but that whenever we made love he'd be holding her in his arms.'

Alli said numbly, 'I'm so sorry.'

Slade's hands closed over her shoulders, holding her in place, his strength pouring through them into her body.

Tonelessly Marian finished, 'Some months later I was contacted because Alison had been killed in Thailand. Apparently she was on her way back to England and our father when she stepped into the path of a truck. I never heard from Hugo again; when we divorced it was all done through our solicitors.' She closed her eyes.

'She must have been mad,' Alli breathed.

Marian opened her eyes and said simply, 'She was seriously disturbed. But I married Slade's father and we were very happy together. I don't think even my half-sister could have stolen him from me.'

'I wish I'd never contacted you,' Alli said fiercely. 'I had no idea of the pain I'd cause.'

'My dear, it's better to know the truth,' the older woman said. 'Although when I realised who you were I was afraid.'

'That I'd be like my mother?' Alli produced a twisted parody of a smile. 'I don't blame you.'

'You're not like your mother,' Slade said calmly. 'You are a warm, responsible, loyal woman.'

His words warmed some part of her that had been frozen since the first time she'd met Marian, in this very room, and heard her talk about her sister's betrayal.

'Exactly,' Marian agreed. 'I couldn't have said it better myself.' She looked at Alli and seemed to be readying herself to say something, but Slade cut in.

'That's enough for the present. Both of you are exhausted, and anything more can wait until later. Come on, Alli, I'll take you home.'

For the first time since they'd met at the door Marian smiled. 'What a good idea.'

Alli said, 'We can't leave you alone.'

'Don't worry about me. I feel as though I've just shed a huge load from my shoulders. I'm sorry you had to hear that, but knowledge truly is power.'

Alli got to her feet. 'I think he—my father—realised that he had always loved you,' she said slowly. 'He cut out the newspaper article about your marriage to Slade's father and kept it with his marriage certificate. That's how I discovered who you were and where you lived.'

The older woman looked bleak. 'Between us, Alison and I made a wasteland of his life.'

Slade said with ruthless logic, 'You had nothing to do with it—it was his decision to be unfaithful. And he spent years working hard and extremely well for the people of Valanu. I don't think his life was wasted.'

On the way home Alli said, 'Thank you for what you said about my father.'

'It's the truth,' he said negligently. 'You can be proud of him because he did an enormous amount of good in the islands. Possibly he tried to atone for his mistakes that way.'

'I hope so,' she said quietly. She didn't want to

think about her mother. Fixing her eyes on the harbour, smiling beneath a late summer sun, she asked, 'Where are we going?'

He'd told Marian he was taking her home, but she had no home now.

'I think we've had this conversation before,' Slade said coolly. 'I'm taking you back to the homestead.'

She sneaked a glance at him; he turned his head and smiled at her, and she knew that she would go with him wherever he asked her to.

If he wanted her she would expect nothing from him but fidelity. As long as she had that, she thought dreamily, she'd be happy.

They drove silently through the blue and gold evening, arriving at the bay with a glory of scarlet and crimson and apricot streaked across the western sky.

'It's going to be a fine day tomorrow,' Slade remarked, lifting her bag from the car.

Alli stood a moment, inhaling. 'I missed the scent of the kanuka trees,' she said, smiling at him without reserve.

'I always do too.'

He put her in the room she'd occupied before. When she'd showered and changed into a pareu, a restrained length of cotton the colour of the red highlights in her hair, she came shyly down the stairs to join Slade on the deck as the first stars trembled into life in the indigo sky.

He handed her a glass of champagne. 'Here's to the future.'

'I'll definitely drink to that.' But she'd barely tasted

the delicious wine before she set the glass down, saying, 'You knew about my mother, didn't you?'

'Yes. When the researchers I employed finally tracked down the details of your birth I told Marian. She was shattered, and it all came spilling out.'

Keeping her eyes on a pair of fantails fluttering around just beyond arm's reach, their black eyes bright as small beaks snapped up night-flying insects, she asked, 'Is that why you distrusted me so much?'

Accurately divining her secret fear, he said bluntly, 'You were right when you accused me of testing you. I did wonder if you were like her, damaged in some basic way. I bought the resort so that I could use it as a lever if I had to.'

'You paid a lot of money for a lever that might not have worked if I'd been like my mother,' she said quietly.

He shrugged. 'It had good prospects. The area was already settling down, and I had plans for it. I didn't expect to lose anything on it. Then I got there and realised that Barry couldn't look at you without salivating.'

'No!' she said indignantly.

His brows rose. 'Trust me. I know,' he said dryly. 'And, although I was as suspicious of you as hell, I hated that.' Irony and something like self-derision curled his mouth. 'Of course I wouldn't allow myself to realise it, but I was jealous—black, deep, dog-in-the-manger jealous. So I offered you the chance of staying on Valanu and saving your friends' jobs.'

Alli said, 'I should hate you.'

His eyes gleamed. 'But you don't, do you?'

She bit her lip.

The fantails' high-pitched squeaks faded as they flew into a bush. Slade put his glass down and walked across the deck to join her in the gathering dusk.

'You stayed on Valanu. Even when you left, you made no effort to contact Marian. And when you thought that your presence was causing Marian real problems you left. As far as I can work out Alison would have pulled the world down around her in flames to get her way. She didn't care a bit about hurting other people.'

'No.' It hurt so much to say that single word.

Very deliberately he said, 'You are entirely normal.' And he turned her into the circle of his arms. When she stared at him, her face coloured by the dying glow of the sun, he asked, 'You've had a hell of a shock. Do you want to stay in your own bedroom tonight?'

'No,' she said on a sigh.

If this was all she could have she'd take it. And as he pulled her into his arms she lifted her face to his kiss and felt happiness flood through her, fierce and elemental.

CHAPTER ELEVEN

ALLI lay in sleepy bliss, so replete with pleasure that when Slade came into the room she could barely summon the energy to smile at him.

'Poor you,' she said dreamily. 'Work…and with boring old politicians too.'

He finished knotting his tie and bent to kiss her. Lazily, gracefully, she looped her arms around his neck and matched his kiss with enthusiasm.

'Stop that, baggage.' Slade pulled her hands away and tucked them under the sheet. 'This is a very important meeting, and politicians hate it if you're late. It makes them feel less powerful.'

She loved the way the gold glints in his eyes lit up whenever he looked at her. In fact, she loved everything about him.

'And I'll bet they're not all boring and old and male.' She sat up against the tumbled pillows while he shrugged into the jacket of his superb suit. 'I noticed a couple of very glamorous creatures in the caucus.'

'Not today,' he said.

A tiny arrow pierced her happiness and lodged in her heart. Looking like that, in clothes superbly tailored to fit his wide shoulders and lean hips, Slade was no longer of her world. They had spent the last three days in isolation, cooking for themselves, seeing no one, hearing no one, making love…

In his arms she had learnt so much about herself— so much about him. Sometimes he gentled her sweetly into an ecstasy that brought her to tears. Other times they loved like tigers, fiercely, without inhibition, losing themselves in rapture so intense she had to muffle her cries in the hard strength of his shoulder.

In bed, she thought, watching him check the contents of a slim leather briefcase, they were equals.

But outside it? She suspected that while she had given him her heart completely, for him this fierce flashfire of desire was enough.

Slade came across and dropped a swift, stinging kiss on her mouth. 'Go back to sleep,' he commanded, surveying her flushed face. 'You're looking very slumbrous around the eyes.'

'That isn't tiredness.'

He laughed beneath his breath. 'I'll be back late this afternoon.'

When he'd gone Alli turned over in the huge bed, holding back stupid tears. This, she thought wearily, was what love did to you—stripped you of independence and common sense.

The low snarl of an engine brought her upright. She snatched a T-shirt and a pair of shorts and hauled them on, just making it to the balcony in time to wave at the helicopter.

Not that she could pick out Slade. He'd be sitting up at the front with the pilot—possibly even piloting it himself. It was stupid to let such a simple thing make her feel desolated, but as she showered she felt as though she'd never see him again.

'Besotted,' she informed her reflection severely. 'You're utterly besotted! You should be working out what you'll do next—at the very least considering some job!—but, no, all you can think of is that you're not going to spend the day in bed with him!'

She pattered downstairs and emptied the dishwasher, then sat out on the deck with a cup of coffee and the newspaper and tried to concentrate on the job market.

Nothing attracted her. Gloomily she put the paper down and watched a tui plunder nectar from the spidery pink blooms of a shrub. The bird's white throat-knot bobbled as it drained the sweetness, and the sun glimmered in blue and green iridescence on its black plumage.

The trouble was she didn't know what Slade wanted from her. She didn't even know what he felt for her. He hadn't told her he loved her—well, she hadn't admitted her love for him either! But he seemed perfectly content to make love to her without any promises or commitment.

This sensuous idyll couldn't last much longer. She certainly wasn't going to let him keep her, even if he wanted to. And she doubted very much whether she'd fit into the life of an extremely rich man anyway; the prospect of spending days like this waiting for him to come home and make love to her did not appeal.

'Certainly not the waiting about part,' she muttered.

What Slade seemed to want from her was mistress

duty—no intimacy beyond wild sex and heady passion.

Exactly what her grandfather had wanted from the woman he didn't marry. Did she love Slade enough to stay faithful to him if he married another woman and had children with her?

Never, she thought, pushing the newspaper away with revulsion. She loved jealously and possessively. If he even suggested such a thing she'd—well, she wouldn't submit to such an unequal relationship.

Women nowadays had more options; she had more pride. She'd rather live alone for the rest of her life than be the other woman in a triangle.

Utterly depressed, she watched the tui for a few more minutes, then rang its namesake at the Lodge and asked how things were going there.

'Very well,' Tui said cheerfully. 'Poppy's loving the job, and with Sim going off to school once the holidays are over she'll be able to give me longer hours. What are you doing?'

'Lazing about in the sun,' Alli said brightly.

The tui chose that moment to burst into song. She held the receiver out to the bird, and waited until the clear paean of bell notes had faded to say, 'Your namesake said hi.'

'And lovely it was to hear it,' Tui said. 'Hang on a minute, will you? Something's come up.'

Muffled voices indicated she was holding her hand over the receiver; when she came back on she said, 'I have to go. Great to hear from you, Alli. Come up and see us some time soon.'

You can never go back. Her father used to say that,

and, God knew, he'd had enough reason to believe it. There was nothing in Valanu for her now, and nothing at the Lodge either. Her whole life was bound up in one man—whereas she suspected that the big bed upstairs marked the limits of his interest in her.

Certainly there had been no trips to local cafés or vineyards. Did he have friends? Presumably. But he hadn't introduced her to any.

Perhaps he was ashamed of her?

The thought stung so much she spent the rest of the morning scouring bathrooms, changing the sheets on the bed and cleaning the kitchen. She cut a bunch of roses that someone had coaxed into growing behind the house and put them beside the bed, lingering a moment to touch the soft, cool coppery-apricot petals.

After a snack lunch she went down to the beach and sat in the old tyre, missing Slade with an intensity that scared her.

She had no idea how long she'd sat there swinging quietly, when the noise from an engine whipped her head around. Slade, she knew, was coming back by helicopter, so who was this driving down the road in a blue car?

Marian.

Heart lifting, she jumped down and jogged back to the house. Over the past few days she'd spoken to her aunt a couple of times on the phone, and she felt that they were cautiously approaching some sort of understanding of each other.

But it wasn't Marian who stepped out of the car. And Caroline's smile—smug as any cat's, yet oddly set—jolted Alli into wariness.

'Hello,' she said, despising herself for the uncertain note in her voice.

Caroline's smile tightened as she surveyed her. 'Hello, Alli. You're looking well. Can I beg a glass of water from you?'

'Of course!' She led the way into the house, trying to emulate Marian's unforced charm—and failing. Something was wrong. 'Is Marian all right?'

'She's fine.' Caroline's tone was clipped.

The cold patch beneath Alli's ribs expanded. 'Let's go out onto the deck,' she suggested.

Caroline followed her and sat down in one of the chairs. She sipped the water, that faint smile still on her lips, and when Alli's fund of small-talk had dried up she put the glass down with decision.

'You're going to hate me for this,' she said rapidly, 'but I think you should know. Has Slade said anything to you about a trust fund?'

Alli's eyes narrowed. 'No,' she said, before remembering that he'd mentioned Marian's fund when warning her off.

Before she could qualify her answer Caroline said, 'No, I didn't think he had.' She looked around the deck, then back at Alli. 'Your English grandfather left everything in trust to his two daughters,' she said. 'And their descendants. It was quite a substantial amount, although not a fortune.' Her mouth widened into a smile. 'Running two households must have eaten up his capital.'

'How do you know this?'

'Marian told me,' she said, sounding surprised. 'After your mother's death no one knew you existed, so

Marian became the sole beneficiary. By then she knew she wasn't going to have any children; after she miscarried things went so wrong she was told there would be no more pregnancies. When Marian married Slade's father she backed his expansion plans with money from the trust fund.'

'What has this to do with anything?' Alli said, worried by the implacable note in the other woman's voice.

Caroline gave an impatient shake of her head. 'I'm sure you know that Bryn Hawkings was a business genius—and Slade is even better than his father was. Hawkings Tourism is now a huge, extremely profitable concern.'

'Why are you telling me this?'

Her companion leaned forward and fixed her with an intent look. 'When you wrote to Marian claiming to be her daughter she knew there was no way you could be that. So she did what she always does—she told Slade and he organised a search for information about you. You know what the result of that was— you are Alison's daughter.'

A chill scudded down Alli's spine. 'Caroline, I know all this. What—?'

'As Alison's daughter, her interest in the trust fund devolves to you.' Caroline sat back, an enigmatic little smile playing around her perfectly painted mouth. 'Any court would grant it to you once you proved who you are—and if the information Slade found convinced him it would convince a court. But even if it didn't Marian is determined to give shares to you. You now effectively own part of his business.'

Alli stared at her. 'Nonsense.'

'It happens to be the truth,' Caroline said calmly. 'You've got power, and if you wanted to you could cause Slade a lot of grief. Being Slade, of course, he's realised this, so he was set himself to neutralise any threat to his business.'

The cold stone beneath Alli's ribs expanded to press on her heart. 'Tell me exactly what you came to say.'

'I told you you'd hate me.' When Caroline looked at her, Alli saw dislike in her eyes. 'And, yes, I do have an interest in this—I love Slade, and for a while I thought he loved me.' A trace of chagrin marred her smooth voice. 'I'll get over it. But he's going to marry you so that he can control your inheritance, and, quite frankly, I think that's appalling.'

She got to her feet and looked down at Alli, her face devoid of every emotion. 'Beneath his sophisticated surface there's complete ruthlessness. His business is his life. As soon as he realised that you were Alison's daughter he dumped me.' Her glance flicked like a whip across Alli's white face. 'I can see you're in love with him. I pity you. But you should at least know what you're getting into and what sort of man you're in love with.'

And she walked away. Alli got to her feet, but she didn't follow; instead she watched in numb silence as the car sped up the hill into the shadowy darkness beneath the kanuka trees.

Walking like an old woman, she turned and went back to the tyre swing.

She was still sitting in it, keeping the motion going with an occasional kick of her bare foot in the sand,

when the helicopter flew over the house and landed—
and she was still there when Slade came striding down
to the beach.

During those long, bitter hours she'd worked out
exactly what she was going to say. But although she
watched him until he stopped a few steps away, her
aching heart blocked her throat and she couldn't
speak.

He said her name, then said it again, this time urgently as he cancelled the gap between them. 'What's
the matter?' he demanded, pulling her out of the swing
and into his arms.

Steeling her will against the shaming desire to forget everything she'd been told and let herself be
seduced into going along with his scheme, she said
distantly, 'Caroline called in today.'

'So?' But he let her go, and she felt the concentrated
impact of his gaze on her face.

Concisely, without letting her eyes stray above the
open neck of his shirt, she told him what Caroline had
said.

When she'd finished she heard the small hush of the
wavelets on the sand for long seconds before he said,
slowly and deliberately, 'She's clever. She's also an
eavesdropper, because Marian would never have discussed this with her.'

'That's not an answer,' Alli said tonelessly, hope
dying.

'Would you believe any answer I gave you?'

Oh, she wanted to—she craved reassurance like a
thirsty man in the desert craved water—but she knew
she wouldn't be getting it.

His expression hardened. 'No, you wouldn't,' he said levelly. 'As I said, she's clever. Before you damn me entirely, however, you should know that she sold that photograph of us driving out of the car park to the newspaper.'

'Why?'

'For spite.'

'Because you dumped her?' she said, white-faced.

'Is that what she told you?'

She nodded.

'I've underestimated her,' he said, his tone so evenly judicial it sounded like a death sentence.

'Is it the truth? Were you lovers?' The moment she asked the question Alli knew she'd betrayed herself.

'No,' he said calmly. 'I'm not a sadist, and making love to a woman suffering unrequited love for me would be cruel.'

Alli digested this, knowing she couldn't afford to let the tiny flare of hope grow to anything more. 'How do you know that she took the photo?'

'I have contacts in the press, people who owe me favours. She did it.' His voice was grim.

'Did she lie at all?'

'Not in the facts,' he said with brutal, intimidating honesty. 'It's her reading of my motivation that's way off. And that, I'm certain, was done with malice.'

Alli desperately wanted him to convince her, but she didn't dare trust her own emotions. During that interminable afternoon while she waited for him she'd made up her mind; she couldn't allow hope to weaken her.

A white line emphasising the ruthless cut of his lips,

Slade said harshly, 'You'll need to apply through the courts for those shares, but morally, and ultimately legally, you do own them. Marian is determined to give them to you. You could certainly use that to damage me financially.'

'Why didn't you tell me?' she asked, at last voicing the question he had to answer—an answer she dreaded.

He had never looked more arrogant, never more ruthless. 'I didn't intend to make love to you the night of Marian's collapse. I couldn't help myself. And I didn't mean to bring you here—but I couldn't stop myself then, either. In fact, Caroline was right; I brought you here to make you fall in love with me.'

Slade saw the colour abruptly leave her skin, then roll back in a silken wave, but her lion-coloured eyes met his steadily. 'So that you could control me?'

'When have I ever been able to control you? I made love to you because I was completely incapable of resisting you.'

'I don't believe that.' Alli fought for control, because if she gave him what he wanted she'd be asking for a lifetime of regret.

A muscle flicked in his angular jaw. 'Then believe this,' he snarled. 'Why should I seduce you into marriage? That's a lifetime sentence. And if you divorced me I'd have to pay you out more than the worth of those shares.'

'No,' she said angrily.

'Oh, yes—New Zealand's law is fairly tough. Assets are split down the middle. The sensible way to deal with the situation would have been to tell you about the shares, offer you their worth—' with savage precision he named a sum of money that drove the last remnants of colour from her face '—and buy them from you. That way I'd have had control of them without having to pretend that I want you enough to enter into some fake marriage.'

'Then why didn't you do that?' she cried furiously. 'Not that I want them. I'll sign them over to you for a cent, or whatever it takes to make a deal. As far as I'm concerned the money's tainted.'

Holding herself together with fierce will-power, Alli began to walk up to the house. 'Say goodbye to Marian for me,' she said, each word an exercise in determination.

From behind, he said uncompromisingly, 'Just like that? Goodbye and thanks for the memories?'

'What do you expect me to do?' Fists clenched at her sides, she turned on him, allowing anger to give her the strength to say what must be said. 'Let this whole farce go on?'

Hooded green eyes burning in his dark face, he said stonily, 'It's no farce. These past few days have been—magical.'

She made a swift, dismissive gesture. 'Oh, yes, a magical time. You're a superb lover, but it was going to end anyway. We can't stay in bed all our lives. And once it was over—when real life intruded—what then? A practical marriage to safeguard those miserable shares?'

'*Practical?*' He astonished her with a furious, humourless smile. 'Do you have any idea what you've done to me? Right from the first? Whenever I look at you I can't even think. My brain seizes up so all I can do is want you. Practical? If you leave me I'll spend the rest of my life looking for you, loving you, aching for you—and you call that *practical*? Damn it, Alli, I love you.' He flung out his arm in a gesture. 'Do what you like with the shares. Sell them on the share market if you want to, put them in trust for our children, scatter them to the winds—I don't bloody care! Just tell me you'll marry me.'

Incredulously she scanned his face, its tanned skin stretched starkly over the bold bone structure. He had to know he could make her say anything if he only touched her—yet he stood scrupulously apart, although every muscle in his big, lean body was taut with the effort.

'Oh, Slade,' she whispered. 'Why didn't you tell me you loved me?'

'Why didn't *you* tell me?'

'You must have known,' she muttered. 'For heaven's sake—I was a virgin. Of course I fell fathoms deep in love with you—'

He said with raw intensity, 'Sex isn't love, Alli. I've discovered that these past days. I thought I could bind you to me with sex, make you so addicted to it that you'd never know the difference between that and love. But while I flew home today I accepted something that's been gnawing at my conscience ever since I realised that I love you. I have no right to keep secrets from you, not even the secret of my love. I have to give you your freedom if you want it.'

Her half-laugh, half-sob silenced him. He groaned and reached for her, and then he kissed her and muttered, 'Don't cry. Please don't cry. Of course I love you, my darling, my precious girl. I am utterly besotted with you. Women are supposed to be much better at this sort of thing than men—how could you not know it?'

'I didn't dare even think it,' she wept, clutching him. 'I love you so much, and it hurt so much… My mother… I look like her…and—'

He kissed the stumbling words away. 'I love the way you look. I dream about the way you look. I don't want to hear anything more about your mother. You're you, not her.'

'But Marian—'

He kissed the frown between her brows, and then her eyelids, and then the corners of her mouth. 'Darling, leave those sad old ghosts where they belong, in the past. The future belongs to us and to our children. Do you trust me?'

She nodded. 'This afternoon I didn't think I could ever trust anyone again, but love is trust,' she said. 'Lots of other things too, but trust is the basis for it, isn't it?'

It was a statement, not a question.

'Yes,' he said simply, and this time their kiss sealed their commitment to a future free of the bitter shadow of the past.

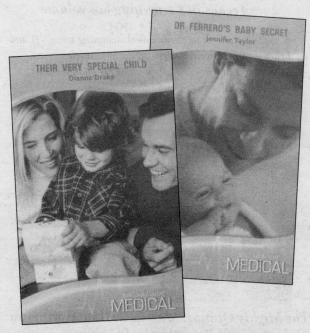